MALIBU 90265

MALIBU 90265

LINDA LANE
NANCY LEE ANDREWS

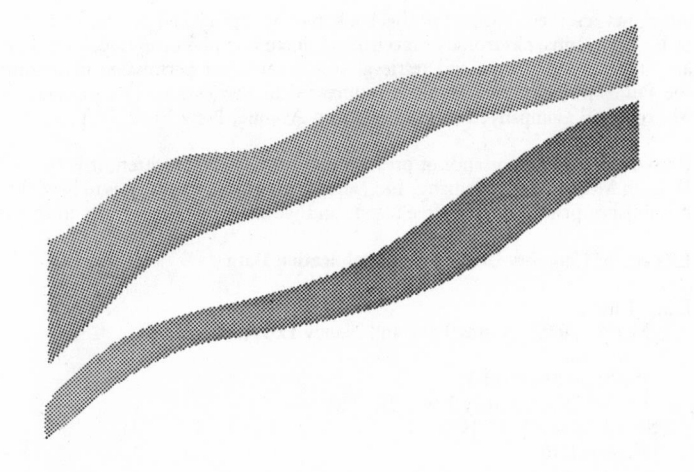

WILLIAM MORROW AND COMPANY, INC.
New York

Library of Congress Cataloging-in-Publication Data

Lane, Linda.
    Malibu 90265 / Linda Lane and Nancy Lee Andrews.
       p.   cm.
    ISBN 0-688-08038-3
    I.   Andrews, Nancy Lee.   II. Title.
    PS3562.A48443M3   1990
    813'.54—dc20   89-13893
                                                                          CIP

Printed in the United States of America

First Edition

1 2 3 4 5 6 7 8 9 10

BOOK DESIGN BY MANUELA PAUL

This book is dedicated to

William "Willy" Royere II
1937–1989

who said, "Yous two should write together"

ACKNOWLEDGMENTS

Bob Rolontz and Peter Cookson, for being there and believing. Lucy Lane-Harrison, Jennarae Andrews, Mr. and Mrs. Lane, Granny Pasuco, Lela Rolontz, Andee and Rick Nathanson, Dane Witherspoon, Pat Turnbull, Lee Garland, Jeff Holgate, Gary Goldstein, Gunnar Magg, Doug Stumpf, Jared Stamm, Uta, Carol Paulus, Paula Dade, Tom Slocum, Zhivago, Cooper, and Taffi Movani, our guide and guru. Thank you and the many others who became the wind beneath our wings when we needed a boost.

CHAPTER 1

*B*onnie Louise was beside herself. This was the very first time in her seventeen years that she'd ventured out unchaperoned. And this was no ordinary adventure, either.

Except for the fantasy chalet outside Aspen, Colorado, she had been nowhere but the lush peanut belt of Plunkettville, Oklahoma. Now, she was about to experience the romantic shores of Malibu, California. She had an idea what it would be like. She had seen so many movies and TV shows in the last few years, but she knew they couldn't compare with real life.

At the Aspen airport she dug her hands into the deep pockets of her jacket and produced a large roll of bills held together by a rubber band. She didn't have a firm grasp on the real meaning of money or what it represented. Why, she could barely add and subtract. She handed the money to the woman behind the United Airlines counter and asked for a ticket to Los Angeles.

The agent peeled off two hundred-dollar bills, wrapped the rubber band around the roll, and handed it back to Bonnie Louise. She stuffed it in her pocket.

Bonnie Louise looked around the departure lounge. A group of teenage skiers, mostly girls, glanced at her, one of them giggling.

How much, she wondered, can other people tell about you just by looking at you? Did they know what she was about to do? She felt as if she had a big red sign on her back that said BONNIE LOUISE IS BEING A BAD GIRL!

Her hair hung down her back in golden ruffles, and spiky bangs surrounded her face. She was wearing a man's hunting jacket with suede trim in forest green, and tight blue jeans that were frayed at the knees, letting a hint of pink skin gleam through the bleached fabric. Her legs were extraordinarily long and rested in snakeskin western boots, which had been scuffed and worn by the elements of the Rockies.

Bonnie Louise self-consciously wondered if there was maybe a way she walked or stood that let other people know things about her, that she herself couldn't tell about them. Codes, signs. Maybe you walked in a certain way if you'd done certain things, and in another way if you hadn't. She'd know more, she thought, if she had friends her own age to gossip with, confide in, and whisper thoughts and secrets.

On the plane the stewardess was struck by the sadness in Bonnie Louise's young and lovely face.

"Are you all right?" she asked.

"No. Scarlett died last night."

"Scarlett?"

"She was our prize mare," Bonnie Louise drawled mournfully. "Everything looked like it was gonna be fine until . . ." She took a deep breath and said, "Foal's head was twisted. Poor little thing couldn't get out. It suffocated."

"What about the mare?"

Bonnie Louise brushed the hair away from her face. Even through tears her sea-green eyes had fire. "Scarlett went into shock. She died not long after."

"Oh, I'm so sorry," the stewardess consoled her.

"I really feel sorry for Rhett. He loved Scarlett so much, and now he's all alone in that big pasture."

The stewardess leaned down and buckled Bonnie Louise's seat

belt. "When we level off, I'll be back, and we can talk some more, okay?"

"Okay," the girl replied gratefully.

Bonnie Louise was finally setting off on the first leg of her journey into the unguarded world. She watched the clouds float past her and the sky change colors, and stared, fascinated, at the constantly changing land below: the ominous sight of the Rocky Mountains, the ocher depths of the Grand Canyon, and the dun expanse of the desert. She felt, she thought, the way some mystic bird must feel.

When the plane landed at LAX, the stewardess protectively walked her to the taxi stand. As Bonnie Louise drove away, waving through the rear window, the stewardess sensed that this was a special person, not quite of this world.

This morning B. J. McClintock's office looked and sounded more like the pit of Chicago's commodities-trading floor than the head-quarters of a media conglomerate.

B.J.'s sponsorship of a $10,000-per-plate fund-raiser had gained the momentum of a runaway train. Little snags like the vice pres-ident's helicopter proposing to land at the site of the event too close to the sacred putting green. The country club had informed MCM that they had been cultivating a special blend of Bent, Bermuda, and other grasses for over a decade. It was off-limits to anyone without golf shoes and a putter.

Lara Miller, McClintock's second-in-command, was trying to arrange an alternate plan. Working with the country-club president on the speaker phone and the vice president's secretary on a line wedged between her shoulder and her ear, she managed to negotiate a deal.

"Okay," she told both parties, "the helicopter lands on the fair-way just below the first tee at six-thirty. We'll have flares out. The Secret Service will have carts waiting to bring the Cravens to the party."

Joan Souchek, McClintock's right hand for the last five years, interjected, "MCM will cover any and all damages!" She went back to her phone lines and lists. Lara passed the message along, and went on to the next item on her schedule.

A young man scurried inside B. J. McClintock's office carrying a garment bag. Five minutes later the founder and head of MCM Studios emerged wearing his new Amir tuxedo.

Through the chaos, everyone in the outer office let B.J. know how smashing he looked in the midnight-blue silk dinner jacket. He enjoyed their approbation. It made him feel young and virile, reminding him of the passion and energy he'd brought with him from Tennessee some twenty-five years earlier.

"There's a Bonnie Louise at the front gate," Lara called out.

The color drained from B.J.'s face. "What?"

"There's a Bonnie Louise for *you* at the front gate!"

B.J. and Joan looked at each other. Lara watched her boss run his tongue across his upper teeth. She had come to recognize this as a gesture of stress.

"Want me to take care of it?" Joan asked.

B.J. nodded. "Please," he said absently, turning and walking back into his office.

"Shit!" Joan cursed under her breath. "This would have to happen today." She disappeared through the glass doors.

Lara found herself running between desks—jumping from her lists to Joan's.

"What do you mean 'they ran out of fabric'?" she called into the speaker phone. "*You* measured it—make it work!" She pressed the next blinking line: "B. J. McClintock's office."

"Put B.J. on the phone," Joan spit out.

Lara shuddered, imagining her superior, the corporate vampire, at the front gate with icicles dripping down her fangs. She wondered what was going on, but today she didn't have time to delve into it. They had but eight hours to pull their $2 million dinner together.

Joan blew through the office, past Lara and into B.J.'s inner sanctum, followed by what appeared to be a gorgeous girl whose eyes were downcast and veiled by a curtain of blond hair. The door slammed behind them.

Joan exited B.J.'s office and jumped back into the fray, picking up exactly where she'd left off.

"I've got Mrs. McClintock on three," Lara announced.

Joan punched the line and said, "Elizabeth, he's out of the office. I'll have him call you as soon as he walks in."

B.J.'s door swung open, and Joan automatically disconnected the call.

"Mrs. McClintock would like a word with you. You can reach her at Georgette Klinger until eleven."

B.J. nodded. "Ladies," he said, motioning them into his office.

Bonnie Louise sat in a daze, looking out over a messy vista of tall buildings, small clapboard homes, and finally, with excitement, to a thin ribbon of blue Pacific water.

"Is that the ocean?" she remarked, but nobody listened.

"This," B.J. said evenly, "is my niece Bonnie Louise. Her luggage was lost on the flight this morning. I want you to take her shopping. Outfit her for the benefit."

"You've got to be kidding!" Joan expostulated.

"Call the Bel Air Hotel and book Bonnie Louise into a bungalow," B.J. said, ignoring Joan. "It's ten-forty-five. Lara, take her into Beverly Hills. Joan, give Lara a list of places where I have accounts."

"Take her to Torrie Steele," Joan suggested. "They have everything."

Bonnie Louise turned around. Her clothes looked and smelled of a stable. She pushed her hair back and managed a shy smile.

B.J. ended the moment with, "Lara, you'd best get her some everyday clothes, too. Shoes. Whatever she needs."

"Ralph Lauren on Rodeo," Joan said. "It's a few doors up."

"I *love* Ralph Lauren," Bonnie Louise drawled. Evidently they had magazines down on the farm, thought Lara.

"Lara," B.J. snapped, "I'll see you at Hillcrest between two-thirty and three. Make sure my niece is settled at the hotel."

He looked squarely at Bonnie Louise and said, "Lara will pick you up at six-thirty, so be ready."

"Good luck!" Joan ventured in her sassy way. She winked at the breathtaking young blonde she'd often spoken to on the phone and had mailed packages to, but whom she was now seeing for the first time. Face-to-face, Joan thought, she's the sort of creature that Botticelli would have glorified.

Bonnie Louise wanted to thank B.J., but he'd scolded her so harshly for having come to town unannounced, on the very night of the most important social engagement of his life, that she couldn't find the words.

"Lara," B.J. called. He lowered his voice and confided, "She's from the side of the family Elizabeth doesn't recognize."

"You can depend on me, B.J."

"Good. Take care of this, and you'll be in the will." He smiled and winked.

Lara gathered what she needed from her desk, happy to be out from under Joan Souchek's iron thumb for a while. "If I didn't know better," she told herself, "I'd swear she's enjoying this Bonnie Louise predicament."

"There's a Town Car waiting for you downstairs with a phone in it—stay on top of your calls, Lara. Check in with me in an hour."

Joan held up a piece of paper. "Here's a list of the stores." She grinned, teasing. "And remember, no rubber, Spandex, or studs."

CHAPTER 2

*T*he Lincoln Town Car turned right onto Rodeo Drive off Wilshire Boulevard and began inching its way past the most expensive real estate in the world.

Elegant façades with chic window displays had been designed to seduce tourists and residents. Silver, gold, china, fine oil paintings, mink, sable, diamonds, emeralds, and rubies—everything the truly pampered treasure-hunter demanded could be found within a four-block radius.

"Joey!" Lara called to the driver. "What's holding us up?"

The young film-school graduate behind the wheel craned his neck to see what was causing them to be gridlocked. Suddenly he burst out laughing.

"Oh man! This is great!" He turned around, addressing Lara and Bonnie Louise. "We've got a classic Beverly Hills fender bender. A hundred-fifty-thousand-dollar Ferrari Testarossa and a two-hundred-thousand-dollar Rolls Corniche are taking up two lanes. Three hundred fifty grand worth of bent metal . . . Oh my God, look at this—here comes a group of Japanese tourists out of Gucci with their cameras!"

"Come on," Lara said, looking at her watch. "We're walking." She turned to Bonnie Louise. "Let's go. Joey, we'll see you up there."

Lara had sprinted the length of two stores before she realized that Bonnie Louise wasn't by her side. A sense of panic swept through her, as if she were a mother looking for her lost child on a crowded street.

There, standing like Alice in Wonderland, was Bonnie Louise, spellbound by the dramatic tableau in Yves Saint Laurent's window. Lara gently took her arm.

"Come on, Bonnie, you can window-shop tomorrow. I'm gonna teach you how they walk in New York." And with that, she locked arms with the girl and strode past all the perfect-looking people.

Beverly Hills had become an international safe haven where women could flaunt their six-carat diamond rings without the fear of an assailant cutting off their fingers. It was a place where a man could sport a $25,000 Rolex watch, carry thousands of dollars in cash, and still be able to wear tennis shorts to a five-star restaurant for lunch.

"Does everybody walk this fast in New York?" Bonnie Louise asked, trying to get an eyeful of each and every store window.

"Faster," Lara teased. "In Manhattan, if you don't keep pace, you're trampled to death. These people are sleepwalking."

"They all look like they stepped off a movie screen."

"Yeah, they do, don't they?" Lara observed. "But this is nothing compared to what you're going to see at the benefit tonight."

Lara caught her reflection in a store window and wished she could make herself invisible. Of all the days to be wearing jeans spattered with pale peach paint that matched her bedroom walls, her blue faded Polo sweatshirt, and well-worn high-top Reeboks!

As a native New Yorker, the twenty-eight-year-old NYU graduate had always prided herself on the way she put her clothes together.

The signal turned green, and in unison Lara and Bonnie Louise stepped off the curb. They could see the police trying to sort out the two rich accident victims and the curious crowd that had formed around them. Traffic, Lara decided, would be at a standstill for some time.

Her dark brown hair sleekly brushed her shoulders with that free but controlled movement that comes only from a precision haircut. Thank goodness she'd washed it and had done her nails the night before.

"Here we are," she told Bonnie Louise. "Let's try to hurry, so we'll have time for Ralph Lauren. Okay?"

Bonnie Louise's eyes sparkled. She was ready for Beverly Hills.

They pushed the heavy glass doors open and entered the austere rectangular salons of Torrie Steele.

A saleswoman wearing a black gabardine skirt with a lavender silk blouse ushered them into a spacious private dressing room.

"Ms. Souchek phoned and told us what you're looking for. Shall we begin with this beaded Krizia?"

"Fine," said Lara, seating herself on the couch and pouring a cup of tea from the silver samovar on the coffee table.

Bonnie Louise didn't budge. She stood with her hands in her pant pockets, looking shy and intimidated.

"It's okay, Bonnie," Lara said warmly. "This is going to be fun." She walked over to the girl and helped her off with her jacket. "What a magnificent gown! I think it's going to look incredible on you."

Bonnie Louise relaxed slightly as she looked from the fabulous array of evening gowns to Lara, whose reassuring eyes put her at ease. She dropped to the floor like a child, and pulled off her western boots. She slipped out of her jeans and raised her shirt over her head. Clad only in panties, she quickly stood up and covered her breasts with the palms of her hands.

Lara was suddenly struck by the girl's nubile beauty. My God, she thought, if this girl can act, she could be the next Marilyn Monroe.

The saleswoman lowered a heavy red bugle-beaded gown over Bonnie Louise's head and zipped her up. Bonnie Louise moved her shoulders up and down and tried to adjust to the weight of the garment.

"I don't know . . ." she said, twisting in front of the three-paneled mirror. "It feels like a piece of jewelry all over my body. I'll never be able to sit down in it."

She dropped the eight-thousand-dollar gown on the floor. Lara helped her into a black velvet sheath with a band of sequins at the neck, hip, and hemline.

"God, how I love Valentino," Lara said, sighing. "You look beautiful, Bonnie."

A worried expression crossed the girl's face. "Don't you think it makes me look so severe . . . and old?" she drawled.

"Okay," Lara said, frustration mounting in her voice. "How about this Monteverdi?"

When Bonnie Louise stepped toward the mirror, she shrieked at her reflection in the seventy-five-hundred-dollar gown by the Italian couture designer. "My Lord! I look like the wicked stepmother in *Sleeping Beauty*. I can't wear this!"

"Listen, Bonnie . . . we're running out of time."

"I'm sorry, Lara. Truly I am. It's just that everything looks . . . well . . . not me."

"You're right," Lara had to agree. All the glitz and pouf didn't meld with the soft, ethereal aura Bonnie Louise exuded. "What's your favorite color?"

"Green."

"Don't you have anything in green at all?" Lara challenged the saleswoman.

"We might have something left over from our sale," she answered, trying to dismiss the idea.

"That's all right."

"I don't mind," Bonnie Louise piped up. "Can you bring it out?"

The saleswoman narrowed her eyes, and after a thoughtful moment disappeared. She returned with a dress and an attitude. "This is the only green gown we have in the store. I really think the Monteverdi is more your style."

"I don't think so at all," said Bonnie Louise, reaching for the seafoam-green dress. "I love the color."

"It is from the spring collection," the saleswoman said disparagingly.

"It matches her eyes," Lara countered.

The gown fit as if it had been made especially for Bonnie Louise. "This is it," the girl said firmly.

Lara was gratified to see that the gossamer creation was only thirty-five-hundred dollars. No wonder the saleswoman had an attitude, she realized. A zero had just dropped off the end of her commission.

"And we have the perfect shoes!" the woman enthused, understanding the Monteverdi was a lost cause. "What size do you wear, dear?"

"Ten and a half."

The saleslady's jaw literally dropped. She tried to mask her surprise and not stare at the young woman's feet.

"Oh my, I'll see what I can do. We don't have very much in *that* size." She left the room.

"Did you go barefoot a lot when you were growing up, Bonnie?"

"I didn't get my very own pair of shoes till I was twelve. I always got my brother's hand-me-downs."

"Well, Bonnie, you just might make up for it this morning. Let's get your shoes and bag. We've got an hour if we're lucky."

"Could I have some lace gloves, too?" asked Bonnie Louise, wringing her hands.

Lara looked at the girl's large, rough hands. Incongruously they belonged to a much older woman . . . or . . . maybe, Lara thought, to a hardworking farm girl.

Once they entered Ralph Lauren, Lara noticed an immediate change in Bonnie Louise. It was homier amid the rich mahogany paneling and display cases, thick Oriental carpets, needlepoint chairs, marble fireplaces, and sterling-silver picture frames. The warm Ivy League colors of burgundy, navy, and forest green combined with faded florals suggested an intimate, Old World ambience.

As they made their way past the antique furnishings in the men's department, Bonnie Louise lightly brushed her fingers against everything. "I just love this place. It's like shopping in a rich person's home."

"I know. It's my favorite store, too—but seven hundred dollars for a pair of sandals is too dear for my budget."

Bonnie Louise made a beeline for an antique table arranged with cashmere turtleneck sweaters. She picked two, turned around, and zeroed in on a Victorian armoire full of worsted wool pants. This girl didn't need lessons from anyone.

Lara was amazed by the teenager's self-assured shopping skills. She went from one department to another, making her selections. From shoes and socks to belts and jackets, Bonnie Louise never had a second thought. She's an Olympic shopper, Lara marveled. It only took her forty-five minutes. I've spent more time than that deciding on one pair of shoes.

The salesgirl arrived with the bill for Lara to sign. "Let's go through this and make sure we haven't forgotten anything. We have five pairs of pants, ten pairs of socks, two pairs of blue jeans, three pairs of shoes, one pair of boots, two cashmere turtleneck sweaters, two cable-knit pullovers, one jacket, five shirts, two belts, one hat, and two skirts. That comes to a total of eleven thousand, eight hundred, and fifty dollars—and with the tax, that'll be twelve thousand, six hundred, and twenty dollars, and twenty-five cents."

The salesgirl smiled at Lara and Bonnie Louise. "Will there be anything else?"

The two shoppers exchanged looks. "I think we've done enough damage for one morning," Lara jested.

"It's going to take at least fifteen minutes to package this up for you. Why don't you go upstairs and have a soft drink or a cup of cappuccino while you wait?"

"That's great!" Lara said. "Just so it doesn't take any longer."

"I'll get right to it."

Bonnie Louise bounded up the spiral staircase, smiling at the portraits of thoroughbred horses and nineteenth-century American blue bloods. She ran over and sat down on a four-poster bed that was stacked with antique American quilts.

"I can't believe this, Lara! My granny made a quilt just like this. It's called Wedding Rings," she said, holding it up.

"I'll take it!" a smooth male voice interjected.

Startled, Bonnie Louise turned to find Zachary Steele, the handsome movie idol, still only in his early twenties, who had starred in many of her most intimate fantasies. Her face turned crimson.

"Is this one just like the one your granny made?"

"Ah . . . ummmm . . ."

"It's lovely," said Lara, maneuvering Bonnie Louise off the bed and over to the hospitality bar. She could feel the magnetic pull between the two young people, and realized this wasn't the time or the place. Besides, Zachary Steele was a notorious Hollywood bad boy. And with that thought, she led Bonnie Louise downstairs in search of their salesgirl.

Zachary Steele stood there staring, waiting for Bonnie Louise to turn around. Much to his surprise, she didn't.

Joey opened the rear passenger door for Lara and Bonnie Louise. "Well, ladies," he teased, pointing at the overflow of packages on the front seat, "looks like you won on *Wheel of Fortune*. If that guy came out again with more packages, I was gonna call transportation and tell them to send a truck."

Lara laughed, savoring the high she felt from having just signed for nearly twenty thousand dollars' worth of clothes and accessories.

"Okay, Joey. Next stop—Hotel Bel Air!"

Joey studied his passengers in the rearview mirror. He wanted a shot at the blonde. "Should I take the scenic route?"

"In Beverly Hills, every route is the scenic route."

They made their way up Rodeo Drive and across Santa Monica Boulevard to the famous "flats." As they passed mansion after mansion, Bonnie Louise began oohing and aahing. She was dazzled by the architecture: a sprawling, Spanish-style hacienda not more than twenty feet from an English Tudor estate. Or a French Normandy château next door to a Bauhaus tribute to the isosceles triangle.

Lara Miller reclined against the soft leather seat. She was surprised at just how comfortable she felt conducting business while cruising through what she believed was the glamour capital of the world.

"Oh my Lord," Bonnie Louise gasped. "These houses are so big! I can't believe the size of them. Too bad they're so close together."

"Real estate's too valuable," Joey chimed in. "These places cost millions! That street up there by the signal," he said, pointing, "used to be a bridle path."

"Is that a fact?"

"Oh yeah. You see that big pink hotel? That's the Beverly Hills Hotel. I think they used to stable their horses behind it."

"Bonnie," said Lara, gesturing out the rear window, "look at the palm trees. Fat ones in between skinny ones. They must be sixty feet high."

"Oh my gosh," the teenager sighed. "They're all so perfect."

"And to our right," Joey said, in his best Robin Leach voice, "is the Liza Minnelli mansion."

Lara could see that Joey was trying to impress Bonnie Louise. She'd known him for over a year, and she'd never seen him this animated.

The car turned left, heading west along Sunset Boulevard. Bonnie Louise was awestruck by the enormous homes. She had seen large ranch houses and lodges in Aspen, but never anything with so many flowers and trees and so much *greenery*. She marveled at how healthy all the plants looked.

"Oh my Lord—what's goin' on over there?"

"Bonnie, those aren't real people. They're Seward Johnson sculptures."

"Yeah," Joey said. "I like the ones taking pictures the best."

"How strange," Bonnie Louise commented, "to want fake people in your front yard."

Around the next curve Joey, still imitating Robin Leach, said, "And over to our left is the Engelbert Humperdinck estate, formerly owned by blond bombshell Jayne Mansfield—the romantic lady who put in a heart-shaped swimming pool and painted the outside pink."

Letting the momentum carry him, Joey pulled over to the side of the road, whipped out a five-dollar bill, and bought a map to the stars' homes. He reached across the back seat and presented it to Bonnie Louise.

"Welcome to Tinseltown, hon. Everybody who's anybody is on this map."

They arrived at the Hotel Bel Air with barely enough time to secure Bonnie Louise and her new wardrobe in a bungalow.

Lara called room service and placed the girl's lunch order: a hamburger, French fries, and a cherry coke.

"I'll be back at six-thirty," Lara told her. "I'll try to make it a few minutes earlier, in case you need some help."

"I'll be fine," Bonnie Louise assured her. "Thank you, Lara. You've been real kind." She wrapped her arms around her mentor and gave her a grateful squeeze.

Lara stepped back, both surprised and warmed by the girl's sincerity.

Walking down the stone pathway and along the narrow bends and turns leading to the front of the hotel awakened Lara's libido. The foliage seemed to reach out and embrace her, while the heady floral fragrances intoxicated her. This place, she decided, was created for lovers.

When she arrived at the bridge, Lara allowed herself one more private moment. She reached inside her purse and found a penny. Making a wish, she tossed it into the pond and watched the swans glide gracefully away from its ripple.

As the Town Car pulled out of the parking lot, Lara shifted into high gear.

"You want me to come back and keep her company?" Joey volunteered. "It's a big hotel."

"Joey, just shut up and drive!"

CHAPTER 3

*E*very major star in the country was either in attendance or had sent a donation. Hillcrest Country Club, the exclusive Jewish establishment famous for oil wells discreetly pumping more profits for its members from beneath the lush fairways of its golf course, had opened its doors for a public fund-raising event for the first time in almost sixty years.

The crusade against AIDS was as nondenominational as the disease itself. It had been at Elizabeth Taylor's behest that the rich, centrally located, securely guarded country club had been chosen for this $10,000-per-plate evening.

They came in limousines, they came in Rollses and Bentleys, all of them looking as if they'd been perfectly assembled by the haute-couture houses of Paris and Milan. Guests had flown in from around the world to participate in what promised to be the most socially consequential event since the unveiling of the restored Statue of Liberty in 1986.

Bonnie Louise's nose was pressing up against the tinted-glass window inside the limousine that B. J. McClintock had instructed his secretary, Lara Miller, to use for the big party tonight.

As the car inched its way along Pico Boulevard, Bonnie Louise was astonished by lines upon lines of people holding burning candles. She'd never seen anything to equal it. Not even Oral Roberts had a turnout like this.

"Why are all those people holding candles?" she asked in her sweet Oklahoma drawl.

Lara Miller was feeling conspicuous and a little self-conscious in the fifty-five-hundred-dollar black velvet Valentino gown that B.J.'s wife, Elizabeth McClintock, had so generously and unexpectedly given her for tonight's benefit. What a wonderful and protective woman Elizabeth was, she thought, as she looked up from her paperwork and peered out of the window at the men, women, and children who'd come from all over the country to show their solidarity.

"The ones with candles have been touched by AIDS. Either a loved one has it or even they themselves," Lara said sadly. She was completely fascinated by this mysterious McClintock . . . this ethereal vision who had turned up at MCM's front gate a few hours earlier. She'd never heard B.J. mention her, but when he heard she was at the studio, he'd put everything else on hold.

The car phone rang. Lara answered it. It was B.J. with a few last-minute details. Bonnie Louise watched Lara's luminous blue-gray eyes flash with excitement.

Before hanging up the phone, B.J. reminded Lara to keep a close watch on his niece. "Don't let her out of your sight!" he commanded.

Lara looked protectively at the golden creature in the seafoam gown. We make quite a pair, she thought, as she fingered the diamond-and-pearl rope necklace she had borrowed from wardrobe's lock-up department. Her dark hair was pulled back into a tight braid and held at the nape of her neck by a black velvet bow. Lara Miller, she mused, this is the coming-out party you missed. If only they could see me in Cedarhurst, Long Island.

On an impulse she picked up the phone, pressed "call," a long-distance number, and "send." Magically a woman's voice crackled across the three thousand miles separating Lara from her family.

"Hi, Mother," she said cheerfully. "I'm calling from a limousine."

Through the static her mother told her she knew everything would work out. "Those large affairs always come together at the last minute, dear."

"I'm beginning to think moving out here was a good idea."

"Yes, dear . . ." Suddenly her mother's voice was drowned out by the loud hacking of helicopter blades. As the vehicle passed overhead on its way to landing near the fairway on the first hole, Lara took a moment to relax into her glamorous new look. As a secretary feeling slightly like Cinderella going to the ball, she knew she would be far from the center of attention. But if she could make B.J. notice her and appreciate her contribution to the evening, perhaps he would give her a chance to take Joan's place.

Lara's head was still reeling from Joan's resignation. Where did Joan get the nerve to walk up to B.J. at five o'clock and quit without giving him any notice? Lara had worked at MCM's West Coast office only six months, and just three of them in B.J.'s office.

"Lara? Lara? Can you hear me? Are you there?" Irene Miller's voice had a desperate edge to it over the car phone.

"Yes!" Lara shouted into the receiver. The static subsided as she concluded, "That must be the vice president's helicopter."

Bonnie Louise craned her neck to see it. She was a sponge, never missing a vital speck of information.

"So he did make it after all!" Irene Miller shouted.

"Yes, Mother. I told you—B. J. McClintock has a reputation for getting what he wants. I have to hang up now. I love you. Bye!" She pressed "end."

Lara turned to find Bonnie Louise staring at her.

"Bonnie, would you like to call your parents?"

Bonnie Louise blushed. "I'd love to, but they don't have a telephone back in Plunkettville."

"They don't have a phone?"

Bonnie Louise shook her head and said, "But maybe they'll catch us on the news tonight, if they go down to the Smiths' to watch TV."

"They don't have a TV, either?"

"Nope."

"Indoor plumbing," Lara said kiddingly.

"No, you still gotta go out back."

Lara's antennae shot up. She knew B.J. hailed from Tennessee. It wasn't impossible for him to have relatives in Plunkettville, Oklahoma. But there was something that didn't jell. She could feel it in her bones.

"Just exactly how are you related to B.J.?"

Changing the subject, Bonnie Louise pointed out her window at the most amazing sight she'd ever seen. "Who's that?"

Lara's question was eclipsed by Ariba's arrival at the entrance to Hillcrest. Guards were pushing the paparazzi back. It looked almost like a riot.

"Ariba's the hottest singer in the world right now, huge in Europe," Lara explained. "She's from Brazil. Joan and I made over two hundred calls to Ariba before she finally agreed to appear tonight."

Bonnie Louise giggled as she watched the dark-skinned, feather-covered singer blow kisses to the frenzied press. Then, as if on cue, Ariba turned around and undulated into the country club.

The media people lost their cool. Ariba's manager held them back, then followed her inside. This night was going to be the big opportunity to dazzle her superstar peers. So far the Brazilian songbird had captivated South America and Europe. Now, she was ready to seduce America.

Bette Midler was scheduled to appear as mistress of ceremonies. Flashbulbs went wild as the Divine Miss M stepped out of her dressing room. The comedienne so widely identified with sex and sexuality struck a pose.

Her outrageous Norma Kamali creation was made up of layer upon layer of iridescent rainbow condoms. She flashed a wicked grin and ripped one of the little safety wrappers off.

"Here, boys and girls," she teased, tossing it into the sea of cameras. "Have a rubber johnny on me!"

Whistles! Foot-stomping. Shrieks of "Take it off! Give it to me, Bette!" rocked Hillcrest's hallowed halls. Even one of the stuffier members stood with his mouth fixed in an ostentatious smile of approval he secretly did not feel.

Amid the whistles and fun the divine lady quipped, "Where was this dress when I needed it? When I graduated high school!"

She was a goddess all right. Bette Midler had for all occasions a unique gift, a chameleon sense of style, and a mouth that was almost protean.

"How much do you think you'll raise tonight?" a television reporter called out.

Bette's mood shifted. She was thoughtful for a moment. "Tickets tonight have already raised six million dollars. Who knows? With this crowd, we'll probably triple it!"

Money. That was what it was all about. Elizabeth McClintock couldn't stand the smell of it. She was grateful that all she had to do was sign here and there. She couldn't remember the last time she'd had to count actual bills. It was all on paper, and as far as she was concerned, her husband, B.J., owned the mint.

As she looked around the exquisitely lush, almost celestial rendering of the Garden of Eden, she couldn't help but notice that the B. J. McClintock empire was silently infiltrating the room. The fragrant scent of Plumaria wafted up to Elizabeth's nostrils. That and the sound of a waterfall reminded her of the happy time she and B.J. had spent on the island of Maui. . . . Black sand beaches and rainbows . . . Making love beneath a waterfall . . .

B. J. McClintock surveyed the dazzling spectacle. MCM's most talented designers and special-effects wizards had achieved the illusion of a tropical jungle. Cascades of red and pink frangipani and hot-red anthericum with stamens that reminded him of erect penises all seemed to grow out of banks of deep green ferns. Even the pathways were made of dichondra grass. He marveled at the dozen or so pink flamingos roaming a mock-lagoon near the stage.

B.J. caught sight of Lara Miller leading Bonnie Louise into the room. His heart began beating wildly. He had to turn away, had to compose himself. How the hell is Bonnie Louise going to fit in? he asked himself. This was a mistake. . . .

He turned back, casually searching the entryway. His eyes landed on a cluster of photographers snapping the unknown blond beauty. A duck to water . . . He shook his head, marveling at the way Bonnie Louise turned on her big, beautiful smile for the group who no doubt thought she was the newest starlet on the scene.

Then he turned his attention to the guests, who were greeting each other, reaching for chilled champagne flutes and—some casually, some directly—searching the tables for their place cards.

As the familiar glitter passed before the founder and head of McClintock Communications Media, Inc., a question flashed into his mind: What are all these people doing here? They haven't come because of AIDS—they're here to honor and admire *themselves*!

B.J.'s mind now drifted over the whole range of events and celebrations—whether for charities or the Oscars or the American Film Institute's annual honorings or any of half a dozen yearly affairs whereby Hollywood had successfully institutionalized, to its own greater glory, a system of mutual admiration under the banner of charity and the public good.

He shifted his body to catch another glimpse of Bonnie Louise, who was now dutifully following Lara. He breathed a sigh of relief. Thank heaven *she* was being absorbed into the perfumed surroundings. His eyes met Elizabeth's. He projected a beaming smile of approval and nodded to emphasize his admiration for a job well done.

Elizabeth McClintock smiled back, soaking up her husband's regard. Uoakti, the Brazilian jazz group, was providing seductive background music, and the soft lighting made everyone look healthy. It was, Elizabeth hoped, an ambience that would relax people into opening up their wallets. Casually she turned away from B.J. and took a long sip of champagne.

Holly Dandridge, Elizabeth noticed, was sprawled in an armchair, managing to look as if she were already in bed with the man she regarded with her piercing sapphire eyes—in this instance, a young priest she had cornered for the last half hour. God knows, thought Elizabeth, if anybody should be a mascot for this charity, it should be Holly, our little prime-time vixen.

That wasn't nice, Elizabeth. God forgive me, she thought, but it's hard at times to hold your tongue . . . even mentally. Perhaps another glass of champagne would take the edge off.

Blast! The press had spotted her. Time to move on. Elizabeth glided away from them in her sleek beaded Schiaparelli gown with its single red flame-stitched sleeve, roaming around the room as if intent on making one final place-card check. She was a notable social chemist whom old-timers referred to as the "Diamond Mesta" of Hollywood.

B.J. was laughing with John Talbot, the only Roman Catholic layman who was an honorary ambassador to the pope. John Talbot was a legend. He had real estate holdings worth hundreds of millions of dollars in the Beverly Hills area, and counseled the Catholic church on its real estate investments.

Elizabeth's lips relaxed into a smile. After all these years, B. J. McClintock was still the only man she desired. She relished his chiseled features, his silver hair shining like a beacon of light. Twenty-five years, she reminded herself. Twenty-five years ago we drove across the country, planning our future. Darlin', if only you would touch me the way you did back then. You always had big ideas. Bigger than any other man around . . .

She felt that familiar tingle at the tip of her refined southern nose. Champagne always had a way of transporting her back to the early years of her marriage, the times when she and B.J. were madly in love with each other. Now as then, she devoted herself to making him happy, but unlike in the past, *he* was more inclined to retire to his own bedroom.

The thought that there was another woman had crossed her mind, but Elizabeth had refused to consider seriously the possibility. No one was closer to B.J. than she was. And having taken her wedding vows seriously, Elizabeth knew that she and her husband would be together until the end.

The McClintocks had been major supporters of the Los Angeles diocese of the Catholic church over the past twenty years. She laughed to herself at the thought of being a pillar in the holy community. And tonight—what a night! she told herself. Elizabeth, you've outdone yourself! And what's more, you've almost certainly had too much to drink. Time to visit the ladies' room.

In the flattering golden light of that venerable emporium, Joan Souchek, until today B.J.'s long-standing executive secretary, was retouching her makeup in a meticulous ritual that mesmerized Elizabeth. No sign of shame or self-consciousness, she observed. A main-chance girl was Joan, notepad in one hand and high heels in the other.

Joan, a thirty-four-year-old blonde, caught Elizabeth's reflection in the mirror and swiveled around. "Hello, Elizabeth. You know, I'm really sorry about leaving on such short notice, but they didn't let me know I had the job for sure until this morning."

"I'm sure you'll do very well for yourself, Joan." Elizabeth's voice and demeanor were cool, measured.

"Well, I know B.J.'s upset. . . ."

"My dear," Elizabeth said, raising her hand to silence the woman who had been her husband's most trusted employee. "This is not the moment for regrets on either side. You have a job to do, Ms. Souchek. May I suggest you take your post?"

Joan gulped. Elizabeth McClintock really knew how to make her feel like two cents. Here she was, about to become VP in charge of television production at a major studio, and her hard-earned self-esteem had just evaporated.

"Everything happens for the best, dear. I believe the person who will prove the ideal right hand for my husband has been waiting in the wings." Elizabeth shifted her head slightly, locking eyes with Lara Miller, who had just walked in with an extraordinarily pretty blond teenager.

Lara was quick to sense the tension between Joan, her former superior, and Mrs. McClintock. She was also intrigued to notice that there was no spark of recognition between Elizabeth and Bonnie Louise. Diplomat that she was, Lara made no introductions.

Head held high, Joan nodded at Lara and exited.

Elizabeth released the anxiety she'd been controlling. Confrontation was not her strong suit. And besides, Joan Souchek wasn't worth agitating herself over. Ironically, at first she had been jealous of Joan's closeness to B.J., but as the years dragged on, Elizabeth started to understand what drove Joan to workaholic heights. Elizabeth had come to recognize Joan's hunger for success, that restlessness masked by efficiency. Even now she had observed the tiniest signs of liquor-loving overindulgence on Joan's face—dry footprints could not be hidden beneath a moist coat of paint.

"Elizabeth," Lara said warmly, "I love my gown. That was incredibly kind of you—thank you again."

Elizabeth's face lighted up. "Lara, you are a picture." Conspiratorially she whispered, "The Lord does everything in our best interest."

The two women giggled as Bonnie Louise kept her face fixed firmly on the mirror as she touched up her lipstick.

Matching Elizabeth's conspiratorial tone, Lara whispered, "And as for what *you've* done, I've never seen so dull a room made so beautiful."

"A true Garden of Eden, isn't it?"

Lara smiled. "This may well go down as the last great party of the century."

"If so, Lara, let's hope it's for the right reason." Elizabeth looked up at a banner proclaiming the fight against AIDS. In the corner she caught sight of Lara's teenage companion admiring her. Their eyes met for an instant. Shyly the stunning blonde turned away.

The ladies' room door flew open, and Ariba arrived. Her ice-blue eyes landed on Bonnie Louise, who had returned to brushing her hair.

Elizabeth was much taken by the feral quality of the Brazilian singer. She couldn't be more than twenty-one or two, Elizabeth mused, about the same age as her daughter, Savannah. It was as if someone had lit a jungle torch, and Ariba had risen in its flames. Elizabeth looked forward to seeing her perform later.

Ariba, for her part, was smiling fiercely at Bonnie Louise. "*Cara*, you have the most *beau-ti-ful* hair! In my country," she said, with rolling Portuguese inflections, "you would be worshiped. And not just for the hair—though also for your hair, they would pay anything!"

Ariba stroked Bonnie Louise's silken tresses. "You a movie star?" she asked.

Bonnie Louise shook her head and tentatively returned the performer's smile. Being close to Ariba was like opening a furnace door.

Ariba continued to smile at her, then, starting to sing softly, disappeared into one of the stalls.

Lara shook her head at Elizabeth, chuckling lightly. "But she is amazing," she whispered. Then, louder: "Thanks to you, they're all here. *Vanity Fair, Women's Wear, The London Times, Der Spiegel, Paris Soir, The Washington Post.* B.J.'s so proud of you."

Elizabeth nodded, trying to shake off the haze that enveloped her. Whenever she had drunk a little, a Tennessee drawl tended to roll off her lips. It was her pampered past, after all, that had bred in her a familiarity with luxury tempered by good form. Being a hostess was second nature to her.

When Elizabeth emerged from the ladies' room, B.J. caught her eye and smiled. He would be watching her. This was an important night for him.

Elizabeth found herself in need of still another drink. If she were home, it would be no problem to catch a discreet nip of Grand Marnier. She looked at B.J. in his glory talking with Maureen and Henry Weinstock, two of the country's most generous philanthropists. New Yorkers. That's right, Elizabeth reflected. Helen O'Brien is their daughter. . . .

Over by the bar Colin and Helen O'Brien were holding court. Actually Colin was, and Helen was there to say, "Yes, dear, that's right."

Being the wife of a superstar who always played Mr. Stud Incarnate couldn't be easy, Elizabeth mused. Especially with Colin's amazing good looks. Those laughing, caramel-colored eyes of his were like magnets. And his body . . . Elizabeth sighed deeply. With his tall, lean frame and rippling muscles in all the right places,

Colin O'Brien was the ideal of masculinity. She couldn't help but enjoy watching him as he went jogging down the beach in the afternoons, his virility on display.

Helen was elegant, Elizabeth decided. Not really a show-business type at all. Delicate features, a thin frame. Not too much jewelry . . . just enough to let you know she was Old Money. And reserved. Maybe too reserved, Elizabeth noted. She's probably taking something—nobody's that calm from drinking straight Perrier.

Elizabeth glanced at her jeweled Piaget watch. This is going to be a long night, she warned herself. She frowned, remembering how B.J. had placed the watch on her dressing table before she slipped into her gown for the benefit. She hated the wristwatch. It was too flashy—New Money at its worst. She knew B.J. had bought it because it was obscenely overpriced. Why did he like hanging glitzy ornaments on her? She wasn't a Christmas tree. Elizabeth gave a silent moan. Time for another champagne.

"Lara!"

Lara Miller turned around. A smiling Joan Souchek handed Lara a flute of champagne and held up her own glass to toast.

"To success!" the new VP cheered. Lara noticed Bonnie Louise hanging back, and suggested she join them. A waiter was summoned. Joan was happily flexing her wings.

But Lara was shocked at Joan's recklessness. "I still can't believe after five years you didn't give B.J. at least twenty-four hours' notice," she told her former boss.

"If the shoe was on the other foot, he'd have done the same thing," Joan opined. "B. J. McClintock is no angel, kid."

Lara's back went up. She'd graduated cum laude from NYU. She was nobody's "kid" except her mother's.

"You did a great job on the benefit. If you ever decide to change studios, give me a call, Lara." Joan lowered her voice and added, "I hope whoever takes my place appreciates you."

Lara wanted to tell Joan what a disloyal, self-absorbed witch she was, but she held herself in check. People like Joan always ran into a brick wall somewhere down the road.

Bonnie Louise was standing on the outskirts of Lara and Joan's conversation when she heard a familiar smooth voice whisper in her ear, "I'll take it."

She turned, and found herself once again face-to-face with Zachary Steele. Joan, never missing a beat, introduced Bonnie Louise to the twenty-five-year-old cinema stud. Zachary seized the opportunity, and whisked her off to the bar for a Coca-Cola.

"Even I'm too old to handle that kind of heat," Joan commented.

"B.J. told me to keep Bonnie Louise with me."

"Lighten up, Lara. She's not going to disappear. Let's mingle!"

Joan spotted a network executive and quickly made her connection. Lara hesitated, wondering with whom *she* ought to "mingle."

"Where is she?" B.J.'s voice breathed down her naked neck.

Lara jumped and turned, facing her boss and an intriguing stranger. "Over there," she blurted. "At the bar, getting a Coca-Cola."

B.J. spotted Bonnie Louise in a crush of people and relaxed. He introduced Lara to Kevin Wenster, an old friend from Australia who—by a great stroke of luck, he remarked—happened to be in town for the night.

"Oh," Lara commented. "You're the gentleman who wanted a date with Holly Dandridge."

"Me and a million others. She's a very . . . lovely lady," Kevin said meaningfully.

What a charmer, Lara thought to herself. B.J.'s Australian friend looked to be about forty-five. Athletic—probably into sailing, because his face and hands bore the sun-kissed stamp of a deep, rich tan. His hair was beginning to take on that sexy, distinguished salt-and-pepper quality. And he had a low, throaty laugh.

B.J.'s hand squeezed her shoulder. "I'd like you to attend to business," he said, veering his eyes in the direction of Bonnie Louise and Zachary Steele.

"Right," Lara said. "Nice meeting you, Kevin."

"My pleasure. Until the next time."

Lara inconspicuously sliced her way through clusters of people, taking her place next to Bonnie Louise. The blonde and Zachary didn't seem to notice Lara's arrival, or the rest of the room full of people.

After greeting Lucy Getz and Harriet Carlmuller and half a dozen of her closest friends, Elizabeth refreshed her glass and stepped aside for a moment of peace. She squinted, trying to attach names to the elegant young couple who had joined the O'Briens and appeared to be hanging on Colin's every word.

The woman was wearing the very same silk-chiffon beaded Galanos gown Elizabeth had herself considered; but she had felt that twenty-five thousand dollars was too much to spend even for such an occasion as this.

"The Capriottis!" Elizabeth said softly to herself. "Prince Carlo Borromayo Capriotti and . . . Elizabeth tried to squeeze the dark-haired woman's name from her memory.

"The royals" as they were foolishly called at the beach. Why did relatively sophisticated Americans continually refuse to distinguish between the holder of a title and members of the royal family! "Eugenia! That's it! Carlo and Eugenia."

His dark Italian eyes flashed with charm and laughter as he threw up his hands, obviously delighted by something the American superstar had said. Jet-setters, certainly, Elizabeth thought, but no Eurotrash. No, the Capriottis were recognized trendsetters. She would have to cultivate them.

Well, well, well . . . Bentine Devorac back in circulation. Dr. Shipp's famous chemical peel must have given her a new lease on life, Elizabeth thought with a smile of inner satisfaction. Her aristocratic bone structure had thus far kept her safely out of reach of Dr. Shipp's scalpel.

Having heard the rumors of Bentine's scandalous divorce, Elizabeth guessed that Helen O'Brien had graciously invited Bentine as her and Colin's guest. The poor woman had lost her home, her children, and probably all of her social privileges. To be alone after forty, Elizabeth thought, would be a curse. Although Bentine certainly looked as if she was having a good time at the moment. And why not? She was resting her hand on a lethally handsome young man's knee, and he seemed to be more than tolerant of her ministrations.

"Elizabeth!" Elaine Shipp squealed. "This is truly fantastic!"

Gooseflesh erupted up and down Elizabeth's exposed arm. She never knew whether Elaine Shipp was experiencing excitement or social terror.

"Why, Elaine, you look wonderful."

"I owe it all to the Sedona Method. It teaches you to release negative energy."

Suddenly the man who had been whispering a running commentary into his champagne flute leaned in and raised his fastidiously plucked eyebrows.

"Elizabeth!" Dr. Morton Shipp exclaimed.

"You know what they'll be saying about tonight?"

"No, Mort, what?"

"You *had* to have been there. That's what they'll say! You *had* to have been there!" The doctor leaned close to her ear. "Looks like that fat farm did its stuff. Thirty pounds? Did Savannah take off thirty pounds?"

Dr. Morton Shipp. The sculptor of many a famous bosom, thigh, and derriere. "Twenty-seven pounds, she told me, to be exact," Elizabeth replied.

"I knew damn well that letting her see my liposuction machine would scare the shit out of her!" He laughed, entertaining himself.

"Morton!" Elizabeth scoffed.

"Morton!" Elaine chastised. "Even in *your* expanding universe, I should have thought there was a time and a place."

Dr. Shipp broke loose, threw his arms out as if to embrace the room, and said, "There *is*—and this is *it! My* time, *my* place, and *my* molding scalpel! Can't you see my signature everywhere? The Shipp who launched a thousand faces!"

"Well, certainly not this one!" Elizabeth said severely.

"Now, Elizabeth," the plastic surgeon said, wagging a finger at her, "let's not get *too* complacent. A stitch in time, they say! Oh yes, better to nip early, so no one notices."

"The only nip I'm interested in, Doctor, is to be found in a champagne glass," she retorted, and made her way to the bar. Elizabeth closed her eyes and thought of Marylou, the first Mrs. Shipp. Her closest friend. A good old southern girl who had ended it all with a lethal potion of alcohol and sleeping pills. It was the only exit poor Marylou could contrive to get away from that man.

Elizabeth was never sure what had sealed the friendship between B.J. and Morton Shipp. She really didn't even think he was a particularly good doctor. He never seemed to be "there" in the way she thought a proper doctor should be there for his patients.

Why, Savannah McClintock. You little she-cat! Elizabeth flashed her twenty-year-old daughter a loving smile. She giggled to herself, thinking that barely an hour ago they had been at each other's throats over the length of Savannah's dress.

Savannah self-consciously tugged on her Gaultier gold lamé micromini and winked at her mother. She could feel eyes bearing down on her with the intensity of headlights on high beam. It was uncomfortable and yet exciting. . . .

She turned and squeezed her way through the crush, holding her heirloom jewelry, the antique rope of seed pearls with the four 1-carat ruby drops that gave her an aura of self-confidence and softness.

Her nose had been sculpted to perfection by Dr. Shipp. Savannah could still hear Uncle Morty's voice echoing down the alley of anesthesia: "When you wake up, your nose is going to be the perfect match for your McClintock chin. Watson," he laughed, "bring me the box of noses!"

Orthodontia had given Savannah a perfect bite. An Oscar-winning makeup artist had instructed her on the art of deception, and she had become adept at disguising what few imperfections remained.

Hollywood meant perfection. Movies meant *creating* images. Even those born beautiful or handsome could always find something to change. No one Savannah McClintock had ever met was entirely happy about his or her self. Even the superstars. People she thought perfect in every way found eyes that were too close or a waistline that was straight up and down or feet too large. Even as a child, seeing *Gone With the Wind* for the first time in her father's projection room, Savannah had heard someone remark—and she never forgot it—that Vivian Leigh hated her hands so much, she hid them whenever possible.

Savannah made up for a lack of self-esteem by becoming a super-achiever. She had been seriously compared to Chris Evert on the tennis court, and had even considered going pro until B.J. laid down the law. He wanted his only daughter home where he could keep an eye on her.

Time was something B.J. had in very limited quantities. It seemed as though he made appointments to do everything. There were no spaces left open on his calendar. If he spent two hours a week with Savannah, she felt bathed in his light and therefore his approval.

It seemed to her that she had spent her whole life trying to get his attention, and tonight she finally had it. She caught a glimpse of her larger-than-life daddy across the room and felt warmed through and through.

She touched her new earrings, the seed-pearl-and-ruby drops that her mother had Cartier create to match her necklace. Yes, they were still there.

This dinner had been a catalyst for Savannah. Finally she had earned her own little spotlight. She'd spent hundreds of hours computerizing every vital piece of information: names and addresses, who had accepted, who had not. Donations, number of reservations, menu selections, special menu selections, seating arrangements . . . all at the tip of her lily-white fingers.

She gulped when she spotted Colin O'Brien leading a handsome man across the room to confer with her father. Colin O'Brien had always been her favorite actor. She knew he was too old for her, but he was the only man she dreamed of kissing when she wrapped herself around a soft pillow at night.

Suddenly Mikey McClintock snaked his arms around his sister's waist. She jerked herself loose and turned to confront her brothers, the poison twins, Mikey and Danny McClintock.

"Hey," one of the sixteen-year-olds said. "What d'ya think?"

Savannah looked at them and laughed. They had managed to bastardize two perfectly nice Armani tuxedos with, in Danny's case, a psychedelic pink tie and cummerbund and, in Mikey's case, neon-green accessories.

"You couldn't leave Melrose Avenue behind, could you?" Savannah asked.

"You should've heard the fight," Danny said. "Dad threatened to send us to school in Switzerland *again* if we didn't pull it together tonight."

Mikey leaned in, closing in on Savannah's long neck. "You want to take a trip to the Alps? Tour the snow country?"

"You know I don't *ski*," she said flatly.

"Well, then, Slim," Danny said politely, "can I bring you a glass of Diet Coke or maybe a Perrier?"

"Hey, you two, if I were you, I'd cool out tonight." She shifted her body in the direction of the dais. "You see that little platform? It's got 'McClintock' written all over it." She flashed them her cover-girl smile and concluded, "We're under a microscope tonight."

Mikey edged closer, reaching for her tight little ass. "Well, all the world can see what's under yours tonight, Savannah."

She stopped his hand. Squeezing it hard, she said, "If wishes were horses, beggars would ride."

"What's that supposed to mean?" the teenager asked frantically.

"It means, Mikey—your skin will never touch mine. Ever!" She released his hand and slipped through the crowd.

"Danny! I'm Danny, Savannah! He's Mikey! I'm Danny!" Mikey lied.

She turned and winked. Mikey turned to his brother and confidently said, "You see that? She's hot for me. I can tell."

Elizabeth squinted at her adopted boys. Handsome sixteen-year-olds who had as much common sense as two fleas. She frowned at their taste in cummerbunds. Why didn't B.J. make his point? Really, she said to herself, I wanted them to look like gentlemen.

Suddenly she was seized by what she called "the uncontrollable" . . . those memories of Bessie Jo she had suppressed so well. No, it was their deep, dark hideous secret—hers and B.J.'s. Something they would pay for every day of their lives.

She felt a warm hand wrap around her sleeveless arm. She sprang back to reality.

"Henry," she said, clearing her throat. "It was so good of you and Maureen to be here tonight."

"Elizabeth," the silver-haired Broadway entrepreneur said sincerely, "I wanted to give this to you personally." He handed her a folded check. She opened it, and her eyes welled with tears.

"Three hundred thousand dollars! Bless you, Henry Weinstock. Bless you."

Henry closed his eyes and said softly, "Maureen and I have lost too many friends and acquaintances." He shook his head, thinking about the many artists and dancers who had succumbed to the deadly virus; the creative foundation of Manhattan was being threatened by AIDS. "The children, the babies . . . they break my heart."

"I know," Elizabeth concurred.

Maureen Tower Weinstock joined her husband with another silver-haired couple in tow. She introduced them as Joseph and Tina Giannelli—good friends from New York who supported the theater, the arts, and more charities than she cared to imagine.

Lara Miller was en route to tell Elizabeth that the vice president and his wife were about to make their entrance when Elizabeth nearly collided with Emil Devorac, the eminence grise of film directors, and his plump wife, Lili. She was now forced to wait for an opening in the conversation.

"I don't go to these things as a rule," Emil announced.

"You're smart," Giannelli agreed. "Me neither, for the same reason."

The two men laughed. Devorac, somewhere in his late seventies, spoke with a heavy Middle European accent. Giannelli, a good ten to fifteen years his junior, had integrated a variety of Sicilian inflections into his New York/New Jersey cadence.

"Just a donation, right?" Devorac asked knowingly.

"Right." Giannelli puffed out his chest, showing off. "They're asking for three hundred per plate. I buy a table now—under the new tax law you can't deduct it if you've gone, because as the IRS sees it, you've had yourself a good time. So you send the tickets back—that's very important. You've sent your money, you've told the charity to give your tickets away—and that's one hundred percent deductible! And you're socially off the hook."

The women chorused their concern. Who would be attending their fund-raising events? Donations were important, but what was the point of planning a spectacular event if all the guests were going to return their tickets? It would put a strain on social chemistry.

"The vice president and his wife are about to make their entrance."

"Thank you, Lara, I'll be there directly," Elizabeth said graciously.

Giannelli smiled. He followed Elizabeth's path with his eyes. He admired a woman who took care of herself.

B.J. diverted Lara on her way backstage. He told her he didn't want Bonnie Louise spending any more time with Zachary Steele. As diplomatically as possible, Lara explained that she couldn't be in two places at once. At least Bonnie Louise and Zachary Steele were sitting at a table in full view of everyone.

"As soon as you've made the vice president comfortable, make Bonnie Louise your top priority." Lara nodded. B.J. took one more look at Bonnie Louise, ran his tongue across his teeth, and made his way backstage.

Lara didn't appreciate being assigned to baby-sit some mysterious blond teenager. B.J., who was old enough to be her father, was acting like a lovestruck teenager himself.

A muscular arm shot out. "I need to see some identification, miss." Lara flashed her badge. She passed the Secret Service guards heading toward the room where B.J. and Elizabeth were greeting the vice president.

"Lara," B.J. called out, "you can take your seat now." Dutifully she turned and headed back to the Garden of Eden.

B.J. placed a firm hand around Elizabeth's waist. "This evening will go down in history."

He looked into her eyes with the look that said, "Are we having a spell?" She flashed back the look that said, "Don't be silly. I'm perfectly all right."

By the look in his eyes he had bought it. He wanted to buy it, because he had no time to deal with the demons in her mind.

"One minute till curtain," he said, smiling.

"Someday someone will invent something to replace that awful dais."

"Place of honor."

"Fishbowl."

B.J. nodded, and they moved on.

CHAPTER 4

*B.*J. McClintock brushed through the crowd. His height, a tidy 6'3", allowed him to see too much. He was an adept politician, always smiling, shaking hands, blanketing one or one hundred with his disarming charisma.

Suddenly he felt a firm hand grip his arm. He turned and found Gordon Stanwick's laser-direct eyes telling him something was urgent. Something needed to be discussed right then and there. But where? As many times as B.J. had been to Hillcrest, he had never really learned the layout. He had no idea where to find a quiet corner.

"How's Muffy?" B.J. asked as he gestured toward a waiter's hand-held tray disappearing down a far corridor. Stanwick nodded and followed his host.

"Muffy's in seventh heaven. All her movie and TV idols are here." Stanwick pointed at someone and said, "My, my . . . if only I were forty years younger . . ."

B.J. turned to see Bonnie Louise laughing with Zachary Steele. The thought of any man looking and talking to *her* sent electric shocks through his system. Lara, he noticed, was just standing there—doing nothing to break up the conversation. He wanted to slip away, but he couldn't.

He and Gordon passed through the guests and were heading down a hallway to the kitchen when Stanwick motioned toward an unmarked door. A walk-in linen closet. Exactly what they needed.

The two men stood eye-to-eye. The heavy scent of their respective after-shaves mingled with the aroma of starch and soap.

Gordon Stanwick was a well-preserved man of sixty-five. Jet-lagged perhaps, but as sharp as a razor blade. "I just got in from Tokyo. I have some information that can give us both a healthy bonus."

"How big a bonus, Gordon?"

"Could be millions."

"Suits me just fine. Do I have to kill my sons for it?" B.J. joked.

Stanwick didn't laugh. "Matsumoto is about to absorb one of your competitors."

"Is that right? Who? And how much do you want?"

"Thirty percent. I'm taking a big risk giving you this information," said the American head of Matsumoto, the largest electronics company in the world.

"We're *both* taking the risk," B.J. said firmly.

"I'm retiring in a few months."

Stanwick's position was not lost on B.J. They had been friends for over twenty years. Ironically, McClintock thought to himself, I'm hiding in a closet with a man whose life has been lionized in *Who's Who*. Gordon and his wife, Muffy, were the perfect slim, trim, gray-haired, golf-playing, charity-organizing couple. They had three strapping sons, who were all seemingly happily married and successful. To B.J.'s knowledge, the Stanwicks attended church almost every Sunday because they found it to be an uplifting experience. Now, after all those clean-living years, Gordon was trading insider information in a linen closet.

A half-smile formed across Stanwick's thin lips. "Constellation Studios," he whispered.

The news put a broad smile on B.J.'s face. Yes, he calculated, this caliber tip-off can make me a fast five million if I put five in.

"Ten percent," B.J. offered, staring him down.

"Ten percent of what?" Stanwick lashed back, insulted.

"Let's just say you'll end up with a cool half-million, Gordon."

"I think it's a deal. And don't forget the insider scandals. I don't want to end up like Boesky and the Milkens," Stanwick said, laughing nervously.

Both men laughed nervously. "You don't have to remind me, Gordon. I appreciate your confidence." B.J. offered his hand. Stanwick took it.

The power brokers took a deep breath, smiled, and exited the linen closet.

B.J. picked up his stride. "Gordon," he intoned, "I think we'd best make separate entrances."

"Right."

They nodded and fanned out in opposite directions.

B.J. was livid. The night was a huge success on one hand, and a monstrous disaster on the other.

He had wanted to slap Joan across her tight scarlet lips when she told him she was leaving MCM "tonight after the benefit." He never had a clue she was moving in that direction.

And Bonnie Louise showing up hours before the benefit nearly gave him a heart attack.

"What are you thinking about, Byron?" Elizabeth asked gently.

"Uh, Joan, my dear. I don't know what I'm going to do."

"I think Lara Miller would be perfect for the job," she said matter-of-factly.

"Lara? She's green and wet behind the ears! Lacks aggression. She's almost shy, dammit! She couldn't handle the pace."

"Oh yes, she could. I wish you could have seen her in action tonight. Why, that bandleader demanding more money at the very last minute—I tried talking to the scoundrel, but got nowhere. Finally Lara said she would handle it—and she did! When she came out of the dressing room, she had talked the whole band into doing the benefit for a tax write-off!"

"Is that right?" B.J. pondered.

"Joan couldn't hold a candle to that girl. Why, she has passion for her work. She'd be loyal, too."

Elizabeth patted B.J.'s hand and rested her head on his shoulder. It was a relief to be in the limousine. She knew B.J. was thinking about Lara Miller.

"I mean it, Byron. I could never have pulled this benefit together without Lara Miller."

"Maybe you're right, dear. I must say, you so often are. I'll sleep on it." He thought for a moment. Then: "But you know what part of the trouble is? She's a lady. And you know what Sam Goldwyn said."

"What did he say?"

"Nothing stinks up the joint like a lady."

"B.J.! That's terrible!" said Elizabeth, laughing.

"Yes, but you know what he meant."

"I'm a lady, I hope."

"Of course. But you're not in the office all day."

Elizabeth smiled, knowing that by morning Lara would be *his* idea. At least she'd planted the seed. Men, she thought. You can lead them to the pot of gold, and only hope they have their eyes open to see it.

B.J. turned his head and looked out the tinted window with only one thought on his mind . . . Bonnie Louise. Seeing her tonight in his world, so close to his family, made his skin crawl. Watching men talking to her . . . men who wanted to do nothing but ravish her perfect young body . . . made him insane.

"Why don't you sleep in *my* room tonight?" Elizabeth whispered while she nuzzled into his neck.

B.J.'s spine stiffened. He took a deep breath. "I don't think so, dear . . . this has been a very trying week. Maybe tomorrow night."

Elizabeth sat up straight, smoothing out her dress. Being rejected tonight of all nights hurt deep down in the pit of her stomach. She and B.J. hadn't made love in nearly a year.

B.J. knew he had hurt Elizabeth's feelings, but he was in the wrong mood after seeing Bonnie Louise put Zachary Steele's number in her handbag The two of them were together all evening. B.J. squirmed in the lush velour seat, silently cursing the young superstar stud touching *his* seventeen-year-old mistress.

CHAPTER 5

*H*olly tried to open her eyes. They were dry and on fire—like a beach towel that had lain too long in the sun.

"My God. How much champagne did I drink last night?" She searched her memory as a little man beat a drum somewhere near her forehead. The thought of moving didn't appeal to her.

Her mind was rumbling with the vision of B.J. waving his million-dollar check at the cheering body of illustrious contributors. She rubbed her eyes and thought, They must have raised almost $4 million last night. I seem to remember donating twenty thousand myself.

Holly Dandridge was a classic beauty. She was gracefully approaching her mid-thirties. She was a combination of Meryl Streep and Sigourney Weaver coupled with the spunk of Cher. Holly was a chameleon. She transformed herself into whomever others required her to be, onscreen and off.

Her reputation was that of a men's lady. Two fast but brief marriages didn't slow her down long enough to change the name on her checkbook.

Every month her gorgeous face was seen in the tabloids, magazines, and trades. Holly with a famous actor, a shipping magnate, a rock star, a real estate tycoon, an Arab sheikh, or an extra from the set of her TV show, which had held the number-one slot on prime-time television for the past five years.

She was a Phenomenon. America loved her no matter what she did. Europe loved her. Fashion loved her. She was one of the ten best-dressed women. Men went to extremes to meet her, be near her.

Holly loved men. She loved the whole game of love. If she wasn't actively engaged in the lusty battle, her mood would drastically swing down.

Holly ached in every muscle of her body as she moved her right leg. She wasn't getting any younger. The lines were beginning to show, and that worried her. A lot of things worried her. She groaned and pushed them all to the darkest corner of her mind. Her makeup man worked miracles hiding her multitude of sins.

Her left leg felt as if it needed to be oiled with the rest of her joints. A steamy shower is what I need, she told herself. A safe, quiet, wet place. Damn, she thought, I never felt this bad when I waited tables—friends were friends, and champagne was cheap white wine. Holly was yearning for a cup of Anna's perfect coffee, which she could smell floating under the crack of her bedroom door.

A moan came from the other end of her custom California king-sized bed. Holly's eyes popped wide open. She turned to find the most beautiful young man. A total stranger. But beautiful.

Holly's brain started to spin. This is ridiculous. I must know him, she told herself. Think! Think! Dammit! No!

That tore it! Once and for all she was going to stop getting ripped out of her mind and clothes. She looked closer. This one was beautiful: full mouth, long black lashes, and dark curly hair just the right length to hang on to. He looked like a young gladiator.

She softly raised the sheet to inspect this heavenly specimen. His large penis was pointing in her direction.

"Thank you, God," she whispered, raising her eyes to heaven.

Until this glorious morning she had been a righteous cunt for weeks. She knew it, but she couldn't help herself. She bitched and moaned at gaffers, grips, wardrobe assistants, and caterers.

But never, ever, at Renaldo, her makeup man. For he held the brushes that made her face flawless.

Holly quietly slipped out of bed and tiptoed into the bathroom. She found what she was looking for; two used condoms were floating in the commode. I may have been drunk, but I wasn't out of control, she told herself, palming a new package.

She smiled and wondered what color his eyes were as she clasped her hand around his throbbing mortal manhood. Blue, Holly prayed as she cupped his precious pouch with the other. His eyes slowly opened. They were bluer than blue!

Feeling invigorated, Holly popped into the shower steam singing. She giggled as she soaped Dino's luscious hairy chest.

"So, you're Italian?"

"*Sì, bella.*"

"And you drive cars?"

"*Sì!* I brrrm, brrrm," he said, as he mimed a steering wheel turning a dangerous corner.

"Oh! You're a race-car driver!" Holly squealed.

"*Sì, sì, bella!*" He cupped his hands under her perky breasts and kissed them.

"Grand Prix?" Holly asked.

"*Sì, sì*, me a weeeener!" Dino patted his chest like a caveman.

"How lovely! Well, my weeeener, you can brrrm brrrm me to the studio."

"*Che?*" Dino looked puzzled.

Frustrated, Holly mimed, "You brrrm brrrm me . . ."

Before she could finish, Dino said, "*Sì, sì, bella,*" smiled the way only an Italian can smile, and pulled her down to the warm, wet safe tile floor and proceeded to drive her out of her mind.

CHAPTER 6

*L*ara Miller liked her new job as B. J. McClintock's administrative assistant very much. And why not? It happened to be one of the better jobs in the film business.

B.J. wasn't sure about her in the beginning, but he soon realized that Lara had a way about her that poured caramel over people as if they were scoops of vanilla ice cream. And that was exactly what was needed to handle the onslaught of stars and movers-and-shakers who ran in a constant stream in and out of his office.

The only thing Lara didn't bargain for was the long hours—twelve hours a day, seven days a week. That included holidays. It was a demanding job, but it paid an extra thousand dollars a month.

"Urgent" was the key word. Today, urgent meant holding a budding young actress's hand while she had her first visit to the plastic surgeon.

It was the most beautiful southern California Saturday she had ever seen. Lara was not amused.

A buzzer opened the door to Dr. Morton Shipp's gorgeous but well-hidden suite of offices. "Hidden" was the key word here.

It had to be hidden, because stars would come in looking like normal human beings, and hours later they would be whisked away from the private loading dock in the bowels of the building looking like creatures from another planet.

Rich women, famous women, paranoid women, women who had

hocked their husbands' income for the next five years just to have Dr. Shipp do wonders to their faces, breasts, and neurotic brains. Men were even more secretive about their alterations. Lara supposed it was cheaper than therapy in the long run.

Dr. Shipp's sanctum sanctorum was nestled somewhere off Wilshire Boulevard in the famous Beverly Hills Adjacent area that had become even more chic to live in than Beverly Hills itself.

The color scheme was black, gray, and white. Stones that looked as if they had dropped off the Parthenon were covered with thick layers of beveled glass. On top of that were all the latest European magazines. A stark black-and-white-check floor made the place seem vast, empty, and cold. What a place to have your face changed, Lara mused.

Lara's thoughts went wild inside these walls: this floating laboratory of evil flesh-rearranging.

The young actress looked terrified as she studied a sculpture that looked like a screaming vulva that belonged to an elephant.

"*Ahhhhhh!* There you are, ladies!" Dr. Shipp breathed out, smelling of a mixture of mint and formaldehyde. There he stood in tennis shorts and a headband wrapped around a wig. Lara stared at him. It had to be a wig. No normal man would put that much lacquer on his own hair to play tennis and, besides, it wasn't quite the same color and length at the benefit.

"Come with me. Please excuse the informality. This is Saturday! I rather like doing my work on the weekend," he beamed, sounding a bit like Captain Kangaroo. "It doesn't have the pressures that normally exist on a weekday."

He led them to a room with one chair in the middle of the floor. Shipp motioned for Vanessa to take the chair. Lara leaned against the wall. Something about this man looked different to her. She couldn't put her finger on it.

"Now let me see, *ahhhh*, what a pretty face you have, Vanessa. Just wait until you see how I am going to enhance what is already there. You are going to be so beautiful!" His excitement was nauseating.

Shipp held a magic marker in his right hand and proceeded to draw on Vanessa's face. He circled her cheekbones and outlined her upper and lower lips.

"There!" he squealed as he handed her a mirror.

She looked at herself and then at Lara with confusion.

"Is this where you're going to cut me?" she asked in a small, trembling voice.

"No, no, no, my dear. This is where I am going to inject you with my magic serum that is going to give you pronounced cheekbones and full, sexy lips like Holly Dandridge."

Vanessa's eyes widened. "Did *she* have this done, too?"

Shipp grinned. "Oh yes," he said proudly. "She's been a client of mine for years. Why, Vanessa, half the ladies you see on the silver screen and on TV have been enhanced by me."

Dr. Shipp's chin! That was it! Lara finally figured it out. He'd done something to his chin. When she'd seen him, at the McClintocks' Christmas party, he hadn't had that chin.

As he smiled down at the naturally lovely actress, Lara couldn't help but feel that Dr. Shipp was totally out of his mind. A modern-day Dr. fucking Frankenstein!

His nose looked as if it had fallen off of Robert Wagner's face. That was the new acquisition last time. And his chin! It was exactly like Kirk Douglas's. Probably #43 in Dr. Shipp's catalog. Lara restrained herself from grabbing the young woman out of the chair and running out as fast as their legs would carry them. Lara took a good look around her and realized this was not a lousy "B" movie; this was real life, and this was her real-life job.

The crazy doctor lined up several tiny needles full of his "magic" serum.

"Now this won't hurt you, really. Just tiny little pricks. Maybe if Lara would be so kind and hold the ether under your nose while I inject the golden fluid into your epidermis." He shot a look at Lara, handing her a dark brown bottle of ether and a large swab of cotton. Lara swooned from the odor.

You vile creature. Someday you're going to burn in hell for the shit you've done to people. There goes my old brain again. Business is business. But this business is against the law of nature.

"That's it . . . why, you're as good as my Billy!"

"Who's Billy?" *Some young boy you're turning into a woman so you can take him out to dinner in a Bob Mackie evening gown? Shut up, brain.*

"Billy is really Wilhelmina, one of my nurses."

I'm willing to bet that Billy is a boy.

The needle must have punctured skin at least two hundred times. Vanessa looked as though she had been beaten by an angry mob.

Dr. Shipp gave her some pain pills and, of course, some sleeping pills to get her through the next few days. He reassured her that all the swelling would go down, and she would be on the set by the middle of next week. His slow but sure method of reaching his goal . . . beauty.

The maniacal pig offered to remove Lara's mole right then and there. The mole that men thought sexy and always gave an extra lick in the height of passion. She never gave it a second thought.

"No, thank you, Doctor."

Get out of my face, you scalpel-happy bastard!

"Well, you think about it, Lara . . . now, for you, Vanessa. We have you scheduled for breast implants on the thirteenth. That's a week from this coming Wednesday." Dr. Frankenstein smiled, exposing his caps from molar to molar.

Sweet Jesus! Is there anything that's real on this crazy man's body? No . . . there isn't. The only thing left untouched on his wife Elaine is the length of her legs.

B.J. wanted cheekbones . . . well, he got cheekbones. He wanted lips . . . he got lips. They were hideous and lumpy. Lara prayed to God they'd miraculously turn into the sexy, pouty, mouth that half the male population wanted to stick their cocks into. Lara didn't believe in the plastic Hollywood system. She believed in Myrna Loy, Katharine Hepburn, Hedy Lamarr, Bette Davis, Barbara Stanwyck, and even Martha Raye.

You didn't have to be stamped a beauty to be a star. You had to have talent, manna from heaven, that magic dust that falls on you in the crib.

Watching Dr. Shipp perform his evil wizardry gave Lara chills. All the human depth of the man seemed to be gone, all the warmth replaced with climate control.

Maybe she was old-fashioned. Maybe she should have an open mind about this business. *Now, I know why Joan complained so much on Monday mornings. I hope this is the worst of it.*

CHAPTER 7

*B*onnie Louise was running through the Malibu Beach house like an out-of-control five-year-old child, one moment squealing with delight at the breathtaking view and the next throwing herself into the deep down-filled pillow of the sand-colored couch.

"Now control yourself young lady. This is only for a few days," B.J. stated in his most authoritative voice. Bonnie Louise ran to him, wrapped her arms around his neck, turned her alabaster chin upward, and sighed.

"Oh, Byron, don't be so businesslike with me! Why, this is the most exciting place I have ever been to outside of Rancho Virgo."

She planted a playful kiss on his cheek and whispered in his ear, "Why don't we run a hot bath up there in that sexy tub and . . ."

"I just don't have the time, honey," B.J. interrupted. "I have to get back to the office."

"There you go again, actin' like a businessman. . . . *You are* different here in California. . . . Don't you love me anymore?" she asked, on the verge of tears.

"You know I love you."

"No, I don't know anymore. I called and called and called, and you never picked up the phone."

"I wasn't there, sweetheart! You know I had that private line installed just for you. Darlin', we've gone days without speaking before."

"But, Byron, I had no idea where you were, and when Scarlett died, I wanted to talk to you so bad." She collapsed into an overstuffed chair and began sobbing.

B.J. felt a sharp pain in his heart. He steadied himself, realizing how insensitive he had been to Bonnie Louise during the last few weeks. He dropped to his knees and cradled her in his arms.

"Baby," he said softly, "I'm so sorry. I'll never do that to you again. I loved Scarlett just as much as you did. I know how important the foal was. It was important to me, too."

B.J. stroked her arms and torso, with a loving, comforting motion. A peace offering. "Remember," he went on, "we spent a whole day pickin' out a name." He handed her his handkerchief.

In a soothing voice he said, "Darlin', did you know that the Malibu Stables is in walkin' distance? Just up the hill, on the other side of the highway."

"So?"

"So . . . I bet they have a horse up there that's just for you. You can ride it right out there—on the sand—right into the Pacific Ocean."

The girl's eyes brightened. "You can?" she asked hopefully.

"You sure can, Bonnie. Come here—have a look." He took her hand and led her out onto the deck.

"You know I love you," B.J. told her. "It's just that I have so much pressure on me right now. I know *you're* not going to give me more. . . ."

"I'll do whatever you say, Byron. I know I've been a bad girl, showing up like this on your married doorstep." Bonnie Louise lowered her head and chewed on her lip.

"I've told Elizabeth that this house is rented to a manager friend for his client. That's *you*. A young starlet, *who leads a quiet life*. So watch your *P*s and *Q*s. That means I don't want any visitors here. Especially *Zachary Steele*." B.J. clenched his teeth.

"He's no good, Bonnie Louise," he went on. "He has a reputation for running after girls until he gets them. Once he's fucked them, he throws 'em away like disposable cups. One drink and you end up on the side of the road like trash."

Her anger began to rise. She hated B.J. for saying those foul words about Zachary. Zachary wasn't like that at all. But it was no use even talking to B.J. about it.

"Now, honey, don't be jealous. Please. He's just a friend."

"He's not a *friend*! You just met him last night! How can you say that?" B.J. heard himself sounding like a father, not a lover. This was not good. It was madness having Bonnie Louise so close to the vital center of his life. B.J. ran his tongue over his teeth, looking at her, starting to convince himself that he could handle the situation.

Assuming a businesslike tone, he began to go through all the rules and regulations of the Malibu Beach house. The maid would come in on Tuesday, Friday, and Sunday. She would cook food and leave it in the refrigerator. The Jacuzzi man would turn up on Saturday. Lara Miller would be at Bonnie's disposal if anything should go wrong with the electricity or plumbing.

After he left, the house began to feel too big for Bonnie Louise. She sat there contemplating the contrast between the Rocky Mountains and the Pacific Ocean. She watched the never-ending waves roll in and out, in and out. Finally she couldn't stand it any longer. A telephone sat temptingly close at hand. She lifted the receiver and called Zachary.

The actor seemed to be the most understanding person Bonnie Louise had ever met. *He knew how she felt.* It amazed her when Zachary wasn't the slightest bit upset about B.J. having forbidden her to see him at the beach house—or, for that matter, anywhere.

"That's ridiculous," Zachary insisted. "There's nothing B.J. can do if I turn up on the *public beach* that leads to your window. . . . I might even bring my guitar."

Bonnie Louise giggled self-consciously. "I've been told what a dangerous man you are with the ladies, Zachary."

"You know what my grandmother always says? 'Believe nothing you hear and only half of what you see.' "

"That's funny—my granny told me the very same thing."

"I can't wait to see you, Bonnie Louise."

After a long, thoughtful pause she asked, "And when might that be?"

"Soon."

"I hope so, 'cause I'm only gonna be here a few days."

"Not if I have anything to do with it." He paused and, almost sighing, said, "I love your drawl."

Bonnie Louise closed her eyes and sank deeper into the down cushions. There was something about Zachary Steele's voice that made her whole body tingle. All at once she was trembling with fear and excitement.

Neither one of them wanted to say good-bye, but when a long-distance call from the director of his new film came through, Zachary had to take it.

CHAPTER 8

*L*ara Miller looked up from her paperwork to see whose foot was tapping in anticipation. It was Holly Dandridge's foot and her nostrils were flaring.

"Hello, Miss Dandridge. May I help you?" Lara asked nervously.

"Yeah! Cut the 'Miss' crap and tell B.J. I'm here!" Holly slammed a script on the desk and angrily waved a letter.

"He's not here, Holly. What's wrong?"

"What's wrong? I'll tell you what's wrong! This reader's report on *Blue Moon*. I told that blond bitch, Joan, I didn't want anyone reading my script except B.J., and not to show it around!"

Holly was pacing up and down in front of Lara's desk, seething.

"Holly, B.J. doesn't read scripts. I think I remember him saying something about your script being too high-budget for us."

"That's bullshit!" Holly leaned down over Lara's desk and lowered her voice. In a confidential tone she said, "Listen, this script is more shocking than Watergate or the Iran-Contra scandal. This is based on stories I heard from the horse's mouth. I had an affair with a soldier of fortune five years ago who laid all the facts on the table about a covert Mafia operation in cahoots with the federal government."

Lara's interest was piqued. "I'd like to read it, Holly. May I?"

"As long as you keep it under your hat. I mean it, Lara. This movie has the magic that puts Oscars on mantels and lines around the block."

Holly stood up and winked.

"High risk, big rewards. . . . Read it, and then get Big Daddy to read it. Bye."

Lara could hardly wait to open the script and start reading.

"Nuke it," Lara commanded, pressing the "start" button on her new microwave. In seven minutes she'd have a perfectly edible three-course, reduced-calorie dinner. Not that ten past twelve was her preferred time for dinner, but the way things were going, dinner at midnight and alone was becoming a pattern.

B.J. pushed her hard as he did everybody else—actors, directors, producers, politicians, even priests—someone was always wanting B. J. McClintock's undivided attention.

Learning the ropes was tricky. The sense of which people were to be admitted and which ones were to be politely put off could be perfected only by time and experience. And, as Lara had discovered, B.J. was a perfectionist. He could be tyrannical if a word was misspelled or a letter not sent when promised. He was a stickler for detail.

The timer buzzer went off. Lara removed her entree and curled up on the couch next to Peter, her six-year-old black-and-white cat. He rubbed up against her; then, smelling the chicken, began kneading her thigh with his paws.

"Stop," she warned. "I fed you first, Peter." His purring became louder. "Now I mean it. I don't beg when *you* eat."

The green-eyed feline looked up at her with an all-knowing stare, then moved his paw toward her plate, purring all the while.

"How can I resist you?" Lara teased, and cut off a small tidbit for the relentless little beggar. Gingerly he took it.

Three bites of her meal and the thrill was gone for Lara. Hunger had somehow been abated, but her taste buds remained unsatisfied. It was time to crawl into bed with Holly Dandridge's screenplay.

Just a few pages, Lara promised herself. Enough to be able to say she was "well into it." The clock on the night table glowed 12:53. The alarm was set for seven. Lara rubbed her eyes and studied the title page. Jeffrey Lascu was considered one of MCM's best writers. He'd created Holly's hit show as well as three half-hour situation comedies that were still running in syndication. Lara knew that Jeff wouldn't work on anything unless it was in some way extraordinary. Holly, as far as Lara was concerned, was ready to follow the likes of Shelley Long, Tom Selleck, and Ted Danson onto movie screens.

Blue Moon. . . . interesting title, Lara mused. Once in a blue moon . . . a blue moon only comes along once every four years. One hundred and twenty-one pages. Right length.

The first ten pages depicted murder, mystery, and mayhem. Chris, the male lead, was described as a Clint Eastwood type. "A man who can fill John Wayne's boots."

The story began by Chris, a former SEAL, being alerted to the disappearance of his younger brother, Johnny. There was a dead girl—Johnny's girlfriend. . . . Did Johnny kill her? The police discover evidence that leads them to believe he did.

Chris knows that his younger brother is innocent. He sets out to find him before the police do.

The writing is good, Lara thought. The story moves quickly. There's a lot of action and plenty of suspense. A love story. A mysterious Swiss bank account leading to drug dealing and double-dealing. Soldiers of fortune working for the Mafia—covertly entering Bolivia, wiping out a village, and making off with hundreds of pounds of pure cocaine paste. The operation appeared to have been masterminded by a corrupt congressman and a Mafia kingpin.

The more Lara read, the more she sensed that *Blue Moon* was based on fact. Holly had probably spent a romantic interlude with a rubber-jawed soldier of fortune. And so many politicians had fallen from grace over the last two decades that it wasn't hard to imagine one of them being the inspiration for the movie's villain.

Real-life villains had been a part of Lara's life since childhood, ever since her brilliant, idealistic lawyer father had pursued the New York/New Jersey drug lords. She pushed her head back into the pillows, returning to the screenplay. Her eyelids were drooping, and Peter had long since fallen into a sound sleep contoured against her torso. Lara kept reading, fast-turning the pages. Holly's role was a great one, one that any hot actress would want to play. No wonder she was so insistent about B.J. reading the script quickly and making an immediate decision.

Who was Holly's soldier of fortune? Lara wondered. The desperado who'd been dropped into jungles and isolated villages and onto mountaintops—paid to kill, paid to steal. One hundred and twenty-one pages later Lara was wide awake and dying to call Holly Dandridge. But it was well past three.

The 8 × 10 portrait of her handsome father, Brandon Miller, standing alongside Martin Luther King, Jr., after King's moving "I have a dream . . ." speech, stood out amid a cluster of framed family photographs. Were her father alive, she knew he'd like *Blue Moon* as much as she did. Then she thought of her mother. No, she'd take the opposite tack. Irene Miller would tell her daughter to steer clear of the project because it was controversial.

Bitter memories of her parents arguing late at night flooded Lara's mind. She recalled her mother telling her about the public debate her father held in Manhattan to discuss the far-reaching problems of drug abuse among young people. As an assistant D.A. Brandon Miller had had the foresight to understand that oppressed and deprived young people, especially those crammed into ghettos, would find unity and solace in altered states.

Irene Miller, Lara thought, had been pressed from a conservative New England cookie cutter. She hadn't had Lara until she was thirty-six and set in her ways . . . a good mother, but *tired* so much of the time.

Lara'd had a strict but privileged East Coast upbringing—church every Sunday, a puppy called Snoopy and a parakeet called Sparky, ballet lessons, tennis lessons, French lessons. . . . How different, Lara reflected, it would have been had her father not died the week after her sixteenth birthday.

The twin-engine Cessna he was piloting exploded in midair. Faulty fuel line, the FAA investigators decided. Sabotage was what her mother thought. Well, nothing could bring him back.

Thank God, Lara thought, Daddy had lived every day to its fullest. She closed her eyes, recalling the dog-eared brown leather diary she had found in the moving boxes they'd taken out of storage before her freshman year at NYU.

Page after page of her father's adventures: smoking pot with a group of fellow lawyers and politicians . . . seeing *Hair* in the Village. Watching the psychedelic sixties give upper- and lower- and middle-class kids an excuse to revamp their values and their morals. He saw it coming. He knew if Organized Crime got its way, it would flood the whole country with drugs.

Lara had smoked grass at a fraternity party and practically passed out. Another time she'd smoked it on a skiing trip with girlfriends. She didn't care if she ever smoked it again. It wasn't her cup of tea. She preferred feeling sharp, living in the moment. And as for anything stronger, she would pass. She had witnessed the compromising effects of cocaine on friends, several of whom had turned into regular Zelda Fitzgeralds. And their husbands hadn't fared much better. She knew at least a dozen people who'd kicked their habit at the Betty Ford Clinic.

She looked at her parents' wedding picture. A stunning couple in their late twenties, radiating hope. She could see why her mother fell so deeply in love with her father.

Brandon Miller was a genuinely nice man. Gentle, intelligent . . . driven. Maybe her own save-the-world bent came from him. It was her hidden desire—deep down she wanted to do something to help people. Lara believed that she'd been blessed with the gift of compassion and a certain amount of foresight. Well, she told herself, you don't have to be a visionary to see the potential in *Blue Moon*.

She leaned back, sinking into her latest extravagance—oversized down pillows. Peter stretched one leg and fanned his claws. He yawned, and Lara gently stroked his soft fur. She couldn't wait for her alarm to ring so that she could place a call to Holly Dandridge.

CHAPTER 9

A full moon cast an eerie shadow over the mountains that embraced Malibu's seaside community. Bentine Devorac's Volvo bounced over the speed bumps and stopped. She cautiously eyed the supermarket parking lot before slipping into a space near the entrance. She checked her disguise in the rearview mirror. "It's fifteen minutes till the store closes . . . I couldn't possibly run into anybody I know."

The electric doors parted, and Bentine grabbed a shopping cart. Only a handful of shoppers were in evidence. She *would* have to run out of toilet paper, Kleenex, and paper towels after having eaten half a box of prunes for lunch.

Paper products. There had to be twenty varieties of bathroom tissue. . . . Bentine reached inside her handbag and pulled out a stack of coupons. She stood there contemplating the wall of choices.

Periwinkle blue, she sighed. It won't match any of my bathrooms, but if I buy that brand, I get a free roll of paper towels . . . and I'll save ninety-nine cents.

Bentine's stomach rumbled as she reached for the bargain tissue. She had the feeling it would be scratchy, but the price was right. She looked up at the clock. Seven more minutes of shopping time. Quickly she crosscut her way to the liquor aisle.

A Robert Mondavi '84 cabernet sauvignon Sterling reserve caught her attention. Twenty-nine ninety-nine . . . Pricey, she thought, but worth it.

On the shelf below, she spotted a Mouton-Cadet within her price range. She picked it up and adeptly peeled off the $6.99 price tag. She replaced the bottle.

Casually, using her other hand, she took the Mondavi wine off the shelf and peeled the price tag off with her index finger. She set it in the basket and pretended to peruse a row of burgundies. Then, as if on cue, she reached down and pressed the $6.99 tag on top of the vintage wine. En route to the checkout counter she artfully scratched the laser readout on the bottom of the label so that the checker would have to ring up the price manually.

Feeling confident, she took her place in line and picked up the lastest issue of *Vanity Fair*.

"Hot off the press," Helen O'Brien had proudly told her. Colin's charismatic smile lighted up the cover. The caption read, "Colin O'Brien: Women love him. Men want to be him."

Bentine marveled at the public's infinite capacity for worship. Colin O'Brien was certainly very attractive, and sometimes he gave an extremely good performance. Laurence Olivier he was not. He was a bankable star—that was how Bentine viewed her best friend's husband.

As she flipped through the glossy pages, she came upon the "O'Brien spread." Helmut Newton's fine focus on Colin, Colin and Helen in Switzerland, at home in Malibu. Colin on the ski slopes of Aspen. If I didn't know you better, Bentine silently told the handsome face staring up at her, I'd believe this article.

She wondered what living with self-absorbed Colin was really like. It couldn't be as good as it looked in these photos, or Helen wouldn't be addicted to her psychiatrist and those little purple pills. But that wasn't Bentine's business. She had never interfered with Helen's marriage, and she wasn't about to start now.

"Isn't it fantastic to have our neighbor on the cover?" a smooth male voice with an Italian accent inquired.

Bentine swiveled around and looked up into Carlo Capriotti's big brown eyes. *She had been caught holding coupons in her hand by one of her wealthiest neighbors.*

"Carlo," she said, laughing nervously and crumbling the bits of paper in her palm. "What a surprise!"

"With that scarf on your head, I almost didn't recognize you, Bentine. Nice wine," he complimented. "And an unbelievable price," he said, squinting at the tag.

"I know," she covered. "I got the last one. Carlo, please, go ahead of me—all you have is cigarettes."

"No, no, no—ladies first!"

"Excuse me, Mr. Capriotti," the store manager interrupted. "Your wife just called and asked if you'd bring these diapers home."

"Oh, thank you, Murray. How considerate."

"That's why we're here, Mr. Capriotti—step over here, and I'll check you out."

"Bentine," Carlo effused, "you, too—you first."

"No, n-no . . ." she stammered. "I'm next. My things are already on the conveyor belt. But thanks—and—and give my regards to Eugenia."

"I will. *Buona notte.*"

Bentine felt a surge of activity in her lower intestine, and she crossed her ankles.

At this moment I'd give anything to be financially independent!

Bentine Devorac and Helen O'Brien were rounding the night out with the vintage Mondavi wine. It had been a slow evening— girls' night in. Colin had insisted on accompanying his friend Derek Middleton to the airport. Middelton's wife, the former Lady Rebecca Ward, was off to London, and not a moment too soon, Helen thought. That Druid witch had made her life intolerable for the last ten days. Fortunately trips to LAX were not on Helen's agenda unless they involved her children or her parents. Colin always used a limousine service.

Bentine couldn't stop talking about the AIDS benefit. How everyone was getting younger. Or, more accurately, how the children of their peers, *babes on the sand*, were now graduating from college . . . getting married . . . landing parts in movies and on TV. . . . She pressed the "on" button. Justine Bateman was guest-hosting a late-night talk show. Her guests were River Phoenix and Chynna Phillips.

"Look at them!" Bentine said hysterically. "They're so young."

"So what? Everybody hits forty, sooner or later. If they're lucky."

"It's not fair," Bentine whined. "Look at Chynna. I could be her mother."

"You're only forty-five," Helen advised.

"Forty-three."

"Get your eyes done. Go see Dr. Shipp. He'll take ten years off."

Tears welled in Bentine's eyes. "The chemical peel was supposed to take ten years off—but it only took off two. I want my whole face—what am I saying, Helen—my whole body redone!"

"Dr. Shipp sets sail every day in Beverly Hills."

"It's easy for you," Bentine asserted. "You can spend whatever you want. I'm on a fucking budget." She paused, filled her wine-glass, and, losing control, said, "Insurance doesn't cover face-lifts and tummy tucks!" Tears flooded down her cheeks. "You wanna know something, Hellsey?"

Helen leaned back on the chaise and moaned affirmatively.

"You wanna know how low I've stooped?"

Helen nodded drowsily. At this point she knew her old friend was swinging across the emotional spectrum. Bentine needed a friend. She needed an ear, even a deaf one.

"No, not how *low* I've stooped. How low I've *had* to stoop because of Randy."

In her drunken state she went into the bedroom, returning with a huge white leather Fendi shoulder bag.

Helen watched through her own haze as her childhood friend plucked a red fabric wallet from a secret, zippered compartment.

Bentine unpeeled the Velcro cover and announced, "Coupons! You see these, Hellsey? Look at this—sixty-five cents off on Tide, twenty-five cents off on Eskimo Pies, a dollar off on Folger's."

"So what, Bennie? Big deal. Everybody uses coupons."

"I'll bet you don't!" the bitter former Mrs. Lloyd spat.

"You want to hold that against me? Fine."

Bentine was suddenly struck by her own bitterness. Helen really didn't care if she used coupons. She was actually sympathetic. Another flood of tears washed across her bloodshot brown eyes. "It's stupid, isn't it?" she said rhetorically. "I know I'm being stupid, but I can't help myself.

"Hellsey, you can't imagine what it's like when you're used to buying whatever you want—whenever you want—and suddenly —zap! You make one tiny, little mistake . . . and you're on a tight budget."

"Sleeping with the Mexican construction worker wasn't exactly tiny."

"No . . . he wasn't."

The two women laughed.

"It wasn't your affair, Ben. It was getting caught."

"Well, I'll tell you one thing. I almost died tonight. Prince Carlo nearly caught me at the checkout stand with coupons in my hand. I thought I was going to have a heart attack."

"Poor Bennie," Helen commiserated. "What do you usually do? Sneak into town in the middle of the night?"

"Almost. I go to Hughes in the Palisades. They double everything."

Helen shook her head. "You lost me."

"Hellsey, every Thursday after I see Dr. Goodwin in Beverly Hills, I stop at Hughes and stock up. I must save sixty dollars a month." She broke down sobbing. She paid her maid sixty dollars to clean the house. "Why am I telling you this?"

"Because confession is good for the soul."

"I want my kids back!"

"Then you've got to do something! You can't sit out here, occasionally going to lunches and dinners hoping to meet Mr. Right."

"But I'm almost broke," Bentine moaned.

"Since when did money make you happy?"

"Since I lost the use of it."

"You're smart," Helen told her. "Do something! Make it on your own."

"You really think I could?" Bentine asked, genuinely astonished.

"I know you could, Bennie. You've decorated everybody's house for free. Why not get paid for it?"

Bentine actually felt as if she might have some talent or value. Yes, she might be able to open a shop or a decorating service. Her mind started clicking over.

Helen closed her eyes and promised, "If you find something that's relatively fail-safe, I'll back you."

Bentine couldn't remember the last time she'd been this hung over. The sun felt like a dull knife across her eyes. She rummaged through the kitchen, making a sure-fix concoction. Plain tomato juice, not that spicy shit. One splash of vodka as she held her nose—the smell of alcohol made her wince. Juice of one whole lemon and two raw eggs with a generous shake of pepper and a splash of Worcestershire. The sound of the blender that fused this witch's brew had her hanging on to the counter.

With darkest shades in place she shuffled out on to the deck that jutted over the glaring sand. Getting drunk was not what she had intended to do. A little wine with Helen and then a couple of nightcaps while reading and watching Johnny Carson seemed reasonable. Wrong. Too many nightcaps.

She separated—gutted was the better word—the *L.A. Times* as she sipped the red liquid. She moaned as she dumped the financial section on the deck. "I'm glad Daddy didn't tie up his money in the stock market. I probably wouldn't be sitting here if he had."

The annoying sound of a jet ski averted her attention. She picked up the binoculars to get a closer look at the hard body of the man who was attempting to beach the noisy piece of machinery.

Bentine gasped and jerked her eyes away from the lenses. "That couldn't be . . ." She took a concentrated look.

"It is! I'll be damned . . . It's Zachary Steele!"

Her eyes followed every motion of his body. His image filled the entire frame of her Zeiss binoculars.

"This is better than a soap opera . . . my God . . . where is he going? . . . What? . . . Who the hell is that? . . . Wow!"

A gorgeous blond girl ran down the beach to Zachary. She was jumping up and down. Zachary dropped the jet ski and unzipped his wet suit. Then he started to chase the long-legged beauty down the beach. Catching up with her, he tackled her and they fell, coming very close to kissing. Bentine was beside herself as she watched the two creatures romp and struggle on the sun-bleached sand.

Her imagination, never far from fantasy, took a sudden involuntary leap: The two bodies disporting themselves in front of her were now on a wide bed, interlocked and naked. That girl was obviously a minor. Both shocked and stimulated by her imaginings, Bentine shook her head as if in self-reproof, to gain control of herself again. She reached out for a sip of her Bloody Mary, not taking the binoculars from her eyes. And then came a flash . . . not more fantasy but of recognition.

"*Oh, oh, oh!* . . . That's the girl who was at the AIDS bash the other night! She looked pretty damn young *that* night . . . now even more so . . . I was never that young. . . . I'll be damned, she's staying at the McClintocks'."

Bentine dropped her arm and took another thirsty gulp. Her headache had gone. What she had just seen so excited her that she picked up the phone and dialed Helen's number. As she waited for Helen to answer, the sound of loud rock music filtered down the beach.

"Ahhhh, a party just for two. . . . Good morning, Hellsey, got your coffee cup in hand?"

CHAPTER 10

*C*omfortably curled up on a sumptuous chair listening to loud rock music, Bonnie Louise thrilled at the sight of Zachary Steele's young, muscular body. No wrinkles. No loose skin. He was tight, athletic, hard, and contoured like a statue in the art books in Byron's library.

"I can't believe you've never heard of the Stingrays," Zachary said, shocked, turning the volume knob on the McClintocks' entertainment center to ten.

He danced across the living room and took Bonnie Louise's hand, pulling her to her feet and twirling her around the white Berber carpet. She squealed with delight.

"Listen to these lyrics," he said, squeezing her tight. "They remind me of you."

Bonnie Louise listened intently as the Stingrays' lead singer, a young man whose voice was raw with emotion, sang:

> "Little girl so far from home
> Made of love and flesh and bone
> You look to see your mother's eyes
> But only hear the laugh . . . the lies. . . .
> Some say she died of heartbreak
> Some say she lived as stone
> Some say she died from that fine ache
> Of living years alone. . . ."

The song brought tears to Bonnie Louise's eyes. It was the first time in her life that she'd heard words that reflected how she felt deep down inside. The first year at Rancho Virgo she'd convinced herself that she was a princess and that that was why she had no friends, only caretakers. The second and third years were more of the same . . . lots of presents and promises—promises of traveling to New York and Hawaii and the Bahamas—promises that she was beginning to realize would never be kept.

"Bonnie, what's the matter?" Zachary asked, wiping the tears from her cheek.

"You're right, Zach, the words *are* like me," she murmured.

"I'm sorry—I wouldn't have played it if I'd known it was going to hurt you."

"No! It's the best thing you could've done. It reached inside of me and made me look at my life."

Zachary looked into those magnetic seafoam-green pools of hers and wondered what she was afraid of. There was something about her that baffled him. She affected him like an addictive drug—the more he saw her, the more he wanted to see her—and the more he wanted to make love to her. He needed another shot of tequila.

The record ended, and Zach led Bonnie Louise over to the bar. He poured the last drop out of the Cuervo bottle and offered her a taste.

"No thanks," she said, turning up her nose. "I don't like the way it smells. I don't like hard likker."

"Oh? Well, I bet I could make you a drink with 'hard likker' that you'd love, Bonbon," he said jokingly, changing the mood.

She went for the bet, wanting to do everything in her power to please him.

"Ooooh, Sauza Commemorativo!" Zach exclaimed from beneath the bar. "Your uncle Byron has excellent taste."

Bonnie Louise smiled, but inside she was shuddering. The sound of Byron's name frightened her to the core. *What if he dropped in right now and found us here?* She looked at the throw pillows bunched together where they'd been lying on the floor. And the liquor . . .

She also thought that if Zachary knew the truth about her and Byron, he'd never speak to her again.

Zachary presented her with a tequila sunrise. "Try this," he said seductively, pushing the tall glass with the iced orange liquid across the marble counter toward her. She took a dainty sip. Her eyes widened.

"This is good! Tastes like fruit punch."

"Yeah," he agreed. "Fruit punch with a punch." He watched her take a larger sip. "My friend Rob's having a major party tonight. I'll pick you up about ten."

The smile on Bonnie Louise's face faded. "I'd really like to, Zach, but I can't. My aunt and uncle are comin' down for the night."

Zach paused, thinking of an irate B. J. McClintock and his cool, correct wife, Elizabeth, and their seventeen-year-old niece.

"Okay," he conceded, "I get the picture."

She wanted to go. She wanted to be with Zachary . . . but she couldn't take the chance. Just thinking about getting caught tied her stomach up in one big knot.

"God, Zachary," she said, holding up what was left of her drink, "I'm already startin' to feel silly."

"Good. Maybe I should take advantage of you." He playfully rolled an imaginary mustache and licked his lips.

"Oh no, you don't, Zachary Steele!"

"Hey! I'm a patient man." He grinned. "How about walking me to my jet ski?"

She nodded and smiled. "I'm ready."

Zachary took her hand, and they made their way down the backstairs to the sand. The sun was still high in the sky.

As Bonnie Louise unlocked the gate, Zachary wrapped his arms around her. He turned her to face him, kissing her tenderly. The kiss deepened, and Zachary knew he couldn't be a patient man much longer.

CHAPTER 11

The shrill gnawing, grinding sound of a chain saw biting into B.J.'s favorite oak tree greeted him as he took his place at the breakfast-room table. Watching the tree's demise was even more painful than listening to the ear-piercing racket.

When he and Elizabeth had purchased the Bel Air acreage, they'd instructed the architect to design the house facing northeast so that the majestic old oak would create a southern ambience. What they called a Tennessee feeling.

The big earthquake had torn some of its roots loose, and the last Santa Ana wind had broken off two huge branches. After those twin acts of God, it seemed to B.J. that the old tree had lost its will to live. He'd called in half a dozen tree surgeons, who, sorrowfully, had all come to the same conclusion: It had to be cut down before it fell on the house or hit electrical wires.

Elizabeth refused to burn any of the tree in their fireplaces. She felt as if a member of the family had died. All evidence of the beloved tree had to be removed from the property.

Evelyn, the maid, served B.J.'s two 3-minute eggs in a Haviland china egg cup. He instructed her to tell the workers to take a break. The noise was intolerable.

He stared through the big bay window at the severed limbs. For fifteen years, he reminded himself, the children had grown up under those spreading branches. He noted the frayed old rope swing limply entangled on the ground. His appetite was gone.

The McClintock home had been featured in every important publication from *Architectural Digest* to *Vogue* and *Town and Country*. It was formal, yet warm and inviting. Elizabeth and B.J. liked to think of it as a tribute to the beauty and grandeur of their American heritage.

The colonial-style home was situated on three prime acres that, on a clear day, looked out over Century City and Santa Monica, and across the water some thirty miles to Catalina Island.

French doors led to a brick basket-weaved terrace with a stone balustrade overlooking a grassy knoll and rose garden. Traversing a winding flagstone stairway, one arrived at the two-story pool house, which could be transformed into a screening room, seating up to fifty people comfortably. Beyond that there was a mosaic-tiled Olympic-size swimming pool and two tennis courts. Between upkeep and taxes, B.J. calculated his Bel Air expenses at $500,000 a year.

He knew he was a lucky man the day he walked into a Christie's auction in New York and watched several Chippendale pieces, identical to the ones Elizabeth had picked up at a Virginia auction house when they were newlyweds, selling for ten times the amount he'd paid. The eighteenth-century oil paintings, the Duncan Phyfe, and especially the Chippendale gave their home an authentic touch of Williamsburg.

Everything in Elizabeth's world was soft and polished. The wood floors were hand-buffed instead of sealed with polyurethane. The silver was antique sterling, and hundreds of pieces of fine porcelain had been handed down by her maternal grandmother, Martha Jackson. The estate was a true reflection of Elizabeth's high-brow English ancestry.

B.J. looked up and saw Elizabeth. He nodded in the direction of the window. She closed her eyes and nodded back.

Elizabeth's long, thick, freshly highlighted blond hair was held back by a maroon satin ribbon that matched her wool slacks. The fall shade was picked up again in her multicolored Missoni sweater. On her feet she wore her comfy lamb's fur slippers.

To change a sour mood was one of a wife's prime duties, Elizabeth had decided early in their marriage. So now she cast a mischievous grin in B.J.'s direction as she peeked beneath the silver muffin caddy cover and took out a blueberry popover.

A pot of hot water, lemon juice, and honey was served. Elizabeth poured the healthy brew and watched her husband devour the *Los Angeles Times*.

"Good morning, Byron. It's so nice to have you here for breakfast," she said sincerely.

B.J. looked up and smiled, watching her sip the hot lemon drink and bite delicately into the popover. Always the perfect lady, he observed.

"While I was getting dressed this morning, I was thinking about all the wonderful birthday parties we've had under that tree. And I always will. So, in that way at least, the old tree will live with us. Yet, you know, Byron, the end of it could be like a sign from heaven that things are changing."

He waited for her to complete her thought.

"When I brought the altar scarf that we ordered from Ireland to Sister Mary Margaret this morning," Elizabeth went on, "I told her about our old oak tree, and she said she wasn't superstitious, but she remembered a similar circumstance from her childhood. Her granddaddy had planted a crop of corn, and when it was reaching maturity, he went out one morning, and it was as if the first rays of sunlight had dried every bit of life out of those stalks."

"What the hell does that have to do with our tree?" B.J. asked impatiently.

"Well, Byron . . . what I'm trying to tell you is how these acts of God affect the human heart."

"Darlin', I've already said how it affects me deeply to see that old tree cut up. Now could we talk about something else?"

Elizabeth thoughtfully sipped her hot lemonade. "Well," she began coyly, "as a matter of fact, I was talking to Helen O'Brien, who informed me that our beach house is the talk of Malibu."

B.J. dropped his paper. "Why, what do you mean, sugar?"

"Well, that little starlet is having a big romance with none other than Zachary Steele."

"Is that right?" B.J. asked in a controlled tone. He ran his tongue across his upper teeth and gripped the chair. "I didn't know he had a place in the Colony."

"Oh, he doesn't. Evidently he arrives on this jet ski, and—according to Bentine Devorac—they play on the sand and in the water like a pair of baby seals in love."

B.J. pushed himself away from the table and stood up. "Got a big day ahead of me, darlin'."

"Byron, we have over a million dollars' worth of art in that house. I think I'd better take a drive out there today and make sure it's all right."

"That won't be necessary," B.J. said sternly. "I'll take care of it myself."

"But, dear, you don't have time to—"

"Let me deal with it, Elizabeth! I rented the house—I'll deal with it!"

Elizabeth watched him storm out of the room. My God, she thought, I've never seen him get so upset over *property*. It's the pressure. She knew he was worried about ratings. The networks and the viewing public had become so fickle. It was a wonder anybody could ever relax in the entertainment industry. To the extent that she could coax B.J. into doing so was another source of wifely pride to her.

CHAPTER 12

*T*he fifty-minute drive from Bel Air to the Malibu Colony had given B.J. the solitude he needed to think about Bonnie Louise. She was his muse. His private fantasy. Now, she had broken his number-one rule . . . she'd been with another man.

He was stymied as to how to handle her. He wanted to turn her over his knee, but he knew that wouldn't help. He reached for the ignition and nervously fingered an antique cuff link dangling from his key chain.

He knew it was in his best interest to put her on a plane and never see her again, but he couldn't do it. He loved her more than anything else on earth. His mind began to wander back to the beginning. Three years earlier . . .

October 1988, Plunkettville, Oklahoma

John Simpson wiped the grime from his neck with a well-used handkerchief. This Oklahoma dirt-road business was beginning to get to him. If it weren't for the phone booth he was standing up against, he would swear it was the Great Depression.

Simpson was in his early fifties, and had been a trusted employee of B. J. McClintock for nearly thirteen years.

Thirteen long, grueling years of finding drunken actors and learning the habits of producers and directors who incorporated their recreational pastimes into their production budgets.

In those days all McClintock cared about were his ratings. Simpson had to laugh when he thought of some of the superstar stakeouts he'd captured on infrared film and surreptitiously passed along to the *National Enquirer* and *The Star*. B.J.'s timing was impeccable. His tactics were worthy of a five-star general; the whole world was his enemy to conquer. Simpson was sure to this day none of the stars exposed ever knew the source of the revelations.

Admittedly in the beginning it was fun, but now, after three years of bloodhound duty, Simpson was ready to take his stash of cash and retire to Miami, where he could lean back and bet on jai alai and the greyhounds.

It had to be worse than being a traveling salesman, this job. In addition, over the past three years he had found five young ladies.

These were special young ladies. All virgins. Pure, sweet, untouched in mind and body.

These were special little girls. They had to have little education. Best if they came from rather large families living in poverty.

Through the years Simpson had a partner, Mabelle Stokes, an elegant professional con woman from Miami. With her posing as his wife, the parents never hesitated to hand over their daughters to such a respectable, rich-looking couple.

Simpson and Mabelle would play road games together.

"Just around the next bend, within a quarter of a mile, there will be a farmhouse with a bunch of hungry kids."

Sometimes he was right, and sometimes it was the second or third bend in the road. He was getting so good, he could smell the scent of a virgin within a ten-mile radius.

On this particular night he cursed his lousy employer who paid him $100,000 a year, plus $20,000 bonuses that were slipped into a Cayman Island account when he did good. *Real good.*

Simpson took a flask out of his jacket pocket and poured a jigger of scotch and shot it down his dry throat, hoping to clean his mouth. Wash away all the dirty lies he had told.

If ever there was a great impostor, it's me, he thought as he filled the tiny cup for the fourth time. When the molten liquid hit his tonsils, the angelic face of his previous acquisition loomed before him.

The Oklahoma peanut belt was thick and lush with greenery that afternoon when their car came to a clearing. Before them was a farmhouse on stilts. The wood was aged to slate gray and white. Several children were running around the haphazard structure chasing a bony dog.

Simpson and his cohort walked up to the front door and peered inside. They could hear someone rattling pots in the kitchen. A clear light bulb hung from the middle of the ceiling. The walls were covered with linoleum of different colors that overlapped layer upon layer. If one were to look at it for any length of time, images would appear.

Mabelle called out, and a tall woman with straggly blond hair appeared in the doorway of the sitting room. Then Simpson began the same rap that had worked time and time again. A glass of water and then a pleasant conversation about the weather. They would work their way outside and talk about the children.

This time there was a girl so beautiful that Simpson found it hard to concentrate on his words as he watched her. Her name was Bonnie Louise. She was fourteen, and her flaxen hair fell in a dazzling curtain to her waist. That was only part of her charm. The look in her green eyes was what caught Simpson. She had the most intense eyes he had ever seen.

She was wearing a flour sack for a blouse. Her jeans were so worn-through at the knees and the butt, they were white. Her feet were covered in mud. At her hip was her two-year-old sister, sucking on two fingers.

Bonnie Louise was a twenty-thousand-dollar bonus. For sure. Simpson went into his sales pitch. *You will receive a ten-thousand-dollar down payment and a follow-up of a thousand dollars a week. This contract is standard in Hollywood. A screen test is the only way to find out if your daughter has what it takes. It will probably take a few weeks, two months at the most. Of course, if you would like to come along, it would be out of your own pocket. A round-trip ticket to California, first class, is about two thousand dollars. Yes, that is a lot of money. Trust is what's needed here.*

Ten thousand dollars is a lot of money and can go a long way.

Good. Then we have a deal.

It never failed. Simpson was the salesman of the century. That was why he was out there. He was B.J.'s man.

"The slimy bastards," he said out loud.

The phone rang. He nearly choked on the Coca-Cola he was chugging.

"Hello. Yes, I have been *very* lucky this trip. . . . She has blond hair and the greenest eyes I've ever seen. She's a quiet girl with something special."

Simpson strained, trying to hear the voice at the other end of the line.

"Yes. No problem. I can have her in Aspen by the end of the week." He cupped his free hand over his exposed ear to hear better. The wind was blowing dust in his face.

"Yessir, I think we've *done good*."

The receiver went dead. Simpson stood there looking at the storm on the distant horizon. What he didn't know was that this would be his last job for Mr. B. J. McClintock.

And what B. J. McClintock didn't know was that this innocent goddess would turn out to be his Waterloo.

Five Days Later, Aspen, Colorado

B.J. paced up and down the length of the Persian carpet staring at nothing in particular. Everything was set to his specifications for tonight's event. He was experiencing an empty feeling in the pit of his stomach; a tiny storm brewing in a sea of loneliness.

This was a special night. A night that had been planned for months. Perhaps it was stress. Stress could affect a person in so many different ways. It ate at your mind and sent impulses to different parts of the body. He had known a host of friends who were slaves to it. Some had suffered heart attacks, stomach ulcers, nervous breakdowns, body sores, and even death.

"You're wearing a hole in my brain," said Morton Shipp without taking his eyes off the blazing fire.

"Sorry, Mort, I forgot you were sitting there."

"What seems to be bothering you, B.J.? Could it be that *you're* nervous?" the doctor teased.

B.J. shot him a hard look. He didn't like to be teased. When he was a kid, he hated the feeling it gave him. He could handle anger and threats from anybody, but not teasing.

Elizabeth once said he was afraid of intimacy and being loved. He had laughed, but deep inside he felt she was right. B.J. had to be in control. Not close.

Ever since childhood Mort had been his closest friend. Shipp knew more about him than anyone. Yet he sensed that Mort was more and more uncomfortable with him as time passed.

His children were like strangers to him, occupying the same house. Elizabeth was a good friend who knew part of him. A better friend, perhaps, than had she known all of him. He was a fragmented man. There were people who knew pieces of him, but never the whole man.

At first he'd preferred it that way. No one person could get a handle on him, find his buttons and push them. That was another thing B.J. couldn't stand, being pushed around. He swore at the tender age of ten that no son of a bitch would ever push him around again.

And so far nobody ever had.

B.J. turned to Shipp, who was still staring into the fire. He thought of opening a conversation on the subject, then hesitated. Best not to expose his emptiness to the plastic surgeon, his trusted friend in many things, but not this.

Kevin Wenster strolled into the warm light of the mahogany-paneled drawing room with a brandy snifter in his right hand. What a crazy Australian bastard, thought B.J.

"Good evening, gentlemen," Kevin said, bowing very low, letting his hands drop to the floor, only to bounce back upright with a gremlin's grin. Mort smiled and poured some champagne and topped B.J.'s glass.

"Who else is with us tonight?" Kevin asked, beaming.

"I'm happy to say, only us," B.J. advised.

"Oh marvelous! This is the smallest party yet."

"Yeah," said the overanxious doctor. "My right foot itches. I feel lucky."

The three men exchanged knowing looks. They were dressed in dinner clothes. There was nothing sloppy about this crew as they sipped their alcohol from Waterford crystal and walked on a Persian carpet that would bring a handsome price at a Sotheby's auction.

The walls were adorned with a Degas, a Picasso, and a small but exquisite Rembrandt. Over the fireplace was a portrait of a bather by Renoir, a naked goddess epitomizing virginal beauty. She was the heart of his collection.

The room was made for comfort, an elegant marsupial pouch, B.J.'s secret hideaway in the mountains outside of Aspen. He only brought his closest men friends here to indulge their fantasies. It was spacious but cozy, warm and intimate.

Each of the five bedrooms was designed and decorated around one painting. Each painting was a nude by a famous artist. A Gauguin, Renoir, Mucha, Bonnard, and a Modigliani. The furniture was carefully selected from B.J.'s world travels.

Texture and color were very important to him. He was a very sensual man, sensitive to lighting and sound. Rancho Virgo was his masterpiece of culture and art.

"Well, shall we cut the cards?" inquired B.J. as he picked up an ornate antique deck. He shuffled while the two men sipped their drinks. His dexterity was impressive. He enjoyed each turn of fate until he intuited it was time to spread them along the highly polished credenza.

B.J. pulled a card out of the line. It was the king of diamonds. He looked to Kevin, who pulled the king of spades. They turned to Shipp, who held up the six of clubs.

"I guess we cut again," B.J. said with relish as he looked at Kevin, who was rubbing his hands together as if it were a cold winter day. He gave one good blow from his mouth and took a card. It was the ten of diamonds.

Kevin and Shipp watched as B.J. pulled and held up the ace of hearts.

"Well! Go on, mate! Have at it then!" Kevin said, giving B.J. a brotherly shove.

"Never once have I pulled the high card," Shipp grumbled.

B.J. moved apprehensively down the long, dimly lighted hallway, recalling the last time he pulled the high card. It had been a disaster. Bad chemistry. *Lousy* chemistry.

So this is what life's come to, snorted B.J.! Crazy old Morton and his brilliant ideas . . . Kevin and his outrageous sense of adventure. It had come to this after two bottles of Martel Cordon Bleu cognac and a discussion on the real meaning of life.

The last time, B.J. had vowed to himself never to do this again. But here he was. He couldn't erase her image. A hysterical banshee.

He rubbed the side of his neck to soothe his invisible scar. Christ! he thought, I pray I never have to go through that again.

Suddenly he was again aware of the empty feeling in the pit of his stomach. He stopped dead in his tracks and leaned against the wall, pulling at his collar. Damn these shoes, he thought. His feet were aching from the Bijan patent leather. He felt like jumping out of his skin. He took a deep breath and turned the heavy handle on the carved oak door.

The master suite was sumptuously decorated around a Renoir painting of a nude lady lying amid the grass swaddled in fabric with colors resembling a fall day. The bed was a high four-poster from an Irish castle.

There in the candlelight, in the middle of the crisp white linen, sat a young girl with yellow hair down to her waist. A pale pink ribbon tied around her head ended in a lazy bow above her left ear.

B.J. lost his breath at the vision. He closed and locked the door, and moved slowly toward the bed. She sat there like a porcelain doll watching him approach. Her eyes were sea green, and dewy from the slight amount of Valium she had been given to relax her.

He sat gently on the edge of the bed. Her fawnlike eyes pierced his being. His penis was standing erect with its head pushing up against his low-hanging black satin cummerbund.

The girl stared at him and his clothes. She wondered why she had been brought to such a place. The man before her seemed kind. His face was a good face. His hands were smooth and cool as he caressed her cheeks. She actually liked him. He looked like a man she had seen in a history book once. Maybe he was the guardian that the nice man talked about on the trip from her home in Plunkettville, Oklahoma.

Yes, she remembered the white-haired lady who bathed her in something that smelled really good and dressed her in the softest material she'd ever touched. "Do what he tells you to," she remembered her saying.

"You're not frightened, I hope?" B.J. asked very softly.

She nodded affirmatively.

"Well, shall I tell you a story? It might make you feel more at home."

She nodded again.

"I know a wonderful story of a king and his long-awaited bride. A story of magic and love and adventure." B.J. looked closer at the girl glowing in the candlelight. John Simpson had found a girl who embodied a Titian Venus. This time a sizable bonus was in order. She was magnificent. He could tell she was open to be charmed. This child/woman was made for love.

Kevin rubbed the dice against his palms. Mentally he pictured double sixes. He threw. Shipp watched them land, smirking when his opponent only managed a five and a six.

"Too bad, Kev. It looks like I've got this one."

Kevin didn't *like* Shipp. He tolerated him because he was B.J.'s friend and doctor-in-the-pocket. He thought him a bore . . . a bore with an absolutely neurotic wife. Elaine Shipp, the bride of Frankenstein.

"And how's Savannah McClintock?" Kevin asked.

"Oh that one's something else. I pity the man who marries her."

"Why, Mort? She's wonderful!"

Shipp tossed double threes. He was lucky at backgammon, and tonight was no exception. Playing for ten dollars a point meant high stakes, and so far he was up close to two thousand dollars.

"Savannah is a southern belle with a Hollywood mentality. That, my Australian friend, is a lethal combination."

Kevin looked at his watch. "I was hoping he'd back out like the last time."

"This one's a beaut. I checked her myself," Shipp said, still relishing the memory.

Kevin took a large sip of brandy and concluded, "It'd be fine, long as we all got a turn."

"Or there were more virgins to go around."

Kevin looked at the board. He was losing, and his throwing

wasn't improving. It's time to cut my losses, he decided. "This, my friend, is going to be my last game."

"But hell, it's not even midnight!"

"Jet lag, mate. Bloody jet lag."

"You wouldn't be jet-lagged if you were in there with the virgin."

"No, Mort, you're quite right. I'd be pumping away like an old fire truck!"

Kevin threw double fives and removed four chips. Mort frowned. He had almost all of his off the board. He concentrated and threw double twos. Kevin took out his wallet and laid twenty-two hundred-dollar bills in front of the doctor.

"You've given me too much," Mort complained.

Kevin sighed deeply and stood up. "No change, mate."

Shipp smiled and thanked him. He watched him wobble across the room and out the door. He patted the crisp hundred-dollar bills and felt warm all over.

Kevin's thoughts turned to Margarite. Six years with the long-legged, sassy bitch. He silently toasted: *To Molly, the tightest little box below the equator.*

Nestled in the crook of B.J.'s arm, the virgin listened with great anticipation to the end of the elaborately embroidered fairy tale.

". . . so when the king saw the beautiful young princess that his huntsmen had found in the woods wandering alone and frightened, he knew that she was to be his queen. She was to live with him in the magic castle forever and ever."

While he spoke, B.J. had not taken his eyes off this perfect creature who, wide-eyed, had followed his every word. He smiled and said, "Because with her by his side, magic could happen at any moment. For, you see, quite by accident, the king had found the lovely princess he'd seen in his dreams. His search had ended."

He lifted her toward him and said, "The king took her in his arms and kissed her, and at that very moment all the kingdom heard beautiful music." He sighed and concluded, "Their love for each other created magic."

The golden-haired girl giggled. Between the Valium, the splendor of the bedroom, and B.J.'s tale, she was beginning to feel lighter of heart and safer.

B.J. looked down at her as she looked up. He kissed her on the cheek and gave her a squeeze. She laughed, leaned up on her knees, and gave him a big hug and kissed him on the cheek.

"Oh! You want to wrestle, do you?" he asked, wrapping his arms around her, rolling down on the bed, laughing. The smell of her hair was driving him wild. He stopped with her on top of him.

The weight of her delicate body pressing down on his erection almost made him come. Not yet, he told himself. I want to enjoy this as long as possible. He did pride himself on his control and staying power.

She suddenly stopped laughing when she noticed B.J. staring at her. He gently pulled her head down and lightly touched her lips to his. She was now shaking from fear and new sensations.

"I want to teach you about love, my princess. I promise I won't hurt you. You must trust me, my dear. You're so beautiful, so delicate."

B.J. lifted the girl to the pillows as he spoke and began to drop her silk nightgown off her shoulders.

It fell to her waist. Her breasts were barely formed, and her nipples were just a shade darker than the rest of her skin. Her alabaster body shivered. Her tiny rosy berries grew erect. She sat there like a small rabbit caught in the headlights of a car.

"Now don't be afraid, my sweet, sweet darling." B.J. bent his head over and licked the soft mound that surrounded the hardened nipple. She shuddered as he sucked on her sweet skin. Her body was responding against her will.

You can't stop nature, thought B.J. We are all basically animals. When the sexual juices start to flow, it's primeval. It's been there since the beginning of time.

She started to whimper and make sounds that had B.J. reeling in ecstasy. He cautiously raised the gossamer nightgown to reveal her golden pubic hair. He lightly stroked her legs until she got into the rhythm of his hands. When the time was right and her eyes were closed and her head thrown back, he parted the golden fleece. He searched with his tongue for the magic spot.

She let out a gasp of surprise and raised her head and looked down at him.

"This is the magic I was telling you about. Just close your eyes and feel, just feel me, and I'll take you on a magic-carpet ride. Close your eyes."

His voice was so hypnotic, the angel closed her eyes and rested her head on the lace pillow. B.J. felt like crying.

She had been bathed in lilac scent. B.J. licked her vagina, savoring the taste and smell. Finding her clitoris, he wedged it between his teeth and expertly kneaded it with the tip of his tongue.

Her body went rigid, and her breathing became rapid. Her light moans had grown into uncontrollable cries.

She tried to pull away, but B.J. had her hips in a viselike-grip. His tongue was fused with her clitoris. Finally she fell back against the pillows. He worried she might lose consciousness from the waves of rapture.

B.J. felt her succumb, and slowly increased his rhythm until he saw her stomach shudder. She grabbed the sheets and let out that cry of first-time released passion.

He finally stopped when he heard the last light whimper escape her dry, delicate lips. He cupped his hand over her heated, wet opening and gently rubbed the clear liquid up over her mound and on her breasts as they heaved up and down.

Her eyes were shining and confused. She looked like an art-nouveau sculpture with her hair ruffled across the pillow.

"Unbutton my shirt for me, my dear," whispered B.J. as he looked down at her. She stood on the bed and took off his studs.

"I've never seen buttons like this before," she said, admiring the flowing gold profiles on his antique Tiffany cuff links.

"Look at that," he said, running his finger down the bridge of her nose. "She looks like you."

"Why, she does, doesn't she?"

B.J. laughed and said, "You're wonderful!" He removed the cuff links and handed them to her. "Here, I want you to have these."

She blushed and meekly said thank you. Her eyes were cast down. She was thunderstruck by the beauty of these objects. Shyly she dropped one of them in B.J.'s hanky pocket. "Since there're two, why don't you have one . . . and I'll have one." She looked away again.

He grabbed her and shouted, "Thank you for sending me this angel!"

B.J. couldn't take his eyes off her as she undid his tie.

"Did you like what I did to you, my dear?" he asked, studying her.

"Yes," she enthused. "The magic-carpet ride was wonderful! Are we going to do that again?" She began bouncing up and down on the mattress with anticipation.

"Maybe later. Now, I want to show you something that I've been saving for you until this moment. Something very special."

B.J. unzipped his tuxedo pants and let them drop to the floor. Her eyes fell on his erect penis.

She pulled back and pointed. "That's what makes the babies."

"Yes," he said, leaning a little closer. "But it's also to make you happy. It's part of the magic." Softly his voice invited her to relax. "Touch it, my angel, and feel it respond to you."

She reached out and placed her hand on the head. It jerked upward.

"Eeeek!" she shrieked, and sank back in horror, staring at the throbbing penis.

"That means he likes you. He likes to be touched by you. You see, he has a mind of his own. You know the way I kissed you?"

"Uh-huh."

"Well, he likes to be kissed, too."

"You mean with my mouth?" she asked, shocked.

"Yes, my darling. Like a baby sucking on its mother's milk."

"Will it make you feel the way you made me feel?"

"Yes. You want to make me feel the way you did when I kissed you?"

"Yes! It was . . . magic!" She was caught up in the game she was playing with him.

He lay down on the soft linens and watched her as she began to fondle him. Laughing at the response of his penis to her cool, inexperienced hands, she watched his face as she stroked the hard shaft the way he instructed her to do it.

He showed her how to handle him just the way he liked to be handled. B.J. was in heaven. This girl was extraordinary. She knew exactly how to click into his pattern of passion, and learned quickly how to stop just before he reached orgasm.

"Put your mouth on it, my dear. Yes . . . Now, part your lips and lick it with your tongue. Yes, yes, now put it *in* your mouth, and move your tongue around."

B.J. thought he would pass out from the sight of this nubile vision sucking on the head of his cock. He took her right hand and cupped it around his scrotum, and gently showed her how to apply pressure that made his cock respond.

She squealed with delight as he moaned and moved up into her mouth. With his free hand he searched for her golden mound and manipulated her clitoris until he felt wetness at his fingertips.

He had to have her soon. He couldn't last much longer. She was whimpering and pushing against his hand. She was sucking on his cock better than any hooker he had ever experienced.

He pulled her to him, driving his tongue into her mouth, searching for hers to respond. It did. He raised himself over her and stopped.

"Now, my darling, we are going to do magic that may hurt a little. Then it will feel good. And as time goes by, it will feel better and better."

Suddenly there was fear in her eyes, and she began to sit up.

"Are you going to put him inside of me?"

"Yes, my sweet. Don't be afraid."

"It's not gonna fit!" she cried.

"Of course it will. It fit in your mouth, didn't it?"

"Yes, but my mouth is bigger than my, my . . ."

"Pussy. Your pussy, your sweet pussy, that will someday have a baby come out of it. So you see, I am much smaller than a baby."

He said this while kissing her gently all over her face and neck.

It sounded logical to the girl. She looked up into his eyes with her green pools that B.J. could swim in for the rest of his life.

"Are you sure it will feel like magic?"

"Yes, my darling. Like magic. First I want to kiss you again on your sweet pussy. Yes?"

B.J. sucked on her magic spot until she was ready for his entrance. Her young, tight body was writhing with want of him. He mounted her, spreading her legs and rubbing her clitoris. He started to enter her vaginal opening.

Their eyes locked. The only thing that existed in the world was the union of his cock with her sweet, wet pussy. Slowly he entered deeper, until he felt the head of his cock up against her hymen.

B.J. stopped and looked into her eyes. Their breathing was in unison.

"Does it hurt, my love?" he asked gently.

"No, it doesn't hurt. Put it all in. I want to feel it all."

B.J. sucked on her nipples and went up on his knees. He could come at any moment. He sat very still and manipulated her clitoris until her hips started to move in a circular motion. She moaned. He moved his hardness in and out up against the thin layer of membrane. He gave it one strong push and heard a cry of pain, and at the same moment felt warm liquid rush over his penis. She was his and only his. He made up his mind right then and there. He wouldn't share her!

He fell onto his elbows and began thrusting himself in and out of her wet vagina. Her moans were loud, and tears were streaming down her cheeks as she watched his face contort with ecstasy.

He moved faster and faster, his body getting tighter and tenser. She felt he was ripping her apart. Fear flashed across her face. He looked down at her and buried his mouth on hers, and went into spasms as he came inside her womb. He thought he would never stop spurting his hot juice, as it mixed with her virginal blood.

His body went limp on top of hers. Their breathing slowly synchronized. B.J. could still feel his heart pounding as if it were going to explode.

Fear was pumping through his veins. Guilt. He felt exhilarated, but as he looked down at this lovely girl, he felt as if he had finally committed the ultimate sin. He'd never felt anything like this. . . .

"Are you hungry?" she asked timidly.

"I don't know. Are you?"

"Hmmm-hmmmm."

He lifted her hand. It was the rough, bony hand of a farm girl. Unlike the rest of her, her hands were too large, and her fingers were too crooked ever to be beautiful. Even good old Morton Shipp couldn't do anything to improve their structure.

"I can cook," she said sweetly.

He smiled at her. He wanted to please her. It was madness. He had never been overwhelmed like this. "If you're hungry," he said, "I'll get us a little midnight snack."

"You know . . ." She hesitated as if searching the air for his name.

"B.J.," he said.

"Mr. B.J., you know what I'd really like?"

He shook his head. He knew what he'd like. More of the same.

"Rice. I make real good rice."

"I'm sure you do, but we've got . . . all kinds of food. Already prepared."

Suddenly she looked as if she was going to cry. "I really want to make it *for you*, Mr. B.J."

How could he resist? If making rice would make her happy, it would make him happy.

Wearing soft, thick terry-cloth robes, they made their way down long corridors and a winding stairway to the restaurant-sized kitchen.

B.J. opened one of the well-stocked refrigerators. Nothing was of interest. All the girl wanted was to make him her specialty: rice.

"If it's here, we'll find it," he said, opening cupboard after cupboard.

"Gee, y'all sure have a lot a dishes."

"I like to give big parties." He finally found a sack of white rice. "You like parties?"

Shipp burst into the kitchen. He was drunk, and from the way he devoured the lovely girl with his eyes, he was ready to take a turn.

"Bonnie Louise," he mumbled. "Am I right?"

She began shaking. B.J. wrapped a comforting arm around her. "Mort, let's call it a night."

"What's cooking?" the doctor asked.

Almost embarrassed, B.J. explained that Bonnie Louise was making a snack. Shipp noticed the rice, and just as he was about to remind his host that he didn't like rice, B.J. pushed him out the door. He was not about to let anything or anyone spoil his first night with this treasure of a girl.

CHAPTER 13

*T*he guard at the gate waved him through, but B.J. stopped.

"Has my *guest* had any visitors?" he inquired.

A young man in uniform disappeared inside the guardhouse. It would be worth the wait, B.J. told himself. He had to know.

The young man returned. "I have two entries. Someone called Orson Welles."

B.J. choked at Zachary Steele's obvious attempt at humor. He got the dates and times and drove to his house. He felt like a bull ready to gore the matador. He was a man possessed.

He let himself in and listened. Loud rock music was blasting upstairs in the master suite. He scaled the stairs two at a time, praying Bonnie Louise was alone.

He pushed the bathroom door open, and there, immersed in the sunken tub in a cloud of bubbles, was his love.

"Byron," she shrieked above U2's song. "You scared me!"

B.J. couldn't find the turnoff knob on the portable CD player, so he kicked it. Bonnie Louise watched in horror as the magical machine smashed into pieces.

"Byron, what's gotten into you?"

B.J. whipped around, walked to the tub, lifted Bonnie Louise out of the water, and started shaking her dizzy.

"You're going home! Pack your bags!"

"No, Byron," she pleaded. "Please, I don't wanna go back to Rancho. Stop it, Byron! You're hurting me."

B.J. pulled her face close to his, and in a low, menacing tone said, "I know all about you and Zachary Steele. *You got that?*"

Bonnie Louise was dripping wet and speechless. She'd never seen B.J. like this, and it scared the life out of her.

"Your coming here was a big mistake! Did you screw him in my house?"

"No, Byron," Bonnie Louise told him. "Honest. I swear on my mama."

B.J. released his grip, and Bonnie Louise thudded against the hard tile floor. She reached for her panties, and B.J. ripped them out of her hand. He sniffed the crotch.

"You're lucky I don't smell anybody else but you," he told her.

Bonnie Louise had never felt so humiliated. She snatched her panties back and slipped them on.

"You disappoint me, Byron. A grown man acting like a wild animal. Why, if you'd been making love to me these last months, you wouldn't be so crazy thinking somebody else was."

B.J. considered her complaint. She was right. She'd hit a nerve.

"Why can't you be more understanding, darlin'?" he snapped. "Your arriving on my doorstep has not helped one bit! Get in there and pack your bags!"

"I'm not going, and you can't make me!" she protested.

"Who the *hell* do you think you're talking to?"

B.J. grabbed her by the arm and threw her into the bedroom. He opened the closet and heaved her suitcase onto the bed.

"Fasten your dadgum seat belt, sugar! You're on your way to Colorado!"

Bonnie Louise didn't want to end up like the CD player, so she did as she was told.

B.J. riffled through a chest of drawers, throwing her clothes at her and on the bed. His breathing was labored, deep and erratic. He was caught in a rage.

"Byron," Bonnie Louise said timidly, "nothing's happened between me and Zach. He's been my friend . . . while you were so busy. All we did was go for a motorcycle ride and walk on the beach."

"Fine, you won't mind going home. Vacation's over!"

Tears spilled down her cheeks, and deeply hurt, Bonnie Louise asked, "Byron, don't you love me anymore?"

"'Course I do, sugar. That's why you're going home. This town is no place for you, honey. I warned you—guys like Steele'll chew on you and spit you out."

She looked at her hands and ran to him, self-consciously hiding them behind his back. She whispered, "Byron, make love to me. I missed you so much."

B.J. wondered if his "best friend" was going to cooperate. He closed the suitcase and threw it on the floor. He checked his watch and noted they had twenty minutes.

He wanted to hold her in his arms and absorb her into himself. He longed to feel her legs wrapped around his waist, and her heart racing with his.

B.J. couldn't resist. He relieved himself of his pants and his jacket. Bonnie Louise dropped her panties and climbed onto the bed, her blond hair falling all around her body. She reached for his cock and sighed, hoping it would make her juices flow.

"I want you, darlin'," she murmured.

B.J. mounted and slowly began to penetrate her. Then, just as suddenly as the urge had arisen in him, it began to ebb. Desperately he closed his eyes and tried to fantasize . . . to fantasize the very creature who was the essence of his fantasies, the one he now held in his arms. To no avail. The harder he pushed, the softer he became. He wanted to make love to her more than anything in the world, but he couldn't. He could neither do it nor face the fact that he could not.

"Byron, what's wrong?"

He rolled over. "I got a lot on my mind," he said calmly. "I'm not a five-minute man. You know that."

Bonnie Louise was confused. She felt rejected. Could he read her mind? Did he know she was relieved? She was afraid to ask.

B.J. ran his fingers through her sweet-smelling hair and said, "Darlin', after waiting so long, we both deserve better." He kissed her on the cheek and promised, "I'll make it up to you."

"All right," she whispered, hugging him. "Then I don't have to go?"

B.J. was more grateful to her for that forgiving hug than he dared to show. "All right, baby, just a few more days."

Bonnie Louise happily got dressed. She loved this place—the beach, the sunsets . . . riding behind Zachary on his motorcycle. This place is fun, she thought, as she descended the stairs in front of B.J.

She could tell he was upset, but she realized she couldn't do anything to change his mood.

"I thought you were gonna take me ridin', Byron."

"I am."

"I'm lonely out here all by myself."

B.J. entered the garage, and after considering the options, he said, "I'll bring Inga out for a few days to keep you company."

"You will?" Bonnie Louise asked, excited. Inga, Rancho Virgo's housekeeper, was her closest friend.

"Yes, darlin'. Then we'll both feel better."

He wrapped his arms around her. "I love you so much, Bonnie Louise. Be patient with me, sugar."

"Of course, Byron," she whispered, resting her head on his chest.

CHAPTER 14

A glorious Sunday in September. Los Angeles, Lara concluded, was a form of paradise. Just as East Coast mythology proclaimed, it was nearly always sunny in the Big Orange. Of course, she still preferred the Big Apple, but, as her job expanded, so did her taste for the pleasures of the sun.

Today, even though it was a Sunday, she found herself gladly doing B. J. McClintock's bidding. He had caught her at eleven o'clock the night before, explaining that he and Elizabeth had to attend a brunch being given for a visiting cardinal. He wasn't going to be able to take his niece horseback riding, and would she fill in for him? For the inconvenience he'd arrange a five-hundred-dollar credit for her at Ralph Lauren. That put a smile on her face.

B.J. had instructed Lara to stop at the Colony Market for groceries, deliver a gift to Helen O'Brien from his wife, and at four-thirty to meet Inga, Rancho Virgo's housekeeper, at LAX—and then drive her back to the Malibu house.

What a job, Lara thought, as she pointed at $19.99-per-pound Norwegian salmon steaks and said, "I'd like three pounds, please." Anything she thought Bonnie Louise would enjoy was all right. And she was learning that money, in these financial strata, was no object.

I wish I had an "uncle" like B.J.

"Three hundred forty-eight, ninety-three," the checker said matter-of-factly.

"It's a charge. B. J. McClintock."

The checker smiled and opened a portfolio. She entered the amount, and asked Lara to sign the charge slip. No muss, no fuss. No challenge. Lara found shopping at this overpriced emporium an instructive pleasure. The fruits and vegetables looked fresh and appealing. The crème fraîche had been flown from Normandy, the limestone lettuce from Tennessee. Being a housewife in Malibu, she decided, must be a pretty pleasant job.

Ten A.M. The sun was breaking through the mist and beginning to warm the sand. The Colony guard checked his list, told Lara where to find the McClintock house, and waved her on with "Have a nice day."

Joan Souchek was a fool, Lara mused. How could she have slammed the door in B.J.'s face? She recalled Monday mornings when Joan would arrive late, then complain about how she had had to spend her Sunday at the McClintocks' beach house *working*. Yeah, Lara reckoned, now I know how she was able to put together her designer wardrobe.

After two hours of equestrian adventure—scaling the dangerously dry Malibu mountains and pounding the wet sand—Lara and Bonnie Louise retreated to the soothing jet streams of the McClintocks' Jacuzzi.

"Boy," Bonnie Louise exclaimed, "this water's gonna cook us!"

"Speaking of *hot*, Bonnie—have you talked to Zachary Steele since the benefit?"

The girl's face gave the answer away. "You have!" Lara squealed.

Bonnie Louise looked away and started stammering.

"You've seen him. I can see it in your eyes, Bonnie." Basking in the blissful expression on her young friend's face, Lara promised, "My lips are sealed. Tell me everything! Come on!"

"All right, Lara—but you've got to swear on your mother's life. Cross your heart."

Lara crossed her heart and asked, "What am I swearing to?"

Bonnie Louise leaned across the bubbling water and said, "You can't tell Byron. He's forbidden me to see Zachary. Byron says he's a bad person—that he'll just use me and throw me away."

Lara leaned back, and after a thoughtful moment said, "B.J. has a point, Bonnie. The boy does have a track record."

"What do you mean by that?"

"Ohhh . . ." she hedged, "it's hard to separate truth from fiction in Hollywood. Zachary Steele's been involved with a lot of girls —but it could all be publicity. Just take it slow."

"Oh, Lara, I am. Nothin's happened yet."

"*Yet?*" Lara teased.

Pushing herself up and out of the hot water, Bonnie Louise said, "This has been so much fun—why don't you come out and go ridin' with me tomorrow mornin'?"

"I wish I could, Bonnie, but unfortunately I have to work."

"Oh, well, then . . . we'll do it next weekend."

"That's going to be a little difficult, since you and Inga are scheduled to fly back to Aspen on Friday."

The information was like a slap in the face. "*What?* But I don't want to go back! I've been in the woods all my life. I love it here! Zachary's promised to take me to Disneyland!"

Lara stepped out of the 105-degree water. "Calm down, Bonnie. You've got five days to change your uncle's mind—better start burning some brain cells."

In keeping with the rest of the McClintocks' beach house, the guest room was large yet cozy. In fact, the brass bed looked so inviting, Lara wished she had the time to curl up on it with a good book.

She was surprised to discover a rather large Picasso—something from his final period, gray, morose, and reminiscent of Vanessa Waters's distorted face after a session with Dr. Shipp.

There's no accounting for tastes, Lara reminded herself. The McClintocks had probably bought it for its investment value. Certainly it wasn't Elizabeth's taste.

Lara pulled a white T-shirt over her head and tucked it inside her white cotton-twill slacks. She was glad she didn't have large breasts, because she loved the freedom of not having to wear a bra. She slipped her feet into a pair of navy espadrilles and tied a navy cardigan around her neck.

As she checked her streamlined figure in the mirror, she was struck by an array of Bonnie Louise's new clothes that were strewn haphazardly around the bedroom.

What's going on here? she asked herself. What's the real story behind Bonnie Louise? She'd never seen B.J. react to anyone or anything the way he did with the young beauty. Even by his own extravagant standards, the man had gone overboard. Oh well, she told herself, don't probe.

Lara laughed, thinking of *Cuntessa* Souchek's motto: Keep your mouth shut and your pocketbook open. Joan, she conceded, knew the lay of the land.

Still aching from the long horseback ride, Lara had to decide whether to walk up the beach or the street to the O'Briens'. She went out to the car, opened the trunk, and reached for Elizabeth McClintock's beautifully wrapped gift.

Ms. Efficiency, that's me. Scripts for the office, clothes for the cleaners . . .

Suddenly Lara felt flustered. As a rule, she was blasé about actors. But Colin O'Brien . . . He was in that rare category reserved for a handful of stars: Streisand, De Niro, Newman, Redford. . . . And Henry Weinstock was probably the most successful Broadway producer she could think of. She had grown up near Manhattan, with "Henry Weinstock presents" on billboards and marquees all over the city. Deep down Lara wished she could spend the whole day with this group of theatrical legends.

Daisies, hybrid geraniums, orchids . . . the O'Brien yard was small but beautifully landscaped. Shady and romantic. An enchanted garden, Lara thought, as she reached for the door.

It was open. She knocked several times, but to no avail. Cautiously she entered. Laughter and voices echoed inside from the terrace. She followed them.

"Good morning," called a man's voice.

Lara turned, and there, standing on the stairs in his swim trunks and T-shirt, was *the man* himself: Colin O'Brien. She was speech-less.

"It's beautifully wrapped," he commented.

Lara held up the present and said, "Elizabeth McClintock asked me to give it to your wife." She noticed that Colin never took his eyes off of her. He was as magnetic off-screen as he was on.

"Colin O'Brien," he said, extending his hand.

"Lara Miller," she responded, as they shook hands. "Thank you for all your support on the AIDS benefit."

"That's right," he said, placing her, "you're B.J.'s new right hand." He gave her his most charming smile and asked, "New York?"

Lara smiled. "Yes."

"I can spot you eastern girls," he teased. "You all have a special look." He grinned and added, "I guess that's what attracted me to Helen."

Lara shrugged self-consciously. She was flattered. "Thank you," she said nervously.

"Join us—we're out here. Lunch. My wife's big on Sunday lunch."

Colin introduced Lara to everyone, somewhat inaccurately, as B. J. McClintock's alter ego. She blushed and smiled.

There were about a dozen people in varying stages of finishing endive salad, iced bowls of vichyssoise with slivered chives on top, cold poached salmon with *sauce verte*, fresh fruit, and imported cheeses with long loaves of French bread. Bloody Marys and Evian water appeared to be the favored drinks.

Helen O'Brien welcomed Lara and thanked her for delivering the gift, which she discreetly asked the maid to put in her bedroom.

"Please," Helen offered, "help yourself. Elizabeth is very fond of you, and that's quite a compliment."

One drink, Lara decided, would take the edge off. She made herself a Bloody Mary and sat down in the only available chair. Derek Middleton, the owlish English director, and Prince Carlo Capriotti, the impassioned Italian entrepreneur, launched into a heated discussion on producing commercial movies. Or at any rate, selecting projects that were artistic and meaningful as well as money-making.

"Do you have any idea how many scripts are sent to me every week?" Colin asked the director and the would-be producer.

"Twenty," Carlo offered.

"How many does Mike send you?" Derek countered.

"Mike?" Capriotti asked.

"My agent," Colin explained. "Six. We have a rule. No more than six scripts a week."

"Jesus, Colin. That's a hell of a lot of scripts," Henry Weinstock called from his vantage point overlooking the water. "You should be able to find something you like."

"They're lousy, Henry! Slick, high-concept, big-budget shit."

Lara chewed a mouthful of poached salmon as fast as she could. "I read an amazing script the other night. I think you'd really like it, Colin. I'd even go out on a limb and say this part is tailor-made for you."

"Then *I* want to produce it!" Capriotti said, laughing and pounding the table.

"What's it about?" Derek Middleton asked skeptically.

Suddenly all eyes were on Lara. She washed the food down with a sip of Bloody Mary and said, "Intrigue . . . murder . . . covert government operations . . . soldiers of fortune. All based on a true story."

"Well, why don't you let me read it?" Colin said.

"Who's producing it?" Derek inquired.

"She works for B.J." Helen interjected. "That should give you gentlemen a clue."

"Let *me* read it, please!" Capriotti insisted. "Because if I like it, I have access to millions! Millions of dollars—please, let's make a movie!"

Derek leaned back in his chair and sighed. To him, Carlo Capriotti was a typically spoiled young Italian nobleman. The sort of man who thrusts himself into the right place, and by some unjust stroke of fortune stands to reap all the awards.

"You know," Capriotti said, "my wife"—he gestured toward his beautiful dark-haired, slightly pregnant wife Eugenia—"her family, her father—they financed Fellini, she grew up on Mastroianni's knee. It's in the blood!"

Eugenia laughed and gestured toward her husband. In her equally charming Italian accent, she said, "Carlo will not be happy till he see his name big on the screen."

People laughed. Not Derek Middleton. He desperately wanted to find a project he could direct with Colin. So far he had found nothing the bankable star liked.

"And by the way, Lara," Derek said, "any time you come across something you think's got substance, I'd really love to have a look at it."

"*Blue Moon*'s got a lot of substance! It's just . . ." Holly had made Lara promise not to give it to anyone unless she cleared it with Holly first. But this was different. If Colin O'Brien liked the script, they'd get the green light immediately. *Think on your feet! That's the key to success. . . .*

Lara turned to her host and said quietly, "Colin, I promised the author not to show it to anyone without asking. I mean, it's very controversial, politically—"

"If you knew me better," Colin said, smiling, "you'd know I'm very controversial politically, too. And if our politics jive, which is more than likely, we could be onto something."

Lara smiled. "As luck would have it, I have a copy in the car."

"As luck would have it, you not only have a copy in the car, but you're going to produce the movie as well," he teased.

"Of course." She laughed nervously, having spoken as if it were the most natural thing in the world. Colin grinned back at her.

"Well, Lara Miller, if it's as good as you say it is, we'll all be happy puppies. I'm dying to go back to work!"

Overhearing her husband's comment, Helen walked over and placed her hands on his shoulders. "I'm dying for *him* to go back to work." She laughed and kissed him on the cheek. He smiled up at her.

"Another Bloody Mary?" Helen inquired, looking down at Lara.

Shyly Lara said, "Half a one—and thank you." She liked Helen.

She liked Colin. She loved *Blue Moon*. She felt a surge of exhilaration. What had been, a few minutes ago, a tentative suggestion, made on impulse, suddenly seemed to take on the contours of reality. Why not? she asked herself. Isn't this how movie deals are made? Over lunch? Over brunch? Having drinks? What a lovely way to spend a Sunday.

"Make mine a double," Elaine Shipp's trained-actress voice projected out onto the terrace from the living room.

Everyone stopped talking and turned around. Elaine Shipp had arrived! Morton Shipp trailed behind her, wearing his bright red pants and a bright red and yellow polo shirt.

"Good Lord, Doctor," Derek Middelton said, "you look like a bumble bee in heat!"

Dr. Shipp struck a pose and said, "Hey, hey, hey! I was the best-dressed guy out there today. This is what you call *golf fashion*."

"I agree with you, Derek. I thought I was hallucinating this morning when he walked out of the dressing room."

Helen handed them each a Bloody Mary. "You remember my parents?" she said, motioning toward Henry and Maureen.

"I'd remember the Weinstocks even if I'd never met them!" Elaine gushed. "How lovely to see you out here on the West Coast."

Henry nodded. He was looking forward to getting home.

"Please do sit down," Maureen suggested politely. "Let me get you a couple of plates."

"But just fruit and cottage cheese for me," Elaine said. "I never eat anything heavy for breakfast."

"I want the works!" Shipp countered. "I'm so hungry, I could eat the eye out of a hurricane."

"Now that's what I call hungry!" Colin said, motioning for them to sit down. "Come on, squeeze in."

Morton Shipp locked eyes with Lara Miller. "I shot a round of golf with your boss this morning. We played for skins. The lucky bastard took me for three hundred."

"I've heard B.J. plays a mean game."

"If Morty beats him twice a year, he's lucky," Elaine complained.

The food arrived, and the Shipps finally stopped talking. Everyone at the table relaxed, and went back to their respective conversations. But Lara silently sipped her drink and thought about Colin's playful suggestion that she help to produce *Blue Moon*. *Lara Miller, producer*. The words had a pleasant ring to them, Lara thought. Yes, very pleasant indeed. . . .

CHAPTER 15

*S*unlight was beating a path across Colin O'Brien's bedroom, hitting a holographic sculpture that cast rainbows across the ceiling. The actor opened his eyes, and upon seeing the multicolored arc above him, bolted out of bed, ready to seize the opportunity he'd been waiting for.

Lara Miller, he thought. What a stroke of luck. It was as if the gods had sent her to present him with the script he'd been searching for.

Whistling and singing "Blue Moon," Colin made his way downstairs to the kitchen, where he made a pot of Jamaican coffee. He looked at the clock and realized that he had an hour and a half to kill before the MCM switchboard would answer.

He inhaled the delicious coffee aroma and sucked in his stomach. Standing tall, he pinched his midriff. Not too bad, he told himself, but if I'm going to play an ex-marine with a drop-dead body, I've got some work to do.

Colin thought of the scenes where his chest and legs would be scrutinized in 70 mm. Time to throw on the jogging suit and make tracks!

Showered, shaved, and energized after an hour of jogging, Colin sat down at his desk and picked up *Blue Moon*. Inadvertently he opened it to the title page and bit his lip.

Holly Dandridge, you illiterate bitch. How could you have written this?

You couldn't have—it's a man's movie. You probably contributed two or three lines and fucked Jeffrey Lascu, whoever he is, into giving you credit. You're a television actress, for chrissake.

He dialed the studio, knowing that once he became involved with the film, it would automatically become a higher-budget, more prestigious project.

"Is that Lara Miller?"

"Yes."

"This is Colin O'Brien. I like that script you gave me, Lara. I couldn't put it down—but I was really amazed that Holly Dandridge was credited as one of the writers. Knowing *her* and never having heard of the other guy—the other guy must be pretty damn good."

Lara laughed nervously and said, "Well, I don't know who contributed what, but I'm glad you like it!"

"I assume Holly wants to be in it?"

"Oh, I know she does!" Lara said enthusiastically.

Colin's worst fears were confirmed. "That's a firm commitment as far as you know?"

Lara suddenly worried that she had overplayed her hand. What was B.J. going to think? He hadn't even read the script. Hastily she offered, "I'll have B.J. call you as soon as he comes in. I'm so glad you liked it."

"Do you know if a director's been set?"

"No, Colin—all I know is that I read *Blue Moon* and saw you playing Chris."

"Good for you, Lara. Speak to you soon."

Colin hung up, feeling good. Clearly this was the virgin run. No director . . . no wonder he hadn't heard anyone mention the project. It was under wraps—now, it would be *his* wraps. He had the town by the balls. With Colin O'Brien *producing* and starring, B.J. and MCM's stockholders would want a female star of the same caliber. Replacing Holly Dandridge would be as easy as flicking a caterpillar off a leaf, he assured himself.

The feel of Helen's arms around his neck interrupted his daydream. He squeezed them and kissed her hand.

"You're in a good mood," she observed.

Colin turned to face his wife and smiled. "Yes, I am."

"Did my first act do this to you?" she asked shyly.

The actor's eyes darted to the pages of Helen's play lying next to *Blue Moon*. Suddenly he remembered he had promised to read it and give her his honest opinion.

"I think you're making progress," he complimented her. "It was fine until . . ." He stopped, trying to recall an earlier draft, trying to fudge his way out.

"The screaming scene? Where he locks her out? Is it too much?"

"Yeah, a little bit—a little too much emotion."

"I thought so. I'll tone it down a little. . . ."

"Sweetheart," Colin said warmly, "I think you're doing a terrific job."

"What about the last scene?" Helen asked earnestly, chewing on her nails.

Colin took a deep breath. He didn't like lying to his wife, but on the other hand, he was tired of reading what seemed like hundreds of versions of something he didn't think she'd ever finish. He was bored with it, but grateful that she had it to keep her mind occupied.

"Needs work, honey," he finally said. "It goes on a little too long—you don't want to put your audience to sleep."

Helen pursed her lips and began walking around the room, thinking. Finally she turned around and said, "You're absolutely right again, Colin. It does drag on a bit. I know exactly where to cut it. Thank you, darling!"

She kissed him, grabbed her pages, and left the room.

Colin breathed a sigh of relief. He didn't have time to read Helen's play yet again. He wanted Derek Middleton to read *Blue Moon* so he could call his agent and put the packaging process in motion.

Without thinking, he began singing *Blue Moon* again as he dialed Derek's number.

CHAPTER 16

*O*n an impulse B.J. had driven out to Malibu to spend an hour with Bonnie Louise. He'd been too busy to make time for her over the weekend, and now, he desperately wanted her out of harm's way—back at Rancho Virgo.

When he arrived at the house, he was greeted by Inga, his Swedish housekeeper. The gray-haired widow had slathered her wrinkled, fair-skinned body with suntan lotion. Embarrassed, she tried to cover herself with a beach towel.

"Bonnie Louise is horseback riding," she explained.

B.J. ran his tongue across his upper teeth and asked when she'd be back. Inga shrugged. "Soon," she answered. "Very soon. What can I get for you, Mr. McClintock?"

"A Heineken will be fine," he said flatly.

Wearing her crisp white uniform, Inga brought him a beer in an iced mug, then retreated to her room.

B.J. wanted to talk to her about Bonnie Louise, but he was too agitated. He took a thirsty drink and leaned against the balcony railing, willing his blond angel to come home. The pressure on his groin served to emphasize his longing for her body—his longing to feel her lying on top of him.

"B.J.!" a man's voice called out. "Open up!"

B.J. pulled himself out of his fantasy to find Colin O'Brien standing at the white iron gate down on the sand.

"B.J.—I've got to talk to you!"

B.J. wondered what Colin was going to ask for now. *Bankable* meant more today then ever before. And O'Brien was one of the last real stars.

"I was just on my way into town. What's on your mind, Colin?"

"*Blue Moon.* I knew it was for me the minute I read it. I'm committed. That's a given."

B.J. motioned for the actor to sit down. He wanted to get this over with before Bonnie Louise walked in, but he didn't want to appear rude. "You know the status of the project, Colin. But I'm all ears. Shoot."

"I do know the status of it," answered Colin, "but Holly Dandridge hates my guts. You know what that's gonna look like in seventy millimeter?"

"Lousy chemistry."

"That's right. Nothing worse than a dead kiss." Colin settled himself into a comfortable reclining chair, then leaned forward. "I've got the whole thing worked out. In fact, it's so well worked out, it's gonna save *you* money on the front end—and make you a hell of a lot more money on the back end."

"Like I said, I'm all ears."

"Okay. Derek Middleton to direct." He waited for B.J.'s reaction, and saw rejection on the horizon. "B.J.," he said heartily, "I know Derek's considered a little avant garde. And okay, I grant you he hasn't made a truly commercial movie yet—but look at Bertolucci. Can you imagine anybody in Hollywood putting up twenty or thirty million for him to make *The Last Emperor*, for chrissake? Derek Middleton's every bit as talented, and he badly wants to make a commercial movie."

"He badly *needs* to make a commercial movie," B.J. corrected.

"All right then. Derek needs a blockbuster, and that's what he knows he can make with *Blue Moon*, and I'm ready to put my own career on the line for the next two years to prove he can do it!"

"If you're this high on the man, Colin, and he's not going to be getting any fancy ideas about what he gets salary- and percentage-wise on account of your interest in him, okay."

"That's terrific, B.J. Lucky I happened to see your car pull in." Colin relaxed. "Another thing: I really want you to meet Adam Snow, the English composer. He's brilliant. I found him in London.

When you hear the score he did for a new ballet based on *Faust*, I'm sure you'll agree he's the one to do the music for *Blue Moon*."

"I'd like to hear him. Get me a tape."

"I'll get one to you this afternoon."

"You know, Colin, this hate thing between you and Holly . . . I'm curious. Did you jilt her at the altar? What are we dealing with here?"

Colin laughed and shook his head. "I don't know why she should hate me. She knew damn well that I was married. I didn't feed her any illusions. . . ." Colin smirked. "Though I did provide some great grass. The good old days—we're talking fifteen years ago. Holly and I had a typical Hollywood date. I was the hot young actor and she was the waitress-cum-budding-actress. Pretty soon she started calling my agent every hour on the hour, and I guess I panicked."

B.J. was mystified. "If that's all it is, I don't see why you're in such a rush to replace her. Holly's show has been in the top five for the past four years. She'll help pull in an audience, too."

"She's not a big-screen actress! She's a glorified soap star!"

B.J.'s voice hardened. "Colin, Holly's name is on the title page of the script! So it's her vehicle in every sense . . . moral and contractual. If it weren't contractual, we might get around the moral. As it is, we're stuck with both."

Colin shook his head and grimaced. He knew what B.J. was about to tell him. Holly was bright and cagey. And, yes, his version of their night together in the Hollywood Hills would no doubt differ dramatically from Holly's. Colin had blocked most of that unfortunate episode out of his mind. How could he have foreseen that, fifteen years later, she was going to write the screenplay for a film he wanted to control? The perfect irony, he told himself.

"So you have no choice," B.J. informed him. "She and Jeff wrote it for her to star in. Period. And frankly, Colin, I'm a little surprised you even thought about trying to bump her off her own project."

Colin looked out to sea, chewing on his lip, thinking about Holly's temper and all the love scenes they'd have to play together.

"Colin, you'll warm up to Holly. Draw on your Oscar-winning talent, and I'll have no argument with your choice of director . . . or even this Adam Snow guy, who to my knowledge has never scored a movie in his life."

Colin O'Brien, having made his pitch, resigned himself to looking for Holly Dandridge's good points.

Bonnie Louise bounced through the front door, running head-on into B.J.

"Why, Byron!" she gasped. "If I'd known you were comin' down, I wouldn't a gone ridin'! Have you been here long?"

"Slow down, baby," he said, taking her in his arms. "I missed you so much, I just had to steal an hour." He drew her body closer and pulled her hips up against his.

At the moment of impact, for the first time in their relationship, Bonnie Louise felt truly repulsed. "Byron," she moaned, trying to break free, "I just got off a horse. I need a shower."

"Oh, honey, I don't care if you just rode a camel across the Sahara Desert, you'd still smell good to me." He gave her a sly smile and whispered, "I have a little surprise for you."

B.J. produced a neatly tied jewelry box from Tiffany. Bonnie Louise didn't want a present from him, no matter what it was. Panic was beginning to set in. She could still taste Zachary's kiss at the guard gate. She didn't want B.J.'s lips on hers or his hands touching any part of her body.

She smiled and untied the blue satin ribbon. Inside, tucked into the sweet little blue pouch, was a fourteen-karat gold-and-diamond tennis bracelet.

"Well, Byron," she said appreciatively, "it's beautiful . . . but it's not really me. It's not somethin' a teenager would wear."

"Since when did *that* bother you? Come on, darlin'—let's see what it looks like on your wrist . . . opposite the *grown-up* gold Cartier watch I bought for you." He was clearly annoyed.

Bonnie Louise complied. She knew that if this had happened a month earlier, she'd have been ecstatic. That was before Zachary Steele . . . and as much as she thought she loved Zach or that he loved her, there were no guarantees. They'd only known each other ten days.

"It looks magnificent! The diamonds match the fire in your eyes, sugar." He pulled her down on the couch and kissed her passionately. He was ready!

"Bonnie Louise, I want you now. Take your clothes off." He unzipped his pants.

"Byron!" she objected. "What about Inga?"

"Don't worry, darlin'—she's in her room. She won't come out."

"But what if she does?"

"Inga knows her place," he said, unzipping Bonnie Louise's jeans and tugging them down around her ankles.

Tears welled in her eyes. "Byron . . . no . . . no," she pleaded. "Not here."

"Yes," he demanded, forcing his erection against her dry, unwelcoming vaginal walls.

Bonnie Louise twisted, trying to push him away, but it was too late. B.J. had managed to enter, and upon doing so, exploded with pleasure.

He fell away, satisfied. "I'm sorry, darlin'—its been so long since we've made love."

Feeling hurt and used, Bonnie Louise tearfully said, "I know, Byron. Today is Wednesday. I've been callin' you all week—beggin' you to come down here. I've seen you more at Rancho Virgo than I have here."

"Well, when I'm there, you have my undivided attention. You called this shot, little lady."

Bonnie Louise wanted to tear the bracelet off of her wrist and stomp on it. She was fed up with being a prisoner.

"Byron, you just don't love me anymore. I think it's time I went back home."

"You are—you're flying to Aspen Friday."

"I'm talkin' about Plunkettville!" she screamed.

"Honey, there's nothin' *there* for you."

"I'll tell you one thing, Byron McClintock, if you send me back to Rancho Virgo, you're never gonna see me again."

Suddenly his little girl was wielding a powerful sword, and it was up against his heart.

"Inga," she went on, "has been waitin' fifteen years to see California. And I haven't even been to Disneyland! You've been promising me Disneyland since the day I first met you."

B.J. zipped his pants and sank into what should have felt like a comfortable chair. Nothing felt right.

What's another week? he asked himself. There's no reason I can't sneak away for a night. The Santa Barbara Biltmore would do the trick. . . .

He gave her his most charming smile and promised, "I'll have Lara arrange a car to take you and Inga to Disneyland. You can stay another week."

"Oh, Byron!" Bonnie Louise squealed. She ran over to him and threw her arms around him. He maneuvered her off the arm of the chair and onto his lap.

"Darlin'," he sighed, "I've been plannin' things for us. Don't ever, not even for one minute, think I want you locked away at Rancho Virgo."

Bonnie Louise looked deep into her lover's tired eyes. The spark was no longer there. She didn't care what he had in mind; she didn't want any part of it.

"I love you, darlin', and I'm going to make you the happiest girl in the world."

She smiled, recalling Zachary Steele saying exactly the same thing to her not two hours before.

"Only I don't want to hear any more talk about you leaving me, Bonnie Louise. Is that clear?"

"I won't say another word. Promise."

"Hmmm . . . I love your face."

Bonnie Louise wished she could think of a compliment for B.J., but nothing came to mind. Instead, she was grateful that he'd only "stolen an hour" and his time was up.

CHAPTER 17

*C*arlo Capriotti checked into the Helmsley Palace Hotel in New York City, put on his Nike jogging suit, and went for an invigorating run through Central Park.

After that he spent two hours in the barber shop getting a facial, a manicure, a haircut, and a shave. It was his way of preparing himself for the meeting that would give him the chips to play the Hollywood movie game. Carlo had the limousine drop him off at the corner of Mulberry and Broome Streets on the edge of Little Italy. As he headed up Mulberry Street, he was overwhelmed by a myriad of delicious aromas. He could smell cannoli shells baking, lasagna fresh out of the oven. His stomach growled.

Memories of Florence regaled him. He loved his homeland, and he longed for the day when he would buy back his family palazzo and return with Eugenia and the children. Carlo stopped in front of Napoleone's, the famous coffeehouse run in the Old World tradition—no women. He entered, and a young man wiped his hands on his white apron and said, "Good afternoon, Signor Capriotti. Let me have your overcoat. Please, follow me."

Carlo was led to a private room at the back of the storefront. The men sipping espresso and red wine followed him with their eyes. The young boy opened the door and stepped aside.

Joseph Giannelli stood up, walked around the table, and shook Carlo's hand.

"Carlo, come! We eat."

Another boy served two salami, provolone, tomato, and basil sandwiches on Italian bread. Carlo didn't mean to, but he stared at the sandwich. He hadn't had one since he was a boy.

Carlo was beginning to feel secure. They had broken bread together, and they were sharing a bottle of red wine. They discussed everything except business. When the dishes were cleared away, the Don offered him a cigar. Carlo politely declined.

"You don't mind if I smoke?" Giannelli asked.

"No," Carlo lied. "Please."

Giannelli leaned back and undid the buttons on his vest and lighted a Havana cigar.

"Okay, Carlo. I found your movie story very interesting." Giannelli blew cigar smoke into a shaft of light and watched it spread out and change shape. "Colin O'Brien must like the script a lot to cut his up-front money in half."

Capriotti became animated. "He loves it! He thinks—"

Giannelli silenced the aspiring producer with a slight wave of his hand. "Two and a half million dollars is a lot to save."

"He thinks he'll make it up on the other end—with his points."

"Carlo," Giannelli said, grinning, "with creative bookkeeping, who sees anything on the other end?"

Capriotti shrugged. "Sometimes you get lucky."

"You make your own luck, Carlo." The Don nodded, slowly taking in Capriotti's princely attire. "That's a nice suit, Carlo."

"Thank you, Mr. Giannelli. It's Giorgio Armani."

The Don raised his right hand and said, "Ah, I figured it was Italian. What about the shoes? Ferragamo?"

"No, Ralph Lauren."

"Oh . . . he's an okay Jewish boy. Smart." He looked down and commented, "I like 'em."

"Yeah," Carlo agreed, extending his right leg, admiring his own foot. "They're very comfortable."

"For me to be comfortable with this film deal, Carlo, it's going to have to be done under very special conditions." Giannelli paused, enjoying his cigar.

"Computers," he went on, "they're a mixed blessing. They tell the IRS too much." Capriotti nodded in agreement. "We'll move the money to Amsterdam and run it through . . ." He removed a small black notebook from his breast pocket and, using his index finger as a guide, he read row after row of corporate names. Finally he smiled and said, ". . . a small company I know there."

"Bene."

"Of course, Carlo, I own the negative. I recoup in first position. *We* share the profits fifty-fifty." Giannelli relaxed and concluded, "I get a hundred and twenty-five percent on my investment."

"I don't know that I can deliver all that, Mr. Giannelli."

"You wanna be a producer, Carlo, you do it this way—or you get your money someplace else."

"I don't want to deal with anybody else."

Giannelli started to laugh. He coughed and said, "Of course you don't, my boy—there's already too much money between us."

"Well, that's what *Blue Moon* is all about!" Carlo enthused. "This is my opportunity not only to pay you back but to make you hundreds of millions of dollars."

"Carlo, Carlo. Calm down. I know your heart is in the right place." He stood up and opened his arms.

Capriotti collected himself, got to his feet, and hugged his mentor, moving his head from Giannelli's left shoulder to his right.

On his way back to the limousine Capriotti felt like dancing in the street. He couldn't believe how easy it was to get $10 million over a sandwich. He felt certain that delivering that kind of money would give him the clout to satisfy the Don's terms.

He wanted to go to the Oak Bar at the Plaza Hotel and pick up the most expensive lady of the night and celebrate!

I'm a big Hollywood producer, baby. Would you like to meet Colin O'Brien?

CHAPTER 18

*L*ara Miller had all but given up finding a man when, out of the blue, Kevin Wenster walked into her office carrying a roll of blueprints.

"Is B.J. available?" he asked, sounding a lot like Paul Hogan.

"Are you Australian?" she asked, smiling.

"Are you beautiful?" he asked, also smiling. "I have a weakness for green-eyed women," he confided.

"Do I know you?" There was something vaguely familiar about him.

"You should." He extended his hand.

Lara took it. This tall, muscular man with thick black hair graying at the temples had a firm grip on her. She had a sense of *déjà vu*.

"Kevin Wenster," he offered.

"Of course! We met at the AIDS benefit." Lara grinned and said, "I believe you were with Holly Dandridge that night."

"After a fashion," he said dryly.

"I know who you are," she teased. "The Australian wildman."

"*Me?* Aw, no! You've got it all wrong—old McClintock likes to tell tall tales. I'm just a simple solicitor from Sydney."

His broad grin oozing with charm told Lara otherwise. She recalled Joan telling her that he was "connected" right up to the Australian prime minister. That he and B.J. went way back . . . that he was one of Australia's top entertainment lawyers.

"That's clever," he said, pointing at a plaque on Lara's desk. "Money talks, ideas listen," he read. "Who's the philosopher?"

"Do you like it?"

"It's appropriate for our business."

She nodded, still smiling. "For any business."

"You wrote it?"

"Uh-huh. I used to work in the publicity department. Catchy sayings were my forte."

He pointed and said, "I'd like one for my desk."

"I'm flattered."

"Well, after all—*you're* the money."

"Well," she bantered, "let's say I'm close to it."

"How about dinner tonight?"

The door to B.J.'s office swung open, and the master himself strode out.

"What in the hell's going on out here, Lara?"

Before anyone could answer, B.J. spotted Kevin. The men pointed at each other and embraced the way rowdy Aussie mates did it in outback bars. Lara watched in complete amazement.

"You scoundrel!" B.J. chastised. "Why didn't you let me know you were coming? Now, you've got me on a tight squeeze." He turned to Lara and said, "Get Elizabeth for me. We've got to whip up a little something for my mate here."

Kevin waved the blueprints. "Here they are—the plans." He turned to Lara and said, "We're going to build the biggest state-of-the-art film studio in the world!"

" 'We'," B.J. said, "haven't come to terms yet."

"A mere technicality, my friend." And, as if for Lara's benefit, he added, "You know as well as I, we have the most beautiful locations in the world. You want to shoot a western—we've got mountains. You want the sea—we've got every aspect she has to offer—twenty-foot waves if you like to surf, the Great Barrier Reef if you want brilliant footage—"

"Kevin," B.J. said impatiently, "I have ten minutes."

"I'm all yours!" Kevin said, firmly locking his arm around B.J.'s shoulder. He turned his head in Lara's direction and said, "I'll pick you up at seven."

She laughed. "You don't know where I live."

He smiled and winked. "No problem."

"I wouldn't trust this guy," B.J. warned. He didn't like this new liaison one bit. "I won't give you her address, Kev. She's my right hand—and my left hand always has to know what my right hand is doing."

"You will, mate! She'll be having dinner with me."

B.J.'s door closed. Lara could hear them laughing.

It was lunchtime, but Lara didn't want to leave her desk. She had come to know B.J. well enough to know that he was serious when he said he wouldn't give Kevin Wenster her phone number or her address. And for the first time in a very long time, she had met a man she was attracted to.

She sat at her desk daydreaming—fantasizing herself with the ruggedly handsome Australian making love by candlelight in her bedroom, her living room, her kitchen—anywhere was fine with her.

Since moving to Los Angeles from New York, she'd dated a variety of upwardly mobile, self-absorbed males. Three years of cruising around discussing business or which hot new restaurant was really *hot*—or how jet-lagged the poor guy was after touring five weeks with a rock band—made Lara appreciate her single status. At least she could rent a few choice videos and curl up with her cat in the comfort of her apartment. Being alone, she decided early on, was better than being with someone you weren't in love with.

Lara placed a call to Vanessa Waters's trailer. Vanessa, thanks to Dr. Shipp's cheekbones and pouty lips, was becoming a popular player. Her face was about to appear on the cover of *TV Guide*. Her rise to fame had been so swift that she wasn't able to go anyplace without being recognized.

Vanessa pleaded for a long weekend. She explained that she was exhausted from sixteen-hour days at MCM as well as inter-views and appearances at charity tournaments. She needed a break!

"Let's skip lunch today," Lara suggested. "Tell Margo that B.J. has approved your long weekend." Lara knew that a happy, healthy actress performed much better than one who was always on the verge of exhaustion. Five years in publicity had taught her how to handle actors. The key, she'd discovered, was *listening* to them—being sensitive to their needs.

B.J.'s door opened. "Get my wife." B.J. closed the door again.

What a creep, she told herself. Sometimes, B.J., there're times when you give "rude" a new dimension.

She took one of her new business cards and wrote her home phone number on the back of it. Discreet was her middle name.

Lara located Elizabeth at Georgette Klinger's Beverly Hills salon, thigh-high in hot wax. Lara connected her with B.J. and proceeded to do something she had never done in her life—she listened in on their conversation.

From the sound of her voice, Elizabeth wasn't thrilled with B.J.'s plan. He wanted her to invite nine *important* guests—preferably including two Australians, if she could manage it.

"Mel Gibson's in town, and so's what's his name. . . ."

In the background she heard Kevin say, "Paul Hogan!"

Elizabeth kept sighing. She wasn't really prepared to give a sit-down dinner for twelve on such short notice. Couldn't Lara arrange a dinner party at L'Orangerie?

B.J. reminded his wife that Lara was busy with studio business. That they paid a cook four thousand dollars a month for just such emergencies. It was, after all, Elizabeth's job to create the perfect ambience.

"And get Kev a live one! Holly Dandridge didn't work out too well at the benefit. How about Vanessa Waters?"

"But, Byron," Elizabeth protested, "I don't think we should call her on such short notice."

Suddenly B.J.'s door cracked open and Kevin Wenster peered out at her. She hit the hold button and replaced the receiver. Kevin winked and closed the door.

God, she thought, I hope he didn't know I was eavesdropping. That would be a terrible way to start a relationship.

It was well past midnight when Lara curled up on the couch alongside her cat with a script that B.J. had told her to read and synopsize for a meeting he had in the morning. She wasn't really into it, but it was her job.

She couldn't concentrate on the plot because her mind kept wandering to Kevin Wenster and how he'd pocketed her business card and then called from his hotel room at the St. James Club to apologize for not being able to take her to dinner.

"B.J. roped me into this 'power dinner,' as you people call it. Maybe I can plead jet lag and sneak out early. Could I interest you in a nightcap?"

A nightcap . . . She knew what *that* implied, and she wasn't ready for it. One-night stands weren't her style. She found herself continually amazed at how nonchalantly, even in this age of AIDS and herpes, people jumped into bed with each other. They're like children, she thought, no common sense.

Her eyes drifted to her own childhood treasures—porcelain dolls, antique lace pillows and family photographs, a needlepoint footstool. She wanted to redecorate—make the apartment more austere and cooler, something contemporary that would reflect a confident career woman.

She admired the black wicker table she'd picked up one Sunday at the Rose Bowl Flea Market in Pasadena for seven dollars. Two coats of enamel and it looked better than the one she'd seen in an antique shop on Melrose Avenue for $275.

A good eye was what the women in her family called it. But she wondered if it was really *her* taste or her mother's? Was her attraction to the supercharged Australian well founded or foolish? She worried that slipping him her card would lead him to believe that she was a typical Hollywood *player* like Joan Souchek—and nothing could be further from the truth.

The phone rang. She hoped it wasn't B.J. with some urgent detail he wanted taken care of. Coolly she answered after the third ring.

"Lara!" boomed the boisterous Aussie. "I've found you!"

Her heart began to pound. "Yes, Kevin . . ." Then, trying to conceal her excitement, she inquired, "How was your dinner?"

"Great, luv! Press the buzzer and I'll come up and tell you all about it."

"You're downstairs?" She had given him only her home phone number, not her address, and certainly B.J. wouldn't have given it to him.

"Come on then, Lara—it's cold down here."

She pressed the buzzer and made a mad dash around the room, picking up books, papers, shoes, a sweater, cat toys—scooping up the telltale signs of disarray. She dropped the offending items on the bedroom floor and rushed to the bathroom to brush her hair and teeth and to apply a fresh coat of lipstick.

Before she could slip out of her purple leggings and oversized T-shirt and into a dress, there was a knock at the front door. When she opened it, there stood the craggy-faced, smiling wildman holding a dozen long-stemmed red roses, a chilled bottle of Dom Perignon, and two Baccarat champagne flutes, which, he confided, he'd "borrowed" from the McClintocks.

Lara was both pleased and annoyed with Kevin. She didn't like him turning up at twelve-thirty obviously intent on going to bed with her. She wanted to set him straight, but she didn't want to alienate him in the process.

Self-consciously she ran her fingers through her straight hair and asked how he'd got her address.

He beamed, exposing a slightly crooked, toothy grin, and explained that he'd slipped out during dessert. "Computer," he said slyly. "I found myself in the library, and—as you well know—the McClintocks' house is terribly well organized." His brown eyes sparked with mischievous pleasure.

He popped the cork, which, like a projectile, flew across the kitchen, missing Lara and the antique cranberry glass vase she was about to use for the roses, by a hair. They laughed nervously at the near-miss.

"Sign of good champagne," Kevin told her. He filled the glasses and said, "You were born May fourteenth, 1962 . . . you graduated cum laude from New York University in 1983. . . ."

"Kevin! That's not fair! It's also very sneaky."

"Well," he said, backing up defensively. "I just wanted to get to know you."

The boyish quality radiating from Kevin's smile took the sting away. Lara relaxed, lifting her glass to toast. The ring of crystal echoed.

"To a seventeen-hour flight that led me to you, Lara."

She smiled and took a sip. She'd never met anyone with the uncanny ability to throw her off balance the way Kevin did. She knew he'd come over because he thought she was ripe for the taking, but he did seem to be getting her message and backing off a bit.

As if reading her mind, Kevin said, "Elizabeth McClintock thinks you're too prim and proper for the likes of me. What do you think?"

"I think she may be right." Changing the subject, she asked, "So . . . how was your 'power dinner'?"

"Pretty bloody powerful!" he said earnestly. His face turned serious as he recounted the list of guests, who included a bank president, two Australian movie stars, three American movie stars, and an Argentinian polo player.

Lara led him into the living room. Instead of sitting down, Kevin proceeded to look around. He appeared to be impressed by a photo of her father with Bobby Kennedy and Martin Luther King, Jr., taken in the mid-sixties. He discovered a sterling-silver paperweight that she had received for winning a sailboat race and carried on about how much he loved the water.

"Do much sailing, do you?" he said, without seeming to focus on anything in particular.

"I love it whenever I can do it."

"I've got a sixty-footer in Sydney Harbor. Took second place in the Queen's Cup finals."

Lara sat on the couch, sipping her champagne and watching Kevin. An hour ago she'd fretted that her apartment mirrored her mother's taste. Now, she was pleased that it did.

"You've got a damn pretty collection here," Kevin said, making his way over to the Welsh china cabinet. He opened the glass cupboard, removed a delicate cup, and, to her surprise, said, "I grew up with this china. Wedgwood doesn't make this pattern anymore."

"My grandmother gave it to me when I moved out here from New York. She insisted I have silver and china so that I could entertain 'properly.' I think I've used it all of three times in five years."

He replaced the cup and turned to face her. "Not enough!" He narrowed his eyes and said, "God, you're a beautiful woman, Lara."

Feeling warmed by his compliment, she watched Kevin top both of their glasses. As he set the bottle down, it suddenly occurred to her that despite his steady glance and square stance, he was drunk.

"Did B.J. dip into the wine cellar?"

Kevin made a fist sticking his thumb up for approval as he sat next to her on the couch. "The liquid," he said, "was the best part of the five-star dinner."

He wrapped an arm around Lara and drew her to him. She thwarted his advance. "Kevin, I'm not in favor of racing into this—I don't even know you."

"Let me clear the air," he said soberly. "I live with a lady in Australia. There's just one problem . . . I'm not in love with her."

"Which means?"

"Which means I find you devastating, Lara."

"Well . . . I'm flattered . . . but I don't want to be with you if you're unavailable."

"I bet you're a mean tennis player." She nodded. "I knew it!" He stood up and became animated. "You've got me all wrong, luv! What turns me on is a woman who's my equal. You're beautiful and intelligent *and* you have my mother's china!"

"That is pretty amazing," she had to agree. There was no getting around the heat she was feeling. Lara knew that her reticence wasn't really fooling anyone.

Kevin took her hand and guided her off the couch and into his arms. Lara felt herself melting as she molded herself up against his tall, muscular body.

"I want you," he whispered, looking down into her eyes.

"I'm not into spontaneous combustion," she said, pulling back, taking his hand, and leading him to the front door. He paused and gave her a nod toward the bedroom. She shook her head and continued to pull him toward the door.

"But you do like to sail?"

"Yes . . ."

"Look, a mate of mine's loaned me his Cal-twenty-nine Saturday. Care to join me?"

Lara searched his eyes and decided that she wanted the adventure more than she feared the adventurer.

"I'd love to go sailing."

"Good! I'll pick you up round about nine."

"Can I bring lunch?"

"Your pretty self—that's all you need, luv." He took her in his arms for one more long, sweet, deep kiss before forcing himself to release her and walk out the door.

Lara closed her eyes and listened to his footsteps tapping down the stairs. She knew that she had just crossed a line.

CHAPTER 19

*E*ugenia Capriotti was introduced all around. She and her handsome husband, Carlo, were new Malibu Colony arrivals. They had taken the Bergdorfs' house for a year. The tariff was said to be excessive—eighteen thousand dollars per month—but the Capriottis were also said to be rich enough not to bother about small change.

Eugenia and Carlo were a matched pair. Prince Carlo Borromayo Capriotti was said to be a direct descendant of the Medicis. Eugenia's father was an Italian count; her mother, an English lady. In fact, one might easily take this to be an arranged marriage. Whatever the circumstances, they fit together magnificently.

Their offspring, Marco, age six, and Daria, age four, looked to be straight out of Italian *Vogue*. Beautiful, impeccably dressed miniature versions of their royal ancestors. Manuela had been Eugenia's nanny, and now she was Marco's and Daria's.

Bentine Devorac sat on the edge of an overstuffed white canvas couch trying to look animated. She had been trying all day to keep Adam Snow's attention. If only he weren't so English and proper, she thought. His dark hair and white skin only made his blue eyes more irresistible. And a composer, too! Bentine let out an audible sigh as the fantasy of Adam lifting her skirt and pulling her panties down her legs flashed across her mind.

Helen went by carrying a cold bottle of champagne and stopped to fill her friend's glass. Bentine snapped out of her hot flash and smiled. Helen grinned and moved on to Eugenia, asking if she would like some champagne. Eugenia declined, explaining that she was, alas, pregnant, and had sworn off anything you couldn't buy in a health store.

"How boring," Lady Rebecca Middleton said. "I never gave anything up, and my seven children turned out all right."

In his typical cryptic English way Derek Middleton said, "*Just*— they're *just* all right."

"Don't be rude, Dekky." She shot her husband a piercing look. He retreated to the bar for another beer.

Helen happened to walk upstairs and look down toward the last rays of sunlight. She caught sight of a couple standing ankle deep in the surf with their arms around each other . . . kissing. A wave of depression washed over her.

"Helen," Eugenia called. "Are you in or out?"

Helen swiveled to digest the question.

Eugenia's pregnancy was urging her to the bathroom, and she didn't really have time to deal with the blankness in Helen's eyes. Helen hadn't realized she was standing in front of the bathroom door.

"The loo," Eugenia said, pushing past her. "Emergency!"

Helen carefully reached into her deep cashmere pocket and wrapped her fingers around a tiny Tiffany pillbox. She had opening it down to a quiet science. Without anyone seeing, she flipped the lid, grabbed one Xanax, and closed the lid again. Using the same hand, she appeared to brush her fingers through her straight black hair. As her hand ascended, she coughed, causing her to cover her mouth out of politeness.

All it took was an instant for her to slip the tiny purple pill into her mouth. No one knew. No one would ever know. She would handle whatever pain she was feeling all on her own.

"Phew, that was close," Eugenia said, coming out of the bathroom.

"How many children do you have, Helen?"

Helen reflected and finally said, "Three. Two boys and a girl."

"Where are they?"

Helen laughed a throaty laugh. The Xanax got stuck in her throat, and she began choking. Her face turned bright red as she vainly fought to catch her breath.

"*Dio mio*," Eugenia said, grabbing Helen from behind. Locking her palms into a tight fist, she performed the Heimlich maneuver.

As Eugenia jabbed her under the breastbone, Helen opened her mouth, ejecting the offending purple pill. She gasped for air.

Eugenia's expressive black eyes widened. She reached down and plucked the remains of the Xanax from the woven white carpet.

"Tsk, tsk, tsk," she clicked, while waving a disapproving finger at her neighbor. "Must never take pills without water. Never."

Helen shook her head and tried to promise she'd never do it again.

Eugenia rejoined the party, having performed yet another maternal feat. Helen slipped out the back door for a breath of fresh air. She'd had enough. She watched Colin through the bay window immersed in a heavy directorial discussion with Derek. They were talking movie talk. Matters of great urgency were chiseling tiny lines of character in their foreheads. Adam Snow, their new houseguest, had joined them.

She opened her silver pillbox and took another Xanax. Thank God for drugs, she said to herself. If it weren't for her purple antianxiety pills, she would never get through the day or the night. She'd never used a needle. Needles had always frightened her. No, that wasn't her worry. And as for sex, she didn't play around. She'd been rejected by her husband of twenty-five years for the last ten. But she was still too much in love with him to want anyone else.

CHAPTER 20

*H*olly was ceremoniously savoring every last crumb of her chocolate doughnut. It was almost as good as sex, she thought, but not quite. Well, at eight o'clock in the morning it was an acceptable substitute.

Renaldo had just finished perfecting her mauve lipstick and was scowling like a mother hen as she carefully ate her bit of chocolate heaven.

She picked up *The Hollywood Reporter*, which she fondly referred to as "the school newspaper." Louella, the hairdresser, started to have a battle with her tresses.

"Well, today we are going to do something out of the court of Louis the Fourteenth with your hair." She began to tease and rat it until it stood on end.

"This will look fabulous with that brocade gown you're going to wear. Even though it may take you a week to comb all this ratting out."

"Go for it," Holly said absently.

Suddenly the star began choking on her doughnut. "What the fuck is *this*?" she screamed, waving the trade paper in the air.

"I told you it was going to be difficult," Louella said defensively, stepping back from Holly's chair.

"How could he do this to me!? *Me!* Of all people! I'll kill him!" Holly jumped out of the chair, still coughing on the doughnut crumbs she'd inhaled when she'd gasped at the news.

"That weasel!" she spit. "This better be a mistake is all I can say!"

The TV star, half fourteenth century and half twentieth century, ran out of the soundstage and down the studio street toward B.J.'s office, clutching the paper in her fist and talking to herself.

"How could they have gone behind my back? I don't believe this!"

Lara Miller was sitting at her desk when she saw Holly with her hair standing on end passing through the glass doors. She stood up and smiled.

"Skip the formalities," Holly spit as she burst into B.J.'s office.

"How could you do this to me, B.J.? Jeff and I wrote this as a vehicle for *me*. I'm the one who brought the goddam project to you in the first place!"

B.J. sat back in his black leather chair watching her, letting her rant and rave, giving her all the time she needed to exhaust herself. He calmly poured a tall glass of water.

"I just read about it in *The Hollywood Reporter*! You could have at least told me yourself!" Holly grabbed her throat and coughed violently.

B.J. handed her the glass of water, and she gulped it down, then smashed it on the floor and leaned in so close to his face that she could see inside his pores.

"He's taken over my movie, B.J.," Holly hissed. "This announcement doesn't even mention me as an actress. Only as a co-author."

"Holly, dear, I had nothing to do with that announcement. Colin's press agent released it without MCM's knowledge." B.J. gestured with his hands in the air.

Holly's mouth opened in surprise. She wondered if the worm was telling the truth. B.J. looked at her with the eyes of a cocker spaniel. The look on his face made her ill. She pulled a Kleenex out of her collar and expertly used it to catch her tears.

"That bastard O'Brien is going to pay for this! One word to the *National Enquirer*, B.J., about what happened on our first date, and the guy will never make another movie! Luckily for him . . . and unlike him . . . I'm too much of a lady. Anyway, he's hated me for years. Well, the feeling is mutual."

"I didn't get that at all, Holly. In fact, Colin has only good things to say about you. He got so excited about *Blue Moon* he jumped the gun, that's all. Lara gave him a script, and he loved it—he committed immediately."

"He really liked the script that much?"

"Yes . . . he cornered me just last week, saying what a brilliant woman you are. I know your history together hasn't been a smooth ride on the lake, but you, of all people, know that business *is* business."

B.J. had her. Holly had stopped crying and was listening to his every word. If there was anything B.J. had learned in all his years in show business, it was how to manipulate actors. They were trained to listen to authority. He had the big-daddy routine down pat.

"Listen, honey, I don't have to tell you Colin O'Brien is the biggest box-office draw in the world." He leaned forward and stated, "Colin's even cutting his salary to do this film, that's how much *your* project turned him on. If there's bad chemistry between you—rise above it!"

"Yeah, the set will explode if we get into the same close-up."

"No, no, no . . . It will be explosive all right, but in a way your public will love. The two of you are pros—young but seasoned actors—you can turn this around and make it into magic in seventy millimeter. I know . . . I'm banking on it, Holly. Literally."

Holly sat back and thought about it. Colin O'Brien was gold at the box office, and to star in her first feature with him was the chance of a lifetime . . . no matter what.

"There's just one thing, B.J. You and I both know that if Colin had even shown interest—let alone commitment—*Blue Moon* would've been worth three times what you're paying us for the script."

"And that wouldn't be the first time *that* happened to a writer or, for that matter, an actress, Holly. It comes under the heading of show business. So look at the plus side of the deal—with Colin O'Brien attached, you have a high-budget major motion picture. Your points, hypothetically speaking, are worth a hell of a lot more now than they were when we negotiated—okay?"

Holly didn't like it, but she'd just have to live with it. She stood up and looked B.J. squarely in the eyes. "You win round one." She grinned and said, "I have a feeling this film is bigger than any of us. But . . ." she insisted, "I'm still top dog in this circus. I don't want that prick to take over and ruin the story . . . deal?"

"Deal." McClintock threw his hand out, and they shook. He knew that as soon as production began, his actors would be too locked in to allow their egos to sabotage the film.

He watched Holly straighten up and exit. Her hair, he mused, looked as if she'd been caught in an electrical outlet. He sighed, Actors!

CHAPTER 21

*A*riba's opening at the Universal Amphitheater was sold out two hours after the box office opened. Her manager attributed the three-night sellout to media coverage and word of mouth following the AIDS benefit.

She was an extraordinarily talented performer, who combined the animal magnetism of a jaguar with the fragile grace of a ballerina. An *L.A. Times* critic wrote, "On the Richter scale Ariba would be eight points." Her dynamism onstage put her in a class with George Michael, Michael Jackson, and Bruce Springsteen.

Tonight was the night! Everybody in Hollywood who was anybody had made it their business to be there. Entertainment-industry people had a sixth sense when it came to spotting a new phenomenon. Ariba, the sexual high priestess of Brazil, had delivered. Now, she had Hollywood's heavyweights in her garter. She had given them three tumultuously received encores before the stage went black.

B.J.'s children, Savannah McClintock and her sixteen-year-old twin brothers, Mikey and Danny, were sitting close enough to the stage to make their way backstage before the onslaught. So many people were pushing and shoving that Savannah and her brothers became separated from each other.

Savannah felt out of place within the crush of music people. They were brash and loud. She wished she could be more open like the twins, but she simply wasn't that flexible. She watched people all around her making fools of themselves—laughing too loud, and drinking too much. They all seemed desperate to be noticed, to be accepted, to be loved, or just simply to get laid.

Instead of sitting on the green room couch, she wanted to crawl under it. But it was okay, she'd be a good sport and wait for the boys.

Savannah took a sip from a can of Diet Coke and giggled. In her black leather minidress with the fitted red leather bolero jacket and Paloma Picasso diamond-X necklace she felt she could get anybody to give her his undivided attention.

A black conga player smiled from across the room and made his approach. He introduced himself and waited for her to respond. When she didn't, he asked if he made her nervous.

"No, no," Savannah lied. "I'm just waiting for my brothers."

"Good. I'll keep you company."

Savannah stood up. "I think I'd better find them, actually." She looked at her watch and moved into the thick of the mob.

The conga player smiled out of one side of his mouth and reached for her arm. "Good," he told her. "I'll be your protector."

Hot on her heels, he leaned in and took a deep whiff of her clean blond hair.

"You American women smell so good," he whispered in her ear.

Savannah panicked. She turned back and forced herself through a knot of people.

"'Bye, nice meeting you," she called as she beat a path out of the green room and down a body-packed hallway. *Where were Mikey and Danny when she needed them?*

Over the din she suddenly heard their unmistakable laughter. She followed the raucous sounds to a door marked WOMEN. Cautiously she pushed it open.

Standing in a sunken shower-tub the size of a small bedroom were half a dozen people schmoozing, hitting on each other, and snorting cocaine from Danny's hand.

Savannah watched in disbelief. One of the Brazilian horn players from Ariba's band beckoned her to join them. And, like a zombie, she walked toward them.

"Danny, when did you start doing *this*?"

"What?" Mikey asked sarcastically. "Snorting coke or standing in a shower with strangers?"

"I think it's time for us to go," she insisted.

Danny approached his sister and gently wrapped his arm around her shoulder. "Oh, you do, do you?"

Biting her lip to keep her rage in check, Savannah glared at him.

"Lemme tell you something, Toto . . . we're not in Kansas anymore."

She looked from Danny to Mikey and realized that they were strangers. The adopted twins had to have sprung from some evil demon seed. Being an only child would've been better than having to endure *them*, she told herself.

Just then one of the backup singers rushed in, locked the door, and shouted, "Everybody! Turn around and face the wall. I gotta pee!"

Bodies turned, facing the wall.

Mikey said, "May we have a moment of silence, please."

This was too much for Savannah. She was appalled at how low humanity had stooped. She went to the door and was fidgeting with the lock when the toilet flushed and the listeners applauded.

Savannah found herself squeezing down the same hallway. At

the far end she spotted Ariba disappearing through a doorway. Everything she'd witnessed tonight went against the laws of nature. She remembered a phrase her mother had used once to describe a certain New York sex club she'd read about in the papers: "A pit of evil, debauched vipers!" Her mother was right. Hell was right here on earth, and this had to be the core of it. Everywhere she looked, she saw the faces of sinners.

Ariba's big coffee-colored Brazilian bodyguard looked down at Savannah as she explained that Ariba had set up her tickets, and she'd like to thank her personally.

The bodyguard sized her up, knocked three times, and waited.

Flavio Gambetti, the elegant, middle-aged founder of Platinum Records, cracked the door open. After recognizing Savannah, he opened it.

Entering the star's dressing room, Savannah felt as if she had just interrupted an intimate moment. "You were fantastic, Ariba! I've never seen anyone hypnotize an audience the way you did."

Ariba sauntered over and put her arm around the McClintock heiress. She led her to the couch. "Yes?" she asked, "So you like me, Vanna?" The blonde smiled warmly.

Flavio, the master of slick, handed Savannah a flute of champagne, saying, "Here, *bella*. We celebrate."

They clicked glasses. Outside the door the natives were getting restless.

"Vanna," Ariba said, patting the couch, "sit down. Be comfortable." She waited while her friend obliged. "You come with us— Flavio's giving a big party for me at Spago."

Savannah's face lighted up. "I'd love to!" *Let the poison dwarfs make their own way home.*

Suddenly the door opened, and Mikey McClintock pushed his head inside, under the bodyguard's bulging tricep.

"Yo, Savannah!" he snorted, clearing his sinuses. "Limo's waiting! Let's go, Sis!"

"Go ahead. I'll catch you later," she said.

"Where you go, I go."

"Not tonight, Bro."

Flavio pushed Mikey's head out the door and closed it.

"Good, Vanna," Ariba cooed. "That makes me happy."

Savannah tried to appear cool, but underneath she was seething. The twins had done nothing but make her life miserable since the day they arrived. She drained her glass, and Flavio refilled it.

"Come, Vanna, I have something to show you."

Flavio watched Savannah's black cowboy boots carry her long legs across the dressing room and into the bathroom. Ariba giggled and closed the door.

"Those girls were made for each other," he said, topping his champagne.

CHAPTER 22

*L*ara strode into Dr. Shipp's waiting room, passing nervous patients on her way to the window. The glass slid open, and Ethel's deeply lined, unsmiling face peered out.

"Dr. Shipp wants to see me for a minute."

The lines around Ethel's mouth twisted hostilely. *Another one of these Hollywood hotshots.* "He's with a patient."

"Would you please tell him Lara Miller is here to see him? He's expecting me."

"No fair using your *connections* to cut in line, Lara," a husky male voice accused.

Lara turned around. "Renaldo! What're you doing here?" But before he could answer, she caught herself. "Never mind, it's none of my business."

"Now, now," Renaldo shot back. "We're all here because we *want* to be. Of *that* I am certain."

"Miss Miller," Ethel called curtly. "Dr. Shipp will see you now."

"What service," the renowned makeup artist sneered. "I've been sitting here all morning."

"I'll put in a good word," she promised. She knew what a bore waiting was, but she wasn't there for her own needs. She slipped inside the electric door, a dozen pairs of anxious eyes searing her back.

Some were easily recognizable folk: an actor, an actress, a TV newscaster, a "wife of," plus a Bel Air beldam. She knew that upon arriving, superstars were ferreted into private rooms.

Lara entered Dr. Shipp's private office. *Well, this is definitely the heart of his evil establishment.*

She immediately noticed the exquisite collection of Japanese nudes painted on silk. Rare and very pricey, she decided, sinking into a deep leather chair.

"This chair reminds me of old, soft flesh," she said, squirming.

"*Memento mori*," he said, and left it at that.

Lara studied the cluster of family photographs fortifying him from behind. Elaine, the redhead, the second wife who couldn't be much older than Lara herself. A plump Savannah McClintock at, she guessed, age twelve, standing next to a good-looking young man who Lara assumed was Mort's dead son, Eddie. The wild boy, she'd heard Savannah say, died tragically in a car accident on Mulholland Drive.

The plastic surgeon sat there fondling a clear plastic baggie filled with what appeared to be water. He couldn't help but notice Lara's inquisitive stare. He grinned and tossed it to her, sitting back, waiting for her reaction.

She caught it and began enjoying the soft, squishy feeling she got from playing with it.

"Don't tell me," she said, "it's a New Age beanbag?"

Shipp rolled his eyes and decreed, "A perfect thirty-six-D." He leaned across his desk. "You'd have men lined up around your desk," he said enticingly.

"I don't want men lined up around my desk, Mort. I want the insurance forms for *Blue Moon*."

Lara took the manila envelope marked MCM from the top of his desk, told the doctor that she loved her breasts exactly as they were, and beat a hasty path back to the studio.

Mort needed a vacation. He had three doctors on staff, but they couldn't relieve the overwhelming pressure. His patients were all paranoid. They didn't want to see anybody else. Only him.

His phone rang. It was B.J., wanting to know if Lara had left.

"I can't take this much longer, B.J.," Shipp warned. "I can't live with myself."

"You're having a bad day, Mort. Take Elaine down to the Springs for the weekend."

"We're not doing well, B.J."

There was a long pause. Finally B.J. said, "Look, Mort, there's a guest role on Holly's show that Elaine could play. Would that help?"

"Maybe . . ."

"Mort." B.J.'s voice was redundant, hard. "You walked into this cushy situation with your eyes wide open."

"That's not what bothers me, B.J., and you know it! It's sick things like the switch you want me to pull on Vanessa Waters. She'll threaten me with a malpractice suit!"

"It's not as sick as injecting an innocent girl with an overdose of insulin . . . is it?"

Shipp wanted to vomit. He quietly returned the receiver to its cradle. *Shit, how could I have done something so stupid? One mistake thirty-five years ago, and that bastard'll make me pay for the rest of my life.*

He felt as if he was on the verge of a nervous breakdown. He'd been taking Valium and Xanax, but now he decided to try something a little more to the point.

One shot of Demerol, and suddenly a feeling of bliss flushed his brain. *God, this is amazing! No wonder so many of my colleagues end up at Betty Ford.*

He closed his eyes and leaned back in his soft leather "God's chair." He liked to call it that because his patients hung on his every syllable. Would they look like their favorite movie star? Could he create their fantasy? What a responsibility. It was getting to be too much, he thought. Maybe he could leave L.A. and start a practice in some small rural community reconstructing accident victims. He sat there dreaming of what it would be like to be free of the horrors he himself was perpetrating.

CHAPTER 23

*I*t had been a long weekend, and after three different kinds of massage, a lesson in color healing, and vegetables for two days, Holly Dandridge was ready for a bottle of champagne.

It was great to get out of town and relax, even if it was only for a couple of days. Leave it to B.J. to track me down in the middle of the desert, she thought. But what the hell, he'd bought her script, and she was the star! *Blue Moon!*

Whizzing past Disneyland in her new Mercedes 560 SEC convertible, she popped a piece of bubble gum between her teeth. With every sweet chomp she silently rehearsed her Oscar acceptance speech.

What a joke, she mused. Colin O'Brien, Mr. Macho, sexiest man on earth. What an asshole.

Even the gum lost its flavor when she thought of having to kiss Colin, although she knew what a good actor he was. Star, anyway. Nominated three times, won twice. She'd seen a picture of him in *People* magazine with his Oscars as bookends.

Too much energy, that was what she was suffering from. So what if the chemistry was bad? Together they'd turn mutual hatred into great art. She wanted to act in a movie that she could sink her teeth into. Also, exercise those muscles and make an actress into a physical legend. A Diana, a huntress.

Colin O'Brien, you son of a bitch! If only I had ignored him that day, she thought. If only he had sat at someone else's station to have lunch. . . . He was so handsome. How could I have resisted his invitation to a party?

She had actually imagined she'd be discovered by some big producer there who would take one look at her and star her opposite Colin. Her life as a waitress/struggling actress, would be over.

Holly laughed at her naïveté. The party had turned out to be big. Loaded with stars. Some of them had eyed her, smiling. Looking back, it was plain to see she was just a little girl way out of her league. Some of the stars had liked her just for that. What a night!

She and Colin hooked up eventually with Grant Thomas, a soap star who was even handsomer than Colin. Holly was on cloud nine when the two hunks decided to go back to Grant's apartment and discuss *her* career. They wanted to help her, introduce her to some casting agents and a few directors.

She thought she was finally in with the "in" crowd. The handsome pair introduced her to tequila. "It's *the* best drink to wash a lude down with," Colin had said, producing a large round pill with the numbers 714 imprinted on it. Hell, why not? she thought. She had always wanted to try a Quaalude, and besides, she felt she was in good hands with these two big, beautiful guys.

In no time those hands were all over her body. It was like a dream in slow motion. Still, bits and pieces hung like laundry on a clothesline in her memory.

Holly had felt like a blowup doll, being maneuvered by Grant as Colin directed, sitting across the room in an armchair, naked and masturbating.

It must have been the Quaalude, she suspected, because it was as if she were standing outside herself, not being able to fully feel what was happening to her body. She recalled that her nerve endings felt numb.

Holly would never forget the way Colin got up out of the old green chair in the golden glow of the room the moment Grant reached orgasm.

When Grant fell away, Colin entered Holly and ejaculated instantly.

The sun had set, and most of MCM's employees had left for the day when the *Blue Moon* preproduction meeting got started. It had taken Lara Miller three days to corral B.J. into setting the time aside. He was not only the executive producer of the film but also the head of the whole studio—which meant that he had the final say on everything.

Carlo Capriotti, however, who had bought his way into the role of producer, had seen fit to telephone at five past four to say that he was having car trouble. Lara found this to be one of the lamest excuses she'd ever heard. The prince had a Ferrari, a Mercedes, and a four-wheel-drive Jeep. Capriotti, she concluded, was either too lazy to drive in from Malibu or, more likely, too scared of displaying his amateurism in front of a group of hardworking pros who'd have figures on budget, schedule, casting, and production at their fingertips.

Derek Middleton arrived promptly at five-thirty. Lara, feeling more like a producer than an executive secretary, led the director into B.J.'s office. She had set a plate of assorted cheeses and crackers on the long walnut table B.J. used for production meetings. There were cans of soft drinks in a silver ice pail. Liquor would be offered by B.J.—if at all—toward the end of the meeting, provided it had reached conclusions he could smile upon. Lara knew she would be lucky to make it home by ten-thirty.

B.J., Derek, Lara, the production manager, the location-unit manager, and the head of the budget department took their places at the table. They began by discussing the contracts: individual ones that business affairs had referred back to B.J. or needed to be signed, and contracts with various unions. They weighed the pros and cons of the cost and convenience of one location over another and how each would relate cost-effectively to the story and the

budget. Throughout, Lara noted, Derek Middleton was coopera-
tive, understanding, and helpful. She had heard he was a beast to
deal with. What a relief, she reassured herself. He couldn't be more
accommodating. His constant and eagerly British "yes, yes, yes"es
soon began to replace his earlier frowns and doubts as the discussion
wore on. Perhaps, thought Lara, his eye was on the farther table,
where scotch and vodka bottles stood awaiting a genial consensus
of the meeting.

After the first two hours, however, it was B.J. who began to run
his tongue over his front teeth at more and more frequent intervals.
She sensed that she had about ten minutes left before her boss
would stand up and walk out.

"The estimable Prince Carlo wants to change the title," Derek
said, smirking. "He thinks he's come up with a better one: *Desert
Fake-out*."

Everyone roared with laughter.

"Next," B.J. predicted, "he's going to ask for a part in the movie."

"He already has," Derek said. "He wants a cameo. He wants to
play one of the sentries in the underground storage area guarding
the drugs. He's even sketched the uniform. I had to point out to
him that American GIs do *not*, so far, wear knee-high jackboots."

More laughter.

B.J. tossed his pen over his shoulder. "Good Lord!" He leaned
on one elbow and said, "All right—to keep the peace, we'll call
Blue Moon a *working* title. Lara, you tell Capriotti that ol' B. J.
McClintock is a skinflint. That the letterhead's been printed, and
I ain't gonna run it through a shredder 'cause somebody *thinks* we
need a new title."

He stood up, put his jacket on, and concluded, "We can talk
about this again when *Blue Moon*'s in postproduction." He shook
hands with Derek. "Good meeting. And, er, anybody wants to
help themselves at the bar, why, you all can see where it's at. Lara,
will you be hostess on my behalf, please?" He headed for the door.
"And pour Derek a *blast*, sugar."

"But B.J.," Lara called after him, "we still haven't set the production designer or—"

He stopped her, saying, "You all can handle that!" He acknowledged the production team, who were hanging on his every word, he thought, because they were anxious to get to the bar.

"You know," B.J. said thoughtfully, "if my mama said it once, she said it a thousand times: 'Opportunities like this come along once in a blue moon.' Those things stick with you—that's why I'm gonna stick with the title." He turned and vanished down the corridor.

Lara and Derek looked at each other.

Imitating B.J.'s southern accent, Derek said, "Well, I guess that *that* is gonna be *the* final word on *that*."

Lara poured their drinks. It was definitely going to be a long night.

CHAPTER 24

*T*hree iced beer mugs clicked. Cheers all around. Then silence as Adam Snow slipped a tape into a new Sony player. Haunting, synthesized tones from his latest round of compositions filled the room.

Colin lifted his glass toward a giant blowup of the Mojave Desert. "To *Blue Moon!*" he toasted.

"*Blue Moon!*" Derek Middleton's deep English voice echoed.

The director pushed himself out of the chair. Not an easy maneuver after putting on another ten pounds in the stomach. For some reason that was the only place he seemed to gain. Rebecca kept telling him it was from drinking too much. If that was the reason, he told himself, then so be it.

Derek handed Adam and Colin a stack of location photos—shots of the sun setting over the Joshua Tree National Monument in the

Mojave Desert, ancient tribal artwork secreted away in the caves near the film's proposed campsite . . . Joshua trees of all sizes and shapes . . . Then the director punched his index finger against a blowup of an enormous boulder resting on top of one of the Santa Rosa mountains.

"Do you remember what H. G. Wells said about eternity?" Derek queried.

Colin and Adam didn't have a clue.

Derek started tapping the boulder in the photo. "Imagine a giant rock—one hundred miles long, one hundred miles wide, and ten miles high." He watched his friends. To Derek Middleton, timing was everything. "Every century a small bird sharpens its beak on that rock," he went on, "and when that rock is worn away, *one second* of eternity will have passed."

"Ohhhh." Colin winced. "That puts everything into perspective."

"Afraid so," Adam agreed, and winked at the actor.

"Yes," Derek said, nodding. He took a stack of 11 × 14 color stills illustrating the desert's incredibly versatile personality and propped them up against the back of the white wicker couch.

"Daybreak," Derek whispered. "Soft salmon pink . . . then," he said dramatically, "we have the red-hot terra-cottalike rocks and boulders. Midday is not a time for man or beast." He moved to the next photograph. "Sunset—when coyotes venture out for dinner and condors flap their wings and rise up—if there're any left by then—to ride the silent wind."

"Oh get off it!" Adam shifted in his chair.

Colin put a finger to his lips and said, "Shhhh."

Derek held up the last blowup, taken with a wide-angle lens. It revealed the desert at the end of the day—heavily textured, blue, and mysterious against the vast arid expanse. "Here we have it . . ." He eyed his audience and said, *"Blue Moon . . ."*

"I have a feeling I'm going to be upstaged by the desert," Colin complained.

"Don't be daft—you're drunk!" Derek chided.

"I thought we were here to listen to my music," Adam said.

"Yes, me boy," Derek answered back, "we are."

Standing near the stairway, Helen could hear them laughing and carrying on as if nothing else mattered. And to Colin, Derek, and her new houseguest, the arrogant young Englishman Adam Snow, nothing else did.

The Annual Cancer Society dinner had been on the O'Briens' calendar for the last six weeks. The tickets had cost hundreds, and Helen's new Givenchy gown thousands.

Now, the lady of the house was slipping into her dress and twisting like a contortionist to reach the zipper at the back of her taffeta bodice.

Where was Colin when she needed him? Her arms felt heavy and awkward as she struggled to push the tip of the zipper all the way up her back.

Helen glanced at the clock and accidently caught her angry expression in the mirror. Yes, she thought, I'm ready to scream. *He's* downstairs laughing, knowing full well that we've got to leave in twenty minutes!

Beneath it all was the fear that Colin would disappoint her. It wouldn't be the first time he'd bowed out at the eleventh hour. All right, she pushed herself, set his clothes out. Make it easy for him. . . .

She'd spoken to Elizabeth McClintock at length about who was going to be sitting at "their" table. They'd tried to devise a plan to eliminate the Shipps, but neither one of the ladies could find a plausible excuse. Mort and Elaine had somehow affixed themselves to a group that could barely tolerate them. They all seemed to be intimidated by Dr. Morton Shipp and the power he wielded with his scalpel.

Helen slipped into her black satin heels and smoothed her gown. Suddenly it sounded as if a raucous English pub had erupted downstairs. Between the loud music and their boorish laughter, she could feel a migraine coming on.

The dressing room was lined with mirrors so that every last detail could be verified. Helen studied herself—her shoulder-length dark brown hair had been pulled back with the gold-and-pearl combs that Colin had given her for their seventh wedding anniversary. For forty-five, she looked sensational . . . at least on the outside. She shuddered to think what years of mood-elevators had done to her insides. If only I had a way of channeling my energy, she told herself. If only I could stick with my play long enough to finish a draft. . . . If only . . . if only . . .

The star's wife took a deep breath and descended the stairs. As she entered the smoke-filled room, the three men stopped talking and turned the volume down. They complimented her on how beautiful she looked. How radiant, how like a shot in *W.* Yes, Helen O'Brien had been born to look grand.

After the pleasantries she said, "Colin, it's seven o'clock. You had better get dressed."

"What I'm doing *right now* is more important than *anything.*" He gave her his best "Don't fuck with me" look.

Shaken, Helen gasped, "What are you saying, Colin? That you're not going?"

The actor rose, letting his eyes and body language tell the story. He walked into the kitchen, Helen on his heels. Derek and Adam exchanged clownish scowls. Fur was going to fly. Great ladies didn't get dressed to the nines so they could stay home.

Colin walked to the end of the white tile counter and leaned against it. He was ready to play the scene.

Mouth tight and quivering, Helen approached. Her dark brown eyes were flashing anger and hysteria.

Beautiful as his wife looked, Colin was tired of accompanying her on the celebrity charity-dinner circuit. If he had to look at one more plate of chicken paillard, he was going to puke.

"How could you do this to me?" she asked, wounded.

"Do what to you, Hellsey?" He paused for a beat and said, "It may appear to you that I'm having a good time in there, but we start shooting the fucking film in less than a month."

Tears trickled down her cheeks as Helen desperately tried to control her feelings of humiliation and despair. "Colin," she pleaded, "you know how important this charity is to me. I was depending on you. We're supposed to be meeting Elizabeth and B.J."

Colin turned slightly, changing his angle. Softly he said, "If it's so important to you, go! Take Bentine."

"Bentine?" He might as well have said Godzilla. How could he be so thoughtless? she asked herself.

"Honey," he said, turning away, "why don't you go upstairs and take another pill and relax. Then call Bentine."

Helen glared at her husband as she swept past him and up the stairs.

Colin ran his hands through his blond hair and opened the refrigerator. They'd gone through the imported beer. Now, they were down to the domestic. *Domestic*, he thought. It's Thursday. No maid. They'd have to send out for a pizza, but it sure as shootin' beat rubber chicken.

Helen lay in her bed, facedown and with limbs so straight she seemed to be measuring herself for a coffin.

The pain . . . the unspeakable pain. It was so great, so intense, that she was numb. No tears. No heavy sighs. Just a jaw locked into position and a heart heavy with grief.

She turned her head, pushing hard against the down Pratesi-covered pillows to see the white light on the landing gear of a jumbo jet making its way through the darkness to LAX.

The purple Xanax had kicked in, and the nightmare of calling Elizabeth McClintock to lie about why she and Colin couldn't make it was still going through her mind. She remembered offering their tickets to Savannah. . . .

"No respect," she cursed. Colin, the superb actor—on and off screen. Nobody really knows . . .

Helen was grateful for the understanding that she shared with her circle of friends. There was a sense of respect and honor among them that even their self-absorbed husbands couldn't destroy.

Colin, Adam, and Derek Middleton were downstairs drinking

beer, "becoming soldiers of fortune," as they put it. Their way of getting ready for *Blue Moon*. To them, she thought, everything can be fixed in the editing room. Even real life.

The phone rang, but Helen didn't want to talk to anybody.

Bastards, she thought.

Colin made his way across the thick white pile carpet. He sat on the edge of the bed and waited. Helen could feel him. She could smell the beer on his breath and the cigarette smoke permeating his hair and shirt.

"Honey," he finally said, "it's Bentine." He paused, waiting for a response. When none was forthcoming, he placed a comforting hand on her shoulder and quietly urged, "Honey, I don't know what to tell her."

In the darkness Helen rolled over. Suddenly the numbness broke. The dam that had been holding the tears back burst. She hadn't cried like this in years.

"Let me unzip you," Colin offered, reaching around, cautiously easing the metal tip down his wife's back. He didn't know how to deal with her. He tried his best to comfort her, but—without a script and a director—his natural abilities in this area were limited. He felt relieved to hear footsteps padding up the stairs and to see Adam standing in the doorway.

"Bentine is still on the line," the Englishman informed them. "What should I tell her?"

"Go away!" Helen told the intruder.

"Honey, Adam's just trying to be helpful."

Adam raised his voice. He was no fonder of Helen than she was of him. "I'll tell her you'll call her back. How's that?"

"Great," Colin said. "Why don't we call it a night?"

Helen kept sobbing.

Colin felt awkward and uncomfortable. He wanted to follow Adam downstairs. He'd give anything to take a long walk on the beach. He was cradling a madwoman, a woman over the edge. His wife was completely out of control.

She fell back on the bed and stopped crying. The numbness was returning.

"Colin," she said softly. "What're we going to do?"

"Shall I turn on a light?"

"No."

Colin sighed deeply. He didn't know what to do.

"Colin . . . hold me?"

Mechanically he folded his arms around her. He could feel a heavy burden of emotion welling from her to him. He didn't like the feeling, but he felt obliged to give her whatever he could.

"Why don't we call the kids? The boys are three hours ahead. . . ." He noted the lateness of the hour at their Massachusetts prep school, and decided it would be wiser to call their daughter in Switzerland.

"I don't really want to talk to anybody right now," Helen said quietly.

"You know I love you," Colin said, gently massaging her neck.

CHAPTER 25

*A*n MCM messenger deposited an envelope marked LEGAL on Lara Miller's desk, turned on her Reeboks, and bounced off to her next delivery.

At the top of the first page Lara saw "*Blue Moon.*" She quickly sifted through the pages until she found Colin O'Brien's signature. Goose bumps covered her bare arms. *It was real!* And, she had been the catalyst! *Blue Moon* was now a "go" picture.

"*Lara, you get B.J. to commit, and I'll give you a finder's fee. I'll even ask him to give you a job on the film.*"

Holly Dandridge's promises were also real. Lara wondered if she would receive the usual 5 percent finder's fee from both Holly and her collaborator, or Holly alone. Funny, she thought, I never bothered to ask.

The job, or at least the prospect of working on *Blue Moon*, got Lara very excited. She loved the subject matter, she loved the project—she wanted to be part of it!

"I think you should push for an associate producer credit, Lara. You put the package together. Remember—without you, Holly'd still be trying to get it off the ground."

Colin had pressed her to approach B.J. for the associate-producer credit. It just wasn't her style to be pushy. If B.J., like Holly and Colin, told her that she deserved a special credit or a bonus, she would accept it happily. Asking was something else.

Lara scanned the lengthy contracts. B.J. McClintock was listed as the executive producer; Carlo Capriotti as the producer. She looked at her plaque—MONEY TALKS, IDEAS LISTEN—and she thought of Prince Carlo. To the best of her knowledge, he'd never produced a film before. *Blue Moon*, budgeted at close to $21 million, would be his trial run. Given the fact that he'd raised $10 million, Lara guessed he was entitled to see his name in 70 mm.

What about you, Lara? Aren't you entitled to be part of the project? If you don't ask B.J. for a job on it, he'll never offer you one.

Lara opened her desk, took out a silver heart-shaped mirror, and evaluated her appearance. She could use a fresh coat of lipstick. She applied a deep autumn red to her lips and smiled. For once in her life she was pleased to have straight hair. She ran a brush through it, and it fell perfectly around the top of her shoulders. She was ready to approach B.J.

Contracts in hand, she knocked on his door, then entered. He was on a long-distance call. He looked up and, never missing a beat, took the contracts and began scanning them.

Lara waited for B.J. to hang up; only as soon as he did, two other lines rang.

"Did you want to tell me something?" he asked abruptly.

Lara shook her head.

"The phones," he said, pointing.

Dutifully she answered, "B. J. McClintock's office." She covered the receiver and informed her boss that Dr. Shipp was on the line. "I'll take it."

Lara handed him the phone and stepped back. B.J. swiveled around to face the tall glass window with the panoramic view of Santa Monica. "I don't care, Mort! She's not going to know the difference between a 'C' or a 'D' once she's out on the table."

Lara sat down and waited quietly.

Oh shit! They're talking about Vanessa Walters's breast implants. God, how unethical—I can't believe these two bastards. Vanessa's always been dead set against anything bigger than a "B" cup.

"Jesus, Mort—get on with it. I guarantee, once she's got them, she'll love them."

B.J. swiveled around to face Lara. Morton Shipp, he thought, is an asshole, but with enough hand-holding, he gets the job done.

Another phone line lighted up. B.J. pointed at it, and Lara retreated to her desk. Her momentum had been lost. Now, she would have to wait to discuss *Blue Moon*.

CHAPTER 26

*L*iving within the posh confines of the Malibu Colony suited the Capriottis. Eugenia's new circle of friends included some of Hollywood's most celebrated actors, writers, producers, and directors. Her children, Marco and Daria, had become beautifully bronzed and happily spoiled—verging on brattiness, she feared.

Being pregnant made her feel more feminine and more beautiful than at any other time. Eugenia Capriotti loved motherhood. She loved nurturing everyone around her. She wanted the world to be aesthetically pleasing, and people to be kind and loving.

She knew that she was an idealist, but she didn't care. If it weren't for Carlo's sudden mood swings, she would be joyful.

It was the movie, she warned herself. Ever since he'd started producing *Blue Moon*, he'd changed. He was nervous, and his insomnia had returned. In the last few days she had even caught him being short-tempered with the children. I'll have to confront him, she told herself. He's disrupting the harmony of the household.

Carlo and Eugenia sat down to lunch at a lovely table situated on the deck overlooking the water.

They had barely begun to eat their mussels marinara when the maid returned and announced that there was a "Mr. G." on the line for Mr. Capriotti.

Carlo practically choked on the mussel he was chewing. He pushed himself up from the table and excused himself.

Eugenia sat there toying with her lunch. Angrily she twisted the crust off the end of the French bread. She dunked it into the marinara sauce, searching for a way she could tell her headstrong husband that he was upsetting everyone—especially her.

When Carlo returned, he smiled mechanically and resumed eating. He tried to make small talk, but Eugenia could see that beneath the bravado her husband was agitated.

"Carlo," she began, "this producer business has changed you. I've watched you talk to people on the phone all day long, but when this 'Mr. G.' calls, you get moody."

"Producing a movie," he said aggressively, "is nothing like stocks and bonds, Eugenia." He averted his eyes, tearing off a piece of bread. "I'm the producer. Everybody needs to talk to me. Joseph Giannelli has nothing to do with my mood."

Eugenia's head snapped to attention. "*Joseph Giannelli?*" she said in utter disbelief. "Carlo, don't tell me you're doing business with Joseph Giannelli!"

Capriotti shrugged. "He's one of the two investors in *Blue Moon*. So?"

Eugenia's dark, passionate eyes mirrored the sense of alarm she was experiencing. "He's not just an investor! How could you go into business with the Mafia?"

"Calm down, *bella*," Carlo said sternly. "It's not the first time. You don't know anything—"

"What do you mean, 'It's not the first time'? Carlo—"

"You don't understand! When the market crashed—when we were about to lose *everything*—Mr. G. was there with six million dollars."

Eugenia's face went white. "You could have gone to my father."

"No," Carlo said. "Then he would have my balls in his hands and prove me the loser he thinks I am."

"My God, Carlo! Better that than to jeopardize your family in the claw of the devil."

Carlo slammed his hand on the table. "You take care of the children, Eugenia. I'll take care of business."

"But I'm thinking of the children. Of our family," she said.

"*Basta!* Two days ago you went to Rodeo Drive and spent twenty-six thousand dollars. Do I not provide for you?"

"Yes, Carlo, but—"

"But what? This is not dirty money, Eugenia. This is a clean investment. Joseph Giannelli needs deals like this to make him legitimate."

Eugenia sat back, massaging her pregnant belly. Her appetite was gone, and she felt nauseated.

"Stop worrying, *bellissima*. *Blue Moon* is the answer to our dreams."

Eugenia pushed herself away from the table. She knew that there was no point in discussing it further. She needed to lie down and close her eyes. She prayed that her father's denunciations of her beloved Carlo were not about to come true—and ruin her life.

CHAPTER 27

A light rain had misted the city, making roads as slippery as oil. Maneuvering her Mercedes up the narrow, winding roads of Bel Air produced more anxiety in Elizabeth McClintock than two kir royales could soothe.

She was still concerned about the disagreement she and Savannah had had over the teenager's impending trip to New York with her new friends—music people. Not Elizabeth's cup of tea, really. The trouble was, as a child grew older, there seemed to be two sides to every question—the two sides in this case being whether to insist upon her own authority or risk appearing to be weak.

Elizabeth recounted to herself Father Malcomb's advice. After mass he had suggested that she let her daughter make more of her own decisions. *"You have given her a strong foundation, Elizabeth. Trying to keep her away from those new friends of hers will only make her more rebellious toward you. Put it in God's hands."*

Well, she told herself, it always *is* in God's hands.

Suddenly, out of nowhere, a car swerved around a corner. Elizabeth hugged the curb, barely missing the mindless woman in a Jaguar who was paying more attention to the telephone conversation she was having than to the blind curve of the street.

Elizabeth caught her breath, wishing that one day soon car phones would be outlawed in Los Angeles for anything except roadside emergencies. Why, the woman didn't even slow down! It was a miracle that they hadn't collided.

Elizabeth rounded another treelined corner—a five-acre walled estate belonging to a fast-food heiress. Food, she thought, we make such a fuss over it.

She had enjoyed a light lunch at the Bistro Garden with Helen O'Brien, who, in order to keep the date, had to have her friend Bentine Devorac drive her into town. One day soon, Elizabeth told herself, Helen is going to have to give up those pills. Deep down Elizabeth felt sure that Helen's pills were the cause of, rather than the solution to, Helen's anxieties.

Bentine was nice enough, but the original purpose of the lunch had been to finalize the brochure commemorating the AIDS benefit. And just as she had suspected, the moment they'd sat down, the conversation had turned to *gossip* . . . good, old-fashioned, titillating gossip.

They had thoroughly discussed Adam Snow, Colin's brilliant musical discovery. Bentine thought he was too good-looking to be interested in anybody but himself. Then Helen reminded her friend that she had chased the thirty-two-year-old Englishman up and down the beach . . . to no avail.

"You're too *mature* for him, Bennie. He has his eye on the blond starlet staying at your house, Elizabeth."

Elizabeth had coolly explained that the girl's manager was a very old friend of B.J.'s. And that, according to him, the starlet was going to be the next Marilyn Monroe.

"Well," Helen had said, laughing, "to hear Colin talk about Adam, you'd think he's going to be the new Mozart—or the new Andrew Lloyd Weber—I wish somebody *really* new and original would come along and knock our socks off!"

"Ariba!" Bentine enthused. "She's unlike anybody I've ever seen. Not since I saw Elvis Presley perform at the Pan Pacific Auditorium in 1958 have I been so emotionally overwhelmed."

"And she's a woman," Helen mused.

"But a wild one!"

"I certainly hope *not too wild*," Elizabeth said seriously. "Savannah's become her best friend. She's even going to New York with her—for her Madison Square Garden concert."

"I think it's wonderful," Helen said. "Savannah lost weight, and now she's blossoming. I've always thought she was level-headed— like her mother."

"But, Helen, she's only twenty. She's never been on her own."

Bentine laughed and said, "Elizabeth, she and Ariba are not going to be alone for one instant. They've got managers and roadies and room service and limousines . . . Ariba's going to be the toast of Manhattan, and Savannah's going to be right there, in the limelight. All that aura around her will give her confidence, help her find herself."

"She'll be meeting the most exciting people in the world!" Helen interjected. "What could be more thrilling?"

Elizabeth pressed the button on her sun visor, and her electric gate opened. As she drove up the driveway and saw the white stretch limousine parked in front of the house with the trunk open, her heart jumped into her throat. Then she saw the driver walking out with Savannah's luggage. So soon? And why on earth did the girl always overpack?

Elizabeth intercepted Savannah on her way downstairs. "You look like an advertisement for North Beach Leather," she complimented her daughter. "You look beautiful—but I didn't think you were supposed to leave for another two hours."

"I know, Mother," Savannah said, wiping a speck of lipstick off one of her front teeth. "Ariba's manager called and said we've got to get an early start because of the rain and traffic."

"But I wanted to talk to you, sugar. Now, there just isn't enough time," Elizabeth said, disappointed.

"I have a few minutes," Savannah said warmly. "What is it?"

"Well . . . you've got to be careful around *those* people."

"Mother, don't start that all over again. Please." Savannah's tone was firm. "Ariba's my friend, and this is the first time I'm having fun that has nothing to do with you and Daddy. It's all mine."

"I know, darling . . . I just worry." Elizabeth hugged her daughter. "I love you, honey."

"I know, Mother. I love you, too." Savannah looked down at her watch and gasped. "Oh! I have to fly. I'll call you when I get to New York. Kiss Daddy for me."

Elizabeth watched her little girl run out the front door and disappear inside a limousine. She had grave reservations about this fast friendship between Savannah and Ariba. Instead of getting up early and playing tennis every morning, Savannah was staying up till all hours and sleeping till noon. It was a lifestyle Elizabeth just couldn't feel comfortable about.

She noted the oil painting of B.J. near the stairs and wished that he weren't so wrapped up in his business dealings. She had warned him about the change in Savannah's behavior, but he didn't take the time to talk to her. He always left the children to her.

When Elizabeth saw the stack of mail on her desk, she poured herself a tiny glass of Grand Marnier and stretched out on the long green couch in her office.

She smiled at her favorite photograph of Savannah, age seven. Her little angel. The lovely, innocent little girl looking out from behind the veil she'd worn with her frilly white First Holy Communion dress. It was all so simple then, she told herself.

The liqueur sweetly stung her taste buds. She leaned back and closed her eyes, remembering her little girl . . . how Savannah had fallen in love with one of the nuns. Sister Carina, Elizabeth recalled, and whenever anyone asked what she wanted to be when she grew up, Savannah would always say that she wanted to be a nun.

In that tight red leather suit, Elizabeth decided, her sweet little angel was going to be venturing into a world in which only God could protect her.

CHAPTER 28

*T*his gloomy morning, with black clouds threatening to rain, reminded Bonnie Louise of the predicament she had got herself into. She thought of her family back in Plunkettville as she watched the angry, roiling gray water. She missed them . . . yet now she was so different from them, she didn't think she could ever live in an isolated place like Plunkettville again. She couldn't even pick up the phone and call them, because she wouldn't know where to begin.

She wondered how they could have let that weird man, Simpson, she recalled, and the tough-talking woman take her. Byron, she knew, would never put her in one of his movies. No, she was just his captive, and that was the way he wanted it.

Bonnie Louise put the kettle on and looked at the phone, praying Zachary would call her from New York. He'd been gone three long days, and he'd only managed to call her once. He'd apologized and promised to telephone that afternoon.

The doorbell rang, and thinking it was Inga returning from the market, Bonnie Louise made her way to the front door and opened it.

To her surprise, there was a young man from a messenger service holding an envelope with a script inside. She scribbled a wavy line and asked who it was from. The man said: "Zachary Steele Productions."

Bonnie Louise retrieved the whistling kettle from the stove and poured the steaming water into a large mug. She could smell the chamomile flowers fusing with the honey.

Not wanting to share her feelings for Zachary with Inga, after removing its contents, she put the large manila envelope into the trash compactor, and destroyed it.

She clutched the script and ached for the young man she wanted to be with all the time. She felt so guilty and confused. Bonnie Louise, she warned herself, you've got to get away from Byron.

The door opened, and Inga came inside carrying two big bags of groceries. She said very little about anything, but her eyes let Bonnie Louise know that she understood her loneliness. The stout woman, with hair as white as snow, adored the girl and, from the beginning, had invited Bonnie Louise to call her "Auntie." She was very protective, especially when being questioned by Mr. McClintock.

"Are we a mite homesick, my little ear of corn?"

Bonnie Louise shook her head. "No . . . bored, I guess."

Inga began unloading the groceries. She had decided to make a good, hearty soup—one of her specialties.

"When Mr. McClintock calls, I'm going to ask him about our little trip to San Francisco. And I think tomorrow would be a good time for us to take the tour of Universal Studios."

"Yes, Auntie. I spoke to Lara Miller this morning. She promised to make all the arrangements."

"You don't seem pleased," the housekeeper said with concern.

"Oh, I'm just havin' a gray day, that's all."

"Here!" said Inga, laughing. "Look at this!"

She produced a supermarket tabloid with a picture of Colin O'Brien and a headline saying ACTOR GETS DEATH THREAT. She began reading the trumped-up piece, but Bonnie Louise wasn't listening.

Next to O'Brien was a photo of Zachary Steele locked in an embrace with Ariba. It made them look as though they were in love and on their way to the altar.

At the risk of revealing herself, Bonnie Louise asked Inga to tell her about Ariba and Zachary Steele. The housekeeper couldn't wait to expatiate on the subject. She had a passion for tabloid gossip.

According to the article, Zachary had attended Ariba's sold-out Madison Square Garden concert, and when the two stars had met at the celebratory party afterward, it had been love at first sight.

Inga quoted, " 'Ariba's manager, Flavio Gambetti, told reporters that he is looking for a project that the two major talents can star in.' "

"Excuse me," Bonnie Louise said hastily, suppressing the urge to break down in Inga's arms and tell her everything. "I think I'm gonna take a little nap," she said softly.

"Are you all right, *älsking?*"

"Oh yes . . . I'm just fine." She started out of the room, still clutching the script. She turned back and said, "If the phone rings, I'll answer it."

"*Ya*," Inga agreed. "It could be Mr. McClintock calling from Tennessee."

Byron had left for Nashville that morning. Only this time he didn't even ask Bonnie Louise to go along. He'd told her that he was liquidating several radio stations in the area, and he would be in meetings day and night. Maybe, Bonnie Louise thought, he took his wife.

Was Zachary lying to her about being in love with her? Byron was right—Zachary was surrounded by beautiful girls, and he couldn't resist them. Good thing, she told herself, I didn't give him what he wanted.

Bonnie Louise settled herself in her bedroom, on the bed overlooking the angry ocean. She thought of Ariba blasting into the ladies' room at the AIDS benefit and running her dark fingers through her blond hair. Bonnie Louise sighed. How could she compete with one of the biggest sex symbols in the world? There was no way.

The phone rang. Byron wanted to see how his little sweetie was doing. She said she wanted to travel with Inga—to see the Hearst castle and San Francisco.

B.J. told her that he was making plans for their future as they spoke. If she'd just be patient, he coaxed, everything would be wonderful for both of them.

"After I conclude my business in Nashville, I'm going to swing down and visit my mama for a day. Then I have to check on something in Florida. I'm gonna make you a happy bunny, darlin'. Just be a little patient. Go shopping with Lara, if you like."

When she hung up the phone, Bonnie Louise collapsed across the bed in a rage of uncontrollable tears, until she fell asleep from emotional exhaustion.

Bonnie Louise forced herself to wake up when she heard the phone ringing. Night had fallen, casting a hazy gray atmosphere over the room. Her swollen eyes ached from all the tears she'd shed.

"Hello," she said flatly.

"Bonnie, Bonnie, Bonnie! Baby, baby, baby!" a male voice shouted into her ear.

"Zach?"

"Yeah, it's me! I miss you!"

Bonnie Louise could hear loud music in the background, and what sounded like hundreds of people laughing, talking, and squealing.

"Where are you?" she inquired.

"What? I can hardly hear you for the noise, baby!"

"Where *are* you?" She raised her voice, getting agitated.

"Oh! I'm at this club in New York . . . Nell's, I think. I love you!"

All Bonnie Louise could see was that awful picture of Zachary and Ariba, smiling at each other, and touching.

"Hello?" he called out. "Are you there, Bonnie?"

"Yes, Zach, I'm here. You sound different."

"I'm a little drunk. Been celebrating with the guys . . . we signed all the papers for *Blizzard* today." She could hear someone talking to him, wanting him to get off the phone. "Listen, did you get the script?"

"Yes."

"Great! We'll talk all about that when I get home tomorrow night. I'll be getting in about nine, so I'll pick you up about nine-forty-five . . . okay, Bonnie baby?"

Her eyes were burning with hot tears. "How can you say you love me when it's all over the papers that you and Ariba are in love!"

"*What?*" Zachary started to laugh. "Bonnie, where did you hear that?"

"It's on the cover of the *National Enquirer*! And what's so funny, Zachary Steele?"

"Baby, baby . . . that's all bullshit! At the party after her concert her manager set up that photo so Ariba wouldn't get any heat about being a lesbian. In fact, you know who was with her?" He waited for her answer.

"No, who?"

"Your cousin, Savannah McClintock!"

Bonnie Louise didn't get the implication—the reference to Savannah being her cousin had thrown her.

"How could somebody write about you and Ariba like that if it isn't true? Can't you do something to stop it?"

"I don't know," Zach said with an edge. "Who cares?" He laughed and added, "I'm floored that you actually believed that crap about me and that voodoo babe!"

"Oh, Zach, I just went crazy when I saw that picture."

"I love you Bonbon, don't forget that. Well, I'm dumping these guys and heading for the hotel. . . . Good night. I love you."

"I love you, too."

Bonnie Louise kissed the receiver until she heard him hang up. She felt hundreds of pounds lighter.

Relieved, she turned on the bedside reading light and reached for Zachary's script. She cocked her head and looked hard at the cover.

"Ba . . . ba . . . le . . . le . . . i . . . i . . . za . . . za . . . bleeza . . . bleezarrddd. Blizzard," she reckoned.

It was the name of Zachary's new movie, the one he'd talked to her about acting in. What was she going to do? She'd been watching *Sesame Street* every morning and every evening. That had helped a lot. Street signs and instructions on labels could be reasoned out, but a script . . . it was too many words. Bonnie Louise felt defeated as she thumbed through the pages. She had never learned how to read.

CHAPTER 29

*B*entine Devorac found herself wheeling a shopping cart down the fluorescent lighted aisles of Hughes Market in Pacific Palisades. She marveled at the amazing number of overweight, sloppily dressed women. How, she wondered, in this affluent neighbor-hood, could they be so out of touch with their physical appearance?

Tall, slim, body-conscious Bentine looked smashing in her new Lina Lee linen suit with matching brown boots. She always looked her best when she made her weekly visit to Dr. Goodwin, her psychiatrist for the last nine years.

There was nothing shabby about her. At least not until she took out her little red Velcro coupon wallet.

She was pretty well organized. She knew too many people who might, by some nasty stroke of fate, have dashed into Hughes instead of Gelson's. Ever watchful, she fanned through the pile of coupons. Diet Coke, yes, she always needed soft drinks. Ten cents for Bounty paper towels. She pushed her rapidly filling cart down aisle after aisle. As the goods mounted, so did her savings. This was going to be a banner food spree.

"Do those things really work?" a man asked.

She looked up. She had been discovered by a tall, dark-haired businessman. A real Brooks Brothers type. Wearing glasses. He looked fortyish. Nice face, Bentine thought. Good teeth. Obviously rich, from the looks of his highly polished Ferragamo loafers. In fact, he reminded her of her ex-husband, Randy.

"Do they work?" he asked earnestly.

Bentine giggled and said, "You'd be amazed at how well they work."

"Funny, you don't look the type," he said. "Does your husband make you pinch pennies?"

She held up her left hand. "See the ring?"

"No, as a matter of fact, I don't."

"There's your answer. I clip coupons for my own edification."

Before they knew it, they were walking and talking, discussing the virtues of one product over another. George Borofsky, as he introduced himself, explained that he and his wife, Jill, had finally got their dissolution.

Freshly divorced, Bentine mused.

"Boy, you really know what you're doing," he observed.

"Thanks, George." She was beginning to feel friendly. "Do you live near here?"

He cleared his throat. "Well, actually . . . believe it or not, I'm still living in Brentwood." She wondered at his apologetic tone.

"The house is still on the market. It's fallen out of escrow three times. So, while we're waiting for it to close, my wife and I are continuing to share the same space. . . . so to speak."

"Big house?"

"Four bedrooms."

"Kids?"

"Two."

"Me, too," she said, smiling.

"How about dinner? The Ivy at the Shore?"

The Ivy at the Shore . . . this showed promise, Bentine thought. "Isn't it a little late to book?"

He shook his head. "No problem."

He spotted the picnic coolers and tossed two of them inside his basket. "For our frozen things," he said thoughtfully.

This guy is too good to be true, she told herself. Great potential was brewing here.

As they checked out, George marveled at how much money she saved as a result of her coupon clipping.

"Twenty-six dollars," she said, holding up the long tape with deductions printed out in red.

"Too bad I wasn't married to you," he said sincerely.

Her brown eyes narrowed as she watched his items move along the conveyor belt. Razor blades, toothpaste, flea spray (must have a cat or a dog), a stack of frozen dinner entrees (that made sense), a carton of OJ, and a bag of flavored gourmet popcorn and a six-pack of Löwenbrau (he obviously had her kind of taste).

The Ivy at the Shore was crowded, but George was welcomed with the promise of a table in ten minutes.

"I'm impressed," Bentine told him. "Are you one of the owners?"

"I might as well be. I'm in here often enough."

"Your table's ready, Mr. Borofsky," the attractive hostess told him. "Lucky you, it's the one you like . . . over there."

Bentine smiled at Gene Hackman as she sat down. She hadn't seen him in ages. Boy, wouldn't Helen be surprised by what her coupon clipping had netted this week!

They ordered strawberry daiquiris. The modern, tropical dining room was packed with well-dressed yuppies from Santa Monica, Brentwood, the Palisades. . . .

"The grilled Hawaiian tuna is great, if you're into fish," George suggested.

Bentine could feel the deliciously disguised rum hitting her brain. Years were falling away. The bad taste Randy had left in her mouth was disappearing. Maybe there was hope for her. Maybe even at this late date she could find love. . . .

"Grilled tuna sounds delicious."

They both ordered the tuna, and instead of white wine they stayed with strawberry daiquiris. Food, no matter how delectable, took a backseat to one's romantic appetite. In the old days it had been sexual appetite. Now, even in the most spontaneous circumstances there had to be a delay.

"Dessert?" the waiter asked, almost apologetically, since they had barely touched their entrees.

Bentine shook her head. She didn't want a doggie bag. She wanted George. And, looking at the hunk waiter, she wouldn't mind having him for dessert. No, Ben, she told herself. No more strawberry daiquiris. Just because George wields a platinum American Express card and can get a table—a great table—simply by walking in, doesn't mean he's 100 percent okay.

She studied her host, wondering what was wrong with him. She wondered if he was thinking the same thing about her.

"I have an idea," he said conspiratorially.

"Yesss," she purred.

"Why not do something really seventies?"

"Like what?"

He leaned across the table and whispered, "Let's stop at the liquor store and pick up a bottle of wine."

"Champagne. Cristal," she specified.

"An expensive date, huh?"

"You get what you pay for," she teased.

He laughed. He actually found her witty, amusing, and sexy. Yes, this could be the beginning of a sizzling affair. He claimed he hadn't been with anyone since he and his wife split. And, in true Hollywood fashion, she swore she hadn't been with anyone since *her* dissolution.

Two clean slates. At least they both silently prayed that fate was doing them a favor.

Bentine parked her Volvo on Ocean Avenue and jumped inside George's Jaguar. It smelled of new leather. The interior was spotless, dust-free. The man obviously took great pains to keep it that way.

He pulled up to the Shangri-la Hotel and parked. He gave Bentine a reassuring squeeze and leapt out of the car.

"Be right back," he promised.

Bentine watched him enter the resurrected lobby. God, she thought, this place's been here a thousand years. I'll bet Daddy's done time here.

She thought of her father, the old-country tyrant. He'd always assumed, rather rightly, that since she was true Hollywood royalty, she'd have no problem landing a suitable prince.

She did. Her first husband, Randolph Lloyd, Jr., had been the eldest son of a wealthy Hancock Park family, a family that owned a brokerage firm, played golf at the exclusive Wilshire Country Club, and used the Bel Air Bay Club for warm-weather activities.

The best part was, they didn't like anyone who wasn't one of them. Hollywood royalty was definitely not in *their* league. Bentine wondered if George was as snobby as Randy. She could picture George registering at the front desk.

Bentine Devorac was a dilettante at heart. She spoke fluent French because she'd been to finishing school in Switzerland. She'd traveled all right. She'd seen the world, but when it came to the

Lloyd family, she'd been totally blinkered. She had assumed that once you became Mrs. Lloyd, you were part of the family. She was wrong.

Half-Methodist and half-Jewish, she had mixed feelings about religion. Her mother had been a gorgeous showgirl. The classic story: director spots a shapely pair of legs, follows them up to the slender waist, and *voilà!*—the face that launched a dozen *Vogue* covers.

Bentine quickly looked into her small light-up mirror. She smiled. If only I'd looked more like Mummy, she thought. What an affront to have the genes of her mother's delicate beauty overshadowed by her father's peasant stock.

George opened the door and waved a room key.

They entered a freshly painted fifties-style room on the sixth floor. Bentine opened the drapery and looked out at the lights twinkling in Santa Monica Harbor. She had never seen them from this angle.

Out of the corner of her eye she watched George take a package of condoms from the liquor-store bag and pocket them. He must be as nervous as I am, she reassured herself. He smiled at her. She smiled back. Her hormones were telling her that this was no mistake. For once in a hell of a long time, fate *was* on her side.

They opened the champagne. They laughed about their frozen food sitting in respective coolers. George talked about his children. How much he loved them, and how he hoped his divorce wouldn't screw them up permanently.

Bentine talked about Randy. How she'd been three months' pregnant when she married him. How in the end it seemed better for their kids to live and go to school in Brentwood. In their old house. The house *he* had kept.

"They only visit me on weekends," she said with a touch of remorse. "Randy's remarried," she said. "He and Sylvie don't like me. . . ." She stopped herself and rephrased her thought. "We don't get along too well. Sylvie's jealous."

"I can see why she would be," George said knowingly. He took her hand and drew her to him. Boy, she thought, he really knows what he's doing. She melted into his kiss. Her suit landed in a heap. They could hear voices blaring from a television in the next room. They faintly sounded like Ingrid Bergman and Humphrey Bogart.

"Is that *The Voyeur*?," George asked.

Bentine listened intently. "No, it's not."

"I think it is."

Their first argument.

"It's not, George. My father directed *The Voyeur*, and that's not it!"

George's mouth fell open. Awestruck, he sat back and looked at Bentine. "*The Voyeur* is my all-time favorite film."

"My father will love you."

"The man is a genius. He was ahead of his time. Even kinky. Wouldn't you say *The Voyeur* was a little kinky?"

"No. I think it was ahead of its time, but I don't really think it was *kinky*. I was only ten when Daddy directed it."

"The film gives such insight into human sexuality. How people think. How they fantasize."

"George, much as I'd like to discuss my father's illustrious film career, I'd rather find out about you." Besides, she wasn't very well versed in her father's early films. She stroked his naked back.

"Well," he said, responsively, "as soon as I get my own place, we'll look at the video together. I'd really like to know what your father was thinking about as he directed that film."

"Knowing him, he was probably thinking about the script girl." She gave him a piercing look. She thought for once in her life she'd met a man who was completely taken with *her*. Wouldn't you know he'd be a film buff, and *The Voyeur*, lowest on *her* list of favorites, would be *his*.

What the hell, she mused. He had a real job. He wasn't an out-of-work actor or a film student who wanted to be a director some-day. He was attractive, and with his pants down, he was becoming even more so.

"Oh, Bentine," he sighed. "I wish I could tie you up. Would

you like that?" He waited, and when she didn't answer, he asked, "Would you like that?"

"Ummmm, I don't know. Would you like me to tie you up?"

"Yes," he said passionately. "Yes."

"*Really?*" Bentine couldn't believe her ears. *I'll humor him*, she told herself. After all, I haven't been with a man in months. "Maybe next time," she proposed.

George led her to the bed and pushed her down. Without much foreplay, he slipped on a condom, and entered her. Suddenly he said, "Let's pretend you have a roommate in the other room, and you have to be very quiet so she won't hear us."

"I don't have a roommate. I haven't had a roommate since I was in college."

"We're pretending, Bentine. We're just pretending."

"Okay."

"And I have to stop you from making any noise," he said, placing his hand over her mouth.

Bentine's eyes widened with fear. This thrilled George even more. He moved in and out of her, his eyes glittering with frenzied anticipation. "You'd like to scream, wouldn't you?" he asked.

"Hmmmm, hmmmm," she said, nodding affirmatively.

"But you can't," he said with great satisfaction. "Can you?"

She felt as if she were being raped. She nodded again.

He leaned in and whispered, "I wish we had some silk ties. I'd like to tie one around your hands. Would you like that?"

She grunted.

"Would you?"

She tried desperately to say no with her body, but he now had both of her wrists pinned above her head with the hand that wasn't covering her mouth. It was a no-win situation. Some two hundred pounds bearing down, saying, "Wouldn't you like that? You would, I can tell."

Oh, Jesus, she was panicking. She had waited in the car, his car, while he got the champagne, and again when he registered. Nobody would know she was with him. They'd probably find her body, with her food still frozen in the cooler. Maybe, she thought, if I egg him on, he'll come and get off of me.

"Uh-huh," she managed.

In the wink of an eye he ripped the pillow out of the pillowcase, twisted the case into a rope, and by the time Bentine opened her mouth, he'd shoved it between her teeth. Her tongue was pressing back against her esophagus. The rest of the lethal pillowcase was wrapped around her neck.

She silently screamed, pleading with every pore of her body for help.

George went wild. His body went into spasms, and he said, "You love it like this. This is the way you like it!"

In her writhing to get away from him, she got caught in the rhythm of it. For a brief interlude she thought she would come.

George came and rolled over, panting. Bentine spit the pillowcase out of her mouth. She was confused.

"That was wonderful, Ben. You're your father's daughter. Give me ten minutes, and we can do it again."

Bentine knew that diplomacy was her only hope. "George," she sighed, "you're wonderful. You're really, really an extraordinary man."

She felt a viselike grip on her upper arm. He said, "I knew it the minute I saw you standing by the cat food. That it would be like this."

Oh shit. For a moment she was speechless. All she wanted to do was negotiate safe passage out of this musty hotel room and take a long hot shower.

"George . . . I'm having dinner at my family's house Sunday. Maybe you'd like to come?"

"Like I said, give me ten minutes and—"

"No," she said firmly. "I have to leave now. But Sunday you can meet my father, and then we can do something." She was sure if there was some future promise, he'd let her go.

"Really? Meet the great Devorac? God . . . that would be great." He squeezed her arm again. He was getting excited. "Why don't we meet here tomorrow night? I'll keep the room. Here," he said, handing her the key. "You take it. And tomorrow night, come in and get in bed and make believe you're sleeping, and I'll come in and rape you! Would you like that?"

"Hmmmm . . . well . . . ummmm, you make it sound very exciting," she said, edging her way off the bed. "I think I'd better take my frozen food and go."

"Well, let me help you!"

George bolted out of bed and threw his clothes on. He was suddenly the perfect gentleman. He helped Bentine on with her jacket and apologized for not thinking ahead.

"If only I'd realized you were wearing linen, I'd have hung it up for you. . . . You're wonderful, Bentine. One in a billion."

He meant it. She could tell. He was crazy about her. Why did he have to be *crazy* on top of it?

George remained Prince Charming. He walked her to her car and made sure she had enough gas to get to Malibu.

"Ben . . ."

"Yes, George?"

"Wear something that's black lace."

"Oh, of course."

She drove away from the curb thankful for Randy's refusal to let her get personalized license plates. Now she was a Volvo, like any other Volvo. Thank goodness she'd had the presence of mind to give him the wrong phone number.

She welcomed the Malibu Colony guards. Oh how she welcomed them! She ran into the house and out onto the sand. What she needed was a fast, cleansing midnight douche in the ocean.

CHAPTER 30

Since marrying Morton Shipp, Elaine had tried everything from transpersonal psychotherapy to group therapy to acupuncture to Swedish massage, reflexology, bilateral breathing, and rebirthing. She knew it wouldn't be easy when she married him, but she'd had no idea it would be *this* frustrating.

Growing up in a big house in Bellingham, Washington, with Republican, churchgoing parents and an older brother who'd served in Vietnam and returned drug-addicted and twisted, had given Elaine the impetus to make it in Hollywood.

From church plays and choir practice she'd graduated to high school plays and little theater. By the time she'd reached her mid-twenties, Elaine Welkey was Seattle's unofficial queen of theater— a mermaid in a pond.

Elaine knew she wasn't a beauty, but when she put herself to-gether and projected, she had presence.

Her baby-fine hair was her biggest headache. Not only had it betrayed her by graying when she was only twenty-six, but now, ten years later, it was thinning out. She'd lost count of the monthly hours spent with Carol, the colorist, Dusty, who'd found the right geometric cut for her hair, Paula the manicurist who knew how to make porcelain nails look real, and Leland, her personal exercise trainer.

She weighed in at 105 pounds, and always felt fat. For a long-limbed girl of 5'6", Elaine was on the anorexic side. Food had become an enemy in her battle to maintain a size five. TV, Elaine reasoned, was her medium, and if she persevered, she'd land a role in a series.

Living with Morton Shipp had become like starring in a nighttime soap. There was always a crisis, a patient calling in the middle of dinner—or worse, in the middle of the night. And B. J. McClintock was always breathing down Mort's neck. All she knew was that when her husband hung up after speaking to his boyhood buddy, he was always overwrought. She'd finally given up asking why.

Bickering had become a way of life for the Shipps. Mort methodically reviewed cupboards and the refrigerator. He criticized her for buying food that tasted good but had little nutritional value. Or food high in fat or cholesterol or containing carcinogens. Even NutraSweet was on trial. The only time they managed to enjoy the same wavelength was after a bottle of wine.

When she'd met him, that first time in his office, he was different. Or, Elaine wondered, maybe she was seeing him through lovestruck eyes. She'd comforted him through Eddie's horrible death—not the actual car crash so much as the repercussions of knowing his son had committed suicide.

Eddie Shipp had driven his mother's Mercedes off Mulholland Drive. He was only fifteen. Mort had been a basket case. Elaine suspected that deep down inside he felt responsible in some way for his only son's death.

Sad commentary, she thought as she climbed naked onto the Rolfing table.

Rolfing, she'd been told, would help release old pain that had crystallized and was blocking her growth pattern. Hit the spot—trigger the pain—trigger the memory—release it.

This was her third two-hour session, and she was ready. Painful as Rolfing was, she knew when it was over, she'd be able to *cope*, and it might even unblock whatever was preventing her from becoming a successful actress.

Bjorn, the hunky Swedish Rolfer, began massaging Elaine's shoulders. She relaxed into his masterful, healing touch.

"Oh that feels good," she moaned.

Her husband's sex drive had become purely missionary, and lately it hadn't even been that. In truth, he hadn't touched her in close to six months.

"Breathe, Elaine," the Rolfer instructed, digging his thumbs into the base of her neck.

She let out a scream.

"Good . . . good. I'm going to go deeper." He pressed harder and said, "Oh my—what's this? Who's done this to you, Elaine?"

"I don't know!"

"Hmmmm. I'm going a little deeper. I want you to start breathing now."

Anticipating the siege on her psyche, she began deep breathing. Having a baby, she thought, couldn't be any more painful than this.

"Oh, oh, oh, oh!" Up the scale she wailed.

"Spit it out, Elaine! That's it," he said, going deeper. "A little more."

Finally, in a low, guttural voice, she moaned, "Mort, you motherfucker. Why don't you want me?"

"Good. Now breathe. Why doesn't Mort want you?"

"I don't know. I don't know."

Her Rolfing exorcist pressed harder. "He's still in love with *her*! He hates himself! He hates me! He's cold—cold as ice!"

"All right, Elaine, relax. That's good."

Bjorn massaged while she sobbed, catching her breath and calming down.

Yes, she felt betrayed by her husband. He even mumbled his first wife's name in his sleep. *Marylou* . . . she thought if she ever heard that name again, she'd die. *Marylou*, Mort's beautiful, miserable first wife. A delicate southern belle like Mrs. Perfect McClintock . . .

She felt the strong thumbs searching for a knot on the other side of her neck. Bjorn burrowed down into her muscle. Her whole body flinched.

Elaine let out a bloodcurdling scream. "My God, what is *that*?"

Calmly the Rolfer said, "I don't know. Tell me what you see."

"I can't!"

Bjorn pressed harder. "Let it out! That's what we're here for."

"B.J.!" she shrieked. "It's all your fault!"

"What's he doing to you, Elaine?"

The excruciating pain made her body contort. "He's ruining my life!"

"How's this affecting you?"

"I have to ignore it! Oh my God, you're killing me! You're killing me!"

"Breathe, Elaine—breathe. Let it out! Let it out!"

"Oh my God, I can't believe he won't give me a series!"

"Get it out." He pressed harder. "Get rid of it! Say it!"

"He won't even give me a movie-of-the-week!"

The Rolfer eased his grip and began gently massaging the tender area.

"Good, Elaine. Don't you feel better now?"

"I think so," she managed through her tears.

Almost more than anything in the world she'd wanted to be a successful actress. She knew she was as talented as Holly Dandridge.

Oh, B.J. had featured her in a few of his shows, but never a starring role or even a supporting one with substance. Be positive, she told herself. All the hard work and training was going to pay off.

She reflected on her relationship with Mort, her negative feelings toward him, the god of plastic surgery. Thank heaven Bjorn's soothing touch had turned firm, releasing the unwanted dark energy. Elaine felt as if a lead blanket had been lifted from her shoulders.

CHAPTER 31

*I*n honor of a day on the ocean Lara Miller had melted plastic in pursuit of a sensational one-piece bathing suit and a navy ensemble with a nautical monogram on the jacket.

Kevin Wenster posed a challenge. She couldn't openly ask B.J.

about him. Joan Souchek, the keeper of the dirt, would be only too happy to dish it, but Lara decided to follow her heart and let Saturday's one-on-one clarify the situation.

Since Kevin's visit to her apartment, he'd sent her four dozen long-stemmed red roses daily. He'd called early in the evening to chat or left a nice message on her answering machine. The man had obviously been chasing her, but now he was using charm and finesse.

The moment the twenty-nine-foot sailboat pulled away from the crowded Marina del Rey breakwater, both Lara and Kevin dropped their pretenses and relaxed.

It was still too early in the day to make much use of the gentle westerly breeze, so Kevin motored north, toward Malibu. He pointed out the multimillion-dollar minimansions, some on stilts, others set back and newly renovated. He observed that Los Angeles had become truly cosmopolitan. The French Riviera had finally made its impact on what he had originally thought a rather architecturally deprived landscape.

Lara took deep breaths, savoring the salt air. She stretched her legs along the deck next to the captain, and told him her thoughts on the Big Orange.

"It's like New York used to be ten years ago. If you don't know some kind of self-defense or speak Spanish or have a gun hidden in your bedroom, you're only a tourist."

"Thank Christ I'm only a tourist," Kevin said cheerfully. "Where I come from, they throw you in jail and toss away the key if they catch you with a gun. You'd love Sydney, Lara." He took his eyes off the compass and squeezed her leg. "I'd love to love you in Sydney."

Lara smiled. Compliments made her feel shy and self-conscious. She marveled at Kevin's confidence. He seemed to be in command of everything around him. He was an adept sailor, he appeared to be extremely well-versed politically, and when he discussed financial matters, he was comfortable dealing in millions and even billions. Lara saw great things in Kevin Wenster's future, and as the yacht lapped through the blue-green water, she wanted more and more to be a part of those things.

"Tell me, Kevin, did you inherit money? Or are you one of those driven Australian power brokers I'm always reading about?"

Kevin shook his head; a boyish smile crossed his lips. "I'm lucky," he said. "When I was fourteen, my uncle Harry took me digging. 'Opals,' he said, 'big as a boy's fist.' We love to exaggerate, we do," he said, grinning. He narrowed his eyes and gave her a lusty look.

"You've got pretty hands, Lara. Nice opal ring would suit you."

"I heard someplace that it's bad luck to wear an opal if it isn't your birthstone."

"Aw, it's an old wives' tale," Kevin scoffed. "They call it 'the patron of thieves,' but that's 'cause of some ancient belief in the evil eye. The real reason it's bad luck, I believe, is because the old lapidaries were responsible for the stones they cut, and opals are brittle buggers. They break easily. And if the cutters broke 'em, they had to pay for 'em. Easy to see how opals got a bad name."

Lara yawned and excused herself, explaining that she hadn't felt this relaxed in as long as she could remember. "Well, Kevin—did you and Uncle Harry find the world's largest opal?"

Kevin laughed, enjoying the recollection. "Coober Pedy's a very special site. The same families have been there for generations. I was lucky 'cause Uncle Harry had a girlfriend living there, and he wanted to make things look a bit more proper by bringing me." He saw something onshore, and headed toward the coastline.

"Old Harry shows me what to do, and sends me down into a mine for a day of exploring. Thanks, Uncle Harry, I think. Then I hit it. By accident I start digging at the end of the tunnel—where nobody else's digging." He snapped his fingers and said, "Like magic—I uncover a vein of black opals, with flames of green and red and blue in a field of black."

He stood up and reached inside his jeans pocket, producing a silver money clip with a cabochon-cut black opal the size of a quarter.

"One of my lucky opals," he said, placing it on Lara's midriff.

"It's magnificent, Kevin! How many 'lucky' opals do you have?"

"Three—this one, and two in my safe."

Lara held it up, admiring the life within the stone.

"I went down a fourteen-year-old lad with nothing much to speak of, and when I came up, I was holding nearly five thousand dollars in stones. That's how I got my start—and no matter what, I know I can always go back to Coober Pedy and do it again!"

"Your uncle Harry must've been surprised."

"So surprised he up and married the lady. He's still there!"

Lara and Kevin laughed. She marveled at how happy she felt.

"You see that house?" he asked, pointing at a modern two-story structure not far from what Lara recognized as the McClintocks' beach house. "I've leased it, with an option to buy. Not bad for an old Aussie digger, hmmmmm?"

"Kevin, so far I think you're perfect—but there is just one little thing."

He gave her a worried look.

"Your nose is turning beet red. I think you'd better put something on it."

"Down in the head, luv. In the cabinet there should be a tube of sun block."

Lara made her way below, deciding to strip down to her bathing suit and get some color. And as long as she was down there, she might as well relieve herself. That morning, in anticipation of Kevin's arrival, she had polished off three cups of coffee.

She slid the mahogany panel back, and there, next to the first-aid kit and a box of condoms, was the suntan lotion.

Condoms . . . she registered. *I wonder who owns the Miss Adelaide? Definitely a man, though by the look of things, no female touches . . . he could be married or unmarried. At least he uses protection.*

A sneaky thought occurred to Lara as she folded her clothes on the forward bunk. She hadn't planned on going to bed with Kevin, but the salt air and the gentle rocking, rolling motion of the boat was making her feel very sensuous.

When they were opposite the Point Dume bluffs, Kevin dropped anchor and served a cold lunch of seafood pasta, hearts-of-palm salad, Brie, and Camembert with French bread, and a bottle of Dom Perignon. Delicious as the food tasted, they only picked at it.

One plastic glass full of champagne left Lara lightheaded. She felt herself leaning back, basking in the noonday sun, feeling giddy.

Kevin pressed his fingers against her thigh and suggested that she apply sunscreen. He slathered his arms and legs, then volunteered to cover Lara's back.

She shifted upright and turned away from him. There was nothing but water as far as she could see. She closed her eyes, enjoying the sensual patterns he was tracing on her back.

Before she knew it, he'd stopped and turned her so that he could kiss her. It was sweet and tender, curious and probing, then urgent and passionate.

All at once Kevin sat back and said, "My God, it's hot! Come on then—let's go below." He took her hand and led her down the companionway.

"Excuse me a minute," Lara said shyly, disappearing inside the head.

She opened the panel and took out a package of condoms. If she was going to enjoy herself, she was going to have to feel *safe*. Kevin's kiss had been so expert, she wondered where he'd learned his magnificent technique. She ran a brush through her hair and smiled at herself in the mirror. She felt beautiful.

When she came out, she found him reclining on the forward bunk singing an Australian folksong. "There's a song in my heart for the one I love best, and her picture is tattooed all over my chest. Yea-ho, little fishy, don't cry, don't cry; yea-ho, little fishy, don't cry, don't cry."

He motioned for her to join him and kissed her. The motion of the boat made their lovemaking even more exciting.

Kevin reached down inside Lara's swimsuit for her breasts, and came up with the package of condoms.

"What's this?" he said sourly.

"Kevin, come on . . ."

"I hate these bloody things!"

"I don't like them, either."

"You know," he said raising an eyebrow, "when you do what we're about to do, they don't work worth a damn anyway. Bloody nuisance," he cursed, tossing the package on the floor.

Lara retrieved it, insisting, "Gotta wear a raincoat."

Kevin could see that there was no dissuading her. Although annoyed, he put it on.

"Thanks," she purred, kissing his neck, then his lips.

Kevin began slowly stroking her torso, then moved down her thigh. Lara had the feeling she was about to learn why Kevin Wenster had a reputation as a ladies' man. Which, she warned herself, explains why he's in his forties and single.

There was something highly erotic about steamy, sweaty, sun-baked bodies confined to a narrow, rolling V-shaped berth. As their skin touched, an electric current seemed to be coursing through their bodies. Then, finally, they merged, melting, fusing—it seemed to Lara—into a single whole.

CHAPTER 32

*B*onnie Louise tiptoed down the hallway and stopped outside Inga's bedroom door. She pressed her ear against it, listening for any sign that might tell her that the elderly woman was asleep. Pressing a little harder and holding her breath, she heard Inga's labored snoring.

Bonnie Louise smiled to herself, pleased that her coaxing had worked. The two extra snifters of B.J.'s vintage brandy would keep the overly protective housekeeper in bed until morning.

She stopped at the front door, disarmed the alarm system, then quietly slipped out, closing the door behind her.

A cold wind was blowing in from the shore, and the sky was so clear, she could see the stars. She pulled the collar up on her Ralph Lauren hunting jacket and buttoned it over her pink cashmere turtleneck sweater. Her Reeboks enabled her to walk soundlessly down the street to the guard gate.

"Zachary!" she exulted. It had been five days since she'd seen him, kissed him, or held him in her arms. Walking in the darkness after sneaking out of the house excited her, made her blood feel electrically charged.

The white stretch limousine was parked outside the Malibu gate down the road to the left. The lights were off, but she could see a glow from inside, in the backseat. As she approached, she realized that Zachary was watching a small television.

She knocked on the tinted window, and the chauffeur stepped out and held the door open for her. There was Zach watching a Lakers basketball game. When he saw Bonnie Louise, he grabbed her, pulling her in and onto the plush carpet.

The chauffeur closed the door and got into the front seat, started the engine, and raised the center window to separate himself from the young lovers.

"Zach!" Bonnie exclaimed. "I missed you so much that I ached. I've never missed anybody like this."

"I missed you, too, Bonnie! This was the longest five days of my life!"

Entwining her body with his in the cushy backseat, Zachary began to share with her his business dealings in New York.

"I can't believe they gave me everything I asked for! The deal is solid, and we go in just eight weeks! Can you believe it?"

"You mean you leave for Montana that soon?"

"Yep, and you're going with me, Bonbon. That's why I sent you the script . . . the part of Josie is perfect for your first time on the big screen."

Bonnie Louise's heart stopped. The script! She hadn't read it! How was she going to tell him that she didn't know how to read?

"What did you think of Josie?" he inquired.

"Josie?" she answered. "I thought the part was wonderful!" she lied, stalling for time.

"I knew you'd love it." He leaned over and kissed her.

"We'll get into that over dinner. Just let me look at you," he said, falling back into the seat, gazing at her with a loving smile.

The limousine slowly wound its way up Malibu Canyon Road, past craggy mountains that were barely illuminated by a slim crescent moon. Bonnie Louise felt a headache coming on. Beneath the laughter, kisses, and hugs she churned with the desire to clear her conscience. She was afraid that Zachary wouldn't feel the same way about her if he knew she was an illiterate hick who bore no blood relation to the McClintocks.

They turned off the main road onto what looked like a wide lane leading to somebody's ranch. Then they drove into a driveway and stopped in front of a huge cabin nestled into a grove of pine trees.

The old three-story lodge was warm and inviting inside. The Saddle Peak Lodge maître d' greeted his "old friend Zachary" with open arms—whisking the movie star and his date upstairs to a quiet room on the top floor, where, due to the lateness of the hour, they could enjoy total privacy.

The dark wood paneling, blazing fire, willow furniture, and shelves crammed with old leather-bound books reminded Bonnie Louise of Rancho Virgo. Her headache was getting more intense.

Zachary was in a celebratory mood. He had called ahead and ordered champagne and oysters on the half-shell. He asked Bonnie Louise to look at the menu and make their dinner selections. She studied it for a long time, then shook her head and deferred to him.

The actor was too busy talking and drinking to notice Bonnie Louise wringing her hands under the table. He didn't even detect her relief when the waiter appeared and told them the specials of the day. She ordered the leg of lamb—which was the only dish that she could remember him mentioning.

"I know Josie isn't a huge part, but what'd you think of the love scene she and Delancy have in the cabin?" He raised his eyebrows, and cast a wicked smile her way.

"I . . . ah . . ." Bonnie Louise stammered. "I guess it was really exciting."

"You guess?" he said suspiciously, leaning across the table. "It's one of the high points of the script!" He paused, looking hard at his lady love.

He sensed something was amiss—maybe she hadn't read *Blizzard* all the way through. He plucked an oyster with his fork and, after submerging it in the spicy cocktail sauce, offered it to Bonnie Louise. She shook her head and apologized for not liking the slippery things.

Bonnie Louise couldn't look Zachary in the eye. She played with a piece of French bread and sipped her champagne. She smiled warmly at him, and he smiled back.

Zachary, he told himself, you're a lucky guy. This is the first girl you've dated since high school who isn't wearing Teflon armor. Something's bothering her—she can't still be bummed over that PR garbage with Ariba.

"So what else do you think about the script?" he probed.

Bonnie Louise popped a piece of French bread into her mouth. Her eyes smiling, she nodded.

"That good, huh?" the actor asked cynically.

"I guess," she answered sweetly. "I don't know much about scripts."

"What'd you think of the way it ends? The chase through Manhattan."

She was thoughtful for a moment. "I liked it," she said.

"You didn't read it, Bonnie! There's no chase scene in Manhattan!"

"Don't be angry with me, Zach. I wanted to . . ."

"What the hell does that mean?" he asked angrily. "You either read it or you didn't." His eyes pierced whatever pretense she had left.

Tears spilled down her cheeks. "I never learned how to read," she blurted. "I'm sorry, Zachary . . . I'm sorry."

The actor sat back, stupefied. He'd never met anybody who couldn't read. He reached across the table and squeezed her hand. It didn't seem to help; she was now sobbing.

"Bonnie, don't cry, babe. Tell me all about it," he coaxed.

She looked up with fear in her eyes.

"I love you. . . ." he reassured her. "It doesn't bother me one bit."

She tearfully explained how she'd grown up on a peanut farm; the only education she'd ever had was at Bible school, and that had only been about once a month. Few of her relatives knew how to read or write.

Zachary took her in his arms and held her close. Held her for quite a while. "It's not so important, Bonbon. It's not so terrible —there are lots of Americans who can't read. You'll learn easily. It's okay."

She shook her head, still crying.

"That's not all Zach. Byron isn't my uncle."

"Who is he, then?"

Bonnie Louise felt relieved that she was about to get everything out in the open. She told Zachary about the talent scout who had showed up one day and offered her parents thousands of dollars if they would let him take her to Hollywood for a screen test.

Her parents, in debt because of crop failure and interest on loans, were in desperate need. She wanted to help them. And the talent scout, taking her aside, had promised her more than living barefoot in the dust for the rest of her life.

"I've been at Rancho Virgo for the past three years. Byron has been like a loving father and friend. . . ."

"And lover?" Zachary interjected.

Bonnie Louise dropped her head, answering Zachary's question.

For the second time that evening he was astounded. His mind raced over her incredible story. Bonnie Louise, he concluded, had been a prisoner—the proverbial bird in a gilded cage, a flesh-and-blood doll for B. J. McClintock to play with.

"We could send that son of a bitch to prison, baby," he said with determination.

"No, Zach," she pleaded. "Please don't . . . please . . . please." She couldn't bear the thought of hurting Byron.

Looking into her by-now red, swollen eyes, Zach could only agree. He wouldn't do anything rash . . . yet. But, at the same time, he wasn't going to take her back to the beach. She was coming home with him!

"What about my clothes?" Bonnie Louise asked, worried.

Zachary explored her beautiful face with his eyes. "Tomorrow we go shopping." She managed a smile. He nodded.

"It's gonna be okay, Bonnie. It's gonna be okay."

"I don't know." She collapsed against his chest. "I hope so. . . ."

"I promise so," he said. "Now, I finally understand a whole lot of things I couldn't quite figure out—not only about you but about that son of a bitch, McClintock. . . ." His voice trailed off. "Come on, babe. Let's go home."

Home. Her mind ricocheted from Plunkettville to Rancho Virgo to Malibu. She knew that when Byron found out she was gone, he'd come after her with the vengeance of betrayal. There was no telling what he would do to her—or to Zachary, for that matter.

Zachary, for his part, was almost grateful to the dirty old studio chief for bringing this exquisite creature into his life. His true love . . . Romantic as his mood was, a sly smile nevertheless crossed his lips as he thought of the weight of the information Bonnie Louise had just handed to him. It gave him, in effect, legitimacy to claim her affection. Besides, if word leaked out, the perverted bastard could go to prison. Jailbait. By the same token, he reminded himself, she's still seventeen when I'm with her, so, until her next birthday, she's jailbait for me, too.

CHAPTER 33

*H*olly Dandridge had found the ultimate trainer through one of the stuntmen on her TV show. She didn't have much time to get in shape for *Blue Moon*. His name was Tomi. He was half-

German and half-Cherokee Indian. He stood 6′ 3″ tall, with light brown hair that hung to his shoulder blades.

Tomi arrived at her dressing room on the MCM lot around noon, and led her outside to a Semi that was parked alongside one of the soundstages. He opened the side door leading her up a few steps into the eighteen-wheeler. She couldn't believe her eyes. The huge trailer had been converted into a state-of-the-art gymnasium.

"If it gets too cold for you, just let me know, Miss Dandridge." His words could barely be heard over the music—music with a driving beat that would help to give a rhythm to the impending physical workout.

"Amazing," Holly said, with wide eyes. "And air-conditioned, too?"

"Oh yes, this used to haul vegetables for Piggly Wiggly, a food chain in the South."

"Is that right?" Holly laughed.

This guy was a piece of delicious work, she thought. His body was so sculpted that no matter which way he moved, his muscles would flex all over his body. His skin was shiny. Holly assumed it was covered with baby oil. And his face—good Lord! He looked like an Indian warrior cast in bronze.

After thirty minutes of lifting weights on the high-tech machines for her biceps, triceps, upper back, lower stomach, waist, and torso, Holly begged for a water break.

Tomi conceded her that, and headed for the spring water cooler at the other end of the trailer. I'm definitely an ass woman, she told herself, as she watched his thighs and buttocks flex, working their way across the gray carpet. During the rigorous workout she had been cracking jokes and trying her best to charm a smile from his cool veneer. To no avail.

"Next we'll do twenty repetitions on the inner-thigh machine," he intoned, leading her to a chrome mesh of metal that looked like something out of a medieval torture chamber.

Once on the machine Holly couldn't believe how easy it was to lift ten pounds.

"You have strong inner thighs, Miss Dandridge."

"Don't I though." Holly grinned.

"Let's put another ten pounds on the machine and see how that feels."

I'd like him to put about two hundred pounds on my inner thighs.

Tomi adjusted the weights, then stood in front of her. Holly felt heat rush into her exposed crevice. Her legs were spread wide open, resting in metal-padded splints, which she had to press, bringing her knees together.

"Try this," he said.

Holly pressed her legs together and moaned. "My God, are you sure that was ten pounds, and not fifty?" she laughed.

"Only ten." He dropped to his knees, studying her legs.

My, my—a smile! I think this inner-thigh machine is turning Sitting Bull on!

"I want you to concentrate very hard on isolating the little muscle right here." He pinched the small bit of flesh at the top of her inner thigh. Holly felt all her senses zoom to the area.

"Breathing is very important. Follow me. Breathe in, then squeeze your legs as you breathe out. That's it. Very good."

Holly could feel beads of sweat running down her back. Her legs were beginning to ache. That little bit of flesh was quivering. She began to shake.

"Is it hurting?" Concern knitted Tomi's brows.

"Yes, I think I'm getting a muscle spasm."

"That's not good."

Tomi got to his feet and lifted her off the machine, then deposited her on the floor, spread her legs, and began to massage her inner thighs. Holly thought she was going to pass out. Those arm muscles flexing were driving her wild with desire.

Tomi looked up at her, eyes half-open. Then she noticed his erection bulging beneath his nylon Nike shorts. "Maybe if you kissed it, it might feel better." She relaxed her legs.

Tomi took her leotard in both hands at the crotch and ripped it apart. She let out a squeal and threw back her head. He pulled her tights off. Holly reached up and tugged at his shorts, exposing the most beautiful muscle on his body.

How perfect, she thought. *Now this is the way I like to work out. . . .*

CHAPTER 34

*S*itting at her desk at nine-thirty in the morning, Lara Miller noted when her private line started blinking. She answered it.

B. J. McClintock's emotionally charged voice bellowed across the country from Tennessee. Lara told Derek Middleton she would have to call him back and hung up.

"I want you to locate Bonnie Louise!" McClintock commanded. "She disappeared from the beach sometime last night or early this morning."

Lara's sixth sense told her that the young beauty had probably run off with Zachary Steele.

"Have you spoken to her in the last day or two, Lara? Do you know where she might be?"

"I don't, but I'll find out by the end of the day."

"And when you do, pick her up and take her right back to Malibu!"

"But, B.J.," she protested, "there're a lot of problems on *Blue Moon*! I just got off the phone with Derek—Holly and Colin are already in some kind of civil war. Maybe you could—"

"My first concern right now is for Bonnie Louise! I'll call you back by noon your time."

"I hope I can find her." Lara heard the line go dead. B.J. sounded frantic. He was obviously in love with the girl. A cold shiver ran down her back. It was one thing to imagine something, to suspect it, but to be confronted by the sinister reality was more than she could stomach.

B.J. could feel his heart working overtime—speaking to Lara had thrown him further into turmoil. It immediately occurred to him that Bonnie Louise must have gone to Zachary Steele, because strong-willed as she was in some ways, she was incapable of making a move entirely on her own. It had to be the fault of that son of a bitch, that cocksure, conceited movie star Zachary Steele.

What the hell was he going to do? The idea of calling the Malibu police station came to mind. But he could scarcely risk disclosure to Elizabeth and others that an all-points bulletin had been put out for a girl he claimed was his niece but was nothing of the sort.

God knew what the consequences of all this were going to amount to. B.J. had reached a kind of Rubicon of the soul that he had always dreaded to cross—the obsessional folly with Bonnie Louise that had now turned to love was coming to a conclusion he had long feared.

Lara went to B.J.'s private Rolodex and turned to Zachary Steele's home phone number. Calling him, she told herself, was going to take courage. The last thing she wanted to do was find herself in the middle of this bizarre and unwholesome triangle. And above all, she didn't want to make matters more complicated than they already were.

The phones started up again, only this time she let the switchboard take messages. She closed her boss's door, relaxed into his leather chair, and meditated for a few minutes, until she felt centered.

She dialed the local number, and when the Latin-sounding housekeeper answered, she asked for Bonnie Louise.

After a long silence she heard Zachary Steele's unmistakable voice ask, "Who wants to speak to her?"

"Tell her it's Lara Miller."

The line went on "hold."

"Lara?" Bonnie Louise's sweet, drawling voice came on the line.

"Bonnie? Are you all right?"

"Uh-huh. Does Byron know where I am?"

"I think he has an idea. He told me to find you and take you back to Malibu."

"Well," the girl said firmly, "I'm not goin' back."

"Ever?"

"Never."

"Never," Lara repeated. "Okay, Bonnie. What am I supposed to tell B.J.?"

"I guess you could tell him I love him . . . and he has to let me go."

"Are you going to be living with Zach?"

"Yes."

"You're not eighteen, you know. You're considered a minor in California."

"I'll be eighteen in four weeks, Lara," she said emphatically.

Lara chewed on her lip. Bonnie Louise sounded firm and in control of herself. Lara had already concluded, after watching the way the young woman had handled a horse, that she was strong-willed.

"Okay, I'll tell him," Lara finally said.

"Lara? I hope we can still be friends. I value your friendship."

"Bonnie, I value yours. But I have a feeling things are going to get pretty damn crazy around here. B.J.'s used to getting his way, too, you know."

"I know, Lara—and he always has up to now. But this time's different. He's just gonna have to understand that it's gonna be this way. I gotta go now . . . 'bye."

" 'Bye," Lara said automatically.

Lara dreaded answering the blinking line. She knew it was B.J., because her watch reflected noon exactly.

"Hello," she said into the receiver.

"Well? Did you find her?"

"Yes, I found her, B.J. She's all right." Lara hesitated.

"She's with that punk actor!" he accused. "Isn't she?"

Nervously Lara admitted, "Yes, B.J., she is."

There was a long silence. Finally McClintock's even though hostile voice asked, "What did she have to say for herself?"

Lara had rehearsed Bonnie Louise's lines, but when it came time to quote them, she found it difficult. Finally her mouth unlocked. "She said that she loves you, and that you have to let her go. She wants it that way . . . she hopes you'll understand."

"Understand? *Understand?*" B.J. started to laugh almost demonically at the irony of his sweet angel's message.

Lara frantically doodled on a note pad: hearts connected by complicated geometric shapes.

"I'll be in the office tomorrow by two," McClintock told her, and hung up.

"Whew," Lara exhaled. God, she had forty thousand things to discuss with him, and all he could think about was a seventeen-year-old nymphet.

Carry on! she concluded. Wing it. That was how Joan Souchek had endeared herself to B.J.

Lara picked up the phone and called back Derek Middleton. They couldn't afford to lose any more time. Going further over budget, she warned herself, could compromise the whole outcome of the project.

CHAPTER 35

S ilence. Savannah pressed her ear to the kitchen door and waited. They must've squared off, she told herself. Then the shrill voices erupted all over again.

Flavio insisted Ariba "date" a man. "Anyone will do!" he shrieked. "River Phoenix, Michael J. Fox, Julian Lennon, Robert Downey, Jr.—I don't care who it is! A carpark attendant!"

"No!" Ariba stood firm.

Flavio cursed her in his native Italian, then explained his record company's position in Portuguese, and concluded his ultimatum in English. If she was going to be a superstar with staying power, she was going to have to give her fans something personal.

"The boys want to make love with you, Ariba. The girls want to *be* you. If you turn that around—it's the kiss of death!"

Savannah heard something fragile smash against a wall and shatter. Flavio flew into Italian, while Ariba used Portuguese to inform her mentor that she would have no part of a record-company romance. Her private life was *private*! She wanted it to remain a mystery; however, if Flavio wanted to squire her to dinner, parties, and galas—okay!

"I have a wife and three children!" he argued.

"So? That never stopped you before!"

"Ariba, be reasonable! It's the system."

"Shove your system up your deep, dark crack, Flavio!"

Flavio sighed deeply. "You're so sexy," he pleaded. "I want you."

"Get away from me!"

"*Cara . . . Cara . . .* go back to the brat-pack boys! Please!"

Silence. Savannah wondered what was going on in there. She knew that Flavio had discovered Ariba singing at a beach party in Rio when she was fifteen. He'd named her Ariba. He'd hired the best music coaches. He'd spent five years training her, molding her, making her a superstar in Latin America and Spain . . . and now they both shared the dream of capturing the prize—America!

Savannah's ear was beginning to throb with pain. Ariba wouldn't make love to Flavio to get her way, she was sure of it. Ariba wasn't like that.

The front door slammed shut. Flavio's voice reverberated: "Think about it!"

A string of Portuguese expletives greeted Savannah as she pushed the kitchen door open and peered into the living room.

"*Filho da peuta! Pórco machismo!*" the ninety-seven-pound singer spit.

"I heard. What're you going to do?" Savannah asked softly.

Ariba's wild dark brown eyes blazed with hate. She vowed not to play the game. Flavio had had her in every way, and—fair enough—he'd kept his word. He'd made her a star. He'd made her rich. He'd done a lot of good things for her and, in turn, for her brothers and sisters, but that could never change the way she felt about the opposite sex. And instead of disguising what she felt, now that she was a star, she could afford to proclaim it!

Savannah cuddled up on the couch and listened. She knew Ariba well enough to know that once she started a tirade, it was best to let it rip. And today she was volcanic.

The phone rang, and Ariba waved Savannah back. "Let the machine get it!"

Flavio had pushed her buttons all right. He'd detonated something long buried. Savannah wished there was something she could do to soothe her, but she was spellbound.

Ariba's inner rage seethed to the surface as she explained how when she was ten years old, she and her younger brothers and sisters watched their father beat their mother bloody because she disagreed with him. She remembered many times when her mother had to have stitches or special poultices for a swollen eye.

"In my country, Vanna, he marry you, you have his babies— he take a mistress, he get bored, he take another mistress. You get bored, you want to go out with your friends, you want to take a class—he kill you!"

"You can't kill somebody for no reason."

Ariba's body was wild with emotion. She gestured frantically as she fought within herself to translate her thoughts as quickly as they were spewing forth. "In Brazil a husband don't need a reason!"

She recalled that the first time her father beat her mother was after a wonderful Sunday dinner. Being a professor of music, her father had a large collection of instruments that family and friends enjoyed playing.

"They were a leetle drunk. My uncle Arturo, he want my mother to dance. My father say *no*. My mother, ah, she was beautiful. A voice like an angel. Legs . . ." Ariba grinned and lifted her miniskirt. "Like mine."

"Great legs," Savannah agreed.

"She danced. Everyone left. My father broke three of her ribs."

"He's a madman."

Ariba shook her head and grimaced. "In my country a *man* can kill you for nothing. I pray to the Blessed Virgin. She no answer me."

"Ariba, my father did the same thing to my mother, only it was psychological."

"On my twelfth birthday," Ariba went on, "my mother, she took me to dance class. Ballet. She believe in me. She love me, Vanna."

Savannah watched the toughness disappear as Ariba succumbed to the tearful memory of her mother. The singer explained that for two years her mother took in sewing to pay for her dancing, and then singing, lessons. When her father found out, he went crazy.

"It was my fault," Ariba confessed. "I want him to see me dance. He want to know how I learn so many things. Proudly, Vanna, I tell him—Mama, she pay for my classes.

"He beat her, he call her a whore. He pour alcohol on her and set her on fire."

"My God," Savannah said sympathetically. "I've never heard of anything like that."

"In my country, it happen."

"What happened to your mother?"

"She died after three days of agony. And my father"—Ariba spit on the floor—"he disappear. Ten days later he walk into the police station. He tell them his wife dishonor him. His wife not an honest woman. She lie—he defend his honor. Fine, they tell him. Go back to work. Take care of your children. Three years pass, then he go to trial. The judge, the jury—they know machismo. They do nothing. They decide my mother was dishonest. It was her own fault."

"That could never happen in this country."

"I know, Vanna."

Savannah was beginning to understand what fueled her friend's passion. Why Ariba was destined to become an international superstar. She had to vindicate her mother.

Ariba explained that after her mother died, she had to take care of her four brothers and sisters before and after school and even on weekends. She had become the little mother. Her father carried on as if nothing had happened. He had apologized a few times, but after his acquittal, he never spoke of the horrible incident again.

"When I was fifteen, I run away. I sing. I meet Flavio. I survive." She smiled through red, tear-filled eyes.

Savannah had been drawn to the depths of emotional memory. Through her own tears she talked about her father—B. J. McClintock, the Beverly Hills megamogul, the man who was always there for his stars and the company, but was rarely, if ever, there for his family.

"You have suffered too, Vanna. Your scars are also on the heart."

Savannah gave her a sharp look. "My father," she cursed. "From the time I learned about sex, he made it clear that I had to *wait* until my wedding night. If I didn't, he said, nobody would ever marry me, because I wasn't a virgin."

"That's cruel!"

"I know. But deep down I still believe him."

Ariba opened her arms and embraced Savannah. They gently stroked each other, soothing the sting of bitter memories.

"So, you see, Ariba—we have a lot in common."

"I know, Vanna. We understand each other. You know why I do not play Flavio's game. It betray me!"

The girls looked at each other and smiled. Thank God they were together. There was no one on earth who could give either of them more comfort right now than they could give to each other.

CHAPTER 36

"*B*entine! My *dahling* Bentine," Lili trilled.

Bentine was forever amazed by her stepmother's affected English accent. She'd even asked her once how a nice girl from Brooklyn, a Russian-Jewish beauty, could end up sounding like England's queen mother sitting on a pincushion.

"Your friend is wonderful!" Lili blathered on. "Papa loves him."

"Who?"

"Oh stop playing with me, Bennie! You know perfectly well who's here!"

Sunday dinner at the Devoracs' had become a much-dreaded ritual for Bentine. Listening to Lili, a former opera singer, trill everything she said made every muscle in Bentine's neck knot. And as for her father, he'd never really approved of her. He loved her in his way, but she was always made to feel as if she hadn't come up to his expectations.

She followed Lili's aqua chiffon designer caftan past the antique aviary of automaton birds and into the den.

"Bennie's here!" Lili announced.

Four heads turned in her direction. Bentine's mouth fell open when she saw George Borofsky seated next to her father, fondling one of his Oscars.

Emil Devorac smiled warmly and greeted her. "Bennie, darling," he said with his heavy Middle European accent, so strong that one would never know he'd spent the last fifty years in America.

"Yor friend is vunderful," he went on, gesturing toward George. "I like this guy—ve're in identical positions. He has the money to produce my next moovie. And so do I. He doesn't have any ideas—and I don't, either. So, ve should get along like vild fires."

Bentine wanted to faint. She wanted to scream. She wanted to wind back the clock, bypassing the aisle with cat food. How the hell did *he* get here?

George had already leapt to his feet and offered her his chair. "Here, Ben, take my seat."

In the background she could hear Sid Shapiro, newly appointed head of picture development at MCM, and his wife of thirty years, Anna, asking George how he met her. She walked over to the wingback chair and dissolved into a contained heap.

George proceeded to rave about her industrious financial wizardry. "There she was, standing by the cat food looking through her coupons . . ."

Anna cackled and said, "It sounds like Bennie's met her match."

George shot her a gleaming smile. Bentine froze.

"Coupons?" Lili trilled. "I've heard of them. Where do you get them?"

"You left us at the cat food," Emil prodded. "Go on!"

"Well, there's not much to say, really. It was just one of those lucky moments. Wasn't it, Ben?"

Suddenly her breathing became labored. She felt as if she were suffocating. If only the floor would open up and swallow her. "I can't breathe," she said desperately.

Devorac sprang into action, directing his troops. Lili was to get a brown paper bag, George a damp washcloth, and the Shapiros were instructed to hold Bentine's arms up over her head.

"She's turning purple," Lili wailed. "Emil, should I call four-one-one?"

"It's nine-one-one. And no!"

Lili nervously took the paper bag and placed it over Bentine's head.

"No, stupid! Not *over* her head. She breathes into it!"

When the bag was removed, Bentine was hyperventilating, gasping for air.

George looked around and said softly, "I'm sorry, but this may be the only way."

He stepped forward and slapped Bentine across the face. She winced, gasped, and came back to reality.

Emil patted him on the shoulder and said, "You made the right choice, George. You made the right choice."

Bentine looked up at George, her father, the Shapiros, Lili, closed her eyes, and took the only door marked "out." She fainted.

Bentine woke up in her old bedroom. She looked at the dusty deep rose-colored drapery, the faded pastel floral wallpaper, bookcases filled with high-school and college textbooks, plays, novels, memories. So many dust-covered memories.

There were photographs of her riding in a dressage competition, at the senior prom, even a wall of collages of her, bits and pieces of teenage Bentine Devorac, beautiful, sassy, and hopeful with a slew of movie stars.

Her first horrifying thought was that she had died and been sentenced to live in her old bedroom.

Suddenly the door cracked open. She locked her eyes shut and listened. She could hear someone tiptoeing across the Oriental carpet, approaching her on the Victorian four-poster. She didn't really want to know who it was. She wished he'd just turn and leave.

A gentle hand was tickling her forehead. Fingers were gliding through her clean chestnut hair. When a hand started moving across her stomach, she bolted upright.

"Bentine," George said sincerely, "are you all right?"

"I'm n-not sure . . ." she stammered.

"I was so worried about you when you didn't show the next night, so I tried your number, and I guess it was a digit off. I couldn't get to you, so I remembered your inviting me to meet your father today. Today is Sunday."

"But how did you find where my father lives?"

He grinned and opened his Armani jacket. Tucked neatly into the inside pocket was a map to the stars' homes. Anyone could buy one from weekend vendors along Sunset Boulevard. She wanted to faint again. This man was just too ingenious.

"So this was your room when you were a little girl? How wonderful that your father left it for you just the way it was. He is amazing, Bennie."

"Don't call me *that*," she barked.

George put his hand over her mouth and embraced her in a viselike grip.

"*Sssshhhh!* Do you want them to hear you? This is the perfect place for me to rape you."

She was stunned. What a wild idea, she thought. That's exactly what I used to dream about when I was growing up. . . .

As she considered his offer, George spotted something by the window. In a split second she watched him untie the velvet cords holding the drapery back. Before she knew what happened, he'd used them to tie her wrists to the bedposts. She marveled at his skill. She'd bet he was faster than a professional calf roper.

Even more stunned, she watched him unzip his pants, rip hers off, and enter her.

She inhaled, her voice rising an octave. His hand came down over her mouth. Fear darted from her eyes. She started mumbling.

"You're wet! I knew you wanted it!"

She bit down on his hand, and he shook it with a quiet "Ow." He pushed his face close to her ear and said, "Yeah, that's it, bitch. Fight me!"

"George," she whispered hysterically. "Untie me. *I mean it!* I . . . ah . . . She gasped and wailed, "My father, what if my father walks in?"

His hand clamped down on her mouth again, and he said, "Wouldn't that be perfect?"

She shook a *no* as best she could, considering her arms were tied to the bedposts.

"Oh, God you feel good," he moaned, pumping away. "Get into it, Bennie. Get into it! We've only got a minute."

Bentine focused on the electric Mickey Mouse clock on the night table. Mickey's eyes were rolling back and forth as if he were enjoying the show. His little white-gloved mitts pointed at time slipping away.

Somewhere in the distance she recognized the old, but all too familiar, sound of someone coming upstairs.

She started gagging and pumping harder. "Oh my God! Someone's coming," she desperately warned.

"Me, too!"

On the brink of her orgasm, George pulled out, untied her wrists, zipped his pants, and was casually adjusting the drapery swags when the door opened.

CHAPTER 37

B.J.'s heart was pounding at the thought of seeing Bonnie Louise. He had booked a suite at the Westwood Marquis, intending at first to have lunch in the room. Instead—fearing that Bonnie Louise would resent the implications—he made reservations at the nearby Hamlet Gardens Restaurant, hoping that its European charm would appeal to her.

The Hamlet Gardens had a large dining area with several smaller rooms tucked away from prying eyes. Waiting for Bonnie Louise, B.J. contemplated the menu. On the one hand he didn't want to spend too much time on the meal, but on the other he wished to avoid the impression of rushing her through it.

Bonnie Louise had to be handled with subtlety. B.J. had taught her about life and art and music. Now, his little Eliza Doolittle was out of his reach. He no longer controlled her. *If only I had given her a little more attention, she'd never have gotten on that plane to Los Angeles.*

The idea that he might not succeed in getting her back belonged to a realm of insecurity he didn't want even to consider. He halfheartedly tried to repress those thoughts by rereading the menu. He had hardly started to consider the virtues of the arugula and watercress salad, to be followed by angel-hair pasta primavera, than his mind had flicked kaleidoscopically into an image of Bonnie Louise's childishly slender arms folded to cover her breasts. Wearing her tiny panties, she had emerged from the bathroom into the bedroom at Rancho Virgo.

Suddenly the wine steward interrupted this vivid reverie by asking if he would care to see the wine list. B.J. ordered a bottle of vintage Cristal champagne to be brought immediately.

He sternly forced his mind to focus on the notion of cracked crab. He had begun to weigh his fondness for the dish when a new and more irresistible in-rush of memory assailed him.

He closed his eyes. . . . There was Bonnie Louise again, now standing beside the bed after her morning run, standing very close and above him. Slowly she peeled off the tiny remaining garment. Even more intoxicating was the thought of her lingering, naked, with the bedside lamp shining golden on her.

Bonnie Louise had dropped away that shred of fabric for one undeniable reason only—so that he, he alone and no other, could readily open and penetrate her.

Dammit, he told himself, concentrate on something else. For one thing, he was going to have to get to his feet at any moment to greet her, and to do so in public, with so evident an erection, would be embarrassing.

He was fortunate to have Lara Miller as the intermediary between himself and Bonnie Louise. Due to Lara's persistence and persuasion, his little girl had agreed to meet him for an innocent lunch.

Suddenly the headwaiter appeared at the table with a phone in hand.

"A call for you Mr. McClintock," he said, as he bent over to plug the phone into the wall.

B.J. was sure it was Lara with another goddam problem regarding *Blue Moon*. The waiter handed him the receiver and left.

"What is so important it can't wait?" he said sternly.

"Why, Byron, please don't be so upset with me," Bonnie Louise shuddered into the line.

B.J. was shaken by the sound of her voice. "Sweetheart, where are you?"

"I thought it best if I didn't come today, Byron."

"Why, sugar, I want to see you . . . I *need* to see you. Get in a cab—I'll wait for you."

"No . . . I'm not coming. It's too painful and—"

"Darlin' it's painful for me, too . . . you still love me, I know you do."

"Of course I love you, but I'm *in love* with Zachary. I don't want to do anything to hurt him."

B.J.'s blood pressure shot up. "Hurt *him*? What about how *I* feel? You're killing me, Bonnie Louise! Don't all those years we spent together mean anything?"

"You're raising your voice, Byron," she stated.

"I'm not shouting!" he yelled into the phone.

Bonnie Louise hung up. B.J. became aware of his surroundings. People at nearby tables were staring at him as he replaced the receiver in its cradle.

He stood up and threw two one-hundred dollar bills on the table, then left the restaurant with the feeling of rejection eating away at the insides of his stomach.

CHAPTER 38

*C*hristmas was coming. Elizabeth loved it and hated it at the same time. There were lists upon lists: presents, cards, thank yous, parties, benefits, charity invitations—and, of course, the tree and decorating the house and grounds. It was a full-time job.

Today she had attended a special 6:00 A.M. mass dedicated to the Blessed Virgin. She usually made it to the eight o'clock service at least three times a week. Getting up so early had thrown her whole day off.

Elizabeth McClintock loved going to church. She loved the nuns. Three mornings a week after mass she and the nuns cleaned the altar and chose the delicate linens to be placed ceremoniously on the slab of white Italian marble. Nearly all the linens were gifts from Elizabeth, lovely things she had sought out on trips to London, Rome, and Dublin, not to mention special excursions to Egypt and to Austria.

Perhaps it gave her a feeling of being closer to God. She had such a special relationship with the sisters. They would have a cup of coffee as they chose the altar cloth for the day, and then they would ask Elizabeth to help arrange the flowers or organize a supper for the archbishop, cardinal, and some visiting clergymen.

She felt needed and pure for her deeds on those mornings. Nothing gave her more peace of mind than to kneel down in front of the shrine of the Blessed Virgin Mary on the left side of the altar and pour out her heart to the Mother of God, her personal patron saint.

B.J. slammed the front door, startling Elizabeth. She followed the sounds and found him in the bar pouring a healthy amount of cognac into a snifter. That means he's had a bad day, she reflected, as she half filled a cordial glass with some Grand Marnier.

Light talk is what's needed here, Elizabeth mused, and started to share her day with her husband. He wasn't listening to a word she was saying. He just looked out the French window and nodded his head at the proper moments. Elizabeth talked about this party and that invitation, which ones to go to and which ones to turn down. B.J. nodded but continued to stay in his own private world. Finally Elizabeth stood up and approached her husband, who was leaning against the back of a sofa staring out of the many leaded panes of glass.

She leaned against the sofa next to him and looked out the window, hoping to see what he saw. Minutes passed. He didn't even seem to notice she was there.

"Byron, if there is something on your mind I could help you with, I would be more than willing," she said quietly, never taking her eyes away from the window.

B.J. flinched slightly. He turned and looked at her as if she had just insulted him.

"Help?" he said incredulously. But he said it almost as if speaking to a servant. Then, coldly: "Of course I know that whenever I ask your help, you're ready with it. I expect nothing less. Thank you, Elizabeth." He continued to sip his cognac and stare out the window.

Elizabeth left the room as if she had been slapped across the face. Her cheeks were flushed with anger. He had never in all the years spoken with such a cold, impersonal tone in his voice. All the same, hold your tongue, she told herself, as she ascended the wide staircase pounding the balls of her feet into the thick Oriental runner.

She went directly into her dressing room and looked at herself in the mirror. As she began to take her jewelry off, she looked down at her hands. They reminded her of Grandma Jackson's hands. Now *she* was a wise old woman, Elizabeth recalled. Grandma Jackson had prided herself on controlling the family. She knew how to make a man happy and how to pull the weeds when the roots were threatened.

Old Grandma Jackson had taught her to look the other way. She used to say, "Elizabeth, someday your husband will stray. They all do eventually. And when you find out, if you want to keep that man, you turn your head. You just keep looking the other way till he gets finished with her. They always come home."

Elizabeth poured some Vitabath into the reclining tub and thought about her grandmother's advice. For months she'd known something just wasn't right with B.J. He had grown so irritable and short with her and the children. His mind was always preoccupied with business, or so he said.

If there was something else, she didn't want to know about it.

She just wanted her husband back to normal. She made herself ready for her evening bath. The hot water would help her to forget how ugly and cold B.J. had just been to her.

Elizabeth lowered herself into the soft bubbles that camouflaged the steamy water. She sighed and relaxed, then rested her head on the neck pillow attached to the edge of the tub. She began to float and dream.

She thought of Savannah as she sank her shoulders under the water. Since meeting Ariba, her daughter had been basking in rock-star perks: private jets, limousines, invitations from royalty, politicians, and social superstars. There were even presents from anonymous admirers.

Her little girl was growing up . . . or should she be honest and admit that Savannah had already grown up? Savannah, she prayed, please meet a fine, eligible young man and marry him. Make me a grandmother. . . .

Then Elizabeth's thoughts turned to her adopted sons, Michael and Daniel. What's to become of them? Those uncontrollable teenagers . . . Their grades are fairly good, which makes me wonder if they have someone else doing their homework for them. . . .

Oh, well, she reassured herself, they're young . . . they'll simmer down when they start college.

CHAPTER 39

*T*raveling first class, being greeted in New York at the arrival gate by the MCM chauffeur and staying at the McClintocks' sumptuous Carlyle Hotel apartment made Lara Miller feel that she had, in appearance at least, the trappings of success.

She stroked her soft black leather coat and wondered if these *trappings* were crumbs from a rich man's table—or was she, in fact, a woman who had now actually arrived?

How did a woman know—what measure did she safely use—to determine if she was, independent of anyone else's whim, a successful woman in her own right, a woman with an unassailable position on the executive ladder?

If she ran afoul of B.J., Lara reflected, as she looked down at the crawling Madison Avenue traffic below her, she could be knocked off that ladder with a mere flick of his fingers.

She considered whether she had any valuable and perhaps unique qualities that would render her a prize catch to a head-hunting corporation if she was fired.

None, she concluded. There was nothing either unique or remarkable about Lara Miller. Except perhaps that she was temporarily the sole occupant of the McClintocks' huge suite at the Carlyle. A few months ago, that would have seemed remarkable enough to her. And there lay the proof: It seemed remarkable to her still. A truly solid and successful woman would be taking this in stride. She was not.

Ergo, she was not a truly solid and successful woman. Lara Miller would have to do a great deal more for herself before that time arrived.

She watched two college boys laden with books trying to hail a taxi. Her days at NYU flashed to mind—a time when she wondered what she wanted to do with her future life. Marriage had always been a possibility, but somehow the boys she'd dated didn't prove to be soul mates of the kind she yearned for. Even her history professor, older and wiser, didn't last more than a year. He was too controlling in the end.

Yet, Lara reflected, she was also very far from being unhappy about her life. She'd managed to take a stand with B.J., telling him that Bonnie Louise was his affair, not hers. And that *Blue Moon* was important to both of them, and someone had better visit the New York location and take charge. They were already three days over budget, and there was no telling where it would end.

She thought of her father, feeling as if he were with her. She knew he was in spirit. Sometimes she even felt as if he were telling her things, guiding her. He was so passionate about human rights, civil rights, education. . . . Lara hoped that *Blue Moon* would have an impact on public awareness the way classic films like *China Syndrome* and *Rain Man* did. If it accomplished that, she knew her father would rest easier.

Bemelmans Bar at the Carlyle Hotel was humming with the type of people Lara thought inspired New Yorker cartoons. Young and old, male and female, they all appeared self-assured. These people were born without sweat glands, she mused.

She slid onto a banquette and listened to Barbara Carroll playing a Gershwin tune on the piano. It was all fitting together so nicely; New York on business . . . Kevin Wenster in for a weekend of pleasure. If only Derek Middleton listens to reason, she told herself, everything will be perfect.

"Lara?" an English-accented voice inquired.

She turned to face an exhausted Derek Middleton. He yawned and slid in alongside of her. Obviously *Blue Moon* was taking its toll.

The cast and crew of *Blue Moon* had assembled in New York for twenty-one days of location shooting. Initially the weather was crisp and clear with cumulus clouds that looked like puffs of cotton floating above the skyscrapers. Then Mother Nature whipped up an early white Christmas, and they lost three days of shooting.

And *snow* was not the only chill factor. Holly and Colin were openly at odds with each other except when the camera was rolling.

"A double Black Label and soda, no ice," Derek told the waiter. "You're looking well," he complimented her. "Did you change your hair?"

Flattered, Lara explained that she had had it trimmed. "I had Carol feather it on top. I'm glad you like it, Derek."

"I'm glad you and B.J. like my dailies," he came back with a wink.

"They're wonderful."

The waiter arrived with a Perrier for Lara and a scotch and soda for the director. Lara knew that they were jockeying for position. Everything was amiable. Lots of compliments to set each other at ease.

"Cheers!" Derek declared.

"Cheers."

After a long, healthy gulp, Derek leaned close to Lara and in a low, conspiratorial tone said, "Wouldn't it be just like you Americans to solve your drug problem by legalizing the stuff and cornering the market?"

Lara smiled. "Makes sense to me. If I had children, I'd be no more worried than I am now."

"Well, I do have children. I have seven, and I wouldn't send them off touring America on their own. It's getting to be like the Wild West—except now there's a gunfight every thirty seconds."

"Lara," Derek said, changing his tone and looking her square in the eye, "my vision of *Blue Moon* must not be compromised. Do you understand?" He drained his glass and held it up for the waiter to see. "This is one action-adventure film that can actually sway public opinion. And if your countrymen get angry enough, they'll do what they did with Prohibition—they'll legalize drugs and put those rotten drug lords out of business."

Lara waited patiently for the director to finish speaking. She wanted him to be her ally. Quietly she said, "I know all this, Derek, but that doesn't alter the fact that you're behind schedule—and I hate to say it, but if *Blue Moon* isn't that big a money-maker and it comes in over budget, it could put B.J. in a tricky position with his stockholders."

"What is your bottom line, Lara?"

"We shoot the chase scenes and exteriors, as planned, in Austria. The hotel room, any interiors, we'll move to the MCM lot. That'll cut the cost in half."

Derek was thoughtful. Finally he exhaled.

Lara went on, "The love scene between Holly and Colin can be shot in L.A."

Derek laughed. "If they're still speaking by then."

"When he finds out she's a double agent and blows up, that'll be dynamite on film."

Derek and Lara broke up over the thought of Colin telling off Holly. There had been so much tension between them off-screen that there was no telling what would happen when Colin vented his emotions on-camera. And Holly would have to listen.

"Derek Middleton? Is that you, darling?" a shrewd Englishwoman asked.

"Daphne, my God! What brings you to New York? A dog show?"

"Dekky, you devil. You know my spaniels can't leave England!" She turned to take in Lara. "When I saw you two in such a close huddle, I was afraid I might be interrupting a business meeting—then I decided that you were far too pretty, and I know that Derek doesn't like to waste his leisure time on business when he can avoid it."

"Lara Miller—Daphne Fitzhugh."

"Oh, how do you do? Are you an actress, Lara?"

"She's my producer!" Derek exaggerated. "Or one of them. And she's a damn sight prettier than the other, I can assure you." He narrowed his eyes at the busybody. "Regards to Henry."

"Are we staying here?" Daphne probed.

"No, Daphne! I'm staying with friends around the corner."

"Of course, dear." Daphne turned to Lara and said, "His wife, Rebecca, is my dearest friend. So nice meeting you, Lara."

The woman turned and joined a group of four on the other side of the room. Derek began fidgeting, feeling as if he was being scrutinized. Under his breath he cursed, "Bloody bitch."

"Don't let's get sidetracked by her, Derek. We've got a full night tonight."

"Right."

When Lara opened her eyes, her view of the McClintocks' chintz-coordinated New York apartment was upside down. Her heart was beating hard and fast. Her body was bathed in sweat.

Kevin Wenster was the first to break the silence. "We've got to stop meeting this way."

"I know," she whispered. "We're lethal when we get going." She gently followed the contours of his chest with her fingertips.

Lara had had a few sexual encounters in her life, but nothing that came close to what she was experiencing with this spicy, erotic Australian.

Without ever saying a word, Kevin was teaching her how to open up and surrender. Although he always took the initiative, it seemed that he was doing what she secretly wanted. When they made love, they were like two seasoned dancers—she followed his lead, and he led them to ecstasy.

Afterward they donned thick terry-cloth robes and made their way through the cozy, lived-in apartment. The kitchen was small, but sunny. Elizabeth, Lara thought, really knew how to set up house. There was everything to accommodate a party of two or twenty.

Knowing that Saturday would be their only time together until after the first of the year, Lara had stocked the refrigerator with what she thought were libidinous treats—food to quench one appetite while heightening another.

She and Kevin proceeded to tease each other with imported long-stemmed strawberries dipped in crème fraîche; soft, runny Camembert with warm dark brown bread; succulent turkey breast and chilled asparagus with a Dijon mustard sauce. They fixed themselves plates and retired to the bedroom. Lara made herself comfortable under the covers, snuggling down, then propping herself up again so that she could reach the food and have a better view of Kevin's firm buttocks as he rummaged through his luggage, producing two bottles of Australian wine. He dug deeper until he found a small, gift-wrapped package. He tossed it onto the bed, into her lap.

"Merry Christmas, Lara."

"I haven't had time to—" she started to apologize.

"Look, luv—being with you is the best present you could ever give me." He sat on the edge of the bed and said, "I'm afraid we'll be on different continents at Christmastime." He motioned toward the package she held in her hands. "Go on, then. Open it!"

Lara carefully unwrapped the shiny gift. Underneath the silver paper was a velvet jewel box that held a magnificent choker made up of cabochon-cut black opals set in eighteen-karat gold. The opal in the center was larger and more elaborately set than the others.

"My God!" she gasped. "It's exquisite!"

He pointed at the center stone and said, "I took it out of the safe."

She caressed it with her fingers. "One of your 'lucky' opals?" He nodded, and Lara suddenly believed that this was Kevin's way of sealing their bond. A necklace of this magnitude and intimate nature could mean only one thing, that he was really committed to her.

Kevin edged closer to her, took the necklace, and opened the clasp. "There is one stipulation," he told her with a sly smile. "It has to be worn with nothing else—just you and your 'lucky' opals."

Complying with his proposal, Lara slipped out of bed and disrobed. Naked and radiating love, she said, "I'm ready."

Kevin ceremoniously placed the gleaming choker around her long neck and stepped back to admire the result.

All at once Lara felt completely vulnerable. She closed her eyes to hold back the tears and buried her face up against his broad chest.

He tilted her head up and caressed her lips. "You're so lovely, Lara. So unspoiled."

She felt that he loved her, and yet she couldn't bring herself to let go, to trust him completely. Since her father's death, fourteen years earlier, she hadn't allowed any man to fully penetrate her heart.

"Come here," he whispered in her ear, pulling her close. "As I see it, I'm going to be spending a lot more time in Los Angeles. There's a little corporate merger under way. . . ."

"MCM?" she asked apprehensively.

"Even bigger," he boasted.

The phone rang. Using her better judgment, she didn't answer it. The message light started blinking.

"You see, luv, nobody knows I'm here. They think I'm still in London."

"You're lucky, Kevin—everybody knows where to find me."

Chills of passion were racing down her spine, and the damn blinking red light on the telephone was reminding her of the calls she had to make, lists she had to check—all the things that related to *Blue Moon* kept nagging at her.

"Stop thinking so hard. Lots of movies go over budget."

Lara shifted her body, turning, looking into Kevin's clear brown eyes. Softly she said, "Kevin, you've spoiled me for any other man. I never knew it could be this good."

He looked away, saying, "I know. Come on, then!" He swept her up in his arms and gently placed her on the bed.

A stream of late-afternoon sunlight burned through their eyelids. Their time together had evaporated.

Kevin remarked that this was the first time in years that he hadn't read three important newspapers before 10:00 A.M. And, once more, he didn't care.

"You're glowing," he commented.

"I'm not ready to face Derek and the gang."

"Don't."

"Right. B.J. would kill me."

Wenster laughed to himself. He knew sides of B. J. McClintock that Lara could never imagine. "He'll manage, luv. B.J. always does."

"I wouldn't be so sure," she said with concern. "He's preoccupied with a girl."

"Oh my God!" Kevin said, picking up *The New York Times.* Purposely changing the subject, he zeroed in on an item on page two. "Speaking of B.J.—listen to this!" He pointed at a short article below a large photograph of Vanessa Waters.

"Actress Vanessa Waters," he began, "one of MCM's most promising young talents, filed a fifty-million-dollar malpractice suit against Beverly Hills cosmetic surgeon Dr. Morton Shipp." Kevin burst out laughing.

"Oh, how perfect—here's a quote from the starlet: 'Dr. Shipp and I had arguments on two separate occasions about the size of the breast augmentations he was going to give me. I wanted a 'B' cup, and he kept insisting on a 'D' cup. When I woke up, I looked like a cow.' "

Lara giggled. She knew it wasn't funny, but the newspaper account made it seem ludicrous. "It's about time Dr. Frankenstein gets what he deserves. Now, poor Vanessa has to have the same operation all over again to make her breasts smaller."

"No wonder you call him that!" Kevin paused, kissed Lara's cheek, and queried, "Dr. Shipp never touched you, did he?"

"He tried. He wanted to remove my mole . . . but I said no!"

"Thank Christ for that!"

Kevin was genuinely shaken. He knew that Morton Shipp did B.J.'s bidding, and that if the mad doctor went over the edge—which Kevin had thought possible from the first moment they had met—he might take McClintock with him.

"You think Vanessa is the tip of Morty's iceberg?"

Lara shrugged. "I don't know. Nobody knows what anybody does behind closed doors."

Kevin folded the newspaper and tossed it across the room. He drew Lara close to him and admired the beauty of his gift against her fair skin.

"There're a few loose ends I have to take care of, luv. You may have to bear with me for a bit."

"You mean your girlfriend?"

"You might say."

He kissed her in a way that made her rule out the possibility of real female competition. As far as Lara Miller was concerned, she had met her soul mate.

They cuddled in each other's arms, quietly sensing the harmonious flow of energy between them. As their bodies touched once again, all unwanted thoughts fell away.

CHAPTER 40

*C*olin telephoned home regularly. It seemed to Helen that *Blue Moon* was running into more than its share of problems. Colin had come down with a touch of the flu, and within a week 80 percent of the crew and cast were down with the same bug.

It looked as if Colin wasn't going to get home for more than a few days at Christmas. B.J. was threatening to sue for breach of contract if anyone took more than three days off for the holiday. When Helen suggested she and the children come to New York for a week or so, Colin didn't match her enthusiasm. Helen was disappointed, but being intelligent enough to know that nothing she said would change her husband's mind, she acceded to his plans.

Deep down she was relieved that Colin was only going to be home for three days. It made declining parties so much easier. Christmas had always been an overwhelming season for her. This year it would be more relaxed, giving her the time to make it *family* perfect.

She took her daughter and sons shopping. They bought twinkling red lights in the shape of chili peppers and holographic ornaments that sent rainbows cascading across the room. The Victorian angel, which had crowned the O'Brien family Christmas tree for over seventy years, now looked down from atop Helen and Colin's ten-foot-tall Douglas fir.

By the time Helen and her daughter, Maureen, had finished, the beach house looked, smelled, and tasted of Christmas.

Helen was in such a good mood she'd begun cutting back on Xanax. No more 1.0 mg purple, only .50 mg pinks, and soon, she hoped, she'd be able to cope using the .25 mg whites.

Late at night, when everyone was in bed, she'd curl up in the living room next to the fireplace with a yellow pad and a felt-tipped pen. Looking at the Christmas tree and the blanket of exquisitely wrapped presents beneath it inspired her.

The play she'd been writing off and on for the past five years was nearly finished. It was in two acts with two changes of scene. Parts of it flowed, other parts were too long and labored. It was as yet untitled. Several titles had been attached to it over the years, but none of them had ever stuck.

If anyone knew the value of rewriting, it was Helen, who had grown up at the helm of Broadway theater. She could remember dinner parties with Tennessee Williams and Arthur Miller. Visiting Lunt and Fontaine in Wisconsin, meeting Kenneth Tynan, the flamboyant theater critic, in London. The greats! She'd met them all at one time or another. Which, she guessed, was what had blocked her from doing anything with her writing.

Writing had become a form of therapy, an outlet she desperately needed but only utilized when Colin was away on location. And this untitled work was good, she thought. It had potential. She crumpled up a page and tossed it into the blazing wood. The felt-tipped pen flew across the yellow pad. A new idea, a more powerful idiosyncrasy for her main character. Her confidence was beginning to peak. She was feeling less afraid to tread on sacred turf. Maybe by spring she'd have something to show her father.

CHAPTER 41

*F*lying into Eugene, Oregon, for Christmas, Bonnie Louise was frightened. She held Zachary's hand and prayed that the Steeles wouldn't ask her too many questions. She didn't want them to judge her by her lack of knowledge, but rather by her love and devotion to their son.

"Will you look at *that*?" Zachary enthused. He pointed at the light blanket of snow that was turning his hometown into a Currier and Ives greeting card. He leaned over and kissed Bonnie Louise's neck. "Loosen up, babe. My folks are gonna love you."

Bonnie Louise gave him a worried smile. "What if your mama asks me to read somethin'?"

"Don't worry," he consoled her. "My mom is cool."

"But she's an English teacher."

"And my dad's an architect, and they're both gonna love you!"

"I love you," Bonnie Louise whispered in Zachary's ear.

"I love you, too," he whispered back.

Valerie and Jim Steele were a remarkable couple. They were about the same age as Byron, Bonnie Louise realized, but they looked so much younger. Their faces were tan from skiing, and their bodies were lean and athletic-looking. They did seem genuinely glad to meet her. It's funny, she thought, it's like I know them. They love Zachary so much. . . . Maybe he's right . . . Maybe it's all gonna be okay. . . .

As they drove up the winding road into the southern hills framing Eugene, Bonnie Louise remarked that the big, beautifully landscaped, gated homes looked like those she'd seen in Beverly Hills and Bel Air.

"But it's cozier here—friendlier than L.A.," Zachary assured her.

Valerie Steele turned to face her son and his girlfriend in the backseat. It seemed like only yesterday, she reminisced, that Zachary was nine years old and appearing in a professional production of *Oliver!* at the Hult Center—a renowned theater downtown across from the Hilton. Today, here he was with serious intent, bringing a very young girl home for Christmas.

"Yeah, I found a young one all right. One who hasn't been spoiled," Zachary boasted.

"Like finding a needle in a haystack?" his mother teased.

"Yeah!" the actor said, beaming.

"Zach tells us you're going to be in his new movie," Jim Steele interjected. "Better be careful, son. With her on the screen, nobody's going to be looking at you."

Everyone laughed, breaking the ice, making Bonnie Louise feel at ease.

"There's the Laurelwood Golf Club," Zachary's father announced. "Do you play golf, Bonnie?"

"No, sir."

"Well, if mother hadn't pushed him into that high-school production of *Our Town*, he'd probably be on his way to becoming the next Arnold Palmer."

"Good push, Mom!" Zachary complimented.

Bonnie Louise thrilled to the stories about Zachary's childhood. She loved the camaraderie the Steeles shared, and she wished that her own family weren't so far away. She had fantasized numerous ways of bringing them back into her life, but, sadly, she just couldn't see how any of them would work out. Zachary's parents were worldly, like the people she'd been meeting in Los Angeles. They wouldn't feel comfortable with her folks, and she knew her kin would feel uncomfortable with the Steeles.

"South won the ball game, son. I think they're gonna make a clean sweep this season."

Zachary turned to Bonnie Louise and informed her that he'd been a real jock—a football player, captain in fact, and a baseball player—he could hit the ball out of his high-school field.

As they reached the winding treelined driveway to the Steeles' modern, wood-and-glass home, Bonnie Louise realized that Zachary Steele was nothing like the press had painted him. He wasn't a big drinker, or somebody who liked to pick fights. She was even beginning to think that most of the stories linking him to one star or another were made up, just as he said they were. Zachary, she decided, was shy and kind and considerate, and she loved him with all her heart.

CHAPTER 42

*T*here is no complacency, B.J. told himself. Not when the devil's got you backed against a hellhole.

His bedroom had all the amenities. There was nothing it lacked except the most important element, Bonnie Louise.

B.J. felt himself being pulled in several directions at once. Like taffy, he stretched to accommodate Elizabeth, Savannah, and even the twins. Like taffy, he stretched in the opposite direction: He was ready to walk away from everything and everyone if he could have Bonnie Louise. He had stretched himself to the breaking point.

Life without Bonnie Louise wasn't worth living. He slumped down in front of the black marble fireplace, opened the black wrought-iron grating, and tossed in another log.

B.J. thought of Lara Miller. Why couldn't he have been passionate about her? Why did he have to get hooked by a nymphet?

"Shit," he muttered. "Virgins. Goddamn virgins . . ."

He took another belt of warm brandy. Smooth was harsh tonight. He coughed. Bonnie Louise was killing him. How could she love that stupid actor?

"Fuck you!" he toasted the air.

He heard Elizabeth outside his door, but he chose to ignore the intrusion. He knew full well she was far too polite to barge in. Tonight he wanted solitude.

The fire spit hot embers onto the border of the Persian carpet.

He stamped them out with his bare hand. The pain felt good in his inebriated state. It reminded him of his humanness. His vulnerability.

For the first time in his life B.J. felt adrift. He was CEO of

MCM, yet he didn't feel powerful. He was a frequent guest at the White House, always listed among the top 10 percent of the Fortune 500, but he felt utterly alone.

B.J. pushed himself up, wavering, catching his balance. Just before he reached the brandy, he bumped into the sharp edge of something. He reeled around and steadied himself. He opened his bathrobe to inspect the throbbing injury.

There it was. The real injured party—below the red welt, hanging shriveled and small. Even that, especially that, had betrayed him. The big-balls image he'd spent a lifetime trademarking was now mocking him. And all because of . . . His body succumbed; the brandy had won. B.J.'s eyes closed. He passed out, whispering, "Bonnie Louise."

Blue Moon was $2 million over budget and climbing. The gods seemed to be against the project. Lara wasn't looking forward to her lunch with Derek Middleton's agent, Barnie Kaplan.

Barnie was trying to woo more money out of MCM. B.J. said that there was no way he would look at *that* face over a meal. Besides, he was convinced that Barnie would get a major crush on Lara—and what better soldier to send into enemy lines? "Wear something that makes *you* feel sexy," was B.J.'s last contribution to the strategy of the forthcoming renegotiation.

Barnie Kaplan was probably the most unattractive man Lara Miller had ever met. The cruel nickname that was used behind his back was "Kermit." He actually did look like the green muppet wearing a pair of thick gold-rimmed glasses. Nevertheless, his sweet disposition swiftly overbore his extraordinarily ugly looks.

Lara wore a sexy, flowing suit designed by Laise Adzer. It was slightly slit up the front so that her shapely legs would tastefully expose themselves when she walked or sat down. Her blouse was of the finest silk, and she was very aware of her erect nipples as she used the raglan coat as a curtain for her personal peep show.

Barnie had booked a table at the Polo Lounge in the Beverly Hills Hotel. The infamous Polo Lounge, where people allegedly had themselves paged just to be noticed by all the power mongers who were enjoying the most expensive Cobb salad in the world.

As the maître d' escorted Lara through the dining room, she noticed a studio head sipping a double martini while smooth talking a deal to Billy Goldberg, the hottest director on the Hollywood block. She secretly wished that Goldberg were making movies for MCM instead of the competition.

Because it was a Friday, a pair of thin blond models, who looked like sisters but weren't, drifted among the tables wearing a succession of dresses that were remarkable, to Lara's eyes, for their imaginative bad taste.

As she approached the table, she noticed two women sitting with Barnie. One looked familiar. It was Derek Middleton's wife, the former Lady Rebecca Ward. She was an interesting beauty, with ravishing red hair the color of an Irish setter's and the wave to match. Her emerald-green eyes were full of mischievous sparks. She never wore makeup, because her face was covered with freckles.

"Lara," Barnie began, "you know Lady Rebecca. And this is her friend Annie."

Lara shook everybody's hand and winced from Annie's grip. To Lara, Annie looked like an English gym teacher.

Lady Rebecca beamed a large smile, showing her perfectly straight teeth—straight except for the small cuspids that framed her two front teeth. Lara found these crooked little imperfections charming.

"I do hope you don't mind me barging in on your lunch with Barnsey? Annie is visiting from England, and I thought it a godsent opportunity for her to meet some of the people Dekky works with."

"Barnsey" gave Lara a pathetic look of helplessness. It was obvious he had been steamrollered by this overbearing creature, whose brothers, sisters, and forebears, Barnie whispered, occupied a full page in *Debrett's Peerage*. Lara put her best behavior in gear to deal with the situation. Besides, her interest was being sparked by her memory . . . the racy history of this eccentric mother of seven beautiful children.

"Dekky talks about *you* all the time, Lara . . . about how he just couldn't do what he does without you. And how thoughtful you are . . . and helpful, even after business hours." Lady Rebecca smiled, a little too much.

"Well my job is twenty-four hours a day, seven days a week . . . no holidays. I grab what little time I can for my personal life."

"I bet you do, you poor dear."

Lara felt a bit uncomfortable without knowing why.

"Well, you seem to talk to him more than I do. And I'm his wife." Lady Rebecca laughed lightly.

"That may be true. I talk to everybody on location because B.J. wants to know every last detail," Lara explained. "And sometimes they don't really have much business to discuss . . . they just want to touch base with home."

Lara remembered the rumor that Lady Rebecca was the most discreet nymphomaniac on two continents. The vision of a passionate embrace between Lady Rebecca and Barnie flashed across Lara's mind. She suppressed a snicker.

"Oh, Annie, you must have the Cobb salad! This place is famous for it," said Lady Rebecca as she snatched the menu from her friend's hand. Annie mumbled agreement. Lara ordered the same, as did Barnie. Lady Rebecca ordered two scoops of cottage cheese, each one on a separate plate. She made a passing comment about her weight. Lara mused at her eccentricity.

When the waiter left, Lady Rebecca pulled out a large stack of photos and started passing them around the table. She had just returned from visiting friends in Australia.

"Here's Johnnie with his floaties on at John Havilott's. And here's Samantha swimming. Don't you love this shot of Augusta in my enormous sunglasses and beach hat?"

Lara looked harder when she heard the name "Havilott." As she recalled, Lord Havilott figured heavily in Kevin's fund-raising endeavors—and his daughter was Kevin's girlfriend.

Lady Rebecca—despite her reputation—was made for motherhood, Lara thought. She wondered how many of the little tots had been sired by Derek. They were all so different-looking. One or two were definitely his, but the one with black curly hair . . . This woman was so overpowering compared to Derek. In his daily life he was a wimpy sort although he suddenly became a dynamo on the set. Clearly this redhead ruled the roost.

"This is rather fun." Lady Rebecca handed Lara a photograph of five-year-old Augusta sitting on a beautiful blond woman's lap.

Pointing at the woman with short-cropped blond hair and a fabulous athletic body, she said, "That's Molly, John Havilott's daughter," and snatched it away again.

Lara couldn't help but be awed by the vast house in the background.

"Are you married, Lara?" Lady Rebecca broke into Lara's daydream as the waiter placed the two plates of cottage cheese on the crisp pink tablecloth.

"No. Not yet." Lara's tummy grumbled as she eyed her delicious salad.

"A woman as lovely as you must have someone in mind." Lady Rebecca probed a little deeper.

"Not really . . ." Lara hesitated, then admitted, "But there is someone I'm very fond of."

"Oh? Is he in this awful business, too?" Lady Rebecca showed her charming crooked teeth.

"Uh . . . yes, he is," Lara replied as Lady Rebecca put her children's pictures back in order as if they were a deck of playing cards. One would have thought she was about to shuffle and deal.

"Well," Lady Rebecca announced, "I have a little secret." She grinned, stretching her upper lip over her protruding little teeth. "Would you all like to hear a juicy bit of gossip?"

They all nodded their heads like children about to be told a bedtime story by the fairy queen.

"Well, then. Lean in, and I'll let you have it."

All present at the table leaned forward, hungrily awaiting the tidbits about to fall from Lady Rebecca's lips. She smiled and—as if to heighten their anticipation—delicately picked up a large scoop of cottage cheese. Then, still smiling, she turned to Lara and flung the whole dollop violently into her face.

"If you ever go near my husband again, I'll smash that face with something so hard you won't even recognize it!"

Lara sat in shock. Cottage cheese dripped from her face and hair. Barnie, white as chalk, had a look of horror on his face that Jim Henson would have paid thousands for. Lady Rebecca jumped to her feet, knocking her chair back against an occupied table. Her eyes darted around to make sure she had the attention of the entire room as she screamed out, *"We Englishwomen don't let trollops like you get away with your filthy little sex games forever, you know!"*

All eyes in the now-silent restaurant were fixed on the redhead, who moved to grab the second scoop of cottage cheese. Lara's hand shot across the table, knocking over a glass as she seized Rebecca's wrist and stood up. Her voice was hardly more than a whisper, but it could be heard across the room: "Try that again and I'll break your arm!"

She had Rebecca's wrist in both hands, twisting it as she spit the words in her face.

Ignoring the pain, Rebecca exploded words into Lara's face: *"You disgust me! Trying to smash up our happy home! And how dare you threaten me!"*

She was actually enjoying her own performance. A man stood up from the next table, wiping the splatterings of cottage cheese off his cashmere sports coat.

"Madam," he directed at Lady Rebecca, in his own English accent, "I was always taught that exposing one's private life"—he looked at Barnie—"in public was in rather poor taste."

Part of the restaurant agreed with him. Lady Rebecca grabbed her sweater and stormed toward the exit, Annie trailing close behind. When she reached it, she screamed, "Barnie! Are you coming with me?"

A woman yelled, "Go with her! Save your marriage! Get up!" A man shouted: "Don't go! Stay in your seat!"

Lara and Barnie sat there looking at each other in silence, stunned, as if they were locked in the same episode of *Twilight Zone*.

"Barnie!"

Barnie jumped to his feet and ran to the exit. Lara composed herself as best she could and gathered her things before standing up and walking calmly through the silence. Suddenly the whole place applauded her.

As she passed through the door to the inside part of the Polo Lounge, a splash of ice-cold water hit her in the face.

"Oh! And this one's from Molly Wenster! Stay away from her husband, too!"

Lara was about to hit her when suddenly something inside her head snapped. *Kevin Wenster married? Molly Havilott . . . Molly Wenster.* She froze.

Barnie and Annie grabbed Lady Rebecca's arms and ushered her out of the front door and through the lobby.

Lara was shaking uncontrollably. She picked up her bag and somehow found her way to the ladies' room across the main lobby.

The icewater felt warm compared to Lady Rebecca's revelation. The opal choker felt like a noose around her neck. Lara reached up, desperately pulling on the clasp until it opened. She stuffed the necklace inside her purse and made her way to a sink.

She looked into the mirror. There was cottage cheese all through her ebony hair, and her nipples stood erect through the soaked silk. She had never been so humiliated—first by an unfounded accusation and then by her lover's betrayal. She filled the small basin with warm water and started to dunk her head, trying to remove the curds from her hair.

She thought of Joan Souchek. "Kevin Wenster's a rogue," she remembered her former superior telling her. Had Joan slept with him? Lara wondered. Joan wasn't above sleeping with anyone who could lift her up to the next rung on the ladder. . . .

Lara raised her dripping head in disbelief. Why was this happening to her? Lady Rebecca was a raving lunatic. She wanted to get even with that English bitch for making people think that she, Lara Miller, was a home-wrecker. Then her heart sank; Kevin Wenster *was* married. . . . By the time Lara arrived home from the Polo Lounge she was disconsolate. Kevin Wenster had created the perfect illusion—he'd written the script and directed their affair, and she had played right into his hands.

Hindsight is twenty-twenty vision, she reminded herself, slipping out of her water-spotted, stained clothes. It was all so clear now: Kevin didn't want her to mention their affair to B.J. because he knew B.J. would tell her he was married. The perfect rogue, she lamented.

Grief-stricken, she took the fabulous opal necklace from her purse and buried it at the bottom of the linen closet. Much as she felt like grinding it through the garbage disposal, her practical nature prevailed. Someday she might choose to trade it in on another piece of jewelry—something she would enjoy wearing.

After a hot shower to remove the gummy flakes of cottage cheese still matted in her hair, Lara called her boss. She reported—accurately, she believed—that Derek Middleton's wife had so embarrassed them at the Polo Lounge that Barnie Kaplan wouldn't dare ask for any more money for his client.

McClintock couldn't help but be amused by Lady Rebecca's handiwork. "It's too bad it had to happen to you, Lara. You, of all people. But as long as the Derek Middleton demand has been put to bed, we can relax. Good work."

"Have you ever met Kevin Wenster's wife?" Lara asked.

"Oh God . . . don't tell me *she* was there, too?"

"In spirit, B.J. Definitely in spirit. I'll see you in the morning." She replaced the receiver before McClintock could delve deeper.

Lara wished she were the type of woman who could seek revenge—concoct a scheme to embarrass Kevin, humiliate him, show the world what a cheat and a liar he was . . . but it just wasn't in her nature to think that way. Deep down she believed that God would deal the Australian a hand as painful, if not more so, than what she was experiencing as a result of his deception.

At least, she decided, she'd find him and tell him off—get Kevin Wenster out of her system once and for all!

Lara called his home office in Sydney, and using B. J. McClintock's urgent need to speak to Mr. Wenster regarding a "personal matter," she was given two London phone numbers. She guessed that one was the apartment that Kevin said he shared with a group of international businessmen. He'd never given her that number, always saying that the best place to reach him was at the office.

London being nine hours ahead of Los Angeles made it just past midnight there. She dialed Kevin's apartment. He answered, clearly feeling no pain and listening to jazz. She wondered if he was alone.

"Kevin—it's your L.A. soul mate."

"My *what?*"

"Kevin, it's Lara."

"My God, luv! Let me turn the music down." He disappeared for a few moments and returned, asking, "How did you get this number?"

"Your *wife* sent it special delivery."

". . . oh, shit."

"My sentiments exactly." She hung up.

Tears streamed down Lara's cheeks. She loved Kevin Wenster, but there was no turning back. It was over . . . Painful as it was, moral compromise was not something she could live with.

She reflected on B.J., recalling his foolish, obsessive behavior over Bonnie Louise. The man was going to end up being ousted by his board of directors if he didn't start paying more attention to MCM business again.

Catching her sorrowful reflection in the bathroom mirror, Lara realized that she was equally a fool, though fortunately not as obsessive. Tough as it felt, she could close the book.

CHAPTER 43

Moviemaking, Carlo Capriotti discovered, was like skiing on top of an avalanche. It was thrilling, hideously unpredictable, and potentially devastating.

As dawn lighted up the World Trade Center like two mammoth bricks of gold, Carlo thanked God that they were finished shooting in New York. He couldn't wait to get Austria over and done with, so he could return to Malibu and put a tan back on his face.

As the stars' trailers pulled away, Carlo experienced a feeling he'd never had before. Up until an hour ago, for seven days, the street where they'd been shooting had been his, he thought. The shopkeepers, the kids on the block, even the old bums in their cardboard homes and doorways, recognized him—looked up to him. This feeling must be what they mean by "movie magic," he told himself, and he loved it.

"Mr. Capriotti?"

Carlo turned to find an old Italian cabdriver approaching him.

"Mr. Capriotti, my name is Tony. Mr. G. wants to see you right away."

"Fine. Tell him I'll call him as soon as I get to the hotel."

"No, Mr. Capriotti, I don't think you understand. Your chariot awaits you," he announced, gesturing toward his weathered yellow taxi.

The neophyte producer knew he had no choice. He would've preferred more comfortable accommodation, but at six in the morning the devil's chariot would, of course, look like a yellow taxi.

On the tape deck Caruso tugged at Capriotti's heartstrings with his soulful rendition of "*E lucevan le stelle*" from the third act of *Tosca*. The cab sped downtown toward Little Italy.

This is not a good sign, Capriotti warned himself. I must have done something wrong.

Carlo was surprised to find Giannelli in a satin smoking jacket and black tie, sitting at the same table they had had lunch at only a couple of months earlier.

"Sit, Mr. Producer." Giannelli gestured at the chair opposite him. "You look tired, Carlo. You could do with a small espresso, I think."

He had no sooner said the words than a cup of espresso was set before Carlo.

"Thank you, Mr. G., I do need some coffee." Carlo thought it politic to let the Don lead the conversation, and so he waited.

"You look hungry, too. Some eggs are coming for us to eat, also." Giannelli smiled.

"Well, actually, I am hungry. Eggs will be good."

"They will be, Carlo."

Carlo, already edgy, was beginning to get more so. He wished Giannelli would just come out and say what was on his mind.

"So, how's the movie going?" Giannelli asked casually, as if it were the last thing on his mind.

"Great! We're a little over budget, but that's normal for a feature this size. The weather has been against us most days. But I think we're soon going to make up for the overrun. . . ."

"Of two and a half million *dollars*," Giannelli said softly.

Carlo looked dumbfounded. His mouth was literally agape.

"Don't look so surprised, Carlo!" And with that Giannelli placed the budget sheets on the table and pushed them over to Carlo.

Carlo turned the pages, not believing what he was looking at. The Don had acquired the over-budget figures to the penny. And it was on *Blue Moon* stationery. This, Carlo realized, meant that there was a mole in the hole. But who?

"So, Carlo? Why didn't you tell me yourself? It would have been friendlier that way." The Godfather smiled.

"Well . . . I saw no reason at this point to . . . to alarm you unnecessarily, Mr. G."

"I don't get alarmed unnecessarily—only when people alarm me by hiding the truth."

"I didn't mean to hide anything from you."

"I know you didn't, my boy. It was an oversight. But now you need more money—am I right?"

"I may, yes, Mr. G.," Carlo answered.

"My people tell me that the proper amount could even be four million . . . yes?"

Carlo thought about the amount and knew that it might have to be that much if the production continued to run further behind, as seemed likely.

"Four million is very outside, Mr. G."

"You get up to four million, but I get twenty percent of your cut—for being a negligent producer, Carlo. My naughty boy."

Carlo wanted to jump across the table and rip the heart out of Giannelli's chest.

"But Mr. G.! Suppose we recover the lost time and we don't *have* any overrun by the end? Then I don't need to forfeit twenty percent?"

Mr. G. smiled. "The offer is good for today only, Carlo. My advice is, take it now. It may simply not be available, that four million, by the time the whole world knows that Producer Capriotti is in deep shit." The Don went on, "Let's just say this is not so much a loss for you as a lesson. You wanted to produce—so *produce*! Like a real *producer*! In the future, watch the money and make every cent work for us. Don't indulge others—at least not at our expense! *Capisci?*" The waiter brought the eggs.

"*Capisco*," Carlo agreed through clenched teeth.

"All right, let's eat," Giannelli said, leaning forward.

Carlo had lost his appetite. Twenty percent! This must be the most expensive breakfast going on in the entire world, he thought. But in another way, he figured he was lucky that Mr. G. hadn't found out about the MCM stock he'd been buying up, little by little. Carlo knew he should stay away from the market—but he knew also that MCM was becoming ripe for a takeover. Particularly if *Blue Moon* failed. If it didn't, his holdings would be that much more valuable.

"I know everybody thinks I'm stupid," he mused, "but what everybody doesn't know is that I should never be underestimated!"

CHAPTER 44

*M*ikey McClintock's red Porsche squealed right onto Lindacrest off Coldwater Canyon.

"Mikey! Cool it!" his twin brother, Danny, demanded. "Slow down so I can see the street signs."

"You know where we are, Danny."

"Yeah, but we don't want to wake up the whole neighborhood. Do we?"

The Porsche slowed, and they snaked around and up the streets, which were barely wide enough for cars to pass in opposite directions. It was, however, a moonless night, perfect for the twins' version of *Mission Impossible*.

Danny started laughing as he loaded his motor-driven Nikon F3 with high-speed recording film guaranteed to get a perfect image in the dark.

Mikey slammed on his brakes and swerved to the right, barely missing a Jeep Cherokee coming around a blind curve.

"Shit, Mikey! You're gonna get us creamed. Slow down!"

"Yeah, we wouldn't be guaranteed a pair of wings, would we?"

Danny instructed his brother to pull over and park. From here they could climb down the hill overlooking Ariba and Savannah's newly acquired Beverly Hills hideaway.

Dressed in fatigues from Banana Republic, the McClintock twins each deposited a mound of sparkling Peruvian flake cocaine on the hollow between their thumbs and forefingers.

"Bombs away!"

Simultaneously their noses vacuumed the white ego dust. Their front teeth and gums went numb. They were ready for an evening of erotic reconnaissance.

One after the other they hiked down the side of a hill that was too steep to build on. The high-pitched, wailful howl of a coyote triggered a round of barking from neighborhood dogs.

Mikey focused his binoculars and smacked his lips. "I think this is our lucky night. The tunas are unpacking boxes in their happy home."

Danny focused his binoculars and determined, "We have to get closer. There's a tree down there to the right. Let's go!"

The sound of twigs and dry leaves crunching mingled with more howling dogs and coyotes. Rabbits and raccoons and even deer were plentiful in these hills.

"Man"—Mikey shivered with excitement—"it's a jungle out here."

"Yeah . . . will you look at that!"

From their vantage point on the mountain they were facing the back of the house and the pool area, which was lighted by flood-lights.

They climbed an old oak tree and found a branch that could hold their weight. The house was in the Cliff May rambling California ranch-house tradition, one story wrapping around the pool. From their tree branch the poison dwarfs had a bird's-eye view of the whole damn place.

Danny checked his watch. It was a little past ten. Too early for the main event. It was frustrating, but then Savannah and Ariba were always good watching. Especially in their lace bikini panties.

During the next hour and a half the boys observed Savannah and Ariba unpacking boxes in the kitchen, the bedroom, and the living room. The intimate moments were close but not close enough. Nothing was film-worthy.

Danny was ready to pack it all in when Mikey spotted Ariba unwrapping a huge dildo. She brandished it at Savannah, who squealed so loud they could hear her in the tree.

"Danny, get back up here! They're getting ready to slam some tuna! Oh, whee!"

"No shit?"

"Oh my God!" Mikey enthused.

They watched as Ariba chased Savannah into the living room and pinned her down on the oversized red velvet sectional, dildo in hand.

"There's no mistaking who's the guy in this relationship," Danny observed.

Savannah wrapped her legs around Ariba's waist. The two women mashed mounds into each other as their tongues danced together.

"Holy fuck!" Danny exclaimed. "I don't believe this!"

"I can't focus! I can't focus!"

"Mikey, you're steamin' up the fuckin' lens."

"Oh my God. She's puttin' it in her."

"Oh no! Oh no!" Mikey moaned.

"What is it?"

"I'm getting a boner, man."

"Give me the fuckin' camera!"

Danny reloaded the camera. When he looked through the telephoto lens, it allowed him to be in the *same room with the tunas*. He clicked off a roll and reloaded again.

"Mikey, will you stop humping the tree! The pictures are gonna be blurred."

"Fuck you, Danny. This is the hottest thing I've ever seen in my life!" He moaned, rubbing his bulging fatigues against the oak bark while pushing the binoculars into his eye sockets.

At the height of Mikey's passion the writhing beauties slid down to the floor and disappeared between the couch and the coffee table.

Danny cursed, "Get back up there, you fuckin' tunas!"

Mikey groaned and fell against the tree trunk, dropping the binoculars to the ground. His body spasmed as he clutched the tree branch.

"Hey, Mikey—which one did it for you?"

"Fuck you, iron man."

"That's the difference between you and me, Mikey. You've got no control. You blow your wad on a tree. I'm gonna blow it in their faces."

"Yeah, well I'm one up on you. I'm doing both."

"That's not the point. It's control. Oh, oh, the fish are surfacing."

With a grin on his face Danny clicked off another three rolls of film: the girls kissing and fondling while pressing up against a doorway, Savannah giving Ariba head on a chaise longue next to the pool, and a few choice moments in between. Danny had a boner, too, but he never told his brother.

"We've got 'em right where we want 'em," Danny concluded with confidence.

On that note, with six rolls of memories, the two evil Peeping Toms slipped back to their Porsche and headed for their guarded, gated Bel Air domicile.

CHAPTER 45

*L*ara walked into B.J.'s office waving a computer printout. She slid the folded papers in front of her boss and waited.

B.J. became more and more agitated as he calculated the number of MCM shares that had been purchased by a company called Tritek International.

"Tritek International . . . ?" he spit. "Who the hell *are* these people?"

"I'm glad you're finally interested."

"Interested, hell! These pirates have come in the back door. Look at this!" he said, pointing at the lines Lara had highlighted in red. "Over the last six months Tritek International—whoever the hell they are—have methodically bought two million shares."

"As of yesterday, that makes *five percent*. They've got nine days to declare."

"Tritek International . . ." B.J. repeated, trying to jog his memory. He'd heard the name, but he couldn't recall in what context. Was it foreign or domestic? Something he'd read about?

Corporate takeovers, B.J. reminded himself, were a devil's game. He was going to nip this one in the bud! He checked the time.

"I want the name of every asshole sitting on Tritek's board. And every other fucking person working there," he seethed. "Run it through personnel and check to see if any of them worked for us. How long will it take you?"

Lara looked at her watch—10:15 A.M. "I'll push for one P.M."

Lara stood there getting off on the adrenaline rush she got from doing business with B.J. She couldn't wait to ferret out the hostile suitor. Sneaky bastard, she thought. Whoever it is has been inching his way in for a long time. But he forgot one vital detail—when you were as well connected as B.J., somebody would tip you off.

"There's something I have to do," he said offhandedly. "I'll be back."

"Oh . . . then I'll see you around one?"

"I don't know. I'll check in."

Lara was astonished by his lack of concern. One minute he was focusing on the company he'd founded, and the next he was on autopilot, going God knew where.

"B.J." Lara implored, "maybe Gordon Stanwick can find out who owns Tritek."

"That's good, Lara. Let me think about it."

"Forgive me, but I don't think you have time to 'think about it,'" she warned. "Otherwise this marauder's going to walk in here and sit in that chair!"

B.J. eyed his chair and firmly stated, "Nobody is going to walk in here and sit in my chair but me! You calm down, Lara darlin'. Don't you worry about your head rolling with a new regime, 'cause there ain't gonna be one! Now, get me those answers!"

Lara watched him leave. She retrieved the computer printouts, wondering what was behind B.J.'s restructuring plan. There was no reason she could think of to sell off the radio and TV stations in the South. The Australian mining operation was running at a loss. Selling that made sense.

B.J. had always known what he was doing, but lately Lara was beginning to wonder. Even she had warned him about MCM being ripe for a takeover. Anytime a corporation started selling off assets like radio and TV stations, it made waves. Waves that reverberated around the international marketplace.

No, it didn't surprise Lara that Tritek was trying to turn the tables. MCM had $150 million in its coffers, the studio property was worth close to that amount, plus they'd just made the richest syndication deal in history. It was no wonder that someone wanted in.

B.J. had been waiting for this day. Bonnie Louise was finally back from location-scouting with Zachary, and he had to see her. Even if it was only from a distance.

He drove to an alley in Santa Monica and started counting garage doors. When he got to five, he put his Rolls in "park," got out, unlocked the padlock, and threw the garage door up.

He grinned at the white 1971 Cadillac convertible. He had been lucky to find it in great condition. A paint job and new brakes, not a lot to ask, he reasoned. Finding this beauty with only 56,542 miles on her had been a real stroke of fortune.

After carefully backing it out, he drove the Rolls in and locked the garage. This is going to be fun, he told himself. I've been waiting two months for this.

He climbed behind the wheel and cruised up Montana—past the posh little shops that reminded him of the Upper West Side of New York.

When he passed the Brentwood Country Mart, his heart started beating faster. "Bonnie Louise . . . Bonnie Louise," he repeated.

He loved the way his lips felt when he formed the *B* in Bonnie. And the tender way his tongue touched the back of his front teeth when he said, "Louise."

For the first time this year he felt signs of life below his lizard-skin belt. He turned onto Bristol, drove halfway up the block, and parked. He slid over to the passenger side, opened the glove compartment, and pulled out a beat-up golf hat and a cheap pair of sunglasses.

Wearing his disguise, he slumped down and reclined across the front seat. He would wait. The detective he had hired had done a thorough job. He knew the Spanish house across the street was costing Zachary Steele twelve thousand dollars a month. Big house, he observed. Well, Zach, if you're doing it for *her* sake, don't worry. You won't have to much longer.

Ten minutes later a stretch limo pulled into Zach's driveway and parked. The chauffeur opened the door, and out stepped Zachary Steele, followed by Bonnie Louise.

B.J. let out an audible sigh. "Oh, baby," he moaned, "your hair's gotten so long."

He crawled back to the driver's side, wishing he had a pair of binoculars. She looked different. She still had the same long legs and arms, but there was something different about her. He couldn't put his finger on it.

As he watched her walk inside the house, he realized that she had made that once-in-a-lifetime transition. Bonnie Louise had become a woman, and he hadn't been there to see it. His little girl was a woman, and he felt cheated.

CHAPTER 46

*S*avannah rolled over and peered at the digital clock on the night table. The sun was high for a good reason. It was one-thirty.

Ariba was in no mood to get up. This was the first break she'd had from touring and recording in a year. This was the first day of her one-month holiday. She'd need that long to plan her next move toward a feature film. Ariba could taste the renaissance acclaim that Cher had so rightly achieved. She wanted it all.

Her *Ariba* album had won her an American Music Award and three Grammys, and she'd won Best Rock Video at the MTV Awards. She was as hot as she could get. But she was smart enough to know that staying there would take planning. She wanted to burn her voice, style, and image onto the public's consciousness.

Savannah stopped squeezing orange juice when she heard Ariba cursing in Portuguese and rummaging through tapes.

"Ariba, what are you looking for?"

"My Uoakti percussion tape! I had it last night."

"It's in the car. I'll get it for you."

Ariba smiled and shook her bare ass in a gesture of deep appreciation.

"Muito obrigado, Vanna bebĕ."

Savannah tightened up the belt on her terry-cloth robe and made her way down the driveway to the carport. Ariba's new black-on-black Corvette was not Savannah's first choice. She'd have preferred a Jaguar XJ6 convertible.

As she popped the tape out of the deck, she noticed a manila envelope on the windshield. On her way to the house she marveled at how far fans would go to touch the life of a star. It made her feel uneasy, knowing that someone had got past the security system and through the electric gates.

Ariba put the tape on. She needed a music fix more than anything in the morning. She took the envelope and asked, "What's this?"

"I don't know, probably an amorous fan. The scary part is they left it on your car, which means they must've climbed the gates."

"You're keeding."

Ariba opened the envelope. She inhaled with a sound not unlike a death rattle. There before her in sharp focus and in crisp black and white was an 8 × 10 of Ariba sucking Savannah's muff, dildo in hand.

Savannah shrieked, "That was last night! What're we going to do? I'm calling the police!"

"Are you nuts?"

Ariba ripped open the envelope and found a note with a number. Savannah rattled on hysterically about this being the end to her career and most likely her inheritance. Ariba silenced her with a slap across her cheek.

"Stop it! We are in control. They want money." Ariba laughed and said, "Last night was an expensive night."

Savannah sobbed, "Your career will go down the toilet."

Disgusted, Ariba dialed the typewritten number. Savannah ran to the kitchen phone to listen.

A young male voice said hello.

"I received the package. What do you want?"

"Well, I think we should talk about a negotiation. We showed them to *Penthouse* this morning, and *they* offered us a hundred grand. Can you match that?"

Ariba and Savannah exchanged looks of horror. Savannah lost control.

"I don't have that kind of money," she wailed.

"But, Savannah, you can always go to Daddy."

Savannah jolted upright. "Mikey McClintock, I'm gonna rip your head off! You lowlife slime bucket! I'm gonna call Daddy and tell him you're trying to blackmail *me*, your own sister."

Mikey casually said, "I'm quaking with fear. There's nothing I'd rather see than *our* father picking out his favorite shots." He laughed lasciviously.

"You're really serious. . . ." Savannah realized, panicking.

Ariba jumped in, asking, "What's your bottom line for the negatives?"

Another male voice came on and said, "One night with you two doing our bidding."

Ariba smiled. "You got it, *bebě*. Tonight! Bring all the negatives."

Savannah could be heard screaming uncontrollably in the background.

"What time?" the boy asked.

"Eight o'clock . . . the champagne will be cold."

Ariba hung up. The poison dwarfs, as Savannah so rightly called them, had gone too far this time. She walked over to her hysterical lover and took her by the shoulders.

"Stop it, Vanna! They cannot hurt you. Trust me."

Savannah had never trusted the twins, and now she didn't trust the situation. If her mother found out that she and Ariba were lesbians, that would be the end of their relationship. Her mother would never forgive her. Elizabeth McClintock was counting on her only blood child to marry a man and give her grandchildren. And Savannah didn't want her father to know, either. She sobbed and sobbed and sobbed, never allowing herself to admit to Ariba just how much her parents' opinion really mattered to her.

CHAPTER 47

*M*ikey and Danny had had to make a special trip to their dealer. The boys needed drugs if they were going to pull off their sweet blackmail seduction. Beneath the individual bravado both sixteen-year-olds prayed that the negatives would insure safe passage from negotiation to consumation. They knew Ariba was crafty, and Savannah hated their guts. Going in, that would make anybody nervous, they concluded.

With numb gums and egos the size of the city, they spent the afternoon in lustful anticipation. They argued over the negatives. Danny insisted they hold one roll back . . . just in case . . . for insurance. . . .

Mikey, whose integrity could fit in the belly button of a flea said, "No, a deal is a deal."

They almost came to blows over who would take Ariba and who would take Savannah. They both wanted Ariba first. Finally they agreed to be gentlemen and flip a coin. Danny won, as usual.

They fought over which cologne to wear. Should it be Ralph Lauren's Polo or Calvin Klein's Obsession? Mixing scents, they agreed, would be a catastrophe. If they looked the same and smelled the same, the girls wouldn't know them apart. They flipped the coin again. Polo took the honors.

Dressed in their coolest Lauren jeans and jackets, they arrived at the love nest, negatives in hand. They sat there waiting for the electric gates to open. Puberty on one side, manhood on the other.

"God, I'm hard, and we haven't even gone through the gate."

"Mikey, beat it down."

"I can't! I can't believe we're actually gonna do it. You know what I mean? I mean, I've had a boner for Savannah as long as I can remember. Even when she was fat. I know what's gonna happen. I'm gonna come, and then I'm gonna die."

"You're probably right."

The electric gate swung open, and Danny drove inside and parked. Both boys took a deep breath.

"Negatives?"

"Negatives."

"Condoms?"

"Condoms."

They slapped five, had one more hit of coke, and got out of the car.

Savannah and Ariba were dressed for the occasion. Ariba wore a red lace bustier, skintight black stretch pants, and spike-heeled black boots. Savannah played the soft southern belle in a pale pink stretch knit miniskirt with a pale pink *charmeuse* chemise. Earrings with strand upon strand of tiny beads and ornaments clicked against each other when she moved her head.

The atmosphere was perfect. Dim lighting, votive candles burning brightly around the room. Suddenly the twins were seized with fear. There was something about Ariba that overpowered them. She seemed cordial enough, but there was something underlying her hospitality.

Ariba produced a chilled bottled of Cristal champagne and poured four glasses. There was mistrust on both sides.

They clicked glasses and toasted to concluding their business. Danny made the first move—he dropped the negatives on the glass coffee table. Ariba looked at them and, masking her emotions, smiled. She looked Danny square in the eye and asked, "Is this all of them?"

Simultaneously the boys said, "Yes."

"How do I know you didn't"—she gestured with her hands and leaned toward them—"save something. A leetle souvenir?"

"Because we made an honest deal with you, that's why."

"Then a deal is really a deal, no?" Ariba cocked her head.

"Yes," they chimed in unison.

Savannah coolly inspected the negatives. Ariba picked up the twins' glasses and danced over to the bar. She turned up the music—her latest CD.

"We gonna party!" she called to the group.

"You two really surprised me," Savannah told them. "I had no idea you were so clever, you little devils."

As Ariba handed them their refills, she blew them a kiss. She winked at Savannah, who continued to question Mikey and Danny about their knowledge of photography. Who taught them? How did they find the perfect vantage point? Had they ever considered working for *National Geographic*?

The teenagers gulped their second glasses of champagne and

boasted about how they strategically made their way down the hill and up the tree. It was a piece of cake.

Savannah laughed and moved closer to the matching human bookends. "Let's get down to business." She giggled and leaned into Mikey.

Ariba gyrated over and shimmied in Danny's face. She reached down and grabbed his hard, denim-trapped cock.

"Oh, is theese for me?"

"Yeah," he said as he was sucked into Ariba's magnetic field.

Gripping his stuffed stone-washed jeans at the crotch, she pulled Danny to his feet and started to dance. She threw her arms around his neck and began gyrating, grinding her pelvis into his thigh.

"Oh, *bebĕ*, you got rhythm."

Danny was in ecstasy. Somehow the champagne had made his insecurities and anxieties disappear. He felt as if he were floating. How could he have mistrusted the hottest piece of chocolate on planet earth? She was a businesswoman, and yeah, she was hot for him! He reached inside her bustier and felt her soft breasts with their dark, erect nipples.

Just then Ariba unzipped his designer jeans and grabbed his stiff cock. Danny quickly flashed to baseball statistics—RBIs—to stop himself from coming.

Meanwhile, on the couch, Savannah was engaged in a most demanding acting role. Using her long, fine nails, she artfully stroked Mikey's denim-covered erection.

Mikey reached for her breast, but she stopped him. "No, not yet. We've got the whole night, Mikey."

Hearing her sensuous voice sent his body into spasms. He fell back into the pillows of the couch just as his brother collapsed on the floor. Mikey wanted to speak, but nothing was coming out of his mouth. He watched in horror as Ariba clapped her hands, and two huge black men appeared. Mikey's eyes rolled back in his head, and he was gone.

Ariba shrieked victoriously. She told her bodyguards to dispose of the black-hearted little pricks. She reminded the men not to physically harm the boys in any way. They were only sixteen. Jailbait for a girl over eighteen.

Savannah began crying. This whole mess was just too much for her. She hated the twins!

Ariba consoled her. "Don't worry, *bebě*. After tonight, theese nasty leetle boys weel be locked up. You watch!"

Danny opened his eyes to flashing red and blue lights and a crowd of spectators. A photographer's flash momentarily blinded him.

Mikey opened his eyes when he heard the police arguing with the fire department about how to get them down. They both looked down and realized they were buck naked, tied to each other, and strung ten feet off the ground in a net at the corner of Santa Monica Boulevard and Rodeo Drive.

They were dead meat.

CHAPTER 48

*T*he upheavals in B. J. McClintock's life had forced Lara Miller to take a quantum leap into his shoes. And they seemed to fit just fine.

Lara leaned back and stretched. She surveyed her living room, noting the piles of MCM papers she had stacked on the carpet. For a moment she imagined them growing, multiplying, burying her.

A loud buzzing noise startled her. She had set her alarm clock for three A.M., thinking that she'd catch a few hours' sleep after the eleven o'clock news. Unfortunately, once again she'd worked straight through.

On the call sheet there were three messages for B.J. from Holly Dandridge, the third marked URGENT. Now what? Lara wondered. *Urgent* was a word used loosely in Hollywood.

Now that *Blue Moon* was on location in Austria, Colin and Holly were being put up at Vienna's elegant Hotel Bristol. In Lara's dealings with the actress, she'd found her easy to work with, certainly reasonable . . . except when it came to Colin O'Brien.

She punched the overseas phone number and waited. The sound of distant crackling static that had made her feel romantic and sexy only a week earlier, now gave her a sinking feeling, as she thought of Kevin Wenster.

"Hotel Bristol," a crisp Austrian male voice announced.

"Holly Dandridge, please."

"Ringing."

"Hello," Holly said tersely.

"Good morning . . . or . . . I should say afternoon. It's Lara."

"Thank God! Finally! I feel like I'm on the moon with all these fucking men out here bossing me around."

"What's the problem, Holly?" Lara asked evenly.

"Derek wants my stunt double to do all the car-chase scenes with Colin." Her voice grew louder and more emotional as she accused, "Colin's put him up to it! I know it, Lara. I've done a million chase scenes—that son of a bitch wants me out so he can look like Mr. Macho Stud for the press."

"Hold it, Holly! Austria in winter can be treacherous. If it's anything but a clear day, neither one of you will be doing it."

After a thoughtful pause Holly concluded, "I'll agree to that, Lara . . . just as long as I'm sitting next to that asshole *on the clear day.*"

Giggles permeated the line. First Lara and then Holly. The giggles grew into laughter and the tension dissipated.

"Jesus, Lara, you know I wrote the script, and these guys muscle me all day long. They treat me like I'm some bimbo. I'm outnumbered."

"Not anymore, Holly. You've got me."

"Well, that's the truth. Where the hell has B.J. been?"

"Cleaning up a personal mess. It's just too much to go into right now."

Holly sighed and said, "I can't wait until you're officially running the whole damn studio!" Loud banging interrupted the actress's train of thought.

"Oh, my God, lunch is banging at the door, Lara. Gotto go! Love ya! Call Derek right now and get me in that scene!"

Lara wasn't surprised when she heard the line click off. Holly was a singleminded woman who usually got her way.

It would be better if B.J. called Derek, Lara warned herself. Then without another thought she picked up the phone and placed the overseas call. Come hell or high water, she thought, I'm not going to let *Blue Moon* be compromised by its stars.

The doorbell rang. Lunch! Holly had called room service a short while earlier. She tightened the belt on her pink satin robe and opened the door.

There, pushing the cart into the room, was Hans, the cutest waiter in the hotel. Holly watched his ass as he wheeled the silver-covered dishes over to the window and began setting up the table.

Hans, she thought, had been making discreet eyes at her for the past week as he had brought in the breakfast trays in the morning and the dinner trays at night. The young Austrian had combined these glances with an exaggerated politeness that had signaled her libido.

"Would you perhaps like me to serve you, *madame*?" he asked.

"Please," Holly replied, sashaying over to the table.

"Are you lunching alone today, *madame*?"

"Yes, all alone." Holly looked into his brown eyes as she held up her plate for the young man to serve her.

"Spaghetti Bolognese," he announced. Hans took the serving forks, scooped up a healthy amount of pasta, and aimed for her plate.

Holly jerked her plate as if to intercept the pasta, but instead it fell into her lap. Hans gasped, and bent over to help. He stopped short when he realized that retrieving the food meant touching the famous actress on her most private area.

"It's okay, Hans. Have you had your lunch?" Holly asked him.

"No, *madame*. I have not eaten today." He smiled at her.

Holly leaned back and untied her robe, partly exposing her perfect 34B breasts.

"Do you like spaghetti, Hans?"

"I love spaghetti, *madame*." And with that, he dropped to his knees and sucked a piece of the pasta through his lips. Holly let out a squeal and ran her hands through his wavy brown hair. She pulled his face to her left nipple, and he happily played with it.

He ran his tongue down her torso, then pushed it through her pubic hair and the Bolognese sauce. She pushed her pelvis against his chin and tightened her grip on his hair.

Lust! thought Holly. I love it! She had been having fantasies about the boy for the past week. Now, it was a dream come true —the most exciting lunch she'd had since she'd been in Austria.

CHAPTER 49

B.J. was outside, chipping golf balls with his Ping nine iron, when Evey's voice shattered his concentration.

"I'll be settin' the table outside, Mr. McClintock," she said crisply, gesturing toward the veranda. "Too beautiful a day to waste eatin' indoors."

He put down the club and checked his watch. He had exactly one hour before he teed off at the Bel Air Country Club with Morton Shipp, Mario Pasuco, and Billy Goldberg, Hollywood's latest fair-haired filmmaker.

Billy Goldberg, like Steven Spielberg, B.J. marveled, was a

torch-bearer of the American Dream. The filmmaker had begun his studio career in the mail room and had managed to spark an executive's interest in his student film. Goldberg had just turned twenty-six, and he had already made two feature films that each grossed over $100 million at the box office.

B.J. savored the thought of signing Goldberg to a long-term contract. "Mayer gave Thalberg a building at MGM," he rehearsed, "Universal gave Spielberg a building, and I'll see that you have *the Goldberg Building* at MCM if—" He stopped himself. *If Zachary Steele thinks he's got the girl and he thinks he's got the director—he's dreaming. When I get through making an offer that Goldberg can't refuse, Steele will be frantically looking for a director to bail out that piece of shit film,* Blizzard. *Your luck is momentary, punk. This is the big league!*

The sun was already too high, he noted, as he padded his way up the stairs to breakfast. He moved the umbrella to shade the table, then gutted Sunday's *L.A. Times*, angrily sifting out the glossy ads, the Food section and the Classifieds.

Evey poured him a cup of coffee. "Mrs. McClintock be down for breakfast this mornin'?"

"No. I think you'd better send up a tray, Evey."

"Is that woman *ever* comin' down for breakfast again?"

Evey had worked for them so long, she was family.

"I'm sure she will, one of these days." He buried his nose in the Calendar section to avoid discussing his wife's increased preference for seclusion.

"One more thing, Mr. McClintock. Miss Savannah said she won't be able to make tennis later today. And the boys have gone to the beach."

"Fine, Evey."

B.J. lifted the cup to his lips and took a sip of scalding black coffee. He spit the burning liquid back into the cup and slammed it against the saucer.

"Jesus Christ, Evey! Did you heat this with nuclear power?"

"I'm sorry, Mr. McClintock," she apologized. "You were so long comin' to the breakfast table from the yard that I reheated it in the microwave."

"Don't do it again, Evey," he said, running his tongue across his scorched lips and opening Section One of the newspaper.

"No, sir, I won't be doin' that again."

B.J. looked down. There in the lower left-hand corner of page two was a photograph of Bonnie Louise and Zachary Steele at LAX. The caption read, "Zachary Steele and fiancée Bonnie Louise had to be rescued by security guards when they were mobbed by fans at Los Angeles International Airport."

Slowly B.J. got to his feet. Blood rushed to his face. His fists clenched the paper until his knuckles showed white.

Fiancée? he screamed to himself, the word echoing through his brain. His Bonnie Louise marrying Zachary Steele was preposterous! It would never happen. He would see to it, if nothing else, that the nuptial ceremony would never take place.

CHAPTER 50

*I*t was another scorching, suffocating day on location in California's Mojave Desert. Lara Miller had even informed the film's stars and its director that B.J. was threatening to drive down to Joshua Tree to oversee the rest of the shoot unless they wrapped it up by the end of the week.

Derek Middleton had directed fourteen motion pictures, and not one of them had been beset by so many problems: unusually bad weather, food poisoning, and the flu; in New Orleans, a demolition truck had exploded; the developing lab had misplaced two reels of film for a week; and Colin and Holly had got to the point where they couldn't speak unless they were running lines.

Every minute had been *pressure*, and as far as Derek was concerned, Prince Carlo was a major part of the problem. From the beginning, Derek thought, Capriotti had distanced himself from the realities of filmmaking. The producer—a title Derek did not think reflected the capabilities of Carlo Capriotti—was always apologizing for his blunders, then going on to ballyhack something else. All Derek Middleton wanted to do was pack up his skeleton crew and head back to civilization.

Colin had made his directorial debut by talking Derek into letting him direct the second-unit footage. On this particular day they had trekked into the desolate expanse of the desert at the foot of Squaw Tank, about five miles northeast of their campsite, in the heart of Joshua Tree National Monument.

Hot, dusty, and sweaty from the day's work, Colin and Derek had taken refuge in a huge tent at the edge of the campground. The ice had melted in the sweltering heat, so the beer was warm, but they didn't care. At this point, any beer at any temperature was nectar.

They were having a heated "difference of opinion" over the script notes when Adam trudged inside, slammed his beer bottle on the folding table, and flopped into a chair.

"Good evening," Colin welcomed him.

"What's so bloody good about it?"

"Straighten up, Snow!" Derek directed. "You never had it so good."

"Don't start giving me that shit, Derek," he hissed back.

Colin had more important business matters on his mind. He turned to Adam. "Stop whining," he insisted. "You sound like an English schoolboy.

"Hey," Adam came back belligerently, "you're the one who's got it easy, Colin. When *he* yells, 'Cut!'—you're free. You have your way no matter what! I'm sick of the whole bloody mess!"

Derek folded his files. "We can go over these after dinner. I'm taking a nap," he said, and headed for his tent.

On his way out, Derek shot Adam a stern look. "Grow up— without Colin, you wouldn't have the possibility of getting a green card, *and* John Williams would be scoring the sound track."

"Thanks, Mum. I needed that."

Colin wondered just how many beers Adam had put down that day. Too many, he guessed.

"Adam, you can be such an asshole sometimes. Come on, let's run some of that alcohol out of your system." He stood up.

"One more beer first."

Colin pulled Adam out of the chair. "Come on—we're gonna run!"

The two men began jogging toward the heart of a gorge. Large, smooth rocks and boulders jutted toward the sky on either side of them.

"Slow down!" Adam yelled.

"Come on!" Colin called behind him. "Just a little further."

Ten minutes later the mountains appeared to converge up ahead. Colin stopped.

"Oh great!" Adam complained. "A dead end."

"Not really. Follow me through one of Mother Nature's glorious cracks." He winked and proceeded to push his body sideways through the narrow crevice. Adam followed.

When they reached the other side, Colin watched Adam's face react to the overwhelming view.

"My God, it's positively prehistoric," Adam whispered.

"Yeah."

Surrounding the two wonderstruck men was the image of huge boulders and flat stones ranging in diameter from three to thirty feet, mirrored in a pool that looked to be about a half-mile in diameter.

The sky went from cobalt to robin's-egg blue as the sun edged its way below the horizon. A hawk's image was reflected as it glided on the soft, still air above the glassy water. Frogs could be heard croaking to each other from far-away distances.

Colin smiled. "Pretty amazing, huh?"

Adam grinned. "Let's dive in."

"Hold on . . . it looks pretty deep."

"Yeah, I forgot. I'll check it out," Adam volunteered.

He peeled off his sweat-saturated T-shirt and shorts and waded in. Then, lowering his whole body, he closed his eyes and let his anxieties fly away with a flock of birds flapping quietly across the surface of the lake.

"Come on, Colin—how'd you find this place?"

"One of the location managers brought me up here yesterday."

"Good God, it's like bathwater," Adam exulted. "Look, it stops at my waist. It's not deep at all."

Colin hesitated. "Walk around—it might drop off."

Adam walked in a wide circle. He knew Colin suffered from hydrophobia, which he'd developed as a child because he was unable to float.

"What do you want? An engraved invitation? Get in here!"

Thoughtfully Colin unlaced his Reeboks. "One of these days I'm gonna learn how to swim."

Naked, he cautiously lowered himself into the still water. "Wow, the bottom's so smooth."

"Over here! I've found the perfect spot," Adam called.

The two men perched themselves on a submerged rock and quietly absorbed the majesty of Mother Nature.

Finally Colin broke the silence. He lovingly wrapped his hand around Adam's neck and whispered, "I've missed you."

Adam tilted his head and kissed Colin on the side of his neck.

Colin turned his face toward Adam and their lips met, parted. His fingers gently followed the contours of Adam's chest and stomach, then moved lower, to close in a folding caress.

CHAPTER 51

*C*laiming Mikey and Danny at the Beverly Hills Police Station in the middle of the night was just one more thing that helped to shatter B.J.'s rosy, well-ordered view of the world. Now, demons pursued him relentlessly day and night.

Elizabeth had all but barricaded herself in her bedroom. She felt that the twins' outrageous behavior was a repudiation of her abilities as a mother. She had tried to instill decent values in them, but these boys had defied her in every way. Apparently they had no respect for adults, or for rules and regulations. They no longer resembled boys so much as furies, elements of a storm.

B.J. had reached the end of his rope. He only had to mention the boys to trigger his wife's tears. Savannah had been warning him about her brothers for over a year. Funny, he reflected, they hadn't seemed so bad. They were arrogant and cocky like their peers, but they were brighter than most, and they had been funny as well.

B.J. hadn't seen their attitude problem as symptomatic of something larger until he'd had to bail them out of jail. Now, he viewed it as a festering disease. If he didn't lock them up and twist their values back into shape pretty fast, he'd be paying for their follies for the rest of his life.

He assigned Lara the task of finding a good, strict boarding school that would coerce the boys into reshaping their lifestyles and attitudes. Unfortunately the national scandal sheets had a field day; *People* magazine and even the *L.A. Times* ran blurbs. "Naked boys netted in Beverly Hills." They had one year left before high-school graduation, and B.J. was going to make sure it changed them forever!

Elizabeth confided their dilemma to Father Malcomb, who in turn informed the bishop, who placed a call to the archbishop, and before it was all over, the cardinal had been consulted.

St. Bartholomew's, located outside of Newport, Rhode Island, was the cardinal's first choice. He wrote a letter of recommendation, giving the McClintock family high marks for their charitable acts and continuous financial support to the church.

Armed with the cardinal's letter and his own checkbook, B.J. flew to Rhode Island. The weather, as it turned out, was warmer than his reception at St. Bartholomew's.

"I'm sorry you've come all this way, Mr. McClintock," Headmaster McBride, a grim-faced, gray-haired ex-marine who reminded B.J. of Oliver North, informed him. "Daniel and Michael McClintock are not St. Bart's material."

B.J. was unfazed by McBride's reaction. He knew everyone had a weak spot. Usually it was money.

"Mr. McBride," he said politely, "I have a letter here from the cardinal." He handed it to him. "Before you close the door, I think we should look at what we have to offer one another."

McBride read the letter and set it down. He handed B.J. St. Bartholomew's book of rules and regulations. It was thick, and from its well-used feel, was referred to frequently.

B.J. liked the prisonlike atmosphere of the school. There was no way in hell that Mikey and Danny could breathe without asking permission.

Under daily duties he noted that beds had to be made prior to leaving for classes. Curfew was 9:00 P.M. Staying out after curfew was a major infraction of the rules.

Fraternizing with others after curfew fell into the same serious category as cheating and stealing.

B.J. was beginning to enjoy the book of rules and regulations. "This looks very fair," he said, a bogus touch of sincerity in his tone.

"According to Daniel and Michael's transcripts, they have only average grades . . . the only sport they've competed in is tennis . . . no other extracurricular activities . . . and a number of disciplinary problems."

B.J. fingered the dog-eared rules and regulations book, avoiding the headmaster's eyes by reading further. Weekend passes had to be applied for no later than noon on Thursday. Anyone applying after that would be denied permission. Leaving the premises without permission resulted in immediate, irreversible expulsion.

"St. Bartholomew's is *exactly* what I'm looking for, Mr. McBride."

"From the look of their transcripts and the publicity, I fully understand why. I doubt, however, that they would last one full week here."

Okay, B.J. surmised, you want to play tough Vatican ball. You're on.

"In all deference to you, sir, my sons are exceptionally bright, capable young men. Under the right circumstances—in a perfectly structured environment like this—I know they will become exemplary students."

The stiff, staunch, former military man sneered back across his desk at the power broker from sunny California, "What makes you so certain, Mr. McClintock?"

"You know, I'd be willing to wager—say, something the school needs—just to prove the twins have what it takes to make it here."

The headmaster reexamined the cardinal's letter urging him to accept Daniel and Michael McClintock for redemption. He shifted his body and motioned toward a blueprint pinned to the right of his desk.

"Is that a renovation?" B.J. inquired.

The wily headmaster sniffed a major coup. "This," he said, pointing to the blueprint, "will be our new arts center . . . when we've raised the funds."

"How much are you looking for?"

"We've raised a million, two. We need another two hundred thousand dollars before we can break ground."

"Consider it done."

McBride beamed a toothy grin and cocked his head. "Before writing a check, Mr. McClintock, I think you'd be wise to consider the precision with which we carry out our rules and regulations.

"For example, we have surprise sweeps. I have a team of students and administrators who periodically check all rooms for drugs, alcohol, sex magazines. Anything that goes against our values."

"I'm not worried," B.J. said confidently, taking out his checkbook. "I know my boys. They're gonna fit in just fine."

"I hope you're right, Mr. McClintock. I'd hate to have to send them back to you."

B.J. handed over his check for $200,000. He knew locking Mikey and Danny up here would be worth every penny of it.

What the headmaster didn't know was that B.J. had a pack of aces up his sleeve. He knew his nasty little boys. He knew how greedy they were. And, upon reflection, he knew it was his own fault.

When the twins were toddlers, he and Elizabeth had set up trust funds for them. They knew they were worth millions before they even started grammar school. To make up for the financial insecurity B.J. had endured as a boy, he'd wanted his sons to know they would be assuming an important place in the world—a place that required a great deal of responsibility.

Unfortunately all the boys had learned was how to thrive like rich brats. Instead of becoming charitable and responsible, they'd become selfish, greedy little satans.

Now, if they wanted those millions, they were going to have to graduate from St. Bartholomew's and go on to college. College graduation had been a second stipulation. Mikey and Danny were going to be two different people when they emerged from their Catholic military-school experience. In fact, B.J. told himself, I think I'll be able to slip them into a nice, respectable eastern college a year from now.

CHAPTER 52

*H*olly was nervous. Of all the scenes in *Blue Moon*, this one, the love scene, was the one she dreaded most. She wasn't worried about the way her body looked; in fact, she was in great shape. She had been working out like an athlete for months.

What was making her as jumpy as a cat was having to kiss Colin. She had to climb under the sheets and make love look believable. Her palms were wet and clammy as she made her way to the set. Thank God, she thought, it was a closed set with just Derek and only a few necessary crew members.

When she arrived, she found Colin already under the sheets, script in hand, studying his lines. He looked up, took off his glasses, and smiled.

"Here's my girl. I've been waiting for you."

Holly wanted to puke. As she climbed between the sheets, she felt the long muscles at the base of her neck tighten. Colin wrapped his arms around her shoulders and pressed his naked body against her. Holly stiffened.

Try as she might, she couldn't relax. She tried to rationalize the situation, but her mind wouldn't cooperate.

"Relax, baby . . . get into it," Colin cooed in her ear.

"I am relaxed. And don't call me baby, okay?" she shot back.

"Okay, okay. Jeez . . . if this scene is going to work, you better warm up at least fifty degrees, honey."

"What are you? A fucking thermometer?"

"Who needs a thermometer to tell them they're holding an ice cube?"

Holly wanted to jump out of the bed. Better still, she thought, if only the scene required her to stab him repeatedly, she wouldn't mind staying in bed all day and night.

This is ridiculous, she told herself. Relax . . . relax. It's only a movie . . . not real life. Make believe he's Hans.

Holly started to loosen up. She got through two takes without much trouble. On the third take her eyes widened when she felt Colin's erection pressing against her pelvis.

"Get off me!" she hissed.

"What's a matter, baby? You should be flattered that you give me a hard-on," he replied, faking an in-and-out motion for the camera.

Holly started to freak out. She began to struggle, trying to free herself from under Colin's weight.

Their love scene was being shot without sound. Music would be added later to create a romantic ambience. Derek was giving direction from behind the camera.

"It's starting to look like an uncomfortable situation. Perhaps you can give me a rapturous expression, Holly, dear. . . . Ummmm . . . no that's not it . . . more like ecstasy. . . . No, that looks painful, dear. . . . ahhh . . . Colin . . . you look a bit menacing there, luv . . . ease up a bit. . . ."

"Roll over, you bastard," Holly demanded.

"No . . . I like it on top," Colin teased, pushing his erection up against her labia.

"Kiss her neck, Colin, and then slowly work your way down to the nipple . . . gently now. . . ."

"Why don't you get into it, baby . . . it's not like we've never done this before." Colin threatened to enter with the head of his penis.

Holly let out a scream and threw Colin off her and onto the floor.

"Cut!" Derek yelled. "What's the problem?"

Hysterical, Holly grabbed her robe and stormed off the set.

"What happened?" Derek asked Colin.

"I think she's got PMS."

"Got what? What did you say to her?" he demanded.

Holly slammed her dressing-room door and locked it. She was shaking with rage. Colin O'Brien represented a part of her life she had buried over fifteen years ago.

She felt like a small toy in the hands of fate. Tears welled in her eyes. She wanted to go to bed and pull the covers over her head.

"Holly dear, it's me, Derek," said the director, knocking at her door.

Holly didn't budge from the sofa. She tightened her arms around her knees and stared into space.

"Holly! Open up the door, for heaven's sake!"

She closed her eyes, trying to forget that she was at MCM studios, making a feature film with superstar Colin O'Brien. From day one, she had rationalized her feelings toward him despite their history together. She had hoped he would make some apologetic reference to the past—but he didn't. Instead, he had the gall to actually try to fuck her on the set!

The despicable creep! she thought, ignoring the knocking at her dressing-room door.

"It's been three hours, for chrissake!" Lara Miller stated in an even yet angry tone.

"She's got to come out sooner or later," Colin offered.

"You said that before! Sooner has past, and later is *now*! We don't want B.J. down here," Lara threatened.

Colin sat weighing the situation. It was because of him Holly had locked her door. It all seemed ridiculous; besides, it was costing a shitload of money.

"I'll go talk to her," Colin said.

Once again Holly heard knocking at her door. Then she heard Colin's voice, low and sweet.

"Holly, listen, this has to stop—you've held up production for three hours. Why don't you open the door? Come on honey . . . this is costing a lot of money—not to mention your reputation in the business. . . ."

Holly snapped to attention. Reputation? Did he say reputation? She got off the sofa and opened the door.

"Come in, Colin."

"That's more like it, baby. Now what happened between us was a long time ago, water under the bridge."

"Wrong," she shot back. "Mud! The water's mud, Colin."

"What's that supposed to mean?"

"I called you at least a hundred times, and you never returned my phone calls. You treated me like a tramp!"

"Listen, Holly, I never held a smoking gun to your head."

"Why didn't you call me back?"

"I was a married man! It was just one of those nights! What the hell do you want?"

"I needed to talk to you! You and your *buddy* gave me gonorrhea!"

"So what? You go to the doctor and get a shot! All gone!" he said, raising his hands up as if he were talking to a baby. "Besides, how did you know it was me?"

"It had to be you, Colin. I hadn't been to bed with anybody for two months. And after that night I was kind of hung up on you. So I waited for nearly five months, hoping you would call. God, I was so naïve. I woke up one morning, doubled over in pain and in a cold sweat. My roommate rushed me to the hospital. The infection had spread through my uterus and ovaries. My reproductive organs couldn't be saved."

Holly watched Colin's reaction. His handsome features went through several changes, stopping at confusion.

"You mean . . . ?"

"That's right, Mr. O'Brien, I can't have babies," Holly answered.

"Oh, Holly, I'm so s-sorry. I had n-no idea . . ." Colin stammered.

"Of course you didn't. You never returned my phone calls! You never let me know about that miraculous shot! Our one night of sin altered the rest of my life."

Colin slumped into a chair, leaned back, and stared up at the ceiling. Holly could see tears welling in his eyes.

There was a soft knock at the door. Derek stuck his head in the room and said, "Are we ready to finish the scene, children?"

"Give us ten minutes," Holly said.

Derek evaluated the situation, checked his watch, and said, "Okay, I'll see you both on the set in *ten minutes*." He closed the door behind him.

Holly looked over at her co-star and felt relieved. She had finally passed the hot potato. Now, Colin felt the heat. She stood up.

"Come on, Colin, let's get this over with."

"Okay," he mumbled, clearly at a loss for words.

The two stars disrobed and climbed back underneath the sheets.

"Quiet on the set!"

"Speed!"

"Action!"

Colin reached up and held Holly's face between his hands. He looked into her eyes and then kissed them. He slowly kissed her cheeks, her ears, her chin, her nose. Gently he rolled her over onto the pillows, caressing her body as if it were the finest porcelain. He took her hand and kissed the palm. Raising his head, he looked into her eyes and whispered, "I wish I could change it, but I can't . . . I'm sorry from the bottom of my soul."

And then he kissed her with such tenderness that she responded.

Lara Miller watched with tears in her eyes. She looked at Derek; his mouth was open. The grips in the rafters were mystified as they looked down at the two beautiful stars totally in a moment.

The cameraman took his eye away from the viewfinder and sat back, quietly watching. Obviously, the magazine had run out of film, and nobody had noticed. Lara believed she was watching that magic that one only hears about. This love scene was going to be talked about for years to come, and she was there, seeing it with her own eyes.

CHAPTER 53

B.J.'s cream-colored Corniche convertible glided into the Bel Air Hotel parking lot.

A solicitous young parking attendant ran to open the door.

"Good morning, Mr. McClintock."

"Morning, Joey."

B.J. walked briskly through the drizzling rain, across the bridge, through the portico, and past the wood-paneled bar to the main dining room. He hadn't felt so invigorated since his last vacation at Rancho Virgo.

As he reached for the brass handles on the leaded glass doors, he was reminded of his great fondness for this hotel, which nestled in the hills like a jewel at the center of a crown. He knew that if he had a choice of hotels beyond the pearly gates, it would be an exact replica of this one.

"Good morning, B.J.," the maître d' welcomed him.

"Morning, Mario."

"We going to get in eighteen holes this weekend?"

"Let's shoot for Saturday at the Bel Air," B.J. suggested.

Mario Pasuco smiled and said he'd take care of the arrangements. Being the maître d' at one of the world's most prestigious hideaways for the rich and famous had it advantages, but being a par golfer put him in league with the people he served.

The dapper fifty-seven-year-old Italian seated B.J. at his regular table, the same table where twenty-five years earlier McClintock had cut his first Hollywood deal. A lot had changed since then— the paint, the carpeting, the furniture, but not the heart of it. To B.J., the hotel felt like an extension of his own home.

Coffee was poured. Scones and home-baked muffins were served hot from the oven. Sweet butter and miniature bottles of raspberry, quince, and gooseberry jam arrived.

Mario beckoned B.J.'s waiter and informed him that Mr. McClintock's regular breakfast consisted of two 3-minute eggs and whole-wheat toast. And it was not to be served until the other guest had ordered.

Two middle-aged women wearing diamonds and tennis outfits waved at B.J. from across the room. He recognized them as Elizabeth's charity cronies. Nameless faces. He smiled, waved, and focused on *The Wall Street Journal*.

God, how he'd been savoring this meeting. Stealing Billy Goldberg away from Zachary Steele . . . from his first independent film effort . . . stopping the little fucker dead in his tracks. The thought of it made his coffee taste extraordinarily delicious.

B.J. ran his tongue across his teeth, remembering his conversation with Goldberg on the golf course. How stunned and speechless Goldberg had been when B.J. offered him his dream project—plus double points, creative control, final cut, and his own building on MCM's lot. It was an offer too rich for any director to walk away from.

By the time superstud Steele finds another director, B.J. mused, he'll have to shelve *Blizzard*. The weather will strangle him, and if that doesn't do it, his commitment to Universal will.

In B.J.'s mind there were no rules, no limits, when it came to getting Bonnie Louise back. She had betrayed him. She hadn't come home. Zachary Steele was to blame, and B.J. was going to even up the score.

The dining room had begun to vibrate with a combination of hotel guests and locals ingesting their choice of power breakfast.

B.J. was suddenly startled by the impact of Zachary Steele's body landing in the banquette.

"Well, I'll be damned," the young star said. "I may be the only person in this town who's seen B. J. McClintock genuinely surprised."

B.J. bit his tongue and asked, "Where's Billy?"

"You made a wrong choice there, B.J. You picked a man with ethics and honor. Hence my arrival."

"Fine, Zachary. Then let's get down to the bottom line." B.J. looked him square in the eye and said, "What the fuck are you doing with *my* Bonnie Louise?"

"Bonnie Louise doesn't *belong* to you. She doesn't *belong* to me. She doesn't *belong* to anybody! She's with me because she wants to be."

"She doesn't know what she wants! She's barely eighteen years old!"

Zach, looking every bit the big-screen movie star in his blue jeans and polo shirt, leaned back and told the aging power broker, "I feel sorry for you, B.J. I'd have thought a man of your experience in such matters would've foreseen exactly how a fourteen-year-old like Bonnie was going to change. And grow up . . . yes—grow *up*, B.J. Get me?"

B.J. suddenly felt like a romantic old fool. He hated Zachary for cracking the safe where he kept his worst demons locked up. For the first time in his adult life he felt the possibility of *losing*.

A smiling waiter came over and presented Zachary with a menu. He declined.

"I'm not backing down, Zach. I love Bonnie Louise more than anybody ever loved her in her life, or ever will. It's just a matter of time."

Steele leaned in and said, "I'll tell you something, old man, that's also gonna be a matter of time. I'm talking about the statute of limitations. I'll have Bonnie Louise haul you through a fucking court for statutory rape. Only you won't get to go to Paris like Roman Polanski."

The waiter placed B.J.'s soft-boiled eggs in front of him, giving Zachary the perfect opportunity to exit.

CHAPTER 54

*M*eeting George Borofsky at his new apartment in Santa Monica led Bentine down Robertson Boulevard—Decorators' Row, as it was called—to Pico Boulevard, a prosperous Jewish neighborhood that realtors referred to as Beverly Hills Adjacent.

Money, or more accurately the lack of money, had been plaguing Bentine for the past ten days. She had paid her car insurance—fifteen hundred dollars for six months—and a few other odds and ends like American Express and Saks Fifth Avenue. Closing her eyes, she envisioned the stack of overdue bills that now measured three inches high.

"What am I going to do?" she moaned, gripping the steering wheel. "What the hell am I going to do?"

She was becoming steeped in debt. It didn't look like old Emil would leave the planet for another twenty years, and even then Lili would end up with the lion's share.

A parking place and a jewelry store! Perfect, she thought. I'll just divest myself of this old bracelet. I should be able to get a thousand dollars. . . .

After applying "attitude" along with a fresh layer of lipstick, Bentine presented herself at the jewelry-store door. A gray-haired man in gray electronically released the lock, and she entered a gated entryway.

"What can I show you?" the man asked reluctantly.

"Well, actually, I'm rather tired of this bracelet." She extended her arm. "I'd be interested in selling it." She unlatched the safety catch and handed it over.

The man sucked in his cheeks as he appraised the tightly woven gold bracelet highlighted with six small diamonds. A fifties trinket that someone had given her late mother. Probably a birthday or Christmas present from an actor or actress.

"How much do you want for it?" he asked.

"A friend of mine," Bentine lied, "a jeweler, thought I should get a thousand dollars."

The man looked at the piece through his glass. "I would accept his offer."

Cat and mouse. "He only deals in antiques." Bentine paused and asked, "Why? How much do you think this is worth?"

He shrugged. "It's a fifties piece. Which personally I happen to like . . . but . . ." He scowled to emphasize the pearl of wisdom he was about to bestow. "Years ago people used to buy gifts— presents, small pieces of jewelry like this. A string of pearls for graduation. Even in the movie business they used to give little presents when they finished a film."

As he spoke, Bentine began wondering if this man were reading her mind. Did he know that this was a movie trinket from the fifties?

"Today," he went on, "nobody does that. They finish a movie —they say 'thank you,' if you're lucky. Which is not to say your bracelet isn't beautiful. I like it very much."

"Do you have any idea who would be interested in it?"

He shook his head and frowned. "Privately is your best bet. Today, rich people shop for jewelry—they look for important pieces, not trinkets. Middle-class people are not buying." He handed the bracelet back.

"What do you think I could get for it? Five hundred?"

"Let's weigh it." He reached beneath the counter and said, "I'll give you its weight in gold."

"But what about the diamonds?" Bentine demanded.

"What diamonds? They're diamond chips. They're made to look bigger 'cause they're set in silver."

He dropped her bracelet onto his scale. "Fourteen-karat . . . eleven grams . . . I'll give you a hundred and fifty dollars."

"For that," she said haughtily, "I'd rather keep it."

As Bentine reached for her bracelet, the jeweler zeroed in on her diamond ring. The ring she had inherited from her mother.

"Now there's a diamond!" he said, reaching for it.

Bentine took her hand away. "This is not for sale!"

The man shrugged. Then Bentine found herself extending the hand after all.

"Incidentally, what *would* this be worth, just a guess?"

"Without looking at it? Weighing it?"

Bentine nodded.

"It becomes a game," said the man.

"Play it."

"We'll start at four thousand," he said without a smile.

"Thanks," said Bentine. In her mind's eye, as she left—not one cent richer—the three-inch-high pile of bills seemed puny beside an imagined stack of forty Treasury notes bearing the portrait of Benjamin Franklin. "At least," she said to herself, "you're a woman of honor."

It had been eight weeks since Bentine broke up with George Borofsky. Not a happy time. She missed him, but she had been forced to take a stand. She wanted someone who saw telephone booths as cubicles in which to use a telephone—not as "thrill boxes."

As she drove toward the beach, Bentine caught sight of a telephone booth. The final straw. Being squeezed into one of the narrow things wearing a skintight cocktail dress and having George artfully stick it to her without anyone suspecting anything.

That and his restaurant fetish. Banquettes with long white tablecloths hanging over the table were his fancy. Between the appetizer and the entree he would suggestively drop something under the table and direct her to retrieve it. After the first time she'd flatly refused, and they'd got into some angrily whispered fights.

George insisted that sexual fulfillment was in direct ratio to the amount of danger involved in its consummation. The more public the place, the greater the danger. The greater the danger, the more explosive the orgasm. She'd gone along with the idea a couple of times. After that, she'd had enough. Living alone was better than courting public humiliation. And, she decided, if George loved her as much as he professed, rather than seek her cooperation, he should seek professional help. But except for his sexual kinkiness, Bentine was crazy about him.

When she saw the monolithic wraparound highrise looming up ahead, she realized George had really done it. He'd taken the money from his house in Brentwood and actually sprung for the penthouse in one of Santa Monica's premier condominiums.

She was greeted at the entrance by a parking-lot attendant. She reached across the backseat for her briefcase, and pictured herself and George in a compromising position. She suddenly realized how much she missed him.

After announcing her, the concierge said, "Please take the west-wing elevator, Miss Devorac."

Bentine was impressed. She entered a beveled-mirrored elevator with a crystal chandelier and pressed PH.

The doors opened into the penthouse apartment. Bentine looked around. The living room appeared to be a good 40' × 40'.

"George?"

When no one appeared, she ventured into the center of the room. The far west wall was glass, framing a spectacular view of the ocean. Leaning up against the north wall were wooden crates containing artwork.

"George?" she called again.

"Out here."

She looked in the direction of his voice and realized that one wall wasn't glass—it was open. Her high heels tapped along the parquet floor. She found George reclining on a $9.99 banana-lounge special from K mart. He stood up. Always the gentleman, Mr. Formal in his three-piece suit.

"Bennie, you look great!"

"Thank you, George. So does your new home. I love it! What's in those crates?"

"A little artwork—a few things I took from the house."

They went inside to inspect the contents. George pulled out a large Francis Bacon oil painting.

"My God!" Bentine said. "You never told me you had a Francis Bacon."

"Well, I told you I collected art."

"What's this? Jonathan Borofsky. Is this a Borofsky sculpture?"

"Yes."

"Are you related to him?" she asked suspiciously.

"No, I saw his retrospective at the Whitney, and six months later I had an opportunity to buy this piece."

"Wow. This is a side of you I've never seen before, George."

George grinned at Bentine, soaking up her appreciation.

"What other treasures are hidden around this apartment?"

"Not much, really. I thought we could start from scratch."

Bentine walked through the dining room and into the kitchen. It was exactly what she'd always wanted.

"This is fabulous, George."

"I know. With your taste, Bennie, it couldn't be anything but."

"Thank you again, George."

He guided her through the rest of the penthouse. The spacious den with a view of the coast all the way up to Malibu. The guest room with a view from Santa Monica Bay all the way to Century City. And, finally, the enormous master suite.

Bentine was speechless when she walked into the bedroom. In the middle of the huge white room, with a sloped ceiling that reached sixteen feet at its peak, was a magnificent four-poster bed.

The only other piece of furniture was a floor-to-ceiling Sony television. Bentine took control of herself and walked around the room surveying it like a professional decorator.

There were two master baths. His and hers. His was gray marble. Hers was pale pink marble, and near it was a bidet. Both baths had unobstructed views of the Pacific Ocean.

Closets within closets. Bentine was opening cupboards when she found George's video collection. The top shelf held every movie her father had ever made. Below that there must have been a couple of hundred tapes filed in alphabetical order. *Now, Voyager; Wuth-*

ering Heights; Gone With the Wind—Fred and Ginger, Katharine Hepburn and Cary Grant, Bette Davis . . . All of the greats were neatly shelved. Romantic movies. And he hadn't gone out and bought them, either, she noticed. The majority were home recordings.

Bentine wanted George to grab her and throw her on the bed and make mad, passionate love to her.

"What's your budget, George?"

"You tell me, Ben."

"Well, George, let me think about it."

She sauntered over to the bed and slowly peeled off her jacket and unbuttoned her silk blouse. She unlatched the gold bracelet, burying it in her pocket.

"There are several ways you could go with a space like this." She unzipped her skirt and let it fall to the floor.

George watched her step out of it. He was hopelessly in love with the woman. He'd bought the penthouse with this very moment in mind.

He rushed over to Bentine, wrapped his arm around her waist, and started to maneuver her out of the bedroom, through the living room, toward the balcony.

"Bennie, Bennie, I've got just the spot!" He frantically whispered, "I've got the perfect vantage point—with a hotel just across the way."

"No!" she insisted, trying to pull away from him. "No, George! Stop it!"

He pulled harder. "You're gonna love this!"

Bentine reeled around and slapped him across the face.

George let go and held his burning cheek. "Oh, Bennie—I've been waiting for you to do that for so long."

"You deserved it. You've been a bad boy for a long time, George!"

"Oh, Bennie," he panted, "I've never seen this side of you before. *I love it.*" He reached for her. She slapped his other cheek so hard it flushed crimson.

Bentine reached over, unbuckled his belt, and, in one tug, burned it out of his pant loops. "I mean it, George. It's going to be different from now on. Get over there by that crate with the Borofsky in it and drop your pants!"

"Yes, Bennie. Yes. Okay."

She followed him, strutting, showing off her peach silk teddy while snapping the leather belt between her hands. She controlled a giggle as George dropped his pants.

"Bend over the crate," she commanded. "You've been a bad boy, George, and now I'm going to spank you."

"I deserve it."

Bentine suddenly felt a sea of aggressions well up. Whack! The belt hit George's bare buttocks. He flinched. A red welt appeared.

"Harder," he begged.

"Harder, George? I'll give it to you harder."

Another wave of frustration surged through Bentine's body. She pictured her ex-husband's face instead of George's lily-white cheeks, and she let it rip. Whack! Now, there were two red welts.

To Bentine's amazement, she was enjoying it. She had never so much as spanked one of her children, yet she was savoring George's moans and groans. She took a deep breath and snapped the belt. "Have you had enough, George?"

"It's up to you, Bennie."

"I think you deserve one more, you naughty, naughty boy." She pictured the jeweler's face and cracked the belt. Three welts, she mused, I guess what they say is true: Inside every sadist there's a masochist pleading for punishment. She thought of her dictatorial father. "Your dad sure cracks a hard whip when he's on the set," an assistant director had told her once, smiling. Yes, Emil directed with an iron fist, and now, in a different arena, so would she.

"Now, get up, George, and follow me to the bedroom."

Bentine climbed up on the carved four-poster and comfortably situated herself among the pillows.

"You're going to make love to me, George. Nice and slow . . . and if at any moment you speed up or don't do as I say, you're going to be a very sorry boy."

George smiled boyishly. "Whatever you say, Bennie—you're the boss."

CHAPTER 55

Adam Snow climbed into the vintage Porsche Colin had given him for his thirtieth birthday two years earlier and sped into the city. He expected to find Colin at MCM, only he discovered when he arrived that the star was on the looping stage at Universal.

MCM was a major studio, but it didn't have a 70-mm looping facility. The Englishman picked up copies of his musical charts and headed for the valley. He was desperate to talk to his confidant.

Colin looked at himself in 70-mm—a close-up. Awesome, he thought. He looked good, actually, for a forty-six-year-old debauchee.

"You've got twenty-seven seconds, Colin," Derek Middleton's voice boomed over the intercom from the control booth. "We'll do a run-through. Mark your pacing, and if you feel comfortable, we'll go for it."

Colin marked his lines for timing and emphasis. In a whisper he said, "I can see the pharmaceutical company up ahead. If Americans really spend three times as much on illegal drugs as they do importing oil, that warehouse is worth more than Fort Knox."

"Let's go for it, Derek." Colin's stopwatch was poised for action.

Once again the scenes appeared on screen. Colin was seen walking through a valley of Joshua trees in the Mojave Desert. A few feet behind him Holly would enter the picture. There was no sound— or, as production people termed it many years ago in Germany, it was MOS, "mit out sound."

Derek called out, "We're going to mat in the pharmaceutical company in the upper left-hand corner of the screen."

Colin delivered his lines. The rugged, courageous character he was playing came through perfectly. Chris, the ex-marine, was part of him, just as every character Colin had ever played was part of him . . . but this one, he felt, had the biggest piece.

He said the last line and stopped the clock. Two seconds under. Perfect, Colin thought. He turned to the control booth, seeking Derek's approval, and noticed Adam standing next to the director.

Derek gave him the high sign. "Good, Colin," his voice resonated through the intercom. "We'll break for lunch. See you all back here in an hour."

"Hey, man. How's it going?" Adam asked.

Colin's face lighted up. He was pleased. "Let's 'do' lunch," he said sarcastically. It was an expression that annoyed both men. Something that had no doubt sprung from a New York agent's speeding lips.

He made a lunch reservation in the executive dining room. Normally Colin would have opted for his dressing room, but they were on the looping stage. No deluxe trailers or even a production office. It would have to be lunch in the commissary.

Colin liked Universal because it was his home studio. As a young New York actor he'd been spotted in an off-Broadway play for a role the studio was casting in a war epic. He'd been flown out— all expenses paid. A big deal, he'd thought at the time.

His screen test had secured a three-year contract. Colin O'Brien owed his movie-star beginnings to Universal. Twenty-six years old and earning a thousand dollars a week with a forty-week guarantee.

"Look at you!" Adam said as they walked into the black glass commissary. *"The Thirteenth Disciple."*

"Yeah, it was the highest-grossing film in '79."

"No wonder they love you here."

Inside the main dining room there was another blowup of Colin, from *Abandoned*, a film he'd made for the studio three years earlier. He waved at the head of the studio. The man gave Colin the high sign.

They eased onto their banquette, and Colin said, "You didn't come all the way over here to have lunch."

"You're right. I didn't."

"Hey! How are you, Marty?" Colin said to a short, balding man who stopped at their table. "Long time, no see."

"Word on the street's good, Colin. I hear you got a winner."

"Fingers crossed," said Colin, crossing his fingers.

"I've got the perfect script for you!"

"Send it over. Send it to the house."

The man winked and said, "This afternoon. *Scorpion*, it's called —but don't let the title fool you. It's a love story with guts. You'll love it, believe me!" He gave Adam a cursory smile and darted to a nearby banquette.

"I couldn't think of his last name," Colin admitted softly, with a chuckle. "He produced a western I made ten years ago. Every time I see him, he's got something *perfect* for me."

A waiter appeared to take their order. Colin wanted a hamburger, fries, and a coke. What he termed his "in-town" lunch. At the beach he rarely ate meat, preferring fish and chicken. Morton Shipp had warned him about the dangers of a diet high in animal fat.

As a boy in Colorado, Colin had been raised on homemade fried chicken, doughnuts from the local Winchell's, hamburgers and French fries at the ski lodge where his father worked. Vegetables were anathema to him. The only ones he could stomach were corn and sweet baby peas.

Adam was a fish-and-chips-wrapped-in-paper man. He could also eat English bangers and mashed potatoes or a plate of flaky crusted Cornish pasties for days on end. The two men liked nothing better than finding a diner that served deep-fried food all night long.

"What kind of beer do you have?" Adam inquired.

"Heineken, Corona, Bud, Miller . . ."

"Heineken."

"Adam, come on—have a club sandwich."

"I'm not hungry."

"Bring him a club sandwich with his Heineken."

Adam was peeved. He didn't like being treated like a schoolboy.

Colin smiled and waved at someone else. The Celebrity Room lived up to its name. It was like old-home week. Colin O'Brien was swimming in friendly waters.

He smiled at the handsome composer. "Maybe you should consider getting married. Have a kid or two."

"Colin, things have to change. I'm not getting married and having a baby!"

"Babies are wonderful! They're what life's all about." He leaned over and whispered, "Men like us need the protection of a family." He sat back.

Bitterly Adam said, "I don't think so. And as for children—I hate them."

"You only think you do. They're not nearly as bad as you think they are."

"What's put you in such a bloody good mood?"

"I think I'm riding a big hit with *Blue Moon*. You should be singing as well. Big changes are coming."

"I am happy about the work, but our private life sucks. I'm moving out. I can't take it anymore. If you want to see me, you'll just have to come into town."

Suddenly it sank in. Colin's smile disappeared. Was Adam giving him an ultimatum—split with Helen or split with him?

The food arrived. There was silence at the table. Colin took a napkin and began calculating, figuring, making notations. Finally he swallowed a bite of burger and asked, "What do you think about the Murdoch place?"

"One good storm and good-bye, house."

"It needs a lot of work," Colin agreed.

Adam knew what Colin was driving at. It was one of the last run-down cottages in the Colony. Something to be torn down to make way for an architect's dream.

"Old man Murdoch and I go way back. If you could come up with fifty thousand, I'll put up the rest. We'll be partners."

"You don't seriously think for a moment that that dump . . ."

"Stop thinking *dump*. If I can pick it up for under a million, I'll be the bank. Instead of paying the mortgage to the bank, you pay it to me."

Adam's mood darkened. It would never work. It was definitely out of the question. The *same* scenario on the beach was too much, he thought, to keep handling.

"It's a great deal for both of us." Colin smiled at him.

Adam drained his beer and motioned at the waiter. He needed a refill.

"Adam," Colin continued, "we couldn't lose on that property— unless California falls into the sea, and I don't foresee that happening anytime soon."

"Colin, it won't work."

"Yes, it will. We belong together, Adam. It's the best I can offer you right now."

Adam stared at Colin, digesting his offer. He knew that Colin was doing all he could for their relationship, considering the circumstances. But he was so bloody tired of the charade.

"You know, once *Blue Moon* comes out, you're not gonna have anything to worry about. You'll be making a couple hundred thousand a film. You'll be able to parlay the Murdoch house into a larger one. Eat up and let's get out of here. I've got a lot of looping to do."

Adam caved in and attacked his club sandwich. *His own house in the Colony* was music to his ears. Maybe he could learn to tolerate Helen.

CHAPTER 56

*L*ara Miller's new office adjoined B.J.'s and enjoyed the same spectacular view of the city. To McClintock, it was insurance. He needed Lara. She was reliable, and for all intents and purposes she was running MCM while he sorted out Bonnie Louise.

To Lara, her new decorator quarters and secretary were a long sought-after reward. A victory well earned. B.J. had become so sloppy about making decisions and keeping appointments that half the time she couldn't even reach him. Anyone who wanted an answer came directly to her.

"Gordon Stanwick on one," her secretary's voice echoed through the intercom.

Lara lifted the receiver and shifted gears.

"Gordon . . ."

"Lara . . . I've got the information you wanted."

"Tritek?"

"Want to risk an open line?" he asked gravely.

Lara was thoughtful for a moment. Considering the immediacy of the problem, she answered, "Yes. Who's behind Tritek?"

"Carlo Capriotti."

"*Capriotti?*" she shrieked, and stood up. "I can't believe it," she muttered. "I just cannot believe it!"

"Hold on. There's more." His voice lowered. "According to my sources—which are damn good—the power behind the pawn is the throne—Joseph Giannelli. The head of the most powerful crime family in the Mafia."

Lara sank down in her chair. Every muscle in her body tensed. "That motherfucker," she said, digesting the information.

"Call me if you need anything, Lara," Stanwick offered genuinely.

"Thanks, we owe you one."

Lara punched the next available line and dialed B.J.'s car phone.

"This is a PacTel Cellular System. Your call cannot be completed at this time. The mobile customer you have called has left the vehicle or traveled beyond the service area. Please try your call later.

Lara slammed down the receiver. "Dammit, B.J.! Where the hell *are* you?"

Like a shark circling its prey, B.J.'s old white Caddie bumped into the driveway of the Brentwood Country Mart. His eyes were firmly fixed on the highly polished baby-blue 450 SL slipping into a parking spot facing the shoe store. He waited, putting on his right blinker and motioning the impatient Volvo station wagon behind him to go around. His eyes never left the baby-blue Mercedes.

Bonnie Louise nonchalantly got out of her new car, obviously something Zach had given to her, and shook her long blond tresses. B.J. moaned. Oh God, how he wanted her! He was staggered by the sight of her long legs and her tight little ass outlined in snug blue jeans. He ran his tongue across his upper teeth and prepared for action. This was it!

The electric window slid down, and he called, "Bonnie Louise!"

She turned around and smiled. "Byron?"

Another Volvo station wagon wanted him to move. He ignored the Brentwood matron and proceeded to put his top down.

"How you doin', darlin'?" he asked, losing himself to his southern roots. "Isn't this a great car?"

"Yeah," Bonnie Louise cooed appreciatively. "It's real cool."

"Come on, darlin'," he implored cheerfully. "Lemme take you around the block."

Bonnie Louise shrugged and got in. It had been a while, and she still had a soft spot for the old B.J., her mentor.

B.J. leaned back against the white leather and let his right foot step hard on the accelerator. He kept running his tongue across his upper teeth. Sure, he told himself, I'm nervous. Calm down, B.J. Relax.

"I miss you, darlin'," he offered sincerely. "I look over at my red phone, and it just never rings."

Bonnie Louise smiled and giggled. She remembered what a big deal the red phone had been. She'd been the one who insisted he have a line she could use any time, day or night. He'd been reluctant to install one, but she'd talked him into it. Right there in his bedroom and one in his office. She was the only one who had the number.

The spin around the block had turned into a fast trip down San Vicente to Seventh Street. B.J. took an abrupt right. The car squealed around the corner and bolted hog-style down the winding canyon. Bonnie Louise's inner alarm was ringing. Something was wrong here. Very wrong! She felt as if she was being kidnapped. This wasn't a trip around the block; this was a trip to the beach. Maybe even as far as Malibu.

"Byron," she pleaded, "I gotta get back. I have an interview . . ." She didn't know what to say, and the more urgent she sounded, the faster B.J. drove.

"I've got everything all worked out, darlin'. Lara's doing a man's job. MCM's in better shape now than when I was making all the decisions."

"B.J.," Bonnie Louise begged, "turn around. You said a spin around the block." She paused, and realizing her request had fallen on deaf ears, she said, "You're scaring me, Byron. I don't like this."

"I don't like being without you," he replied. "I have planned, oh how I have planned." He stepped hard on the brakes in time to turn left on Pacific Coast Highway.

Bonnie Louise sighed with relief. B.J. was heading back toward Santa Monica. He was still driving too fast and cutting in and out of lanes, but he seemed to know what he was doing.

"I got the boys locked up," he bragged. "Good Catholic military school. Not an easy order, Bonnie. But by God, I did it. Once they're in there, they'll be no problem!"

"God, Byron. It sounds like you put 'em in jail."

"That's where they belong. Same difference, except this cost me two hundred grand."

"Byron, why are you goin' on the freeway? The mart's back the other way!" She was getting desperate.

B.J. could feel her hysteria, and like a good horse, he was ready to bolt.

"Take it easy, darlin'! I got it all worked out!"

He slipped his free hand under the seat and came up with a beautifully printed brochure of Sotheby's better homes. He told her to open it and take a good look at *their* dream house.

Bonnie Louise felt frozen as she looked at a sprawling tropical Bahamas home. An island. B.J. had bought a small island. The asking price was $22 million.

"You like it, darlin'?"

"I don't know what to say, Byron. It looks big." Adrenaline was pumping through her whole body. *How am I going to get away from him?* she asked herself. *What am I going to do?*

B.J. was pleased with himself. He had his little sweetheart right where he wanted her. Next to him. "Soon we'll be on the plane, darlin'. You're going to love the Bahamas."

"Elizabeth, your wife. What about her?"

"What about her? Ever since the twins got skinned, she's kept to her side of the house. We barely talk now. She'll probably be relieved."

Bonnie Louise suddenly knew her worst fears were real. B.J. McClintock would rather see her dead than with another man. He *was* trying to kidnap her; it wasn't her imagination. He was really trying to get her on a plane to the Bahamas.

"My p-passport," she stammered. "I don't have it. It's at home."

B.J. applied his foot to the brakes, sliding over two lanes to the shoulder of the road. He rammed the gears into park and turned on his frightened lady love. He was furious. His features contorted with rage. He grabbed Bonnie Louise's straw purse and turned it inside out. He sifted through the contents. No passport.

"I taught you to keep your passport with you at all times!" he chastised her. "How could you be so stupid? How could you *do* this, Bonnie?"

"Byron, listen to me now. You drive me back to the mart so I can get my car. I'll just be a minute. I'll run home and get my passport. I mean, how else am I goin' to get it?"

B.J. didn't like it. He didn't like the idea of letting Bonnie Louise out of reach, even for five minutes, but he didn't have a choice.

"I'll drop you off in front and wait. Don't do anything foolish, darlin'."

"Zach's not home, if that's what you mean. He's in New York."

"He left you all by your lonesome?" B.J. shook his head. "Now that untalented brat's gonna get what's coming to him."

B.J. sped up to Twenty-sixth Street and exited. He drove to Bristol Avenue, furious that his plan had not come off perfectly. He'd taught her to keep her passport next to her driver's license. That had always been his fantasy. He'd always wanted to take Bonnie Louise away. To have her all to himself. And now that he was finally doing it, she'd forgotten to take her passport.

"Give me a few minutes," Bonnie Louise pleaded.

B.J. calmly parked the car in front of Zach's two-story Spanish home.

"Just hurry it up," he snapped.

B.J. watched and waited. He didn't like waiting. If Zach was in New York, why couldn't he go inside with her? Of course, he reasoned, she was going to try to escape!

B.J. flew out of the Caddie and across the street. Madly he punched the bell, which kept playing and replaying "God Bless America." He knocked, but no one came to the door. He called her name, but Bonnie Louise didn't appear.

Fired by adrenaline, he rushed around the side of the house. Dogs barked. He could see two Dobermans cursing him through a chain-link fence.

The back door was open. He couldn't see anyone in the house. The gate! B.J. opened it and looked around. No dogs there! He rushed inside the house and through every room, calling Bonnie Louise's name.

A frightened Latino maid rushed after him, telling him that Bonnie Louise wasn't at home. When B.J. started breaking things, throwing crystal and silver picture frames, she pressed the panic button, alerting Westec, the security brigade.

In his frenzy B.J. suddenly realized what the maid had done. He couldn't be discovered this way! Bonnie Louise had tricked him. She'd run out the back door.

"You tell her I'll be back!" he threatened. "You tell her that!"

The black-eyed maid stood by helplessly, watching a fifty-five-year-old man go mad. She didn't know much English, but he communicated his message nonverbally. She just stood there shaking as he rushed out the back door and down the side of the house.

B.J. wasn't about to give up. No, sir, he vowed grimly as he revved the engine and sped down one alley after another, searching for his blond beauty. She was on foot. She couldn't escape!

On and on he drove, up one street and down another. Cat and mouse. Stop and wait. . . . Start and rush down one street and then another. No Bonnie Louise.

Out of the corner of his eye he noticed a white security patrol car. He'd been spotted. "Shit," he muttered. "I'll get you, Bonnie Louise. I'll find you if it's the last thing I do!"

B.J. was a pro. He knew how to play poker. He knew when to leave the table, and this was one of those moments. Better to get back to the office than be confronted by a bunch of bogus policemen.

CHAPTER 57

*T*his morning as Carlo Capriotti slipped into his royal blue and white Fila sweatsuit, he felt as if all the world were a stage, and he were about to be bathed in the warmth of its spotlight.

The beach was socked in with fog, but that didn't stop Carlo. It excited him. He savored the number of MCM stock options he'd accumulated over the past six months. He thought of his good friend the Don, and how proud he was going to be when he heard the news. . . .

With every footprint Carlo made in the cold, rough sand, he felt more confident. Each tiny toe print was a step closer to making his mark in life. Seven thousand miles, he told himself. I've come seven thousand miles to prove I'm the smartest Italian bastard on the face of the earth.

He puffed through the fog, anticipating the sunrise. He could feel the muscles in his calves tightening as he passed his two-mile mark. Today was the day he'd go for it. He'd push himself an extra half-mile.

Eugenia was in labor. He prayed for another son. Girls were wonderful, but boys carried the family name.

He squinted, thinking he saw a shape, a moving form up ahead of him. As he was trying to make it out, he heard a voice.

"Mr. Capriotti?"

Carlo stopped dead in his tracks. "Who's there?" he called.

The figure approached. He was facing a man who was the size of a linebacker for the NFL. He had to be 6'4", weighing no less than 250 pounds. Carlo knew, because he'd had occasion to cross paths with men like this before. His blood ran cold. His relationship with Joseph Giannelli pushed the ominous thought of a hit man to the front of his brain. He fully expected the man in the black cashmere overcoat to reach out and grab him by the throat.

"Mr. Capriotti?"

Carlo collected himself, stretching as tall as his 5'8" frame would take him. "Yes," he answered. "I am Carlo Capriotti. Who wants to know?"

"My name is Frank. I work for Mr. B. J. McClintock." He smiled and gestured inland through the fog. "Would you follow me, please?"

"No! This is a private beach. You tell *Mr. McClintock* I don't conduct business this way. If he wants to talk to me, I'll be in my office at ten o'clock."

Carlo started to jog in place. Frank stopped him with a firm hand to his shoulder.

"I don't think that's a healthy decision, Mr. Capriotti."

"Are you threatening me, Frank?"

Frank stepped back. "No, Mr. Capriotti. I'm only following orders." He motioned inland again and waited.

Carlo considered his options, and rather than risk disfigurement, he followed the brute through the dense gray atmosphere to an open gate, and along a narrow walkway to the deserted Colony street.

Frank spoke into a walkie-talkie, alerting a white stretch limo that quietly cruised up to the men and stopped.

Frank opened the door, and out stepped B. J. McClintock, looking powerful in a navy pinstriped suit. He towered over the barefoot jogger, B.J. being a good 6′2″ tall and looking as if he'd stepped off the cover of *Forbes* magazine. The man with the fortune that Carlo Capriotti had been stalking since before *Blue Moon*.

B.J. smiled warmly and extended his hand. "Carlo, *buona notte*."

Carlo was silently amused by B.J.'s faux pas. After all, the sun was rising, not setting. "*Buona mattina*," he corrected, and extended his hand.

B.J. seized it with a viselike grip and pulled Carlo toward him with lightning speed. Before Carlo knew what was happening, B.J.'s fist made contact with his right eye. Carlo's body smashed against the cold pavement, and for a moment, it was lights out for the nobleman.

"You greasy little piece of pepperoni. How dare you try and stick it to me? Who the fuck do you think you're dealing with? Did you think I couldn't find out who Tritek was?"

"What are you talking about?" Carlo screamed.

"Shut up!" B.J. growled. "I know you don't have the brains to put a corporate takeover in motion. This is what you're going to do . . . you're going to call Giannelli and tell him to reverse all buys on MCM stock!"

"You are wrong, B.J. Giannelli knows nothing about this. . . . It was my plan. I *am* smarter than you think," Carlo bragged.

"Good. Then make the phone call to *your* broker."

Carlo rubbed his injured eye and shuddered. "And if I don't?"

"Then you die right here . . . in the fog . . . I'll cut you up into greasy little pieces and feed you to the fucking seagulls off the Santa Monica Pier."

Frank appeared with a wireless phone, and Carlo took it. He dialed his broker in New York.

B.J. stood over the little Italian as he argued with the stockbroker. You coward, B.J. thought. You lousy Mafia pawn.

"You don't have to call Mr. G. to get permission!" Capriotti yelled into the phone. "You listen to me! I bought the fucking stock, and I can sell it when I damn well please!" He listened, then added, "I take all responsibility. I'll deal with Mr. Giannelli!"

Carlo was so frustrated, he punched his fist against the side of the remote phone, turning it off, and handed it back to Frank.

"I feel sorry for you, Capriotti," B.J. said. "You have until the end of the day to straighten it all out—MCM stock, Giannelli. This is the last time I want to see your face."

B.J. ran his tongue across his upper teeth and nodded to himself as he climbed into the limousine and slammed the door behind him.

Carlo could feel his eye throbbing and turning color as the white limo disappeared over the speed bumps and into the fog.

"Too bad you burned a bridge that was needed, Carlo," Joseph Giannelli said.

"I came so close to taking over MCM. Another week and the studio would have been ours," Carlo said, sweating, gripping the phone.

"You're a greedy man. You couldn't be happy going in the front door like a respectable person. You, of all people, should know the *right* door!"

"I'm sorry, Mr. G. I'll make it up to you," Carlo said meekly.

"Sell all the stock, and stay away from McClintock. I'll send a clean business boy to deal with him. I was looking forward to making movies with him for the next twenty years. Too bad."

"Maybe after a little time has passed—"

"No!" Giannelli cut him off. "It's too late. The damage has been done. I'll be in touch."

"But, Mr. G., what am I supposed to do in the meantime?"

"Stay away from the stock market, Carlo. It brings very bad luck to you. You'll be hearing from me very soon . . . you owe me."

Carlo sat there with the receiver to his ear, listening to silence. He was flipping out. He owed Joseph Giannelli! He shuddered to think what the payoff might be. Maybe he'll want me to kill someone, Capriotti imagined. Or reduce me to a loan shark in the streets of Brooklyn or the Bronx.

Capriotti felt tears streaming down his face. He had put himself behind the eight ball, and there was no way out.

CHAPTER 58

Colin O'Brien had worked up a healthy sweat. Not so much from jogging as from trying to rid himself of the anxieties and dramas he had come home to face.

Adam was becoming far too comfortable with their relationship, to the point of being openly aggressive, Colin reflected. Helen was suffering. He could tell by the way she had become obsessed with finishing her play.

Colin collapsed on the sand to catch his breath. He wished he didn't feel so guilty about Helen . . . and about Adam . . . and about his children . . . and about his *image*. People were depending on him—his fans were depending on him. There was no way he could walk out of the closet at this point in his life.

He thought back to sweeter times. The early eighties . . . 1984 . . . the end of an era, he reflected. Colin drew his legs up to his chest and wrapped his muscular arms around them. He smiled.

On a day exactly like this one he could remember cruising Santa Monica Boulevard—picking up some strange trade. Yeah, he lamented, those days are over. Now, West Hollywood's a forbidden zone.

Those boys . . . those beautiful boys just in from the sticks . . . Colin savored the memory of his last conquest, an evangelical preacher's son from Tuskegee, Alabama. A hundred bucks. He laughed. Poor kid, he'd said, "Mister, you look so much like Colin O'Brien." "Yeah," Colin had told him, "I hear it all the time. Wish I had his money."

God, what a hoot. Life used to be fast and free. One shot and gonorrhea was history. I guess I'm a lucky son of a bitch. With my past . . . before I met Adam . . . phew . . . The boys on the 134 freeway—jeez—I don't even want to think about them.

He looked up in time to notice Eugenia Capriotti, her children, and their nanny zeroing in on him. He pushed himself up and sprinted in the opposite direction.

I can't even jog on *my own* beach anymore!

Bentine spotted Colin and Adam soaking in the sun on the O'Brien terrace. She trotted up the sand, bursting with good news.

"Where's Hellsey?" she asked, letting herself in the gate.

"At the computer," Colin said dryly.

Bentine took her wicked little grin upstairs. She found Helen sitting at her keyboard, tearfully looking at a blank screen.

"It can't be that sad," Bentine said, announcing herself.

Helen nodded.

"I thought you were happy with your play."

"I am," Helen said. "I'm right at the end." She looked up and smiled. "The Irving-tells-all part. It has to be *just right.*"

"So far I think it's brilliant!"

Bentine plopped herself into a comfortable wing chair and,

sounding like Mary Poppins, said, "You're catching me at the peak of my happiness!" Her well-tended teeth gleamed. "George and I are moving in together! I've given up the shrink! I'm free, Hellsey! I'm free for the first time in my life!"

Helen was baffled. "I thought you and George were finished?"

"That was three weeks ago. What can I say? The man's crazy about me!"

"That's great, Bennie. I'm so happy for you."

Bentine extended her arm and dropped her hand down. A broad gesture, one someone with perfectly manicured nails and wearing very expensive jewelry would use to make a point.

"I guess our coupon-clipping days are over, hmmm?"

Bentine shrieked with laughter. "Wrong! George loves it! The more I save, the hotter he gets."

The women couldn't contain themselves. What a joy, they agreed, to have something go right!

Bentine bounced up, gave her old friend a quick hug and a kiss on the cheek, and decreed, "Finish your play! Every time I talk to my father, he asks me when he can read it. Well, what should I tell him?"

Helen shrugged.

"Hey! Now that you've cut back on those mood-elevators, there's no reason you can't wrap it up! Hellsey, you've got real talent! Share it!"

"You *are* in a good mood."

"Well, wouldn't you be?" Bentine said coyly, backing out of the room while displaying her new ring. "George is coming for lunch. If you get my drift?"

The women giggled.

Bentine, buoyed by her newfound happiness, navigated her way back to the beach.

Helen watched from the window. She was having a relapse. She couldn't seem to knock the lingering feeling of rejection. Seeing Colin and Adam basking below made her feel like an intruder in her own home.

There was nothing she could do about Colin. Their relationship suited too many of their needs to change it. Stepping out as a playwright, however, would give her her own identity.

CHAPTER 59

*B*entine sat at the old kitchen table, the one on which, over the course of years, she'd spilled everything from oatmeal to marijuana seeds. The dark, square table was a comfort. It conjured up so many memories. Cozy and good memories. Bits and pieces of growing up movie-star rich in the heart of Bel Air, a vast residential enclave that—to discourage sightseers, prowlers, rapists, burglars, or mere autograph-hunters—had no sidewalks.

This is the chance I've been waiting for all my life, she told herself. If Daddy says yes, we're all on the map!

"The map" meant real life. It meant more than *talking about* producing at parties. Or writing, in Helen's case. If she could pull this off, it meant individual recognition. Respect. That's what they were all after. They wanted the people who mattered to care about them. To acknowledge their taste and talent as more than mere birthright.

She reached for a golden, brown-flecked Asian pear and bit into it. Juice dripped from her chin. Memories . . . always being told to "eat properly" by Hedda, the German governess. God, how clumsy and inept she'd always been made to feel.

The pear crunched pleasurably between Bentine's perfectly bonded teeth. She was nervous. Waiting had never been one of her strong suits, but then neither was dealing with Daddy.

Her eyes circled the country kitchen, resting on the glassed-in pantry that held three shelves of her mother's finest china. How extraordinary, she mused. It's exactly as she left it the day she died.

As she stared up at the delicate Bavarian Franconia china, she could hear her mother's high, girlish laughter, peals of it. Scenes of garden parties, hot Bel Air afternoons with the sun beating down on white umbrellas with pink tablecloths and white linen napkins. Binnie and Eddie, the black couple who'd lived there, had taken care of everything. They were gone, too.

But those plates, Bentine comforted herself, they're still there. Surviving a second boorish wife, earthquakes, and theft. They'd come through it all: Her mother's fine china remained loyally intact.

She closed her eyes, drifting back two decades to pretty wives with long red fingernails, their unfiltered cigarettes burning as they laughed and gossiped through the swirls of smoke. Yeah, Bentine thought, in those days smoking was glamorous. So glamorous I couldn't wait to see myself with a cigarette between my sophisticated fingers. All *healthy* meant in the fifties was drinking a glass of freshly squeezed orange juice when you woke up at 11:00 A.M., before the first cigarette of the day.

How different her childhood had been from that of her children. Bentine's had been ordered by her father's films. When he went off to Athens to direct a movie, the whole family took up residence in the Grande Bretagne—or whatever the best hotel would be in all the other cities—Rome . . . Paris . . . London. It was all supposed to have been the prelude. The prelude to what? she wondered. What had shaped her, made her the way she was? Sent her on this endless quest for *true* love? The dishes?

She opened a built-in drawer and felt around for a tiny key. She hadn't touched these precious memory-makers for too long to recall.

Carefully she removed a plate: Franconia's Mandarin pattern with the tiny, exquisitely painted pink and blue flowers. An exotic bird placed here and there for emphasis.

The Bavarians really knew how to create fairy-tale magic. Service for twenty-four. Yes, twenty-four cups hanging two by two and twenty-four soup bowls with delicate gold handles hanging two by two.

Hollywood parties. Dreams of playing *wife* opposite a Robert Stack or an Errol Flynn.

Bentine smiled. Errol with his sparkling Robin Hood persona had always been her man.

Maybe that was why she liked George so much. He was as wild as old Errol, yet he looked even straighter than she did. George knew, all right. He knew how to shock her into being completely in the moment. She would never get over his cleverness . . . finding her by using a map to stars' homes. What a guy.

She sought out her mother's favorite Limoges teapot. Dust had settled around the top. High time, then, she thought: Two or three cups of Earl Grey from that lovely pot would go down pretty well right about now.

She put the kettle on. A new one, one of Lili's Revere Ware classics.

"Daddy, where *are* you?"

Her impatience was turning to anxiety. What if he doesn't want to direct Helen's play? Or worse—as George warned—what if he wanted a rewrite tailored to himself? Emil was an old grouch when it came to being in control.

Bentine lifted the delicate china lid. Just as she was about to rinse the inside with hot water, she noticed something. Paper? An old letter. Faded, yellow, and cracked with age. Her father's almost illegible scrawl said, "My darling, she meant nothing. You, Delores, and you alone are the only woman I have ever loved. I will never love anyone but you."

Tears welled. Bentine replaced the lid, turned off the gas, and sat down. How many more things were there she didn't know about her parents? Their sorrows had reverberated in her dreams.

The front door banged open, and Emil's deep, throaty laugh echoed through the downstairs. Bentine took a deep breath, exhaled, and smoothed her dress. She could hear George's voice: "Don't argue with your father. Agree with whatever he says, and I'll take it from there." She locked the cabinet, taking the key and the letter with her.

She walked out, looking her best but deep down expecting the worst.

"Bennie! Bennie!" Emil greeted her. "I love it!" His lips pursed with thought, and shaking an all-knowing finger, he warned, "Of course, there are *a few little things*, here and there."

Bentine beamed. George had been right. This was the perfect coup. Helen would get her life's work respectfully produced. Emil would be welcomed back to the theater with his rusty though formidable megaphone, and Bentine would show all her so-called friends that she was up to more than shopping and socializing. George really did love her. He accepted her for herself, and she accepted him, kinks and all.

Maybe, she thought, that's what love is really about. Maybe her father really did love her mother in ways she had never considered.

Emil launched into his list of proposed changes. Bentine smiled, nodded, and took copious notes. She knew that George would smooth all the edges. He was her other half.

CHAPTER 60

*M*orton Shipp slumped in his God's chair, leaning against his desk. His mouth formed a tense, tight-lipped purse.

He opened the top drawer, reached under the bottom, and pulled out a tattered envelope containing photographs of the old gang: B.J., Elizabeth, his first wife, Marylou, and himself—taken thirty-five years earlier. Tears moistened Mort's vision. The ugly, weak-chinned boy with the broad nose was him. Wrong, he corrected himself. Had been him.

His newly woven hair extensions were killing him, pulling his face so tight that he felt as if the top of his head were going to explode.

He flipped to another shot, a group shot. God how he hated

B.J. McClintock! He'd ruined his goddamn life. There they were as college students, drunken fraternity boys holding up the newly crowned Homecoming queen, Bessie Jo Beesmyer. So beautiful, he recalled. A lot like B.J.'s daughter, Savannah.

The phone rang, but he knew who it was. Elaine was the only person who'd track him down at his office on a Friday at midnight. She'd have gone to a screening and some party afterward. She'd be home wondering where the hell he was, thinking he was out with another woman.

Mort laughed out loud and started to run his fingers through the mass of tiny braids that now thickened his hair. He winced from the tenderness of his scalp. A face-lift isn't this painful, he told himself.

The ringing stopped, and the plastic surgeon breathed a sigh of relief. He looked at a smiling 8 × 10 of his wife. Elaine had been such a terrific girl when he'd met her. Now, she was self-absorbed like all the other women he had known.

He shifted again, staring sideways at the photograph of Bessie Jo Beesmyer. He uncorked a bottle of Chivas Regal and swilled a hefty mouthful. He noticed the bottle was half-empty. How could he have consumed so much with so little result?

Demerol, that was what he needed. One shot of Demerol would put him square. Then his headache would go away, and he'd be able to face Elaine.

A nagging inner voice challenged him, *"Morton, you can't face anybody, because you can't face yourself! You murdered that girl!"*

"I did not!" he screamed.

"You did."

Make the voices go away. "Go away!" he demanded, downing the shot of scotch.

But the voices wouldn't go away. It was as if Bessie Jo Beesmyer had stepped out of the tattered photograph. She was sitting on the edge of his desk.

"Why'd you kill me?" she asked, her voice a thick Tennessee drawl.

"Bessie Jo, it was an accident. You had too much to drink—you were havin' a seizure. I gave you too much insulin." Beads of sweat were sprouting above his upper lip. His hands felt cold and clammy.

"Then why didn't you come forward and tell the truth, Morty?"

"I couldn't. B.J. wouldn't let me. He said it'd ruin my career. I'd a' been kicked out of medical school. I wouldn't a' been able to become a doctor," he said, hyperventilating.

He took a shot straight from the Chivas bottle. The alcohol coursed through his body. He relaxed, sinking back in his chair, looking away from the ghostly apparition of Bessie Jo Beesmyer, wearing her blue taffeta gown and rhinestone tiara.

"You can try, Morton Shipp, but rest assured, you're never gonna get rid a' me. Just like you're never gonna get rid a' B. J. McClintock. You never shoulda' listened to him. If you'da stayed in Nashville, Marylou'd still be alive. So would Eddie."

"Shut up!"

"No, sugar. I won't shut up till your ears are deaf. And even then I'll find a way. Your guilty conscience will never die, Morty. *Not as long as you're alive.*"

Shipp took another gulp of scotch and wearily slumped over his desk, burying his face in his arms. He felt as if Hulk Hogan were holding him by his hair. He broke down into uncontrollable sobs.

Suddenly the phone rang again.

Paranoid, he peered at it. He watched his hand move slowly toward it as if he were underwater.

"You don't really want to answer that?" a familiar female voice said.

Mort froze. He was terrified. He didn't want to look. He didn't want to see. The phone stopped ringing.

"It used to be me on the other end of that line, worrying about you. Wanting you to come home," she drawled.

As if some outside force moved his head against his will, he turned, and there, sitting in the consultation seat, was his dead wife, Marylou. He started gasping for air.

Marylou calmly leaned on the desk and rested her delicate chin in the palm of her lily-white hand.

"Calm down, Morty. I wouldn't want you to have a heart attack."

He crashed backward against the chair, gripping his chest, trying to regulate his frantic heartbeat.

"Marylou, I'm sorry."

"It's a little late for that, Mort."

He watched her pick up the bottle of scotch and fill his glass.

"What you need is another drink."

He didn't move.

"That's what you used to tell me. 'Marylou, take your medicine, and you'll feel better in the morning.' Her voice echoed into the distance.

Mesmerized, he watched her image dissolve into thin air. The filing cabinet across the room came into sharp focus. He reached for the glass and threw its contents down his throat.

Paper. Something to write on. He madly searched the cluttered mass of paperwork on his desk. Nothing. He opened his desk drawer and, after rummaging through it, settled for a prescription pad. He began scribbling what he believed to be the truth.

"I'm guilty," he wrote. "I am a murderer. I killed Bessie Jo Beesmyer. B. J. McClintock was there. I'm responsible for the death of my wife . . . I'm responsible for the death of my wonderful, innocent wife, Marylou. . . ."

He tore the small sheets off, tossing them to one side.

". . . I could have saved her, but I didn't. I deserve to burn in hell for my sins."

He ripped off the note and tossed it on top of the stack. He fingered the tablet and retrieved his pen.

"Elaine," he scribbled, "we should never have got married. I'm sorry I ruined your life . . . maybe there's still time. In my own warped way, I love you. B. J. McClintock, I'm going to be waiting for you at the gates of hell."

He tore off the last page and stared at the cardboard backing.

Now, out of nowhere, a young man's voice asked, "What about me, Dad?"

"I didn't kill you, Son."

"Yeah, you did. I wanted your attention. I wanted you to notice me, Dad. You never came to Little League. All those home runs were for you."

"But I did everything for you, Eddie."

"No, you didn't, Dad. You thought you did, but your heart just wasn't there."

Morton Shipp picked up the hypodermic needle, pushing the metal point through the rubber top of a Demerol bottle.

He quickly tied off his bicep with a rubber tourniquet and injected his favorite vein. He untied the tourniquet and fell back in his chair.

Fifteen-year-old Eddie stood there with his hands buried in his black leather jacket. He smiled and turned on his heels.

Mort's lips formed a gentle smile. He followed his fading son.

Ethel unlocked the office at precisely 8:00 A.M., just as she had done for the last twelve years. Saturday was a short day, for which Dr. Shipp paid her a little extra.

She made a pot of coffee and scanned the patient roster. *Ummm,* she thought, *a light morning. Thank God, it looks like we'll be out of here by noon. I can get to that white sale at Robinson's.*

Dr. Shipp's private line lighted up. She ignored it. The ringing persisted. "It's probably a wrong number," she said to herself.

"Hello."

"Ethel," Elaine's worried voice boomed, "have you seen Mort?"

"He doesn't come in this early on Saturday. What's wrong, Elaine?"

"Well, he didn't come home last night. I'm so worried. Maybe something's happened to him. I don't know what to do."

Ethel let out a low sigh. "Well, I don't know what to tell you, Elaine. Did you try beeping him?"

"Yes, of course! I've been beeping him all night!"

"Calm down. Dr. Shipp will probably walk in any minute with a perfectly logical excuse. I'll ask Dr. Kessler the minute he gets in if he's heard from Dr. Shipp. I'll call you one way or the other."

"Thank you, Ethel."

Ethel disconnected and smirked. Serves her right. She doesn't deserve him. Never did. What a man-eater. No wonder he stayed out all night. I hope he had a good time.

She padded her way to the coffee machine, whistling. She noticed that Dr. Shipp's door was closed. She opened it, complaining, "Those cleaners, they never do it right anymore."

The offensive odor of alcohol blasted her nostrils. She saw Dr. Shipp slumped over his desk.

"Well," she chastised in a whisper, "I guess we tied one on last night, didn't we?"

She tiptoed over to the blinds and twisted them open. She turned, waiting for the doctor to meet the morning sun. When he didn't respond, she walked over, lightly prodding his shoulder.

"Dr. Shipp . . ."

Ethel froze. His shoulder felt rigid. Snapping into her nurse mode, she reached for his neck and pressed on his jugular vein. No pulse.

She straightened up and surveyed his desk. Over his shoulder she peered at the prescription papers scattered around him and on the floor.

"Oh my God!" She saw the syringe. "Oh my God! You stupid man! How could you have done this?"

She heard Dr. Kessler's key in the door.

She quickly pocketed Dr. Shipp's last words and screamed.

CHAPTER 61

*E*laine Shipp climbed inside her Mercedes and burned rubber away from the Beverly Hills Police Station.

"How dare you patronize me, you son of a bitch! How many times did Mort pick up the phone and do you a favor in the middle of the night? I don't have enough fingers and toes," she spit.

B. J. McClintock was going to pay for Mort's death! Even if their old friend, the chief of police, refused to use Mort's suicide notes as evidence, she'd find a way to make the world see B.J. as a criminal. Not the nice Tennessee philanthropist he'd like people to think he was.

"Oh, if they only knew!" she said in a frenzy.

It was time to confront the matter head-on. She could make it to MCM by three. The perfect conclusion to a perfectly horrible day, she thought, as she cruised down Santa Monica Boulevard toward Culver City.

The chief's voice rang in her ears: "Dr. Shipp's notes aren't very coherent, Elaine. I wish I had something solid to go on."

"What about Vanessa Waters's lawsuit?" she'd said. "That's the tip of the iceberg! B.J.'s been blackmailing Mort into doing his bidding since they were in college!"

"Elaine, Mort died from an overdose. The coroner's report indicates that he's been using drugs for at least a year."

"That's because B.J. was blackmailing him!"

"I need proof! I can't use these hen scratchings on prescription papers to get an indictment against anybody. Morton Shipp *was* a pillar of the community, Elaine. Drug addiction takes away a man's credibility."

Tears of loss and bitterness and hate rolled down her cheeks as she vowed to vindicate her late husband—even at the risk of being blackballed throughout the industry.

Elaine pulled up to the MCM guard station. "Hi! Elaine Shipp to see B. J. McClintock."

The guard sifted through his passes and drew a blank. "Is Mr. McClintock expecting you?"

"Oh that Lara Miller! They're so busy up there, she forgot to call you. It's not really necessary. I know exactly where I'm going."

"I'm sure you do, but I'll lose my job if I let you on without a pass." He retreated to his telephone for confirmation.

Elaine bolted. She floored the accelerator and entered the MCM lot with mounting determination. She was ready for B.J.! All she had to do was find him. His office in the tall, smoky copper building was her best bet.

She skidded around a corner and clipped a wardrobe rack, sending dozens of costumes flying through the air. Roving actors, extras, secretaries, workmen, carpenters, gaffers—anyone and everyone who saw the wild Mercedes ran for cover.

"Why does it have to be so difficult?" she cursed, trying to find the street that led to B.J.'s new office building.

"Stop your vehicle!" a man called over a bullhorn. "Stop your vehicle!"

So what if studio security was on her tail? So what! She didn't give a flying fuck. Chase me, she thought. Go on, you dumb bastards—chase me through Fantasyland!

She watched people scatter, jumping up, flattening against soundstage walls to get out of her way. Now, the security police had resorted to golf carts. Isn't that cute? she thought. Little electric carts pursuing a Mercedes 560 SL. She wasn't about to surrender. She had a gun, and she was going to use it!

At the end of the narrow street two security carts and a real policeman on a motorcycle cut her off.

"Shit!"

She swerved into an open soundstage, applying the brakes but too late. The wheels locked, and the car slid across the *Santa Fe* set, crashing through the cocktail lounge that was about to be used for a key Holly Dandridge scene.

As the car thundered through the set, Holly and her extras jumped behind the bar, barely missing furniture and lights, which went flying over their heads. Some members of the cast and crew weren't as lucky.

Holly instinctively popped up, peering over the bar to get a look at the culprit. To her complete amazement, she saw Elaine Shipp sitting stunned behind the wheel of her mangled Mercedes, about to be bodily removed by security guards.

"Wait! I know her!" Holly yelled. "Hold on a minute!"

The director yelled, "Let's clear the set!"

Elaine was still gripping the wheel when Holly got to her. The show's still photographer captured the harrowing moment—*series star helps crash victim.* The cinematographer pointed the video camera in their direction and turned it on.

The assistant director grabbed a bullhorn and said, "We don't want anyone to get hurt! Clear the set!"

Holly overheard the director say that he smelled gas. That meant that Elaine's car might explode. "Come on, Elaine. Lean on me. Let's get outside."

B.J. and Lara arrived as the cast and crew were filing out of the soundstage.

"Oh my God!" B.J. was horrified. "Was anybody hurt?"

The eager assistant director rushed over to him and reported, "Artie Epstein, our producer—I think he got a concussion. Renaldo, the makeup man—he broke his arm jumping out of the way. And," he said, grimacing, "Holly's cockatoo flew away. The set's a wipe, Mr. McClintock. And so's some of the equipment. I think we're going to have to shut down."

"You are shut down," Lara told him.

"Jesus Christ—where's Elaine?"

The A.D. pointed to the hunched form of a woman being supported outside by Holly Dandridge.

"Poor Elaine," Lara observed. "She looks like she's out of her mind."

B.J. gave his right-hand woman a knowing look and said, "Yeah, not surprising after having lived with Morton Shipp. Considering all the damage she did today, she should be locked up."

B.J. and Lara moved toward Elaine Shipp, assessing the damage to people and property as they went.

"Mr. McClintock!" the director called. "Could I have a word with you?"

Elaine looked up and saw B.J. only a few feet away from her.

"You," she accused him. "This is all *your* fault! You made him do it! *You*—B. J. McClintock—you killed Mort! I know all about Bessie Jo Beesmyer!"

B.J. felt his muscles tense. He felt a contraction across his chest and popped a Di-Gel into his mouth.

Elaine opened her purse and produced a .38 caliber pistol and pointed it at B.J.

"You're gonna burn in hell, B.J.," she threatened. "I know about Rancho Virgo, too."

The security men froze. Everyone watched quietly. It was as if a "B" movie were being shot right there in front of them.

Holly had been enjoying the show, even mildly relishing the discomfort her illustrious overseer was suffering, until she saw the gun. But death by Elaine Shipp—that was too much. Using her long right leg, Holly deftly karate-kicked the gun out of Elaine's hand. The security men seized Elaine, dragging her, kicking and screaming, to the waiting ambulance.

The cast and crew cheered and applauded. B.J. thanked Holly, saying, "I owe you one." The director threw his arms round her.

"Holly, you were great!"

B.J. and Lara took a quick, curious look inside the soundstage. Insurance would cover most of the damage, but it would put them behind schedule. B.J. would have to call the head of the network and personally explain the delay.

Walking back to the office, B.J. railed about how crazy both Mort and Elaine were. But the so-called madwoman threatening him with Rancho Virgo was a deep shock. What had she discovered? Notes? Photographs? No, he decided, if she'd found hard evidence, she wouldn't be waging a one-woman war. She'd be down at the D.A.'s office. Fortunately, he thought, the D.A. doesn't prosecute on hearsay.

"What does she think I did? I didn't do anything. He was a grown man—he overdosed, for chrissake."

Lara thought back to her meetings with Dr. Shipp. She never really knew what Machiavellian schemes the two men were devising, and she sensed that she was better off in the dark.

"Damn," B.J. said. "You know, Lara, Elaine couldn't have picked a better soundstage. Call publicity—get some stills of the disaster before they clear it. I can see the headline: 'Holly Dandridge Disarms Madwoman!' "

"I can see another headline—'Doctor's Wife Accuses Studio Head!' "

The implication wiped the smile off B.J.'s face. Deep furrows creased his brow. If Elaine would crash through studio barriers and pull a gun on him, there was no telling what lengths she'd go to to seek revenge. And the press had already had a field day with the twins. . . . Lara was right, he concluded. He had to come up with something sweeter than revenge. . . .

As they neared the office building, B.J. picked up his stride and said, "Call Mort's lawyer and tell him to come over right away. I want my lawyer here, too."

"I know it's none of my business, B.J., but it looks like you've had a brainstorm."

He chuckled and opened the heavy glass door for Lara. "Give her what she wants—touch her where she lives."

"A part?" Lara asked tentatively.

"Exactly. We'll write her into Holly's series. Either she gets blackballed from the industry she lives for—or she takes a twenty-six-week guarantee on a hit show. To Elaine Shipp, work is sweeter than revenge."

"I think you're right."

"I know I'm right. She and Mort were always at each other's throats. The only reason she married him was so he'd surgically make her into a star."

"I think she just played her one and only starring role."

B.J. nodded and pressed the elevator button. The doors opened, and they began their smooth ascent to the top.

Lara shook her head and commented, "A winning move, B.J."

"I only play to win." He winked.

Lara smiled, but she could see the fatigue lining her boss's face. This had not been a winning year for him. His obsession with Bonnie Louise had cost him more than heartbreak. Savannah had fallen in love with Ariba, Elizabeth refused his calls, and the twins' scandal would no doubt be added to Hollywood's nastier legends. B.J.'s batting average, Lara decided, put him in the cellar.

CHAPTER 62

*E*ntertainment Tonight had sent a film crew to the MCM lot to interview Holly Dandridge and Lara Miller about *Blue Moon*. Co-incidentally, they had selected a day with more real-life drama than anything ever filmed there.

Lara turned on the TV in B.J.'s office. The late-afternoon news came on, blaring. She turned it down.

"Turn that up, Lara!" B.J. commanded. "It's about today."

The roving camera crew showed MCM's fire chief standing in front of the soundstage that Elaine Shipp had nearly demolished.

"What can you tell us about the wild chase through the MCM lot today, Chief Dillard?"

"Well, it didn't set off any fire alarms, or I'd have been right there," the veteran fireman said.

"Thank you," the commentator replied, quickly turning back to the camera.

"According to a studio spokesman, actress Elaine Shipp"—a

glamorous shot of Elaine taken from one of her television roles appeared in the upper left-hand corner of the screen—"was filming a scene from *Santa Fe* when the accelerator pedal of the car she was driving stuck."

The camera pulled back to include more of the ravaged sound-stage in the background. The commentator continued, "The actress was taken to Cedar Sinai along with five other members of the production company."

The camera moved in close for the commentator's wrap-up. "This is the second time in less than a week that tragedy has struck Elaine Shipp. Three days ago, her husband, Dr. Morton Shipp, whose roster of stars and celebrities was a *Who's Who* of Hollywood, was found dead in his Beverly Hills office from an apparent drug overdose.

"Friends of the couple say that Dr. Shipp was severely depressed over Vanessa Waters's impending malpractice suit. And that other suits were about to be filed.

"We'll have an update at eleven."

"Call publicity and tell them I personally appreciate the way they handled Elaine's 'accident.' Good work, Lara."

The news moved on to gridlock around L.A. Lara pushed the *Entertainment Tonight* tape into the VCR. The magazine show opened with highlights of the upcoming thirty-minute segment.

"Tonight we'll be talking to Holly Dandridge about her new movie, *Blue Moon*—critics are calling her performance an Oscar shoo-in—and to Lara Miller, one of the producers."

A shot of Holly and Colin kissing between the sheets sizzled across the screen. Both B.J. and Lara were thrilled with the provocative *Blue Moon* promo that MCM's publicity department had crafted together.

"And on a beautiful spring day we're going to take you to the Rockies to visit the set of *Blizzard* with director Billy Goldberg and Zachary Steele, who's producing as well as starring in the western saga. And we'll meet newcomer Bonnie Louise—Zachary Steele's real-life wife."

Real-life wife seared into B.J.'s mind. He pressed "stop," then "rewind," then "play." Mary Hart repeated the phrase. ". . . real-life wife."

A shot of Bonnie Louise kissing Zachary Steele in close-up hit B.J. like a bucket of icewater.

He stood up and leaned on the desk with his fists. His eyes were riveted to the tube.

"I didn't know they got married," Lara said softly. "They must've eloped."

She watched as B.J.'s face went white.

The commentator began, "Billy Goldberg's first two films have each grossed more than one hundred million dollars at the box office. Zachary—do you think *Blizzard* is going to make it an even three?"

The actor grinned and, gesturing toward the diminutive, bespectacled director, said, "You're looking at Mr. Midas over here."

"Okay, Dad!" Goldberg quipped.

"Are we expecting?" the commentator asked.

"He is!" Goldberg said playfully.

Zachary Steele's face turned red.

The commentator excitedly asked, "So you and Bonnie Louise are expecting your first child—when is it due?"

"Near Christmas," Zachary said shyly.

"Congratulations to both of you," the commentator said.

Lara heard a crash and turned to find B.J. rolling off the desk, clutching his chest. She reached him as he hit the floor. Panicking, she unbuttoned his collar.

B.J. tried to speak. His left arm was contorting spastically inward toward his body, and his back was arching from the seizure.

Lara grabbed the phone and ordered a paramedic squad.

"You're going to be okay, B.J.! Stay with me!"

B.J.'s eyes were riveted to Lara's. His right hand was gripping her arm so tightly, it was cutting off her circulation. She didn't care. It meant he was fighting and alive. He tried to speak again.

"Don't try to talk! Just lie there and breathe! Breathe, B.J. . . . breathe."

His grip relaxed, and Lara feared the worst. She got to her feet and ran out into the corridor. A young secretary stood by the watercooler.

"Where in God's name are the paramedics?" Lara screamed, and ran back inside B.J.'s office.

She fell on her knees beside the ashen mogul. "Oh my God! B.J.! B.J.?"

In a desperate attempt to bring him back, she started to administer CPR. A crowd had gathered at the door. As she pumped on the dead man's chest, she screamed, "Come on, you bastard! You're in this room somewhere. Get back in your body!"

Just then, the paramedics arrived, and in less than a minute they were electroding B.J.'s chest and searching for vital signs.

"We have a heartbeat! It's faint, but it's there!"

"All right! Let's get him out of here!" the other paramedic said, putting the cords back inside their case.

Lara stood to the side, amazed by the speed and skill they'd used to bring B.J. back to life. She had actually prayed for him.

In less than five minutes she and B.J. were speeding toward Cedars-Sinai in an ambulance.

CHAPTER 63

*E*lizabeth stood over B.J.'s bed, listening to the beeping of the monitor that was hooked up to his heart. His mouth was taped to a hose that was connected to a respirator. Intravenous tubes ran out of both arms. She had never seen him so vulnerable and helpless.

Elizabeth sat down and pulled her needlepoint out of her bag.

When she had got the phone call to rush to Cedars, she'd been shocked but not surprised. The last year had taken its toll, what with the twins' despicable behavior and Savannah living with that black rock singer. It was by the grace of God that B.J. was alive.

Elizabeth took it as a sign from God. Her husband had to be stopped. He had to be humbled. He had to be reminded he was mortal. Yes, she was relieved that it was only a stroke instead of a fatal heart attack.

Now she would have B.J. all to herself. Time was something she had never really shared intimately with him. It's as if God were giving us a second chance, she said to herself, as she pushed the needle through the canvas and pulled the blue thread taut.

With every stitch she felt stronger and more secure about herself. She planned the future for herself and her husband.

Frank, the McClintocks' chauffeur, popped his head in the door. "Just wanted to let you know I'm here, Mrs. McClintock."

"Thank you, Frank. I'll be right out."

Elizabeth gathered her things, leaned over the bed, and kissed B.J. on the forehead.

"Bye, bye, dear. See you in the morning."

As she approached the entrance of the hospital, she heard a commotion and saw a group of people around her limousine. She pushed the glass door open and was barraged by reporters. Microphones were shoved in her face, and flashes momentarily blinded her.

"Is your husband going to press charges against Mrs. Shipp?"

"Is it true he was blackmailing Dr. Shipp?"

Elizabeth couldn't believe the audacity of these people. She stopped and looked at them. A bright light from a television video camera clicked on.

"Is there anything you would like to say to the press, Mrs. McClintock?" one smart reporter asked.

"Yes, there is," Elizabeth found herself saying. "My husband has been the innocent victim of a madman."

"What about the accusations made by Mrs. Shipp?"

"They're all lies. My husband would never knowingly harm another human being."

"Mrs. Shipp says she isn't going to give up until your husband is exposed for his crimes."

"I can understand why Elaine Shipp is upset. But I believe it's time she faced the fact that her husband was a sick man and unable to cope. He turned to drugs for comfort. In the McClintock home, we turn to each other."

Elizabeth pushed her way through the press and climbed into her waiting limousine, like the southern lady she was.

CHAPTER 64

*O*n the advice of her accountant Lara Miller was house-hunting. Between her 5 percent finder's fee and producer's salary on *Blue Moon*, two raises, and assorted bonuses, she had amassed close to a hundred thousand dollars in less than a year. Being thrust into the 50 percent tax bracket was making it necessary for her to consider long-term investments and tax shelters.

Lara entertained the idea of living in Santa Monica or Brentwood until she discovered that on the West Side a million dollars would buy only a handyman's special. For the last week realtors had been showing her condominiums and townhouses in a recently renovated section of Venice Beach.

Several times she had walked through a brand-new three-story townhouse overlooking the Pacific. She loved the views and hearing the sound of the surf, but she still had "first-time jitters" when it came to committing to a sale price of three hundred thousand dollars. To bolster her resolve she invited Bonnie Louise to lunch at the Rose Café, a popular, trendy restaurant that just happened to be across the street from the building in question.

Circumstance had thrown them together, but a genuine fondness for each other had developed. Lara had been too busy at MCM to keep up with old friends, and Bonnie Louise hadn't really had the time or opportunity to make any lasting ones. Most of the people she'd got to know were older, and not really the type she felt she could confide in.

Appreciating the salt air, the ladies chose an outside table that afforded them sunshine and just enough privacy. As they caught up on each other's news, Lara marveled at how Bonnie Louise had—on the surface at least—evolved into a sophisticated, self-assured young woman.

"Both our lives have taken such big leaps in the last six months," Lara said enthusiastically. "You look so much happier and more relaxed, Bonnie."

"Well, so do you, Lara." Bonnie Louise took a bite of a croissant and softly drawled, "I'm sorry Kevin disappointed you . . . but . . . you're gonna meet somebody—somebody really wonderful. I hope he's as good to you as Zach is to me."

Lara smiled and said, "I'd like that. A lot."

Upon noticing several people reading books and newspapers, Bonnie Louise started talking about her tutors and how much her reading and writing skills had improved since that fateful day when Lara had taken her—"B.J.'s niece"—shopping in Beverly Hills for the AIDS Benefit, where she met Zachary. Now she was married to America's number-one heartthrob.

"And about to become a star yourself," Lara told her. "Word around the industry is that your screen presence—even in a small part—is enough to get you a starring role."

Bonnie Louise cocked her head and looked directly into her friend's eyes. "What do you think, Lara?"

"I thought you had something special the first time I met you."

The teenager shook her head and dove into her oversized handbag, producing a well-worn hardback book. She handed it to Lara and waited.

Seeing the title, Lara said, "This is a great novel. People have been trying to make it into a film for years. I think Universal owns the rights."

"Not anymore," Bonnie Louise said proudly. "Zachary's been watchin' the calendar and we got lucky. I think he picked it up before the studio even realized their option had expired."

"That was a coup."

"I got another one for you, Lara." Bonnie Louise leaned across the table and in hushed tones confided, "Zach's had a falling out with Brady, who was running his production company." Lara nodded. "Well, I think you'd be great running Zach's company." She held up the novel and said, "*Wildcats* is gonna be our next film."

Lara thought a moment. Heading up a bankable star's production company would guarantee her top status as a motion-picture producer. She would get a green light from any major studio in town for any of the superstar's projects. Awfully tempting, she thought.

"Bonnie Louise, I wish I could say yes, but between us, I've been running MCM. I don't know what would happen . . . I can't really leave right now. Not till *Blue Moon*'s in the can."

"Why don't you come to dinner Thursday night? Get to know Zachary a little better."

"If it's done right, *Wildcats* could be the *Giant* of the nineties."

Bonnie Louise waved at a young TV director who was waving at her. She swept her long blond hair over one shoulder and turned her attention toward the huge pink complex looming kitty-corner from them on Main Street.

Two hot young actors wearing Gold's Gym T-shirts and bicycle pants that left little to the imagination sat down at the next table and smiled. The sunlight in Bonnie Louise's hair created a kind of halo effect. Lara could understand why B. J. McClintock had become completely obsessed with her. She still didn't understand, though, why her boss would have risked everything in his life by kidnapping her. B.J. was lucky that he hadn't ended up in scandalous disgrace, she reflected.

Bonnie Louise turned away from the amorous muscle men and gave Lara a sly smile. "There's somethin' about the beach that makes guys hot-blooded. Zachary and I are thinking about buying a house in Malibu."

"Not in the Colony, I hope."

"No," Bonnie Louise said ironically. "We won't be doin' that."

Lara studied the building across the street and said, "I've always wanted big white walls so I could start filling them up with contemporary art. And L.A. is the city for it. Art-wise, this is the place to be."

"Then let's walk across the street so you can sign the papers."

Lara lifted her mineral water and toasted, "Let's do it!"

CHAPTER 65

One Year Later

Lara Miller's promotion to president of MCM positioned her center stage. Now, she was holding the reins. B.J. had survived and been named CEO so that he could gracefully retire—to be wheeled out for formal occasions. Recuperation had become his life's work.

Nonstop had become Lara's mode. Business and pleasure overlapped. She had been the one to collect *Blue Moon*'s prize at the Cannes Film Festival. She had been the one to option Helen O'Brien's play before anyone else had even read it. And *Blue Moon* had grossed close to $90 million prior to its video release.

Lara climbed inside her new BMW with smoky, gray-tinted windows. Perks like this were all part of the trappings. First on the agenda tonight was the American Film Market cocktail party. It was a special event for mainstream studio executives and stars.

It was still hard for her to feel that she deserved the power and money she was earning. There was a melancholy place in her heart for what might have been had Kevin Wenster not been married.

The signal turned red, and she eased to a stop. This is going to be an intense evening, she warned herself. After the cocktail party she was meeting Derek Middleton at Spago. The director, still riding high on the success of *Blue Moon*, had been given the green light from MCM for his next film. As usual, he was already screaming about an increase in the budget and certain artistic changes.

Lara knew how to deal with the Englishman. First she would smooth his ruffled feathers, reassure him that MCM was going to push him in the Oscar race. Then she'd give him the ultimatum.

"Derek," she rehearsed, "the difference between proceeding with *Undercover* or allowing it to fall by the wayside and eventually go into turnaround is *compromise*. If you want to go forward, you'll have to cut back. Otherwise, no deal."

Pleased with herself, she stepped on the accelerator. Prissy Derek and his vile, cottage-cheese-throwing wife. Tension shot across her abdomen. The very thought of Lady Rebecca at the Beverly Hills Hotel enraged her.

She drove up the long, winding palm-tree-lined driveway to the hotel. In spite of Lady Rebecca, it was still her favorite landmark.

Looking every inch a power broker, the thirty-year-old president of MCM glided up the steps and inside the lobby. She couldn't help but stroke her new mink coat, the security blanket Elizabeth and B.J. had given her for Christmas.

Men and women turned to look at her. Who was she? An actress? An heiress? Lara could feel their stares as she crossed the lobby and disappeared inside the Crystal Room.

Attitude, as Colin O'Brien liked to tell her, *was everything*. Now, she had mastered it. She knew how to set the right tone without saying a word. That was what the sleeked-back hair secured by an antique diamond barrette and the Paloma Picasso diamond-X necklace and matching earrings were all about.

Lara gave herself forty minutes to work the room. And what a room, she thought. The turnout was impressive. A representative from *The Hollywood Reporter* flashed their picture.

She spied Michael Ovitz, CAA's wunderkind agent, looking like he was about to lead Hollywood out of the doldrums. Bonnie Louise and Zachary Steele were crossing the room, and Billy Goldberg was talking to a columnist from the *Los Angeles Times*. He looked up and smiled upon seeing Lara.

A waiter brought her a Perrier. Casually she turned toward Billy and smiled back. There could be no question of a love affair, Lara told herself. Equally, there was no doubt in her mind that Goldberg wanted to be friends, probably for other reasons. And anyway—in the sense that she had been accustomed to regard such matters—he wasn't in the least good-looking. All the same, she thought, he had looked at her in a certain way, and she had been attracted by it.

"Genius," her mother had once remarked, "is usually kind." Lara had no way of evaluating the truth of that somewhat curious observation. Goldberg had a quality she had met in no other man in Hollywood. Brilliant as this young man was, there was also an aura of gentleness in his manner. He seemed to be reaching out to her when he had looked at her in that certain way.

She made her way to the buffet table, listening for vital snippets of information. There was lots of small talk with "friends" she saw only at social gatherings such as this one.

Lara marveled at Bonnie Louise's transition from naïve blond goddess to wife, new mother, and, Lara suspected, after her next film, in which she was going to star opposite Zachary, a movie star.

Lara would always recall the day Bonnie Louise had arrived on MCM's doorstep eighteen months earlier. Lara was pleased to note that the teenager was as sweet as ever, and was even developing an air of sophistication.

Lara backed away from the table and collided with someone. She turned and came face-to-face with Kevin Wenster, who was brushing someone else's spilled drink off of her black wool suit. For a moment they were both stunned.

"Lara?"

She nodded, trying to keep her cool.

"We broke ground. The studio's under way."

"I'm glad it worked out for you," she lied.

"Oh it did, Lara. I'm going to have the best state-of-the-art equipment in the world. Australia has every kind of scenery you'll ever need."

"You don't have to sell me, Kevin. You did once before, remember?"

A pretty, very pregnant blond woman stepped between them and told Kevin she was going to find the loo. She excused herself and walked away. Kevin looked noticeably shaken.

"Your wife, Molly?" Lara asked.

He nodded affirmatively.

"In the interest of fair play, Kevin—when your studio's finished, send us the particulars. The production department can take care of it. Good-bye."

She turned and strode across the room, knowing that Kevin's eyes were probably bearing down on her. She knew there was still heavy chemistry there, but it didn't matter. Their personal business had concluded.

"Lara Miller!"

Lara swung around to face Joan Souchek, who was waving an empty champagne flute at a waiter.

"Lara," she effused, "you look fantastic! Success really suits you."

"Thank you. You look like you're doing well yourself."

Joan heaved a heavy sigh. "I *was* doing great. We've been taken over by some Japanese conglomerate. They think they know more about making movies than"—she scanned the room and gestured—"Billy Goldberg. Hence, about six of us are *quietly* looking for new jobs. You wouldn't happen to have anything for me at MCM, would you?"

"No openings at the moment."

"Well, keep me in mind, will you, Lara? I always liked it over at MCM."

Colin O'Brien and Adam Snow entered the party with Helen O'Brien and a young actress trailing behind. Directly behind them Lara spotted Savannah McClintock, Ariba, and two actors she guessed were regulars on a daytime soap. It was like old-home week.

"How's B.J.?" Joan pressed.

"Oh, he's improving—talking in complete sentences. It's a miracle." Lara turned and walked over to greet Holly Dandridge.

Holly and Lara kissed each other's cheeks and smiled like two partners in crime.

"Who's the hunk with Savannah?" Holly whispered in Lara's ear.

"What're you up to, you naughty girl?" Billy Goldberg said, approaching Holly.

"Billy!" Holly said, blushing. "You busted me."

"I know what *she* gets up to," Billy told Lara. "I liked your film."

"Really . . ." Lara found herself saying.

"Why don't you come up to the house?" Billy suggested.

"I'd love to."

"Shall we say seven-thirty?"

"You mean tonight?" Lara asked.

"Sure," Goldberg said.

Lara thought she ought to say, "Well, I'll have to make a phone call." Instead, she asked only, "Your address?"

Billy smiled and explained that his house was not far from the McClintocks'. Lara knew exactly which gate he was describing. She politely excused herself and went off to call Derek Middleton.

Lara was amused by her actions. She had never liked people who, like the wind, changed direction when a better offer came along. Now, here she was, canceling one director for another . . . only, as she knew, her real reason had little to do with business.